Dearest Kathy
Speedy recovery
my friend
lots of love
Elizabeth

Where The
Truth Lies

Susan Rae Fox

PO Box 99, St Francis Bay, Eastern Cape, 6312

susanrf@mweb.co.za

Where the Truth Lies

ISBN 978-0-620-80717-3

First edition 2018

Editor and proofreader: Peta Vardy

Cover design: Rory Morrison

Cover photograph: Sharon Wellman

Typesetting: Quickfox Publishing

From the author of
Unravelling

Where The Truth Lies

SUSAN RAE FOX

For my husband Ron and sister Peta – with thanks
for their unwavering support and love.

'Allow the love of a good ghost. They possess all that emotion, trapped.

Bow to it. It will assuredly never release them but who knows what relief it may give to them, who knows how they may quieten in their chains, in their glass jars.'

'No Man's Land' — HAROLD PINTER, 1975

CHAPTER ONE

PLUM

The first time I saw the house it was like a hand reaching into my chest and squeezing tight and swear to God my heart stopped dead.

The house had a face – two upstairs windows, square and blazing with light for eyes and the door a tight mouth clamped shut. The roof was high with grey tiles – some missing – and scraggly birds' nests in the eves. That's her hair I thought and the roof is her pointy hat and I couldn't stop staring because it was like meeting an old friend which was weird because the only time I'd seen the house was when Dad showed me a fuzzy black and white picture printed off his computer. "Here's our new home," he'd said. "Do you like it?"

I never wanted to leave 88 St Stephen's Place where Mom died in the upstairs bedroom seven months, three weeks and four days ago after what her obituary said was a 'long struggle with cancer'. I cut it out of the paper – the obituary – and stuck it in my diary. *'Survived by loving husband William, daughter Plum and sister, Frith…To live in the hearts we leave behind is not to die…In lieu of flowers, donations can be made in the name of Lily Westwood, to the UK Breast Cancer Society.'*

I have a memory that switches on and off which means there's sometimes an empty space in my head but mostly I remember things nobody else does.

My aunt started crying when we got off the plane at the airport – fat round tears sliding down her cheeks and plopping on her chin. She said it was because her head was ding-donging from a migraine but I knew we were both thinking of Mom and how happy she'd have been to be standing with us on the scorching hot tarmac. It's kind of freaky coming back to South Africa *after* Mom died because she was the one who was homesick – me, I didn't care – I was happy as long as we were together.

Mom never wanted to leave South Africa in the first place and by listening to whispery conversations and filling in the missing ends of chopped-off sentences I learned we had to move to England because Dad had done something really bad.

I thought maybe he'd murdered a man but it turned out the man had killed himself after Dad had stolen money from him.

Mom told me about the money and the man who'd jumped out of a window twelve floors up but made me pinky-swear I'd never tell Dad – "It'll destroy your father," she said.

Anyway, back to my memory. Not long ago I reminded Aunt Frith about her crying when we landed at the airport and her skinny black eyebrows did a dance and she said, "What on earth would I be crying about?" We both knew the answer. "Mom," I told her. "You were crying about Mom," but she blinked fast and said, "Oh, Plum, that didn't happen."

I've come to know memories shut up tight inside my head aren't the same as the ones in my aunt's or Dad's heads and you can't work out whose memory is true and whose isn't because feelings get knitted into memories. Aunt Frith was desperately sad after Mom died so all her memories of that time are like lumpy grey jumpers while mine are more bluey and Dad's are black because of the three of us he was the saddest.

It's not only feelings – imagination gets knitted into memory especially if you're like me and have what Mom called an 'overdeveloped' imagination. I used to think that was a good thing and I'd grow up to be a famous writer or film director but it turns out it can mean you sometimes make things up and pretend they're true, like being a liar.

FRITH

I distinctly remember the day we moved into *North Wind Manor*. It was surreal, the entire experience. I kept asking myself what I was doing back in this godforsaken country. Plum said I was crying over Lily but that's nonsense. I was in shock. That house!

Serve him right for buying it on the internet. William's got a reputation for being an investment genius but hasn't a clue when it comes to property. I knew the minute I clapped eyes on it: Lily would've loathed that ugly monstrosity skulking behind a row of dead trees.

The last time I'd seen Lily, I hadn't known it would be the last time. Her cheeks were flushed pink that day, not the chalky white we'd all grown used to and, for once, I felt hopeful.

When she asked, I grasped her hand and said, "Yes, yes, of course I'll help take care of Plum. I could never take your place, but I'll do my best. And don't worry about William. I'll stay till he's well enough to cope alone. You can trust me, Lily. You know that, don't you?"

Even now, I shudder at the look she gave. My first thought was she knew about me and William – either that, or she knew I was lying.

I gave her my word, but, if I'm honest, I wasn't planning on staying long, just until they were settled with William back on his feet. I didn't want to be William and Plum's caretaker and told myself she'd never know if I stayed for a month or a year. The thing is, I was scared stiff. For a start, there's always the danger of someone recognising William – and the consequence of that doesn't bear thinking about.

And then, Plum's not normal. There, I've said it. With Lily gone, it's easier to stop pretending. "*There's none so blind as those who will not see*" – as our mother used to say.

When she was a toddler, I thought Plum might be autistic.

"Just a slow developer." Lily said. She'd never admit Plum has some – not all – of the symptoms of Asperger's syndrome. Bright lights and noise used to make her anxious. She'd start spinning in widening circles, knocking things over, seemingly unaware of what she was doing. "She's clumsy," Lily said. "Takes after me that way."

But there were other signs. Plum would flinch if I touched her and draw back when I came too close. Sometimes she'd be remote and withdrawn – other times talking nineteen-to-the-dozen, words tumbling out in a never-ending stream. I don't deny she's as bright as a button, but she's odd too, not like other kids her age. Show me another girl of eleven who thinks her dolls are alive! We squabbled on the plane. I'd told Plum to pack her doll in her trunk. "I don't want you taking that doll on the plane, not at your age. People will laugh." We'd been in the air a couple of hours when we hit an air-pocket and I reached for her arm. "You okay, Plum?" I couldn't believe it – she had Dahlia in her lap! Right away, I lost it. "I told you not to bring that doll! Why must you always go against me? Put her away in your bag."

I've never known anyone as stubborn. She shook her head, cradling the doll. "Dahlia's frightened, she's never flown before. Look at her eyes, how scared they are!"

The woman sitting next to Plum was shooting glances at me. I gritted my teeth.

"Oh, do put that damn doll away! This is silly – big girl like you!"

"Dahlia's got a tummy ache. She wants a cuddle."

Plum settled the doll lovingly in her arms. For a second, it resembled a new born baby with a sweet, pouting mouth and tiny starfish hands grasping for something out of reach.

But then the doll's eyes clicked open and they were cold and glassy.

I made my voice low and reasonable. "Plum…please…put that doll in your bag."

"Go to sleep, Dahlia," she whispered. "I won't let anything bad happen to you. Not ever."

She never listens. This is what I have to put up with and she's not even my child.

Honest to God, if it weren't for Lily's love for Plum, we wouldn't be coming back to this bloody country. William would've been able to stay out of harm's way in England with his daughter and I could've gone back to France. Lily was the one who begged us to take Plum home and, even as I agreed, I knew we were making a dreadful mistake.

PLUM

This is all Dad's fault – her coming with us to South Africa. "I can't do this on my own, Plum." He was using his 'sorry-for-himself' voice.

I shouted, "Do *what* on your own? I don't need looking after. I'm nearly twelve!"

"It's not that simple. We need Aunt Frith, darling."

"But *why?*"

"She's family, Plum. You two…you're all I have now."

I hate how he lumps us together. I'm his daughter and she's Mom's sister who went off to France to be an artist and only came back because Mom got sick and begged her to.

When the taxi dropped us outside *North Wind Manor* my aunt was dabbing her eyes and I said, "I know what you're thinking! Mom would've loved this house!"

She gave me this look like she'd just remembered I was there and said, "Please take your bag. The driver's not an octopus – he can't handle all these cases on his own."

She used her sharp as scissors voice and the driver winked like he felt sorry and I started shrinking – that's what she does – makes me feel small as an acorn fallen from a tree.

I was staring at the house and it was staring back with shiny window-eyes when this awesome idea flew into my brain fast as a bee zooming into a pot of jam. I couldn't help it. I laughed out loud. Aunt Frith asked, "What's so funny?" and I had to think quickly. I lied. "Look! This house has a face, can you see?"

Now I'm going to describe *North Wind Manor* the way it was before Dad changed it.

First there's the front garden with mossy cobble stones and a round pond of bilious green, oily water and way down at the bottom swirling little fish like sparks of silvery light.

A path winds behind the house where there's a mowed lawn and, at the edges, long rows of bushes with purple flowers – I can't remember their name but if you rub a stem in your fingers a sweet smell buries itself in your skin. Cracked pots, a broken statue of a man's head with his face all worn off, piles of rotted leaves under trees with hunched backs.

Lavender – that's the name of the bush with the flowers! I remember because Mom had a lavender pillow spray when she was sick.

At the front of the house you climb six steps to a ginormous door where Aunt Frith was wrestling with a key stuck in the keyhole. She was growling like a bear, kicking the door. "Bloody, bloody thing! Stuck fast, won't budge. Plum! Stop prancing like a giddy goat and give me a hand here."

I'm good with keys. She had the wrong one in the hole so I jiggled it a bit until it came out and then fitted the smallest key on the bunch and twisted right and left until there was a little click and the door opened. *"Ta da!"* I sang, throwing out my arm.

"What's that silly look doing on your face?" my aunt asked. Then her mouth went soft and she said, "Sorry, Plum, don't mind me. It's this headache."

Inside the house you walk from one huge shadowy room to the next across wooden floors with your shoes clip-clopping like pony hooves so you'd never be able to creep up and surprise anyone. There's a dim passage – long and winding – with doors shut tight on both sides and then you go up a wide staircase like the queen has at Buckingham Palace and along twisty passages into more rooms. You could probably fit a hundred people into this house, if you wanted to, maybe two hundred. There's a second staircase – this one shorter and crooked – and at the top there's a door smaller than the others with a curly black iron handle.

I touched the handle and it was icy and rusty flakes came off and stuck to my skin which was kind of creepy so I wrapped my t-shirt over my hand before I turned the handle.

The door opened into a cobwebby room full of dead spiders and floating dust balls.

There wasn't much inside except a baby's crib like you'd find in a museum, a dirty wooden rocking horse with half its tail missing and a cupboard with the doors spotted with teeny-weeny worm holes.

I rubbed the glass of a window that hadn't been washed for years and saw rows of trees standing stiff and tall like soldiers.

In the corner of the room I poked a dark stiff shape with my shoe and it turned out to be a dead bat and that's when I hugged myself because the room was...*perfect!*

FRITH

I was grappling with the Samsonites, when this man, sidling like a crab, appeared from nowhere. I let out a piercing scream. I don't know who was more terrified, him or me, we were both shaking. "Who are you?" Probably a homeless squatter taking refuge in the outbuildings, I thought and tried to see if he was carrying a weapon but he was old, *really* old, frail, stooped and thin as a reed and harmless, couldn't harm a fly.

"I'm Oom Jacob," he said, so softly I strained to hear. "I've come to help madam with the luggage." I was confused. William hadn't mentioned staff. "You *live* here?"

He made a series of bird-like bobbing motions. His eyes were rheumy.

"Yes, madam. *North Wind* has been my home for many years."

I let out a long breath because, in a way, it was a comfort knowing we weren't alone in that shambling house, miles from anywhere.

Plum's voice was echoing. "Hurry, Aunt Frith! Come and look. It's like a...like a *castle!*"

Castle my foot. I asked the Oom to help with the cases and took one myself, bumping it over rough cobbles. When I went back for another, the Oom was bent double, chin touching his hollow chest, puffing like a steam train. I had visions of the old man collapsing in a heap so I waved my arms. *"Stop!"*

I grabbed the handle and, between us, we heaved the case up the steps and into the hallway. "Thanks," I gasped. "Will I see you in the morning?"

The old man did that bird thing with his head again and limped away. I waited until he'd gone and then locked the door behind me.

There was a disgusting smell in the hallway – a mixture of damp and dust and something sweetish, like rotting wood. Oddly, it was bitterly cold indoors, with mean little draughts sweeping beneath doors and gaps in the window frames.

I'd been sweltering all day, tugging the fabric of my cotton blouse, pulling it away from an unpleasant dampness beneath my armpits. I've always loathed the intensity of African heat, how it makes me perspire, beads blistering my top lip, hair turning wet and stringy – but a few minutes inside that icebox and I could feel the sweat cooling rapidly on my skin.

My headache ratcheted up a few notches. I'm on intimate terms with this agony. If I don't pop a migraine pill right away, the headache mutates into a raging monster reducing me to semi-blindness and unstoppable weeping.

I fumbled in my bag for my stumpy brown medicine bottle and went to look for water.

After a few wrong turns, I came upon a behemoth of a kitchen. *God!* – it defies description – an endless, filthy space with an immense, unworkable black stove anchored in the centre.

I smelled the unmistakeable reek of mice and noticed the filthy linoleum was sprinkled with a tell-tale trail of tiny black droppings and…could it be…wood shavings? Presumably, leftovers of a meal mice had made of a gnawed table leg.

The kitchen sink was nauseating – stained enamel – pre-Victorian by the look of it, with something pink and mushroomy growing in the plughole. The tap leaked a stream of rusty water and I let it run until it was as clear as it was ever going to be and then, drinking from my cupped hands, I gulped down my pills.

"I'm sorry Lil. I know I promised, but I don't know if I can do this."

I've been talking to her since she – I can't make myself say 'passed away' – such a ridiculous expression – since she died. We were very close. I've never loved anyone like my sister Lil. We used to talk about absolutely everything until…*oh, Christ,* until I ruined everything.

PLUM

I found my Aunt in the kitchen with a face like flour and a mouth all pinched and I knew she had one of her headaches.

"I have something to tell you!" I shouted and she closed her eyes and said my voice was like a foghorn and would I mind whispering but what I had to say wasn't something you'd whisper.

"There's this tiny room at the top of the stairs," I told her. "And…and there's a…*ghost inside!!*

Aunt Frith opened her eyes and rolled them back in her head the way she does when she thinks I'm being 'theatrical' – that's her word – and said in her dead voice, "Not now, Plum, if you don't mind. I simply haven't the energy."

But I couldn't wait. I blurted it all out…about a kind of electric buzzing against my skin and invisible fingers tickling my backbone, moving slowly up and down. Then the fingers stopped and it was like a heater switched on making the air warm and toasty and I could feel something…no… *someone*…watching me. I made my eyes huge. "It's that kind of house, isn't it? The kind with a ghost?"

I'd been holding it in for so long, a big loud laugh fell out of my mouth.

She sounded so tired. "You're hysterical, Plum."

My aunt half-shut her eyes and stared through slits. "You've had an *episode,* haven't you? That's what this is about."

She's the only person I know who says '*episode*'. I don't even know what that means. Episode is like a chapter or something – it doesn't make sense.

"Why do you use that stupid word?"

15

Her mouth was a straight line. "Seizure then. What word did your mother use?"

We used to call it a '*blank*', Mom and me. I haven't had one for so long I may have grown out of them and that's *not* what this was. This was a feeling like I was being watched by someone I couldn't see.

My Aunt opened her mouth in a yawn and said she was half-dead on her feet and would I look for the case with the sleeping bags inside and I knew she wouldn't listen to anything more about the ghost so I shut up.

I made it up – that thing about the ghost.

My plan was to scare her so much she'd fly back to England and leave me and Dad alone but here's what really happened.

I was pressing my nose against the smeary window when I saw a small black furry creature rushing into the bushes. I followed it with my eyes as it scuttled from bush to bush and a kind of tingling moved from the middle parting of my hair all the way down to the tips of my toes. The air in the room got heavy and wrapped around me like a blanket and – this is going to sound weird – it was like being hugged by a person who loved me. I don't know how long the feeling lasted but I felt sad and kind of lonely when it went away.

So now I'm all confused. Did I make the whole thing up or did I really feel a ghost in the small square room at the top of the stairs?

CHAPTER TWO

FRITH

Our mother, Julia, didn't like children and, given a choice, would never have had any but our father was desperate to leave a legacy.

He'd set his heart on three or four children, at least one boy somewhere in the mix, and was bitterly disappointed when, after two girls, a deadly tumour the size of a grapefruit grew and our mother's womb had to be surgically removed.

When we were young, we'd listen engrossed as Julia told grim tales about when we were born, how the epidural didn't work, how she felt every bone-wracking contraction and shrieked and grew mad with pain during a labour lasting sixteen hours. Our birth she said, turned her 'inside out' and 'split her from stem to stern' and she was never the same again. First thing Julia did when she came home from the hospital was hand us to our nanny and went on a liquid diet to lose weight gained during pregnancy. She swore she'd never have another baby and, as if on cue, her obedient womb began multiplying deadly cancerous cells.

Our mother never smiled, laughed or showed outward signs of happiness when recounting the story of our birth. Her gruesome tales were of spilled blood and excruciating pain.

I lay the blame at her feet – she's the reason why I've never wanted children although, given my awkward relationship with Plum, I'd have been pretty useless at parenting. But Lily…well, Lily, was a born mother.

17

When our mother Julia was pregnant, she had no idea she was carrying twins.

Her doctor heard one heartbeat instead of two hearts beating in unison and it was a shock when, during the delivery, he cried out, "We're not done yet, my dear…there's another on its way!"

We were identical twins – a mirror image of one another – although mentally and emotionally different in every conceivable way.

People used to say Lily was cheese and I was chalk. We weren't pretty… thin and angular with dead-straight black hair. Taken individually, our features were good – large, deep-set brown eyes, small nose, generous mouth – but, fitted together they seemed slightly *'off'* in some way which made us more 'interesting' looking than attractive.

All that altered as we grew older and Lily traitorously changed. Her teeth grew in straight while I wore braces to correct overlapping incisors. Her ears stayed folded petals as mine kept getting larger until they peeked out between curtains of hair. And though we were identical in everything but the details, she was known as, 'the pretty twin'.

Skinny kids, we developed into skinny teenagers with pointed elbows, knobby knees and long, thin, arched feet with five metatarsal bones as visible as if we were skeletons in an anatomy class. As adults, our bodies grew rounder but when the cancer came and Lily shrank to nothing, I stopped eating until we weighed the same.

Lily and I were raised in Johannesburg where our father, Jacques du Buisson, owned an antique shop: a great dusty barn crammed to the ceiling with heirlooms from once great country-house slings. That's where we played as kids, on ancient rugs from Persia beneath nineteenth century winking French chandeliers. Dress-up was a favourite game and, unlike other girls who wore their mother's old castoffs, we donned embroidered slippers from the souks of Marrakesh, glorious pashminas from Kashmir and beaded Chinese Xinjiang hats.

Melville was our address – an area no longer considered fashionable but, back then, the hub of exotic Bohemia. Our home was a restored farmhouse from the 1800's with broad-panelled Oregon floors, pressed ceilings and a wide, shady stoep. Here, an old, striped canvas swing chair sat in a crescent of shabby rockers whose cushions had been left out in the rain so often that the covers had bleached to uniform grey.

Mother used to perch in one of those chairs, chain-smoking through a pack of Dunhills while jiggling one skinny crossed leg and endlessly tapping red-tipped fingernails, pointed as daggers, on the wicker arm.

At four-thirty each afternoon, father would bring Julia a cocktail of vodka and tomato juice with a stuffed green olive bobbing on a toothpick.

Mother sipped two cocktails before dinner and went to bed as the grandfather clock chimed eight and only after she'd retired did our house truly come alive.

I suppose Julia was a part of our lives, she must have been, she was our mother after all. But, all I remember is her husky voice harping on about dogs crapping on the verge, neighbours playing too-loud music, an unoiled squeak in the gate hinges, an ink stain on Lily's school-dress, my unwashed hair, our father's stained tie...*everything*.

Dad didn't stand a chance. Julia querulously complained about his lack of ambition, money and backbone and accused him of growing old before his time. She'd married a handsome man, fifteen years her senior, and while she was still lithe and lovely, his face became unforeseeably wrinkled and his once thick hair fell out, all but one sprout combed comically over his shiny spotted pate.

As if that weren't enough, Dad's teeth turned elephant-tusk ochre and crisp white hairs sprang from his ears, nostrils and facial moles. Lily and I adored and pitied our gentle, good-natured father and did whatever we could to protect him. Sadly, he was no match for our mother who was at pains to constantly remind him how very much he disappointed her.

At thirty-eight, I recognise disturbing signs of my mother in myself. I see her cruelty in the glitter of my dark eyes, her sarcasm at the edge of my dry voice and there's something coldly dismissive in my manner that brings Julia to mind and makes me shudder.

Our father showed up in Lily's warm, forgiving nature and her desire to see the best in everyone. My whole life I yearned to be more like Lily, but then I also dreamed of flying planes, fighting fires and scaling jagged mountain peaks and all these were unattainable to a twin commonly viewed as somehow *less* than her sister.

First impressions of people often change over time but one thing about William that's never altered for me, is his likeability. He's one of the nicest, most charming men I've ever known and it's easy to see why Lily found him irresistible. They met when she was nineteen and he twenty-three and were married eight months later. For years, they tried to have a baby and had three attempts at in-vitro fertilisation, but nothing worked and finally they gave in and signed with an agency to adopt Plum. After she got sick, Lily's greatest sorrow was she'd never see her little girl grow into a woman.

I'm told these days most adoptive parents tell their children they're adopted but Lily and William never told Plum. William says it's too late now and he's not breaking her heart by letting her know she's not their natural child although, frankly, I've always thought it glaringly obvious.

PLUM

Aunt Frith told me to start unpacking and I was carefully lifting out my dolls when she yelled at me to be sensible and take out clothes and shoes first. I found one pink trainer and was hunting for the other when my eyes fell on the butterfly cases Mom said I should give away but I couldn't because of hurting Dad's feelings and then all these memories crowded suddenly into my head.

Mom used to say memories are precious but that's not true and some, like the ones about the butterflies, make me cry inside. When Mom got sick she said Dad and I needed to get out together more.

She thought a hobby would help and Dad said, "Why don't we start a butterfly collection?" so that's what we did. We threw ourselves into *lepidoptery* – that's its proper name – and I spent all my pocket money on cork-lined storage boxes, an organza net, entomologist pins and proper labels for identifying dates and places where we caught our butterflies. You're supposed to call these '*specimens*', the word collectors use for the butterflies we netted flying above the purple heather on the common near our house.

Dad took me to the library where we learned that the village common used to be an airfield during the war which is why there's an old runway hidden in the grass and an air-control tower that's collapsed into a pile of crumbly concrete.

Mom made egg salad sandwiches and tea in a flask and I carried the net and Dad packed envelopes and tweezers in his backpack. We'd spend Sunday afternoons hunting butterflies and looking for rabbits, polecats, weasels – and once we saw a red streak that turned out to be a racing fox.

I loved the common with its boggy ponds and powdery catkins but when we caught a butterfly I had to *pretend* to be happy because, deep down, I was terribly sad.

Dad used to put the butterflies in envelopes to keep in the freezer for twelve hours and I had to shut my eyes tight to stop seeing their wings struggling and flapping when he stuck down the envelopes. Dad said this was kinder than using deadly toxic poisons but I wondered whether he'd like to be smothered in an envelope and frozen till stiff like ice.

I said I thought it took longer to freeze to death than be chloroformed but Dad patted my head and said, "There, there, no long face, please. There are hundreds of butterflies on this common, maybe even thousands, and we've taken only *one* for our collection."

"I'm sad for just that one," I said and he smiled and said, "Irrefutable logic, I agree, but sacrifices have to be made for scientific studies."

Mom read my mind and knew something was wrong. "If this is upsetting you, tell Dad you don't want to catch butterflies, any more. He won't mind."

But his face showed how much he minded and I heard Mom whisper, "Please, Wills, don't make her feel worse," and Dad gave a long breathy sigh and said he'd had a fish tank when he was a boy and maybe we could try that next, what did I think?

All this was in my head when I was looking at the '*Silver Studded Blue*' – the last butterfly we caught – pinned through its thorax in my cork box. I can still see Mom wearing a worried look and Dad saying, "Don't baby her,

Lily, you baby her too much," and her saying, "But, she's a sensitive child, Wills, you forget that sometimes. Promise you won't when I'm not there to remind you."

FRITH

The first time I met William was at the club. They'd been playing tennis and when he shook my hand, his was slippery with sweat.

"Good God!" he'd exclaimed, grinning, "I didn't believe it when Lily said there were *two* of you. How lucky can one man get?"

He kissed my cheek with loud, smacking noises and Lily took his arm in hers, hooking it in a hungry, possessive way that wasn't like her.

William was being kind with his '*two of you*' remark. Lily was shapely while I was still reed-thin, flat chested as a boy. I'd chopped my hair to my chin and wore it with an untidy fringe over my eyebrows. Lily's hair, long, to her waist, was thicker with a lovely soft wave from a body perm. For some perverse reason, I'd left my hair natural – the dull black of a crow's wing – while Lily highlighted hers with reddish-auburn tints that glinted in sunlight.

At six-three, William towered, taller than most men I knew, but it was his eyes that got to me – deep, dark, corduroy blue – they gazed directly with an intensity that made me catch my breath.

That day, Lily asked stiffly if I'd like to join them for lunch. I knew she wanted me to say 'no' but I accepted and saw her frowning, puzzled I'd ignored her signal – something I'd never done before.

They sauntered ahead, swinging their racquets and from their easy familiarity and the way his hand couldn't stop caressing the curve of her bum, I knew they were sleeping together.

It hurt she hadn't told me – she who'd always confided all her girlish loves – and I felt the first disloyal stirrings of jealousy for my beloved sister. "It's not *fair!*" I remember telling myself. "Why's she always the one who gets *everything?*"

Over lunch, I'd tried to fathom why I was so attracted to Lily's new boyfriend.

He was good-looking, bright, laughed a lot and made us laugh with him – but it wasn't any of those things. Only later, I realised that William's friendliness towards me was genuine enough but he wasn't remotely interested. In his eyes there was only Lily and this, of course, made him irresistible.

They threw a party the night they got engaged. I drank too much. Made William dance and held him too close, rubbing up against him, kissing his mouth. He must have said something. Lily drew me aside. "You're making Wills uncomfortable," she whispered. "And people are talking, Frith – they think you're behaving like a slut. Don't do this, please. You're only embarrassing yourself. Think how humiliated you'll feel tomorrow."

I told her I was only having a little fun. "You're so *uptight*, you and William. You take yourselves too seriously. It's a *party* for Christ's sake. You don't think I'm trying to steal him, do you? Oh, Lily, please! I'm just being nice for your sake."

She touched my mouth with a finger to make me quiet. Her eyes glowed with kindness. "You think you're losing me, but you're not Frith, I swear. You'll never lose me, even if I marry Wills. You'll always be the sister I love most in the world."

"Ha! That's because I'm the only sister you've got."

Lily smiled tearfully and we hugged and neither of us mentioned my shameful performance at their engagement party again.

I woke after a restless night at *North Wind Manor*, heavy with dread.

Plum was still sleeping and it dawned on me how vulnerable we were; a woman and child alone in a huge old house in the back of beyond with only an old, crooked man for protection.

I haven't had it for years, this feeling of nervousness that comes from being in one of the most dangerous countries in the world. I don't like it. You forget a lifelong habit of bolting doors and windows and alarming rooms when you live in rural England. You stop looking over your shoulder on a crowded street or when drawing money at an ATM.

Nobody in a UK country village drives with car doors locked in case of a hijack or sleeps with a baseball bat propped at the side of the bed, ready to crown an unwelcome intruder.

If not for my promise to Lil, I'd never have come back to this wretched country, not if you'd paid me millions.

Weeks before the end, Lily complained about England.

"This is no place to raise a child," she would say. "Truth is, I haven't been happy here what with the bitter cold and rain, the dark coming early. And I worry how safe Plum is with Isis terrorists blowing themselves up around every corner and then there's this damn-stupid Brexit-Government lowering living standards."

Surprised, Wills interjected. "Oh, darling, come on! It's a lot better than living under Zuma and his crooked cronies!"

Her voice was husky. "Don't fight me, Wills, *please*. I want Plum to grow up at home. We're only here because…well…I don't have to tell you that, do I?"

"We'd be taking a risk, Lil. Think about it. What if I'm recognised?"

Lily shrugged. "That's a chance we'll…*you'll* have to take. Besides, it's been forever. Surely no one will remember you?"

He frowned. "It's not that long, actually."

Lily broke down, her body wracked by harsh sobs.

William reached for her hands, gripping hard.

"I'll do it, Lil. I swear. I'll take Plum back home."

She looked beseechingly at me. "You'll go too, Frith?"

"Yes," I said, the words wrung from me. "Yes…if that's what you want, Lil."

Six weeks after Lil's funeral, I caught William scanning property on the internet, '*Houses for Sale – Western Cape*'.

He jabbed a foggy image on the screen. "What do you think of this place?"

"You're going to do it then? Go back?"

"We made Lil a promise, you and me." His wheedling voice. "Come closer, Frith, you can't see from there."

William chewed his bottom lip, clicking the mouse, squinting at the screen, scrolling down, reading aloud.

"*'Situated on the brow of a hill overlooking Paarl, authentic Georgian Manor, built in 1812, listed as a national monument.'* I've a good feeling about this house, Frith. Paarl is the most *wonderful* place to bring up a child."

"What do you know about Paarl?"

"Famous for its mountains, winelands, graceful historic Cape Dutch architecture, the Berg River, fruit orchards…"

"You're reading that from the screen."

Calmly, his eyes met mine. "You don't know this, not many do, but I lived in Paarl for a while before I met Lily."

Turning to his laptop, William carried on reading. *"Renowned for its illustrious past and scenic beauty…"*

"This is a bad idea and you know it. It's too risky. She's gone, Wills. She'll be none the wiser if you don't go back."

I might've been talking to the wall.

William bowed to the screen. "Six bedrooms and bathrooms, large reception, spacious living and dining rooms, kitchen and separate scullery. Three outhouses, slaves' quarters and – oh, look – a wine cellar!"

His face lit up. "This place would make a perfect guest house. Lily always said she'd like nothing more than to run a bed and breakfast."

"Yes, well, don't look at me. I'm not Lily and that's the last thing I plan on doing."

Momentarily deflated, William gave an apologetic smile.

"Think about it. We could be completely self-sustaining. Rely on no-one but ourselves. Grow our own vegetables and fruit. Hang on, it says something about, ah, yes, here it is, *'Deciduous fruit trees and a small vineyard'.*"

Wearing his most amiable expression, William gestured at the computer. "It's called *North Wind Manor*, this house. At least take a look at it."

The photograph of a shabby relic from a bygone age grew distorted and blurry before my eyes. I tried to imagine living in the wantonly large house, keeping it clean, the endless upkeep of sprawling gardens with their scabby grape vines and fruit trees.

William tapped the picture. "It's the most perfect hidey-hole. No one would dream of looking for me there."

My voice trembled with emotion. "Don't be so sure! It's a small world. You should stay here. Plum's settled at school, and there's this house – all paid for – and your job. And what about me, Wills? I can't stay with you two forever. I've got my own life to think of. You must see that, surely?"

"But, you promised, Frith. You gave your word, you know you did." He spoke as if explaining something fundamental to a child. "It's what Lily wanted. It's time to go home."

PLUM

When I woke I heard a loud hissing like air being sucked in and puffed out and I thought it might be the ghost trying to make contact but it was only the house breathing.

I could hear other noises mixed up with the breathing. Water sloshing through pipes…a tap dripping in a bathroom where there's a fairy bed of spongy moss between the cracked tiles…pigeons cooing at the back of their throats…tree branches scraping walls…my aunt's slippers slapping up the stairs.

I *love* old houses. Our last house was spanking new and all you could hear was the dishwasher humming and the microwave pinging or the front door bonging like a church bell when somebody rang.

Before that we lived in an older house – not nearly as old as *North Wind* – but old enough to squeak and creak and groan. I think old houses are like orchestras with violins and flutes, horns and harps, piano and kettle-drums all coming together to make music that's achingly sad or jangly or thrilling depending on how you're feeling the moment you hear it.

That got me thinking about *88 St Stephen's Place* but I switched off the picture in my mind before it made me sad and went looking for my aunt.

She was sitting on the bottom stair rubbing small circles between her eyebrows. Her face was snowy as the bowl in Mom's room where she kept dry rose petals called *potpourri* (that's French) to cover the smell of her sickness. There wasn't a smell – Dad said it was in her head but I could tell she didn't believe him.

You can see fangs biting down when Aunt Frith holds her head and she has to swallow two blue pills and one red stripy capsule and rub the nerves at the front of her head with her thumb and pointy finger to make the pain go away.

When Aunt Frith looked up and saw me, she told me to wash and brush my teeth with a jug of boiled water she had left in the bathroom.

"But for God's sake, Plum, *don't touch anything!* This place is utterly filthy and there are beastly mice skittering all over the floor. Careful you don't step on one."

I swear I tried to make my feet walk to the bathroom but they don't always obey and my shoes skipped up the queen's staircase and then up twelve twisty steps to the teeny room at the top of the house. I couldn't touch the gross rusty handle so I used my elbow and when the door opened I breathed in the same smell as yesterday, dry and papery and dusty and even a little gluey.

I hadn't had time to look at everything properly before so I started with the cradle.

There are three pretty carved wooden roses on the headboard which means it was made for a baby girl with wood the colour of butter starting to burn in a pan. The rocking horse has only one foggy blue eye and half a tail. I felt the tail with the tip of a finger and it was hard and bristly like my hair brush but I couldn't tell if it was real horse hair because I've never touched a horse's tail before.

I pushed the cradle to make it swing but staring at the seesawing rockers made me kind of dizzy so I sat on the floor. In my ear, I could hear a teeny-weeny voice, very thin and high, singing at the window. I thought it might be the ghost speaking a foreign language but it turned out to be a fly whirring tiny gauzy wings against the glass.

I wanted to open the window and let the poor fly swan-dive into the garden but my eyes kept closing and there was this feeling – like silky sea-water washing over me and pulling back and spilling slowly forward again.

'Oh, I remember!' I thought as sunlight wrapped around me like Mom's loving arms and then I had the most awesome idea…*What if the ghost was Mom, flown down from Heaven to take care of me and Dad?*

FRITH

The stream of vile water coughing from rusted taps was dirty brown, probably alive with e-coli bearing deadly cholera. I made do rinsing my face in boiled water from the kettle and got the fright of my life as my reflection gazed back from a cracked, spotted mirror – *Christ,* I looked a hundred!

I'd have murdered for a cup of tea but didn't dare risk an onset of dysentery so I called for a taxi to take us into Paarl to hire a car, shop for groceries and organise a team of cleaners to make a start on the house. I shouted for Plum to hurry and get dressed.

At the foot of the stairs, a door opened into what must once have been a formal sitting room – a space as big as a town hall. The air in the room was weighted with cold and I could smell the sickly, sweetish odour of decaying wood. It was dim and dust clouds flew as I dragged aside the heavy velvet drapes to let in a little natural light. Only then did I notice the walls were papered with a hideous design of charging horses following a baying pack of dogs on the heels of a frantic, panting fox. Why would anyone in their right mind choose to paper their walls with a bloodthirsty hunting scene?

I tore off a curling strip and discovered, beneath this, a pattern of blue willow trees and Chinese long-legged birds. There was another layer underneath this, vaguely familiar, a botanical design with leaves and twisty vines in muddy shades of green and faded gold. My heart sank. What would William do when he discovered he'd invested millions in the kind of God-forsaken manor in which one of the Brontes might have hidden a lunatic?

A wave of self-pity washed over me.

I buried my Lily seven months ago…and now I'm expected to deal with this mouldering house!

I shouted again for Plum and when she didn't answer, went looking and found her in a small box room at the top of the stairs.

She was sitting cross-legged on the floor, staring vacantly. This is typical of the *petit mal* seizures she started having when she was about three. It's as if she's been hit on the head. She stops talking, stops whatever she's doing, gazes like a blind person with eyelids fluttering and then, minutes later, she's back as if nothing's happened.

"Feeling alright, Plum?"

"Know what I think, Aunt Frith?" She didn't wait for my reply. "I think the ghost could be Mom's spirit."

Tears crowded my throat. I swallowed. "Oh, Plum!"

Honest to God, she breaks your heart sometimes, she really does. I heard the taxi hooting and gripped Plum's hand to help her up.

I made my voice ordinary. "We're going shopping. Sure you're okay?"

She looked blissful. "Mom promised she'd never leave me and I think this is what she meant. She's here to protect us, like she said. Aunt Frith… what's the matter?"

"Nothing." I shook my head, blinking. "Speck of dust in my eye."

CHAPTER THREE

PLUM

I couldn't wait to show Dad *North Wind Manor* with the royal staircase, winding passages, and awesome attic at the top of the stairs. I'm certain Dad will feel Mom's spirit the same way I do…it's the only room in the house that's warm and bright and that was how Mom was when she was alive.

Aunt Frith doesn't believe in God and says people use religion as a crutch which is silly because a crutch helps you walk when you've hurt your leg or your foot and hasn't anything to do with God. Mom believed in heaven and said there were angels.

"I'll love you all the way from there," she told me. "It'll be as if I'm still with you."

When we got back after shopping, Aunt Frith's head was pounding like a tom-tom so she went upstairs for a little lie-down.

"Don't go wandering off, Plum, okay? For once, just sit and read *Anne of Avonlea.* Think you can do that?"

I read almost a page of my book but the attic was calling so I raced upstairs.

I had to tug hard at the knob before the cupboard door swung open. Inside were four empty shelves and – shoved right to the back of one – a bundle of dirty cloth, a black cracked lamp and a roll of dusty paper.

I heard my aunt on the stairs and she came into the attic looking cross with hands on her hips.

30

"It's impossible to rest with you making this din!"

"Look what I found!"

"Mmm, pile of old junk, by the look of it!"

The lamp had made my hands sooty so I set it on the floor and opened the roll of paper.

Inside was a wishy-washy, half-finished painting.

"Let me see that!" Aunt Frith snatched the paper out of my hands.

"Oh, look! This is *North Wind*! You can see the hipped shape of the roof…the bank of upstairs windows, the rim of the fishpond just visible in the front. That row of trees has grown three times that size. This must've been painted *years* ago. It's good. I like the bleached sky. This artist has a lovely, delicate touch."

My aunt is an artist – that's why she knows about stuff like this. She reads mountains of art books and buys paint in small tubes and camel hair brushes and visits galleries where she spends hours staring at paintings and talking to other artists.

Mom didn't do any of those things but her paintings were better than my aunt's even though Aunt Frith trained in Paris. Mom used to say my aunt was the real artist in the family and she was only a 'dabbler'. Ha, ha – that's all I have to say about that.

There was a dirty bunched cloth that smelled like a towel put away damp. The cloth was stiff like cardboard, dusty-grey dotted with weeny black specks though you could see it was once pale green with little white flowers.

I shook the cloth and there was a loud bang. Aunt Frith jumped in the air and shouted a rude swearword as a book fell onto the floor, near my feet.

Aunt Frith held out her hand in a bossy way, "May I see that, please."

"I found it," I said, but quietly so she couldn't hear.

I looked over her shoulder as she opened the book.

"Gracious!" she said. "It's a diary! There's a date, um…1904. It looks authentic. Oh, Plum! What a lucky find!"

"It's *mine*," I said loudly. "That – *and* the painting, they are both mine. Finders keepers, losers weepers."

FRITH

Plum has discovered a diary in the attic. The cover is of worn, soft red leather freckled with mildew and the pages are yellowing and fragile. The owner of the diary had written it in an ornate calligraphic script which is difficult to read and made more so because, over years, the ink has faded from black to sepia.

Curious, I flipped through the pages.

Clutching her heart, Plum gasped out loud. "Oh...oh! I've just thought of something. Can I say what it is?" She halted, dramatically. "Aunt Frith! What if we were *mean*t to find this diary? What if there's a message for us inside?"

I swallowed a sigh. I've learned a rapid change of subject can sometimes stop Plum from getting carried away. I held up the open diary. "Can you read this handwriting?"

She peered closely and shook her head.

"It's tricky, I agree. Let me see if I can decipher a few pages for you."

I convinced Plum to lie quietly on her sleeping bag and sat beside her with my back against the wall and the book in my lap. The silk binding was coming away from the cracked spine and some of the pages were loose. A spidery signature ran across the frontispiece: *Charlotte Jane Butler, 1904*.

Taking a deep breath, I began to read.

October 19th, 1904

I have, this morning, taken up this journal to record events as they transpire. It seems prudent to write it all down if only to keep my sanity for sometimes I fear I shall go mad with all that is happening, with all the unexpected and unwanted changes in my life.

Marriage does not suit me. This comes as no surprise. I warned Edward I might not be the perfect wife, companion and helpmeet, but he would not listen and now we are, both of us, paying the price.

32

There are thirty-five years between my husband and I – an eternity that may never be bridged.

I am shocked anew whenever I see the pair of us reflected in one of the many mirrors gleaming upon these walls.

My ambitious mother engineered this union between her youngest daughter and the wealthy son of a Lord. As a consequence of Mama's machinations, I find myself wed and living in South Africa in a place called Paarl, so strange a destination it might as well be the moon. I am a castaway, cut adrift from all I know, buried deep in an isolated valley sheltering beneath Paarl Mountain – or the Peerlberg – as it is known by the locals.

How well I recall the day Edward brought me to North Wind Manor.

Entering through the gates, we passed beneath an avenue of trees, their branches curving overhead like a bridal bower and, as I set my eyes upon this most elegant house, the sun broke through a bank of clouds. It seemed like a miracle...

"I have long dreamed of inhabiting such a house as this," I told Edward, happily. "What a precious gift you have bestowed upon me!"

Alas, Edward misconstrued my meaning and was at pains to clarify the house is his alone and mine to share only for as long as we remain man and wife.

Such misunderstandings occur often between us. A few months into our marriage, I sense a widening chasm as Edward, seemingly bored with his dull young bride, seeks fresh distractions.

My husband has invited his English friends, the Talbots and the Brooks to visit this weekend, although the manor, still only partially furnished, is quite unprepared for guests.

I believe Edward has extended these early invitations to pique me though I shall do my utmost to make our visitors comfortable and they may count themselves fortunate to spend time at the manor whether it is fully furnished or not.

A shameful thought occurs – if I cared half as much for Edward as I do for this house – how contented I should be!

October 20th, 1904

We are in the process of redecorating after I complained the manor bears too much of Victoria's touch with all the rooms reflecting Edward's first wife's taste in furnishings.

When we met, Edward informed me Victoria had passed away from consumption but I have heard rumours, too many to ignore, that the cause of her death was an excess of laudanum prescribed to calm shattered nerves. Poor Victoria had been buried no more than six months when Edward took me as his second wife.

My husband never utters Victoria's name in my presence. I cannot say whether this is due to his sorrow at her passing or if she has already been cast from his mind.

It grieves me to admit I believe the latter is true.

October 25th, 1904

Praise God, our weekend guests have departed after four days consumed with idleness...eating, drinking, dancing, flirting and playing endless games of whist – surely the dullest game ever conceived!

Stocks of wine and reserves of venison have been depleted after so many rich meals with barely pause between luncheon and dinner. I suspect I may be too puritanical a wife for Edward for I cannot abide such wantonness and greed.

As we were bidding farewell to our guests, Edward kissed Edwina Talbot's cheeks and then, rashly, touched his mouth to her lips! His motive was likely to make me jealous although my only emotion was shame that he should behave with such impropriety in the sight of Edwina's clearly offended husband and our shocked assembled guests!

October 29th, 1904

Now that I am, for better or worse, Mrs. Charlotte Butler, I have learned a good deal about my husband. I know a shield of ice encases his heart, making it brittle and impenetrable. I know he has a violent temper and is, besides, a mean and nasty bully. I know Edward is stubborn and refuses to listen to reason, particularly if it comes from me, a mere woman and, in his eyes, a lesser being.

As for his physical appearance, Edward is not attractive. His everyday countenance is one of scowling bad temper and his small, dark brooding eyes closely resemble those of an angry hedgehog.

I'd hoped my husband's homely face might hide a warm heart but he is ugly inside and out.

Yesterday, after an argument, Edward stood close enough for me to smell wine on his breath.

For a few moments, I feared he was about to strike me and I found myself shaking. Perhaps he noticed for he walked away at once. I suspect Edward may be abusive in nature. I tell myself to take great care not to provoke him in the future.

November 2nd, 1904

I have begun taking brisk, solitary walks to improve my health and sanity though I make it a point not to wander too far since we are neither liked nor respected in these parts.

Edward, a former Captain in the Imperial Yeomanry, is regarded as an enemy in this Boer town, still simmering with hatred two years after the war. Unhappily, the townspeople's loathing for my husband extends to me, his wife. I find this hard to bear. Surely my youth precludes me from blame? When war began in 1899, I was an innocent pupil at an English school, far from this bitter conflict between the British and Boers in South Africa.

Edward is equally despised for buying North Wind Manor from a family called Steyn, who built this house in 1812. The loss of a father and three sons in battle brought ruin upon the Steyns and Edward is said to have taken advantage of Mrs. Steyn, forcing her to sell the property for a fraction of its worth at a time when the grieving widow was both desperate and in poor health.

I believe Mrs. Steyn now lives with her daughter in a modest cottage in the valley. I should dearly like to pay my respects and apologise most sincerely for the ruthless actions of my husband but I am not brave enough to face that poor woman. Besides, it would be a mistake to meddle in Edward's affairs and risk incurring his vile wrath.

November 11th, 1904

Life grinds on.

Edward makes it known he is dissatisfied with our 'marital relations' and complains I am frigid. If frigid means shrinking from my husband's attentions, this is true.

There is something so cavalier in Edward's lovemaking – as though the act exists for his pleasure alone. Small wonder his first wife, the melancholy Victoria, became addicted to laudanum!

November 14th, 1904

We have made excellent progress decorating the bedrooms at North Wind and I am confident our guests will find them most welcoming. I have also convinced Edward to improve the Spartan bathrooms, replacing tarnished copper baths with those of gleaming white enamel.

A delivery arrived this day direct from Paris…a crate of perfumed Belvoir potpourri ordered for the purpose of filling the urns above the stairs. North Wind Manor smells like Heaven!

November 15th, 1904

Today we received the Senior Butlers, Edward's parents: Lord Redvers and Lady Henrietta who live abroad. The parents arrived laden with belated wedding gifts, mountains of silver plate, a marble bust of an unrecognisable soldier and a lovely navy carpet patterned with arum lilies, purchased in Rome.

Lord Redvers has most generously offered to cover the cost of building stables for the manor although he is not a fan of Georgian architecture and says these new buildings are to be erected in the more modern Cape Dutch style.

Lady Henrietta has merry visions of my producing a large family and suggests we build two additional laundries. I have managed to dissuade my kind mother-in-law of this extravagance and requested, instead, a contribution towards landscaping the grounds.

November 20th, 1904

"What joy to see you two newly-weds together," Lady Henrietta murmured after dinner, last evening. "It does my heart good. I have never witnessed my son more content than he is now with you, my dear, as his devoted wife." Since Edward, poker-faced as always, had not uttered one word during a dreary meal, I found Lady Henrietta's comment at odds with circumstance. Is Edward's poor mother blind to reality?

The in-laws depart early in the morning and we can, thank God, put an end to this silly charade of marital bliss.

December 3rd, 1904

Oh, Lord help me! This blot upon the page comes from my hand trembling so that I can hardly grip my pen.

Edward has killed a man! The deceased is one of the youths recently employed by my husband to work the land.

Edward's version of this terrible deed is that the boy spoke insolently to him and, as punishment, Edward struck him with his fist. The boy toppled backward, falling against a plough and splitting his head open. He died, Edward said, from a cracked skull and severe loss of blood.

Edward immediately reported the boy's death to the magistrate as a 'deeply unfortunate accident' and the youth has been buried in haste in an unmarked grave near the servants' quarters.

Soon this site will be covered over with grass and few will know the earth holds the body of a boy, not yet eighteen, who lost his life for daring to speak out against Edward's cruel treatment.

December 10th, 1904

I have passed an agonising week, ill with shock and horror. On top of this, there is the dreadful burden of loneliness. How I wish I had someone in whom I could confide – a mother, a sister, a close friend. The knowledge of my husband's cruel nature keeps me awake at night and anxious every day.

Living with Edward is more than I can bear!

December 15th, 1904

This morning Edward told me he is making plans to travel abroad. I wonder if guilt compels him to flee? Or is Edward growing increasingly frustrated by a wife he accuses of being remote, cold and withdrawn? Lately, there has been no intimacy between us. The sight of this man sickens me so that I flinch at the touch of his hands upon my body.

I shan't be sorry to see Edward depart and would be glad if he would leave the house this very hour!

"When will you return?" I asked, praying he name a date many months hence. Edward bestowed a heavy purse of money and stiffly said he had business to attend to and would be back 'in due course'.

December 16th, 1904

Without Edward, I feel lighter – as if floating several inches above the ground. Life is simpler and natural and, as I write, I can hear carefree chatter and laughter from the housemaids, the cook, the men in the fields.

I have shut up half the house, shrouded furnishings and barred windows and doors. With just a kitchen, sitting-room, bedroom and bathroom for my personal use, I find I breathe more freely as I claim North Wind Manor for myself!

December 17th, 1904

How happily occupied I am, in these peaceful days leading to Christmas. I have been putting up preserves using ripe fruit from our trees.

I found a recipe in the Ladies' Almanac that calls for twelve pounds of fruit with as much sugar, boiled in a copper pan over an open fire and then ladled, still boiling, into mason jars and…"

Plum's eyes were at half-mast. I pulled a grip from my hair and used it to mark the page. "Let's leave it for today. I'll read to you again tomorrow."

Plum yawned. "Do you think the lady who wrote the diary is our spirit?"

"I don't know anything about spirits, Plum," I answered, firmly. "Get your jammies and I'll run a bath for you."

38

November 20ᵗʰ, 1904

The frankness of the diary has caught me unawares. I'd skipped over quite a few 'unsuitable' sentences describing the intimacy between Charlotte Jane Butler and her revolting husband, pretending I couldn't read the cramped handwriting.

Lily taught Plum words like 'vagina' and 'penis' when she was just a toddler. I think Plum was about four when she'd asked how she'd been born. Lily's answer had been straightforward.

"I have a uterus here in my pelvis and that's where you lived until you were big enough to be born and the uterus pushed you out through my vagina."

Doggedly, Plum had gone on. "But, how did I get to *be* in your uterus in the first place?"

I'd shot Lily a helpless look. "We made you," my sister smiled. "Me and Dad made you together."

"But, what did you make me *with?*"

"We used a cell called an egg from me and a cell called a sperm from Dad. When you put the egg and the sperm together, that's the start of making a baby."

Plum had accepted her mother's explanation without further questions. I'd searched Lily's face. She'd looked guileless. Later, when we were alone, I'd asked, "Will you ever tell Plum the truth?"

"If you mean about her being adopted, then no," she'd said. "There are some things she doesn't need to know and this is one."

Lily's frank discussion with her toddler had made me think about our mother who never spoke to us about sex. "I don't know how you do it," I told my twin, a couple of days later. "I would be as awkward and uncomfortable as Julia."

Lily laughed. "I didn't do such a good job. Soon after, I was beating eggs for a cake and Plum asked if I was making a baby."

I ran a bath for Plum and added a generous dollop of bubble-bath to the brackish water.

Plum soaped herself, staring at a long-stemmed mushroom sprouting at the edge of a corroded tap. "What's *laud-an-um*?" she asked, pronouncing it phonetically.

Laudanum! All I could think of were names of Victorian writers who'd been doped up on the stuff: Byron…Keats…Dickens…Edgar Allan Poe. Samuel Taylor Coleridge wrote *Kubla Khan* after a laudanum-induced dream…Mary Shelley's Frankenstein took it to help him sleep.

"Don't you know?" She kept her eyes fixed on the sickening mushroom.

"It's…um…a medicine…or rather it *was* a medicine at the time the diary was written. Doctors don't prescribe it anymore. It's too dangerous."

"What makes it dangerous?"

Keep it real, Lily always said. "Um, well, because it was made with alcohol and opium which comes from poppies and people became addicted to it, which means…um…they couldn't stop taking it once they'd started."

"You mean like a drug?"

I nodded and, before she could ask another question, I savagely flicked the mushroom across the room.

"*Ugh!* This house is *crawling* with fungus!" I offered a towel. "Hop out. That water's getting cold."

"It was so pretty, that mushroom," Plum said sadly. "It had dainty white spots on top, like a fairy cap."

CHAPTER FOUR

PLUM

It was still dark when my eyes opened and my heart was boom-boom-booming very loud. *The diary!* I wanted to think about Charlotte Butler who lived in our house like a hundred years ago. I got the diary from under my pillow where I hid it for safety and switched on Dad's powerful double-D battery torch and shone it onto the pages.

Aunt Frith says the curly handwriting is 'calligraphy' and William Shakespeare used the sharp end of a bird's feather in ink to write the same way. It's hard to read because it looks like a pattern and if I hold the diary away from my eyes the letters turn into armies of ants marching up hills and down into valleys. There's one page nobody can read because drops of water have blurred the ink and washed the words away – no, not water – tears, I think and if I shut my eyes I can see Charlotte Butler crying over the page.

I closed the book and breathed out a long sigh and Aunt Frith whispered from her sleeping bag, "What's the matter, Plum?"

"Nothing," I said though it's *her* – she's the matter – and I feel funny when I look at her because it's like looking at Mom except it's my Aunt Frith and I don't know why she's with me – she's like a total alien.

Mom was funny, she made me laugh and was good at loving and hugging and listening and explaining stuff but Aunt Frith *never* listens to anything and she's not a good hugger.

She makes stupid rules about when and how you should do things and has a fat fit if I take out my dolls because in her mind girls of eleven are too old to play with dolls even though we lived next door to a lady with a wrinkly face and snowy hair who had nine beautiful china dolls she liked to talk to.

Another thing – my aunt is a muppet when it comes to plaiting hair or sewing on buttons or baking muffins – and if I wrote a list of what she can do it would end up a whole lot shorter than a list of things she can't do.

Aunt Frith crawled over to my sleeping bag.

"We're going to fetch your Dad from the airport today," she said in her pretend-happy way. She put her hand on my arm and it lay there not moving like a dead thing. I could tell her sinuses were playing up because her voice was thick and drippy.

"You know we can't stay in this house, don't you? Your father will have to find us somewhere warmer to stay until the manor is habitable or, pray God, he puts it back on the market."

A market is where you sell vegetables and stuff.

"What's that mean?" I asked.

She sniffed. "It means selling *North Wind* to another gullible buyer."

Dad's always saying, "Don't be rude – remember she's Mom's sister," but I told Aunt Frith if she didn't like *North Wind Manor* she should go back to England or France where she really wants to be and she opened her eyes wide and said, "Do you want me to go?" and I didn't even have to think "Yes!" I shouted.

I don't know if I hurt her because her face didn't change and that's another way my aunt's not like my Mom whose feelings were in her eyes for everyone to see.

FRITH

After our arrival in South Africa, I'd staggered through Cape Town airport in a stupor, exhausted after a tediously long flight. This time, I made sure we were early with time to spare and tried to imagine the scene through William's eyes.

It was one of those perfect days with a sky more blanchingly bright than any he'd have seen in years. He's missed this climate – the intense heat, the glare of the sun, the air so pure it's like a narcotic. The tarmac was burning through the soles of my shoes. Passengers were eddying and flowing, speaking in the easy, familiar South African accents that would make him feel at home although, these days, my brother-in-law talks like an upper-class Brit.

I saw Will through the glass, waiting to reclaim his luggage from the carousel.

He'd shaved his beard and his hair was closely cropped, darker than his natural straw.

He'd lost weight since Lily had died and looked thinner, younger and somehow bruised and vulnerable.

Plum hadn't spotted him yet. I savoured the next few minutes wondering what I'd think if he were a stranger in an airport. Open face, honest eyes, curving laugh lines around his mouth.

William gives the impression of being an affable, thoroughly decent person with a kind heart. Looks nothing remotely like a man who'd lie, cheat, steal or be unfaithful to his wife – and yet I know he's done these things. Even so, Lily loved him to the bitter end.

Wills wheeled his Samsonite through the automated doors and Plum crowed, *"Dadeee!"*

He steadied himself, face lighting the way it does when he sets eyes on his gangly daughter. She yelled again in that annoyingly childish, high-pitched way. *"Dadeee!"*

He flung his arms around her, hugging tight. "God, I've missed you!" I heard him say. "My world is empty without my darling girl."

"Mine too!" she laughed, wriggling free, jumping impatiently on the spot. He turned, head inclined, sizing me warily. I could tell he was nervous.

"How are you holding up, Frith?"

This is how we always start out – like graceless strangers at a party.

"So-so." I answered stiffly, "Doing the best I can, considering."

Dramatically, Plum held out a warning hand, palm facing me. "Aunt Frith – I *beg* you! Do not say *one* word about the house. I want Dad to see what it's like for himself."

"Oh dear." He looked rueful. "You don't like it, then?"

"Don't answer, Aunt Frith!" Plum shouted. "You'll *ruin* everything. Come Dad! I must be the one to show you everything."

"I'll drive," I told William, but he took the keys from my hand. "Relax," he said, stowing his luggage in the back. "I'm pretty sure I can still find my way around."

Wills' eyes met mine. "You're looking tired. You okay?"

"I've been busy," I replied, off-hand. "The house is a pig-sty!"

I jumped as Plum bellowed in my ear. "I told you not to say anything! Now Dad's got the wrong picture in his mind. You *never* listen!"

I glared. "Don't shout at me like that."

I glanced at William for support but he took Plum's hand, kissing it with loud smacking noises. "You seem meters taller, darling. How much have you sprouted since I saw you last?"

Plum giggled. "I'm so happy you're here. I absolutely *hate* it without you."

This is how it is when these two are together, there's no room for anyone else. He treats her like a spoiled baby, lets her get away with murder. No rules, no discipline, no boundaries. She's allowed to do and say whatever she wants. For her part, Plum's manipulative...winds him around her little finger.

That familiar sick feeling lodged in my stomach. I'll go mad if I have to put up with these two. A couple of months at the most and then I'm gone.

PLUM

I knew she'd ruin things, that's what she does, tries to make everyone think the same as her. Like she keeps saying there are no ghosts at *North Wind Manor* or anywhere else.

"I've never seen a ghost and I've lived a lot longer than you."

"But some people say they see ghosts."

"There's no real proof they've seen anything, Plum. These people imagine they've seen a ghost when it's their mind playing tricks. Sometimes it's a lie people tell themselves because they can't face knowing the person they've lost has gone forever."

I thought about that. "So everyone who says they've seen a ghost is lying?"

"No, of course not." Aunt Frith clicked her tongue. "I suppose they imagine they've seen something because they so desperately want to believe there's an afterlife and it's not just ashes and worms after we die."

I saw slippery worms slithering through a pile of ash and felt sick and shivery until, clear as anything, I heard Mom's voice, *"Don't be scared, Plum. I'll be right beside you, loving you through all the years of your life."*

That's what Mom said to me the day before she died.

All the way from the airport to *North Wind Manor*, Dad kept looking at me in the mirror and smiling while he was jibber-jabbering to Aunt Frith who had her nose to the window.

"These are all new, these road signs," he told me. "Named after apartheid struggle heroes, most dead by now. Sat next to a chap on the plane, a developer, who says there's a massive boom in the construction of office parks, hotels, apartment blocks, shopping malls. Mostly from foreign investment, I suppose. Good to know there's still confidence in the government."

"Huh!" Aunt Frith said. "Confidence in this government. That's a laugh!"

45

"Cheer up, Frith," Dad said and gave her knee a friendly pat but she picked up his hand and dropped it in his lap like a cockroach.

He can be so stupid sometimes. *Don't think you can make her like Mom because you can't…not in a trillion years!*

We got jammed in cars and Dad slowed until we were crawling past all these teeny falling-apart Lego-land houses stuck in mud and dirt and piles of stinky garbage with a smell so bad I had to pinch my nose.

Aunt Frith gave Dad a fierce look. "Nothing's changed, by the look of it, not a bloody thing! Hundreds – no, make that *thousands* – of squalid, makeshift cardboard and plastic shacks. Mountains of rubbish…look at all that disgusting filth! No sanitation, no electricity. Nowhere for kids to play. Goats, pigs, hens, cows, all roaming free. No water, no fencing, nowhere for animals to graze. Your friend didn't mention a massive boom in building RDP houses, I suppose? All these years under an ANC government and nothing's changed for the man in the street. If anything, it looks worse."

Dad started getting smaller like a balloon with air hissing out so I said, "I spy with my little eye, something beginning with C!"

"Chickens," said Aunt Frith.

"Wrong!' I yelled though she was right so I started thinking of another C-word – harder this time – there was a lady selling coconuts at the side of the road.

"Coconuts," my aunt said. "I'm right, aren't I?"

FRITH

William slumped as we drove out of Cape Town. He looked troubled, probably assailed by long-buried memories, battling with remorse, dwelling on Lily who'd adored this country and begged for years to come home. I know for a fact this is the last place on earth he wants to be. He's making this pilgrimage for Lily's sake. His way of atoning and keeping his pledge to bring Plum back to South Africa.

The traffic thinned. William put his foot down, accelerating away from the flat-topped mountain and the salty sea, racing to Paarl and *North Wind Manor* where my brother-in-law is going to put on a convincing show of pretending to believe he can make a new life for himself and Plum in a country he once fled.

It's a good forty minute drive to the house – William made it in just over half an hour.

He was grinning as we sped through the wrought iron gates and up the steep driveway to the graveled semi-circle at the front of the house, narrowly missing a stone obelisk at the steps.

He switched off the engine and stared up at the manor. I suppose it doesn't look *that* bad from the outside. The proportions are handsome. The roof is solid and the front door well-preserved with two sturdy columns framing the entrance. The interior, however, is quite another story.

Wills looked smug. "That photograph on the internet doesn't do this place justice."

We ambled slowly behind Plum as she skipped through the neat, brick-paved terrace with its statuary, fountains and flowerbeds, freshly forked by the faithful Oom.

"See this, Frith!" He jerked a thumb at his feet. "These bricks have been laid in the traditional Victorian herring-bone fashion."

Pompous arse, I thought. *Just you wait!*

William's eyes were sparkling.

"No word of a lie, Frith, it's exactly as I imagined it. *North Wind* has an air of…" he paused, searching. "An air of *refinement*. The grounds have been superbly designed. Over there…can you see…from the way it's laid out, that was probably once a Knott Garden."

William let out a breath. "Phew! It's a relief to finally see the house for myself. Damn dodgy business, buying property on the internet. If you're not careful, you can end up spending a fortune on a pig in a poke."

I smiled thinly.

Plum was bursting with impatience. "Dad, I can't wait to show you what it looks like inside! There's a *glorious* staircase like the one in…"

"Just a tick, darling, I almost forgot…gifts for my girls."

William scrabbled in a zippered case and pulled out two duty-free bags. "Yours," he said, pressing one into my hand.

The bag held an extravagantly large bottle of Chanel No. Five – Lily's signature perfume.

Eyes wide, Plum cried out, "That's *Mom's* perfume!"

"Oh, God, you're right!" He looked stricken.

After an awkward silence, Plum dipped into her bag and drew out an obviously expensive silky scarf, patterned with blocks of yellow and violet.

All wrong. Why would anyone buy a matronly square of shimmery silk for an eleven-year old? William's gifts are often utterly inappropriate, like the pair of white kid skates he gave Lily when she was so ill she could barely walk.

I sent Plum a sympathetic glance. Pointedly ignoring me, she tied the scarf bandanna style, around her head. "*Brilliant* Dad!"

I gave her the Chanel. "Please take this."

She aimed a burst at her wrist, inhaling deeply, closing her eyes. "I'll spray my pillow and have Mom's smell in my nose when I go to sleep."

William rallied. "Right, well, I'm keen to see that staircase. Lead on McDuff," he urged.

We trooped inside. It wasn't long before William's nostrils started quivering as he gingerly tested the air.

"*Christ!* That smell! What is it? Bad plumbing?"

Bad plumbing, wood-rot, centuries of damp, dust and dirt piling up, families of mice, spiders, pigeons, bats – take your pick. I shrugged. "Dunno. Could be anything."

"Why haven't you opened the windows?"

"Stuck tight. You try."

William made a manly show of jerking at a rusty latch, swearing as it snapped like a twig. No longer swaggering like the Lord of the Manor, his eyes roamed, taking in acres of rough, flaking walls, dull worm-eaten floors, chandeliers grimed with dirt, hanging askew.

Aware of my sleety eyes boring into his, he broke into a sweat. Perspiration darkened the back of his shirt.

Plum waved from the staircase. "There's one like this at Buckingham Palace, Dad!"

I don't know where she gets that from but the staircase *is* beautiful – if you like the *Gone with the Wind* somber, antique, dark-wood thing. Each baluster is carved with a delicate grape and vine motif and there's a raised leaf design on the newel posts. The wood is maple or teak and despite no one taking a duster to it for years, it still shines with golden luster.

We trudged up the staircase, Plum leading. At the first bend, we came upon an indented space. William is a master of little-known facts. "This used to be known as a 'coffin corner'," he told Plum. "You'd turn a coffin around in this space when you were carrying it to one of the upstairs bedrooms."

Thrilled, Plum whispered, "Why would you carry a *coffin* to a bedroom?"

"In the old days, people often died at home in their beds. Corpses would be laid out in a coffin so friends and family could pay their respects before they were carried away to be buried."

Plum gasped.

"Mind if we desist with the grisly details?" I interrupted.

William walked cautiously through a maze of shadowy, gritty corridors into cavernous bedrooms. I saw him visibly wince in a sour, mildew-spotted bathroom as his eyes fell upon ripe clusters of leggy mushrooms growing around a bath tub.

With mock-innocence, I asked, "So, still think the manor has...what was it you said...an *'air of refinement'*?"

William never admits to being wrong. "Oh, I'll admit it needs a bit of work," he said mildly, pretending to be distracted by a rusty stain blooming across the ceiling.

In the master bedroom – the size of a ballroom – Wills was showing Plum the marble mantle of an antique fireplace when his shoe sank into a rotten floor panel. I tried not to laugh as he struggled to pull his foot free.

"Be honest," I urged. "Tell me what you really think? This is not what you expected, is it?"

William made a scratchy noise at the back of his throat. "I think the bones of the house are excellent." He sounded defensive. "And, naturally, when a property is just over two centuries old, you expect this kind of wear and tear. I see there's a lot needs doing, but I anticipated that."

He gave his lopsided smile – the one that used to charm me. "And, let's not forget, Frith, I bought the manor for a song, for less than half its true market value."

"You never told me how much you paid."

"Didn't I? Well, trust me, it was a bargain. I've been able to put aside sufficient funds to cover the cost of a total restoration." He looked beseechingly at me. "I thought we'd do it together – you, me, Plum. That's partly why I bought the manor. Help take our minds off things…you know. The beginning of a new chapter…a project to bring us closer."

PLUM

I didn't know Mom and my aunt were identical twins until I saw photographs taken when they were little and they could've been the same person. Mom said they changed as they got older but then turned back into twins after her cancer grew inside. First, Mom shaved her head and Aunt Frith shaved hers '*in solidarity*' (whatever that means). Second, Mom needed glasses and picked the same thin silvery frames that Aunt Frith wore.

After Mom died I used to see her standing beside my bed though it was only for a few seconds before she melted away like sugar in water. When I told Dad, his sad-dog eyes got wet and shiny.

"Oh, Plum, how lucky you are! I keep willing myself to see her. Waiting for her to enter a room and walk towards me but she never does and that's when it hits me – I've lost my Lily and I can't bear that I'll never see her again as long as I live."

Yesterday I jumped when I saw Mom in her soft hairy blue sweater with her tiny winking jeweled Chinese slippers on her feet but the other voice in my head shouted, *"It's not Mom, stupid!"*

"How come you're wearing Mom's sweater and slippers?"

"For comfort," my Aunt said.

"I don't want you wearing them."

"Sorry, I wasn't thinking."

My aunt got changed and came back with a bar of nut chocolate and we sat on the stairs and she broke off pieces of chocolate for us and we didn't talk for ages.

"I upset you," she said at last. "I didn't mean to, it's just…I was missing her but, selfishly, I didn't stop to think how sad you would be, seeing me in her clothes."

I didn't know what my face was doing because you can't see your face unless you're looking in a mirror but I could feel it getting hot and prickly and I knew I was going to say something hateful.

"Wearing her clothes doesn't make you more like her," I said. "You're still the same person that nobody likes very much."

I was sorry after but at least she won't wear Mom's stuff again.

"I want to show you the attic!" I told Dad and we started climbing the wonky stairs to the little door at the top.

"You said I was taller. Am I looking more like Mom?" I asked.

He gave me one of his slow smiles and said, "Why yes, I think you are."

But it's not true – I don't look like Mom or Aunt Frith or Dad or Jo'burg Grandpa and I've been through all the photo albums and nobody in our family has my curly hair or nose or mouth or eyes or chin and I'm taller than everyone except Dad.

Mom explained that's because I'm an original and I'll start looking more like her as I get older though I'm almost twelve and I think once you've settled into your skin you don't change that much.

I stopped at the attic door and whispered to Dad. "You'll feel something truly awesome when you go inside."

I opened the door. It was just as I'd pictured it. Sunlight pouring over the floor like Lyle's syrup…dust sparkling…the fossilised bat in the corner…the girl-baby cot…the rocking horse with one unblinking glass eye.

"Isn't it *beautiful?*"

But Dad was coughing and thumping his chest and when he could talk he said, "This room hasn't been dusted in centuries!"

"It's a bit dusty," I mumbled.

He shook his head. "I can't even breathe in here. And it's claustrophobically small."

"What's that mean?"

"Like walls closing in."

I showed Dad the cradle and rocking horse and he said they were genuine antiques and should be in a museum so I quickly made him pinky-swear never to give them away because they belonged at *North Wind*.

I couldn't wait a minute longer. "There's a spirit in the house," I said. "This is where I feel her mostly – in the attic." Dad's eyes got bulgy and he made a funny bleating noise and said, "There's a…*what?*"

I didn't want him to be frightened. "Not like the spirits you read about in books, not spooky or scary or the haunting kind," I explained. "A *kind* spirit and loving in the way Mom's spirit would be if she'd changed her mind about going to heaven and stayed behind to keep watch over us."

"*Christ!* Is that what you think?"

"In the beginning I made up the spirit to scare Aunt Frith so she'd go back to England. But then I really did feel something warm and loving in the attic but I don't know for certain if it's Mom's spirit or the spirit of Charlotte Jane Butler."

"Who the hell is Charlotte Jane Butler?"

"The author of an old diary we found in that cupboard."

Suddenly, Aunt Frith was in the doorway looking cross with eyebrows hooked and her mouth sewn up all tight.

"I've been reading the diary to Plum but if she keeps harping on about spirits, I'll hide the damn thing away where she can't find it."

I shot a look at Dad. *See what I have to put up with?*

"I can talk until I'm blue in the face," she said. "but your daughter never listens to me. You're her father. You tell her there's no such thing as this 'spirit' she keeps obsessing about."

52

Dad laughed. "Let's be honest, Plum's always had a vivid imagination. And, I have to say, if you were making a film about a haunted house, this old manor would make a pretty convincing setting."

She made her eyes like slits. "Not helping, William."

Dad winked. "Plum, any chance you could try to put this spirit out of your mind?"

Aunt Frith rolled her eyes. "That's *pathetic,* William! Use logic and science. Explain properly why there are no ghosts."

Dad was quiet for a bit and then he said, "It all boils down to physics, Plum. When a person dies, the energy in the body is released into the environment as heat which is absorbed by living animals and plants. No energy survives after death, so, that being the case, there can't be spirits – do you see?"

"Mom said after she died her spirit would ascend into heaven and if she didn't have a spirit because all her energy had been sucked up by animals and plants then how could she be in heaven?"

Dad combed his hair with his hands until it stood all spiky on his head. "She has a point, Frith."

"Good grief – is that the best you can do? Listen, Plum, be sensible. If there were ghosts there'd be *proof!* You'd have photographs, videos, recordings, documented films – but there's no credible scientific evidence, none whatsoever to verify…"

"Okay, Frith, that's enough." Dad put his finger to his mouth to make her quiet.

He bent to whisper into my ear. "Mom's in heaven – trust me, darling. I can't explain it. I just know she's with the angels, where she belongs."

CHAPTER FIVE

FRITH

I heard Plum talking in her sleep and shook her lightly. "You've been dreaming."

Opening her eyes, she started babbling.

"I heard a baby crying like this…*hoo, hoo, hoo, hoo*. It was coming from the attic and Dahlia was in the cot, crying her eyes out but when I picked her up she went deathly quiet. Her arms and legs went floppy and when I put my hand on her chest she'd stopped breathing and that's when I knew she was *dead*."

I patted a hump and dragged the doll from where she lay concealed beneath the blankets.

"Here she is!" I jiggled the doll. "See, there's nothing wrong. Dahlia's certainly not *dead*." I laughed, ironically. "Listen to me! I've lost my marbles. Come downstairs. I'll make tea and toast. Okay?"

William was scribbling notes on a notepad. "I'm drawing up lists of what needs doing," he said, cheerfully. "Been at it since daybreak."

I couldn't resist. "If you want my advice, hire a bulldozer, reduce the place to rubble and start over from scratch."

He looked imploringly. "Be nice, Frith. Please."

"What am I to be nice about?"

"Well, can we talk about the house? I have permission from the local heritage authority to alter the place and I plan on starting the renovation right away, if that suits? With any luck, we should be done before Christmas."

I shuddered inwardly. "What are the chances of our moving elsewhere while you get the builders in?"

William looked down. "I'd prefer to remain on site, if you don't mind. I thought we'd begin upstairs and once that's all done, get on with things down here."

I groaned, dramatically.

He gave what I'm sure he thought was a winning smile. "I grant you, it won't be easy. There'll be noise and dust, workers all over the place."

"Then why can't you rent a cottage for us until…"

"Because I've never done a conversion on a listed house before. I'll have to micro-manage this to stay on top of things if I want to redeem myself."

"*Redeem* yourself?"

He nodded.

"In whose eyes?"

"Lily's, of course, she's the one who matters most. But in your eyes too. Frith – and, of course, my own."

"Lord! You need no redemption from me! As for Lil, she forgave you everything, you know she did."

"Yet, I've so many regrets, Frith." He presented his earnest face. "There's so much I wish I could undo. I just pray Lily knew, in the end, I never meant to make her unhappy."

Too late! I wanted to shout. *Too late for regrets now!*

"We none of us mean half the things we do," I said sharply, "yet we do them all the same."

The previous night, unpacking my case, I'd found a pile of Lily's letters in a Roses chocolate box. My tart comment brought one to mind.

"Dearest Frith,

Something shocking and shameful has happened and, as always, you're the only one I can tell.

You'll remember I wrote that Wills got that job at the firm of stockbrokers – Van Dam & Associates.

I haven't the foggiest how he landed the position but, knowing him, he probably lied through his teeth to get in. I was terribly nervous, but he was so confident, so convinced he'd be a success.

Right away, Wills was out of his depth. He knew nothing of stocks, bonds, currencies, securities and something called 'futures'. Van Dam money managers are cutthroat and were openly scathing, waiting like vultures for Wills to be dismissed for incompetence. This attitude brings out the best in William. He enrolled in an online college, studying global money markets long into the nights.

It wasn't long before the senior partner made him manager of a promising hedge fund and clients started calling him, 'King Midas.'

The promotion went to his head. He grew cocksure. "You, my darling, are married to a financial manager of one of the biggest brokers in the country. It's like a dream, Lily. I earn a fortune to play with other people's money." It was about that time he bought our new house...our new car...then we spent two weeks in Mauritius. I called after our holiday and you asked why I sounded so down when we were living the high life, remember?

Here's what you don't know. Wills' luck ran out. He started making more losses than gains, telling no-one in the company, covering the losses, faking steady profits, producing fictional accounts and robbing Peter to pay Paul until his funds crashed.

One night, he confessed to me. He blamed the markets, blamed his partners – even blamed his clients for being so naive as to put their eggs in one basket. I thought he'd own up to his mistakes and try to pay back the money but he panicked and insisted we run away like common criminals.

We packed what we could, left the rest behind and drove like thieves in the night from Johannesburg to Robertson. That's where we are now. Wills has a job selling wine for the Celeste Estate. We live in a small house near the farm.

I'm desperately unhappy, Frith. There's something broken between us. I've stopped trying for a baby – it's not going to happen after all this time and, anyway, I'm not sure I want one with William now.

Who is this man? How could he do something like this?

I must see you – it's been forever since we were together. I've been thinking of coming to stay for a month or so. I've money of my own, enough for food and I can help with utilities and so forth.

I'm suffocating here. So ashamed I can barely bring myself to go out in case someone recognises me…"

Plum came into the kitchen, carrying Dahlia. The sight of the doll set my teeth on edge. "Would you like a boiled egg?"

She nodded. "Don't make it slimy – it *has* to be hard-boiled which means six minutes in boiling water. Will you read the diary to me today, please?"

PLUM

I've been having dreams so real it's like I'm living inside them.

First there's a dream where I'm sitting on the rocking horse and it changes into a real horse of muscle and blood and starts snorting and pawing the ground. I bow my head over the horse's neck and grip hard with my riding boots and we fly right through the attic window and thunder across the wide flat fields that go on and on forever.

Even now, if I close my eyes, I can bring the dream back to where I hear the horse panting and see its lips opening to show square yellow teeth and there's this thud, thud, thud behind as its hooves kick up lumps of mud and grass.

If anyone asks if I can ride I'll have to say 'yes' because that's what I did in this dream and it was so real I smelled horse on my fingers next morning.

Then there's this dream where Dahlia dies in my arms and I try to wake myself up before I get to the place where her heart stops. I described the dream to Aunt Frith but left out the part where the attic door slams and I'm locked inside with my dead baby and the air gets thick and cotton-woolly and then there's only blackness.

I was thinking about this when I heard Dad's voice in my ears, "Plum… *Plum!"*

I opened my eyes and his face was so close I could see threads of wispy gold hairs on his cheeks. "You've had a blank, darling," he said.

"Not a blank," I said. "I've just climbed out of a dream about a horse."

Aunt Frith came in. "She's been having these seizures since the day after we arrived. Five so far by my count."

She doesn't know what she's talking about.

"I feel sorry for a person who can't tell the difference between someone thinking about a dream and someone having a blank," I said.

There's a big difference. The way Mom explained, 'having a blank' is like sleeping with my eyes open and after this I can't remember anything that happened.

When I'm thinking I might have a funny look on my face but I'm right here and I remember *everything*.

Aunt Frith told me in her snippy way to eat my egg before it got cold.

Dad gave his crooked smile. "Would you like to venture an opinion as to why your aunt is dressed for the North Pole?"

"Because this house is bloody freezing!" Aunt Frith snapped.

Dad's appointed me 'Senior Foreman' on the restoration and I promised I wouldn't let him down.

Dad says building's in our blood. Our family have been builders for hundreds of years and when he was my age, Dad could point out roads, bridges, libraries, schools and even a city hall his father and grandfather once built in shiny white marble.

Dad has a theory that building's been *'calculated into our genetic code'* (I haven't worked out what that means yet) and says he hopes he's inherited the skill of his forefathers because he could certainly do with it now.

I made Dad tell me again how his father died when a steel girder fell from very high up hitting the back of his head and decapitating him. Decapitating means having your head cut off. I had to look up *'girder'* – it's a beam made of steel.

Dad sliced his toast into triangles. "Your average construction worker is six times more likely to be killed at work than any other man on the job."

I *love* it when Dad talks like I'm a grown-up.

He counted on his fingers. "There's the obvious – falling from a roof or a ladder, a collapsing scaffold or broken safety harness. Then there are electrocutions and power-tool accidents. Fires and explosions. Accidents from defective cranes, dumpers and forklifts. And then there's falling debris – like the steel girder that killed my father in his prime."

Aunt Frith wiggled her eyebrows at him. "But nothing like that will happen on this building site, *will it?*"

It's funny how she wants me to be what she calls 'a big girl' but talks over my head like I'm a dumb little kid who doesn't know what's going on.

Dad said, "No, no, of course not! You and me, Plum, we're project bosses so we're quite safe. Our job is to keep our eyes peeled and make sure all work is done to best practice standards."

Dad was shiny from the shower and smelling of aftershave – something lemony – and I said he didn't look like a proper builder.

"Ah, but you haven't seen me in my hard-hat and cement-splattered work boots."

"You should have a big blue ink tattoo on your muscly arm," I told him.

He laughed. "All that is easily remedied, my sweet. Now, first order of business – pass the *Yellow Pages* and let's get cracking."

FRITH

For no reason I can fathom, I keep thinking back to that first year in France. The hideous flat I shared with three other students near *The Paris College of Art*. That kitchen with its distinctive pong of garlic and onions…the grimy shower stall…the mucky, narrow bedroom with its dreary, uninspiring view of the Metro.

'Lily has the brains. Frith is the artistic one.' Something in our mother's early judgement always felt wrong. It's too easy to slap on labels because one is good at maths and the other can draw. Our mother didn't care one way or the other where our talents lay, but father played along, encouraging art at school, paying for classes with a tutor who'd studied in Florence. That's how it begins – Lily the brilliant neurosurgeon, Frith the arty-farty painter, potter, sculptor – whatever she finally decides to do with her life.

I went to live in France after Lily and Wills got married and started trying for their baby.

They were so lovey-dovey, so convinced they were the only happy couple in the world and it turned me sour as a pickle. None of the men I knew could hold a candle to William.

It wasn't only his looks – they lacked his sex appeal, brains and personality. On top of this, they bored me rigid. It frightened me I couldn't stop thinking of my sister's husband, couldn't stop wanting him for myself.

Lily and I had never lived apart before. It took every ounce of courage to pack a bag and say goodbye. I chose France and Father, bless him, paid my tuition at *The Paris College of Art*.

In those days the school was known as '*Parsons Paris*' because the college had had a relationship with the famous 'American Parsons School of Design'. It's always struck me as ironic that in a city thronging with French artists, I ended up in a class of mainly American, English and even a few South African students.

I lost my confidence that first day at *Parsons Paris*. A wall of self-portraits painted by first year students both enraptured and terrified me. Compared to these, my bulging portfolio of etchings and watercolours seemed mediocre at best.

Driven by a fear of being judged and found wanting by peers and teachers, I spent that junior year working day and night. Friendless and alone, I longed desperately for Lily, missed home and never stopped dreaming of William.

I suppose I chose Max because he was the antithesis of Wills – lanky as a lathe with acne-scarred skin and a smoker's tarry cough, bubbling up from his lungs.

Max seemed indisputably French right down to his clichéd black beret worn at a rakish angle but he told me in a lazy drawl that home was Santa Barbara, California, where his folks owned a dog-grooming parlour.

Two years ahead of me, Max saw himself as a tortured Jackson Pollock, laying canvases on the floor, crawling around them on all fours, smearing sand and broken glass into pools of wet acrylic.

It was Max who introduced me to Pollock's work and explained how the artist died tragically at 44 when his green Oldsmobile smashed into a tree near his Long Island home. The story stuck with me. Pollock had been driving too fast in an alcoholic haze with his mistress, Ruth Klingman – who had survived the crash – and her beautiful friend, Edith Metzger, just 25, who'd died standing up on the back seat screaming until the last second of her life that she wanted to get out of the car.

Why am I thinking of this now? It's so odd, all these long forgotten memories and chunks of irrelevant information flooding back after all this time. The story of Pollock's death means nothing to me though it was once a subject of grim fascination for Max who might be dead himself by now, for all I know. I think it may be something to do with living in this old house that's unlocked the memory compartment in my brain.

I told this to Wills who made a typically obscure William comment about the human brain being roughly the size of a grapefruit with the consistency of warm butter. He stores random information in his two hemispheres while my memory is rooted in the past and mostly about Lily and me when we were younger. I can't seem to stop rehashing our history, doggedly retracing my steps, working out where I went wrong and what I should've done to fix things before it was too late. Regret is such a wasted emotion.

"Max plays my body like a violin!" Hard to believe but I wrote this cringe-worthy, Mills and Boon drivel in a letter to Frith. Violin my arse!

My sexual fantasies were of Wills and when Max and I made love, his blue-white sunken chest with its coarse black hair would morph into Wills' smooth, tanned muscular torso. I'd try to imagine the smell and taste of Wills' skin – cedar and soap – I'd decided, traced very faintly with salt. Max smoked Gauloises and his mouth held the flavour of smoky liquorice tinged with espresso.

I was lost without Lily but my time at *Parsons Paris* made me who I am today.

Parsons was where I learned to paint and Paris taught me how to make love, dance, dress like a French woman and drink red wine.

I learned to be free in Paris. To be the only person on earth who looked like me, talked like me and thought like me. When I called Lily to tell her of my new freedom, I think I used the awful cliché, '*finding myself*'.

I remember laughing over the phone. "It's taken long enough, but I think I'm finally an individual…independent, unencumbered…*original.*"

Silence at the other end.

"Lil?"

"Good for you!" Lily had answered, bluntly. "But, I'm still your twin, no matter where in the world you are. We'll always be half of a circle. And, by the way, I've never felt – '*encumbered*' – as you put it."

When I received Lily's letter asking if she could come to stay with me, I did something shameful. I wrote back with a list of excuses. I was studying for mid-term exams…the flat was poky…Max and his canvases had moved in and there was no room for another guest…the landlord would have a fit.

The real reason was simple. I wanted to keep Lily away from my new life. I hadn't told anyone I was a twin and didn't want fellow students meeting my sister and drawing comparisons in which I'd, inevitably, come off worse.

I ended my letter with: "*My advice, for what it's worth – patch up things with Wills. It's one mistake, Lil, anyone can make a mistake – you can't hold it against him forever. And if you can't have a baby, why don't you adopt?*"

Wills spoke about regrets. Not offering Lily a safe harbour when she needed it most will always be one of mine.

PLUM

Dad kept making phone calls so I sneaked away to talk to the Oom who was chasing leaves with his broom in the garden.

"My name's Plum."

The Oom's face was soft and droopy like the chamois Dad uses to clean the car and he had silvery veins on the backs of his hands and no shoes on his feet.

I asked how long he'd been at *North Wind Manor* and the Oom said, "Since 1972."

"What was it like then?"

He was quiet a long time and then he said, "In the old days we had six horses in the stables…grew grapes in those fields…made good wine."

The Oom had no teeth only smooth shiny gums and I wondered how he managed toast but didn't think he'd like me asking so I said, "Is there a spirit living in our house?"

The Oom looked like he didn't understand.

"A ghost," I explained. "Is there a ghost living at *North Wind Manor*?" But the Oom didn't answer and started sweeping again and if I'd been a detective I'd have thought he was acting suspiciously so I stopped this line of questioning until I could win his trust.

I liked the soft, sleepy whisking noise the broom was making on the stone path and asked if I could have a turn.

"We got plenty weeds."

"Oh, *good!*" I clapped my hands. "Show me what to do!"

The Oom shook his head like he couldn't believe his ears. "You saying you *never* weeded?"

"Not once in my entire life!"

The Oom took me to a shed where he took a tool from a hook – a funny-shaped fork with a sharp prong in the middle and pointed to a patch of weedy lawn.

"You want to pull up the blackjack and goose grass." His knees creaked like old doors when he knelt down. "You got to dig deep to take up the root. Watch what I do."

I loved the soft flump the weeds made coming up with a ball of soil still clinging to the roots.

"I think I'm going to *adore* weeding," I told the Oom.

I pulled up a mountain of weeds and when I was nearly finished the Oom brought two chipped mugs of hot tea that tasted sweet and smelled like honey.

"This is funny tea!"

"You never heard of *Rooibos*?"

He drank with rude slurping noises and then lay back against a tree and started snoring with his mouth open. I stretched on the grass listening

63

to Turtledoves cooing in the trees and watching leaves float and fall on my body and last thing I thought before I fell asleep was if I got buried under them would anyone find me?

FRITH

I found her asleep on the lawn in a wide-brimmed straw hat which cast a finely meshed shadow on her face. I recognised the hat as belonging to Oom Jacob. She looked grubby. Half-moons of dirt under her nails, a streak of mud on her chin, plaits coming undone. I had an urge to lie beside her, pull her close and listen to her breathing while she slept in my arms. I didn't do that. If I touch her she immediately draws away with that *'You're not my Mom'* look on her face.

"She'll come to love you," Lily had promised. "Be patient. Give her time."

"But she won't Lily! She won't ever love me because I'm not you. We argue non-stop, rubbing up against one another. All this friction can't be good for Plum, with her seizures and everything. As for me, I say things without thinking and wish I hadn't but, by then the damage is done. Your daughter is like you. She has an instinctual bullshit monitor. 'Sorry' doesn't hack it with Plum, if you don't mean it. I can't stay here for long, Lil, not even for you. Please understand. Soon I'll go home, back to my apartment in Paris. I'll take up painting again, look up old friends. Who knows? I may find a man to marry me, ha, ha. The other day I snapped at Wills about how he'd hurt you. "We none of us mean half the things we do," I told him from the lofty position of my high horse, "but we do them all the same." Afterwards I wondered…who was I talking about – him, or me?"

CHAPTER SIX

PLUM

Dad set up a table in the hallway where we'd be interviewing people to work on the restoration.

"Your role will be to separate the wheat from the chaff."

I didn't know what that meant.

"Really? Mmm. Well, chaff is the dry, inedible husk around the ripe wheat grain. Separating these is called '*winnowing*'. So, Plum, my sweet, quite simply, your job is to winnow the good from the bad. Or, put another way, you'll be the one 'separating the sheep from the goats'."

I wasn't sure what that meant either.

Dad gave me a pen and a notebook and on the cover he'd written, '*Plum Westwood – Senior Foreman. Project: North Wind Conversion*'.

I divided the first page into two columns and above one I wrote '*Wheat (Sheep)*' but then I got stuck. "How do you spell '*chaff*?'"

Aunt Frith had organised cleaners and eight ladies in blue overalls with white doeks arrived with buckets, brooms, mops and feather dusters and started sweeping, stirring up a swirly tornado of dust. I thought of the *Twelve Days of Christmas* and started singing, '*Eight maids a-sweeping*' until Aunt Frith put her finger to her lips and said, "These women are domestic workers. It's not pc to call them 'maids' anymore."

Builders began coming and I listened to them answering Dad's questions. You can tell when someone's lying – the clue is in the eyes – they never look right into yours, they slide from side to side or stare at their shoes.

I liked the builders who smiled more than the serious ones but wasn't sure writing *'Looks kind'* was what Dad meant by 'winnowing'. Then I heard him saying things like, "See you Monday," or "I'll need a quote – that'll be the deciding factor – just how competitive you are."

I told him, crossly. "You don't need me to winnow. You made that up."

"Not true, darling! I rely entirely on your feminine intuition. That last chap for instance, what did you think of him?"

Dad tells lies sometimes. Small lies like when Mom was very sick and he said she was still as beautiful as when they'd first met and whoppers like the night he said he'd been working late when he'd really been with Aunt Frith.

I wish I hadn't told Mom. When I think about her crying I have to twist a bit of skin on my wrist and dig in with the nails on my thumb and middle finger until I bleed.

It doesn't change anything but it hurts and makes me feel like I'm being punished and that's a good thing because I should be.

I heard Aunt Frith calling me. "It seems your Dad has things under control. We're not wanted here," she said. "Let's find out what Charlotte Butler is getting up to."

She was feeling sorry for me. I couldn't see it in her face but there was a bit of sorry-ness in her voice.

FRITH

I stood in the draughty hallway watching William wearing his inscrutable Chinese face as he consulted with conversion specialists. He was annoyingly jaunty as he outlined his fuzzy vision of bringing the manor into the twenty-first century. He's such an imposter!

You'd never guess Wills' knowledge of building can be written on the head of a pin. Elbows planted on the table, a genial smile on his face – he comes across as an expert, taking in an unsuspecting audience with his little act. I'm the only one who knows what a tit he's making of himself.

Catching my eye, he winked across the room. That wink made me angry. It felt strangely *proprietorial*. But Plum's the one I feel sorry for. There she sits, scribbling pointlessly in her notebook, totally under her father's spell.

I asked her to join me outdoors and we perched side by side on the cold stone bench near the pond. It was a perfect morning. Beetles were skimming across water, lily pads turning yellow in the heat, curling at the edges.

*Lily…*oh, please don't think of her now.

I settled my reading glasses on my nose and found the place in the diary.

December 18th, 1904

I hold myself supremely blessed – so this is how it feels to be truly happy!

I must confess this emotion is foreign to one resigned to a calm, steady ticking of the heart – not this joyful exuberance pervading my entire being.

My happiness is not only the result of Edward's absence but of being granted the freedom to do as I please. Reveling in my new-found independence, I had the servants take down the heavy velvet bed-hangings and replace these with floating drapes of muslin. Walls and ceilings have been covered with an ivory distemper and we have painted dull wooden panels in a soft shade of blue-green made by mixing the earth pigment – terra verde – with white of egg and buttermilk.

I am not convinced my husband will approve of these changes to the manor though, since he is entirely consumed with self, perhaps he will not notice.

Our industry extends to the garden where the men have set out an arbor of rose trees encircling a tranquil pond. Winding stone pathways have been laid beside a flourishing vegetable garden and this very day we have commenced with building a wine cellar.

I take great pleasure in spending Edward's money. Lately, I have purchased a mowing machine, one dozen laying hens and two crowing cocks, six wide-mouthed stone jars and a statuette of a splendidly naked Venus with which to beautify the grounds. (The hens are more a prudent investment than an indulgence. Cook has promised to show me how to pickle eggs for the stone jars.)

December 25th, 1904

I find myself alone yet quite content this Christmas day.

Our servants are gathered in the barn, singing hymns of praise. Their festive luncheon, a pig roasting with sweet potatoes and pumpkins in a fire-pit, has been paid for by money left by their lord and master whose purse has also provided each of our workers with a stout pair of new leather boots.

I lift a glass of ruby claret to make a season's toast of gratitude to my husband for his uncharacteristic acts of charitable generosity.

December 26th, 1904

Boxing Day holiday – a day of delightful repose!

To stop myself growing dull from solitude, I have been sewing a quilt: cutting squares, circles, hexagons and diamonds from scraps of cretonne, taffeta and brocade: some patterned, some plain.

My dear spinster aunt sewed exquisite quilts and I am hopeful this intricate craft is not beyond my capability and will keep me happily occupied for many months to come.

Why, I wonder, do I so dread periods of idleness? Can it be because, with time hanging heavily upon my hands, my thoughts are helplessly drawn towards Edward's inevitable return – a terrifying prospect that brings with it dark feelings of consternation and wretchedness.

January 10th, 1905

I am resolved to walk a little further every day, straying from the boundaries of the manor and edging, little by little, into the town of Paarl where I am considered an interloper and not made welcome.

Despite this, I venture forth claiming a need for fresh air, exercise and a visit to the drapery for needles and thread- when what I truly seek is human contact and the possibility, however remote, of friendship.

A dreadful calm has settled on Paarl as on other towns in South Africa. Beneath this deceptively still surface, memories remain fresh. The war is not yet forgotten, wounds are raw and many harbour anger and resentment against the English for committing harsh acts of oppression and insult towards the Boers.

This morning, on my way to town, I passed by a small cottage where two young boys were milking a goat. I waved and was gratified to see how the boys waved and smiled in return.

From there I proceeded more lightly – thankful to these innocent children for perceiving me as one untainted by my country's terrible deeds.

In town, I purchased a gift for myself – a charming box of Windsor & Newton watercolour paints in nine essential shades. I am only a dabbling amateur, yet I shall take pleasure in setting my easel in the open air and painting my beloved North Wind Manor against a backdrop of sky and tattered clouds.

January 14th, 1905

My little maid, Pretty, informs me the house where I saw the two boys is owned by Mrs. Aletta Prinsloo – a widow who lost her husband and eldest son in the war. Pretty says the family survives by living frugally on homegrown vegetables, fruit and milk from their scrawny goat.

Today I began sketching an outline of the manor. I have found when I am rendering an impression of North Wind Manor, tranquility descends. I tore up several poor attempts before I was even moderately satisfied with my drawing. It seems so elemental – a simple sketch of a large, square structure – yet it proves beyond me to capture the house with complete accuracy. I may have to create a more impressionistic drawing.

January 15th, 1905

I am in a state of suspension...spending time in idleness, unpicking my quilt and starting over, tearing up drawings and beginning again. I cannot focus my attention on any task other than daydreaming.

How I love sitting in the garden with the healing sun upon my face and the cheeping of scattered hens filling my ears. In such moments I allow my thoughts to idly consider a life exactly like this – but without Edward! How blissfully happy I should be.

January 20th, 1905

I could not stop thinking of the impoverished Prinsloo family – this mother and her two boys weigh heavily upon my conscience. I made up a basket with meal, coffee, eggs, sugar, butter and honey and took it to them.

After knocking, I observed a figure, presumably Mrs. Prinsloo, peering from behind a window.

At once drapes were drawn and the door latched and bolted. With a heavy heart, I set my basket upon the stoep and made my way slowly home.

Later, I heard banging at our back door and there, on the steps, stood the Prinsloo boys, barefoot and smiling, the eldest carrying an enamel jug of fresh goat's milk.

He spoke in Afrikaans. "Ma se baie dankie, Mevrou,"

'Their mother thanks you,' Pretty translated. (To her credit, my maid speaks this language fluently.)

I gave the boys a pot of stewed peach comfiture for their trouble and they ran back down the path, happy as you please.

February 6th, 1905

It has become something of a regular routine, this exchange of gifts between me and my neighbour. Every week, I leave a basket at the gate and sooner or later, regular as clockwork, the Prinsloo boys turn up with a squash, an armful of spinach, a jar of milk or fresh picked strawberries.

This morning, Aletta Prinsloo beckoned me into a neat, scantily furnished cottage. She speaks no English and I have only a few words of Afrikaans so we made do with mime and understood one another well enough. She offered breakfast – a bowl of mealie pap – and after this we took coffee in the garden where I was proudly shown a grove of fruit trees: lemon, apricot, plum, peaches and loquat.

Here in a cool, dim space beneath an almond tree, Mrs. Prinsloo pointed to a shaded grave marked with a humble wooden cross where a young daughter, lost to typhoid, lies buried. A tear gleamed when the mother spoke and I saw how this painful loss grieves her still.

Before my departure, Mrs. Prinsloo gripped my two hands in hers. I believe I may have made my first true friend!

I am, at last, well-pleased with my latest pencil sketch of North Wind Manor. Tomorrow, if the day is fine and I am able to sit outdoors, I shall begin painting.

February 20th, 1905

This morning, I left the green and tussocky country lanes to venture into Paarl where I wandered down a wide street, beyond the drapers and seed shop, to a place I have never been before.

As a caution, I wore my wide-brimmed black bonnet to hide my face from the inquisitive glances of townsfolk and tradesmen.

The Great Depression afflicts us still, yet I am encouraged to observe increasing signs of prosperity in Main Street. I counted three wagon builders, a bustling carpentry workshop, an ironmongers, a shop selling paint, two flourishing blacksmiths and a hansom carriage works.

There are two churches in the town, the 'Het Gesticht' and the 'Strooidak'. It was the latter that called out to me – the stark white gables summoning me like graceful beacons.

I took refuge in the quiet, dim sanctuary of that church and a comforting silence pressed upon my ears.

I had been there for half an hour or so when a young man seated himself at an organ and began leafing through sheet music. I observed the straightness of his posture, the way his thick black hair curled into the nape of his neck, the slenderness of his pale hands riffling through a binder of pages.

He began to play and so soothing was his touch upon the keys, I dipped into momentary slumber and when I woke it was to discover the organist looking down upon me, smiling.

The organist spoke Afrikaans in a most mellifluous voice but, seeing my confusion, changed swiftly to English and asked politely if I were new to the parish and when I nodded, said, with genuine warmth, "Then I am pleased to welcome you to our church."

He gave his name as Dirk Barnard and his occupation as church organist, choir master and music teacher. He paused to allow me to reveal my identity and

I did so with reluctance though, since there was no alteration to his agreeable countenance, Mr. Barnard has not yet made acquaintance with the reputation of Captain Edward Butler of North Wind Manor – a small mercy for which I am deeply grateful.

February 28th, 1905

During this past week, I have visited the Strooidak Kerk no less than three times. Vainly, I attempt to convince myself I am seeking out the church for solace and prayer – yet, in my heart, I know my intentions are far less pure. I shall never admit this to a living soul but, for the life of me, I cannot stop thinking of the organist, Dirk Barnard.

Last night, in a dream, he was playing a piece by Bach – expressly for me. The music was everywhere, filling my being to overflowing. I woke trembling, astonished at the depth of emotion this man has unleashed after the briefest meeting.

Mortifying shame overwhelms me. How unseemly for an older married woman to fill her foolish head with improper thoughts of a handsome bachelor and, what's more, a clearly devout man of the church!

March 10th, 1905

Fine weather keeps me in the garden where our blooming rose trees scent the air with dizzying sweetness. There is a new swallows' nest in the eaves of the shed and often I see the parent birds darting, unafraid, above my head. Swallows bring luck, they say. Oh how I pray this is so!

I have been at my easel, painting the house in palest tints against a misty sky. I lack a true artist's skill to render North Wind Manor as fine as it deserves, but, perhaps with practice and patience, my art shall improve.

Inappropriate visions of Dirk Barnard still crowd my head. How is it possible to dwell so much upon a man I barely know?

March 12th, 1905

With the cellar complete, we have turned our attentions to digging founda-tions for the stables where Edward has plans to keep a fine pair of greys.

An hour ago, a group of riotous young boys made mischief hurling eggs at our front door! Many hit the two white columns rising on either side of the door, staining them most dreadfully with yolk.

I am appalled at such acts of sinful wastefulness when so many of Paarl's townsfolk are starving.

This was no idle practical joke. These boys were shouting obscenities, calling out in Afrikaans and there was no mistaking the hard, ugly contempt in their voices.

When I asked Moses, our head gardener, what they had said, he refused to tell me for fear of causing offense. If I am to fend for myself in these parts, I shall have to learn to speak this language.

March 22nd, 1905

Today I joined the Strooidak choir – a large assembly of ladies with excellent singing voices.

I was gravely disappointed to learn the organist, Dirk Barnard, has taken leave of absence to visit an ailing aunt in Pretoria. I see God has seen fit to punish me for my conniving. He knows how little I care for singing.

The replacement organist – stern-faced and formidable, Miss Emeline Kriel – wasted no time informing me that she, like so many in this war-torn land, had been imprisoned and subjected to monstrous indignities in a filthy, over-crowded British camp.

What was I to say? I apologised most sincerely on behalf of my countrymen. I am appalled at injustices committed by the British army – but surely there must come a time when Miss Kriel and others like her look beyond the war and recognise the courage it takes for an Englishwoman to live in a land where so many still view her as an enemy?

Miss Kriel made me stand at the back where my soprano is drowned by loud alto and contralto voices...I consider this a fitting punishment for my deceit!

April 5th, 1905

I arrived early for choir practice and had been waiting only a few moments when, to my surprise, Dirk Barnard advanced. "Mrs. Butler," he smiled. "I hear you have joined our choir!"

Immediately, I turned to stone – struck dumb – opening and closing my lips like a gasping goldfish in our garden pond. I had a sudden sharp pain in my chest, as if Dirk Barnard had seized my heart between his two hands!

Praise God, a group of choristers entered the church at that moment. I searched their faces for signs they may have seen my blushing confusion. Thankfully, they remained expressionless, so perhaps my feelings are not as transparent as I imagine them to be.

How foolish I feel – behaving like a simpering schoolgirl.

April 7th, 1905

A telegraph has come. Edward will return home within the week!

Oh, God, I have dreaded this day for so long and, now that it is here, I find myself becoming, by degrees, utterly dejected and weepy.

I have put away my quilting. My painting is not yet finished. I have no heart for such pastimes now.

April 10th, 1905

Worn to fiddle strings with preparations for Edward's homecoming, I am taking a mixture of Phosphorus and Nux Vomica for nerves and exhaustion.

The maids have been polishing and dusting, the men mowing, pruning and setting everything to rights. With Edward gone for many months, we have all grown forgiving of dust on furniture and leaves on lawns.

Linens have been washed and the silver brightened with Goddards paste. Garden bulbs are sending out shoots and small, hard fruits are beginning to ripen upon the trees. Despite this activity, these are bleak days. I do my utmost to conceal my distress from the servants though I cannot fail to notice they too are downcast. A cloud has settled over North Wind Manor. Now we must wait for the storm.

FRITH

Plum's face was rapt. "That painting in the cupboard – *she did it!*"

"Yes." I nodded.

"She never finished it." Plum lowered her voice: "Something happened after her husband came back." Dutch-doll circles flamed her cheeks. "I *desperately* want to find the house where Mrs. Prinsloo lived with her two boys and the goat and…and I want to see the church where Charlotte met the organist – what was it called? It had a weird name."

"The Strooidak Kerk. *Strooidak* means *'roof of straw'* and *kerk* is 'church'. The church is in Main Street. I've seen it. We can go there together, if you like."

"There are bits of broken statue in the grass – do you think that's the naked Venus Charlotte bought with Edward's money? The pond she talks about is our pond – at least I think it is – and the stables are…"

"Whoa! Slow down! Take a breath."

"I *have* to know what happens to Charlotte, it's absolutely *vital*. Promise you'll read to the very end of the diary. Promise you won't hide it away, like you said."

I promised. Tentatively, without meeting my gaze, Plum laid her hand on my knee.

She's *never* done this before and I was secretly thrilled. Very lightly, I stroked my thumb against her knuckles, back and forth it went, back and forth. And the simple fact she allowed her hand to remain docilely on my leg for just shy of a minute made me hopeful.

CHAPTER SEVEN

PLUM

There's a rusting sign outside our gate that says *North Wind Manor* and as we passed I tapped the square of curly iron and made it sway with a thin tinny squeak.

"Touch for luck," I told myself.

We were walking to Main Street to explore the church and Aunt Frith took off her sweater and tied it around her waist. "I feel as if I could walk forever," she said, like I wasn't there and she was by herself. "Walk to the back of beyond, to the very ends of the earth."

I said the earth is round and doesn't have an end and she blinked at me and I knew she'd forgotten I was with her.

"Your father's using his BBC television presenter voice this morning, have you noticed?" She laughed like a small dog barking. "I can't believe the audacity! It's such a farce – posing as an authority on listed buildings when he knows bugger-all."

But she wasn't laughing – her mouth was a straight line.

"Dad comes from a family of builders," I said. "Building's in his blood!"

"Ha!"

By the time we reached a signpost pointing to *Main Street* I had a blister where my shoe was rubbing my heel and Aunt Frith was dying for a coffee so we stopped at a café and sat at a table next to a spotted dog asleep on a red sofa.

A waitress with a button: *'My name is Zoe'* – brought a pamphlet – a *'Tour guide to Paarl'* and inside I found a teeny black and white picture of the Strooidak Kerk – *'the oldest Dutch Reformed Church in South Africa.'*

"Look!" I showed Aunt Frith.

Zoe flicked a cloth over the table and crispy crumbs flew into my lap. "I'm guessing you two are on holiday, right?"

Rudely, Aunt Frith stuck her nose in the pamphlet so I said we'd moved here from England and were living at *North Wind Manor*.

"Oooh!" The waitress made her eyes pop out. "Aren't you the lucky ones?"

"Lucky!" My aunt's face was all twisted. "You must be joking! That house has been standing empty for years. You've no idea what it's like inside."

"But, I have – I've been there!" Zoe said. "You can't see much because of the windows being dirty but you get an idea and I think it's awesome, I really do."

'Thank you.' I shaped my lips to say the words without making a sound – like talking to a deaf person – but Zoe spoiled it by answering, "My pleasure."

She went off to get our drinks and I nudged Aunt Frith: *"See!* It's not only me and Dad – this Zoe person also loves our house and she's only looked through the windows!"

FRITH

We stopped at an outdoor café with pavement tables and striped umbrellas and, incongruously, a crimson brocade chaise with a large, spotted Dalmatian sprawled against the cushions.

The waitress, a nosy little thing with a vapid expression, told us *North Wind Manor* is the most authentic Georgian house in Paarl. "Good to know," I mumbled, making it obvious I didn't want to talk. Naturally, Plum was overjoyed at the girl's comment.

She gets this annoying 'point scoring' thing from her father. Who gives a toss if a silly little waitress approves of the house? It's always a competition with William and Plum – who's right, who's wrong – one endlessly attempting to outdo the other and trying to trip me up in the bargain. They didn't do this with Lily – or not that I noticed, anyway.

It was a lovely morning with a cloudless sky. I leaned back, lifting my face to the sunlight.

I hate to admit it, but Paarl is starting to grow on me. Main Street is wide and well-kept, lined with spreading trees and elegant Cape Dutch, Georgian and Victorian buildings, it's really quite charming.

Sipping my cappuccino, I watched Plum poring over a pamphlet. I'm no longer used to the African heat after too many sunless summers spent in Europe. The sun makes me lightheaded and drowsy, as if I'm floating in a soap bubble, a spectator idly watching what's going on through a fragile, soapy membrane.

I caught Plum staring curiously and reluctantly roused myself.

"Let's find that church," I said.

On the way, we came upon a square of neatly-staked vines between two stately homes and, behind these, a field of fruit trees in bloom with pale pink blossoms falling like confetti.

"There it is!" Plum shouted, recognising the church gables in the distance. I heard bells and we stopped to listen until their pealing faded.

We entered the churchyard through a squeaky gate and followed a trodden grassy path to an enormous wooden door, half open. Cool, worn flagstones underfoot. Stacked piles of old, leather-bound prayer books. Pews worn to silky smoothness. Light filtering through arched stained-glass windows. Dying roses, petals browning and withering, leaves turning crisp.

A lingering fragrance of beeswax candles, furniture polish and slimy water left too long in flower vases. It's been forever since I was in a church and for some reason, it brought a lump to my throat until I remembered… it wasn't so long ago, the day of Lily's funeral.

Plum beamed. "There's the organ." As she pointed, her finger trembled. She turned, face glowing. "It's *his*, isn't it? The one Dirk Barnard played."

"We can't be certain."

"I think it is. It *has* to be."

I eased off my shoes and slid into a pew while Plum tiptoed around the organ, lightly touching the keys before wandering through the vestry to the altar with its melted candles. As she reached to turn the vestry doorknob, I called out: "*Don't* go in there!"

My voice echoed.

Plum lifted a finger to her mouth. "Shhhh! You have to be *quiet* in a church."

Seconds after we left, Plum begged me to bring her back next day.

"I haven't soaked it all up enough yet," she said. "I need more time." I should have known the diary would become another of Plum's obsessions. She's been this way since a toddler. Dolls, butterflies, stamps, she gets stuck on something for months and then, when her interest finally wanes, she immediately fixates on another thing.

Plum's obsessions consume her thoughts and dreams and monopolise her conversations. This intense preoccupation drives me mad – but there's a small chance the diary might stop her pining for Lily and fantasising over this ghost she imagines she's seen.

I worry about Plum but there's no point talking to Wills. He and Lily would never admit she had a problem. I once drew up a list of Asperger's symptoms and Lily balled up the page and flung it at me, shouting, "She's developing at exactly the right pace, like a normal little girl of her age. There's *nothing* wrong with her. End of subject!"

I spotted a tall, narrow building in a winding side street with a shingle reading: *'Venter & Swart, Attorneys.'*

"Just a tick," I told Plum. I had my face pressed up against the window, peering inside, when a lofty, spare man carrying a briefcase emerged.

"May I help?"

Pin-striped suit, polished loafers, glinting spectacles. "Are you a lawyer?"

He nodded politely. "Attorney," he said.

His teeth gleamed white against tanned skin.

"How may I be of assistance?"

I've been thinking about talking to a lawyer about Lil's will but it wasn't the right time, not with Plum's ears flapping.

"Um…do you have a card?"

Fumbling in a pocket, the man withdrew a business card. "Louis Venter, that's me, I'm the senior partner. We specialise in family and commercial law. If there's anything I can do, don't hesitate to call."

Louis Venter stared frankly at Plum. "You're new to this area, aren't you? I haven't seen you before. What's your name, young lady?"

"Plum Westwood. We live at *North Wind Manor*."

"Well, well!" Another grin. "So you're the people who bought the manor. Congratulations!"

I was mildly surprised. "You know the house?"

He looked amused. "Oh, everyone in these parts knows *North Wind*. We call the manor the *'Pride of Paarl'*. I'd go so far as to say you've bought yourselves one of the most distinguished Georgian houses in the country."

That didn't sound right.

"Well, if that's the case, why has it been for sale for so long?"

Venter's eyebrows soared. "Few of us can afford a house like *North Wind*."

All the way home, I could feel Plum quietly gloating at my side.

PLUM

If I want to remember something I play, *'I am a Camera.'* I stare at a scene or a person or animal or whatever until…*click…freeze…click…freeze…* pictures are locked inside my head and I can take them out and look at them whenever I want.

I have a whole library of Main Street saved in my brain. There's that spotty dog lolling on red cushions. Zoe's lopsided smile when she heard we live at *North Wind Manor*. The man with the briefcase telling Aunt Frith our house is *'The Pride of Paarl'*. A fruit-seller with a wobbly basket of prickly pears on her head. A museum I wanted to visit called *'Die Oude Pastorie'* but my aunt said. 'There's always another time.' People walking very fast with heads down like they're counting pavement cracks.

When Charlotte Butler lived in Paarl there were three wagon-makers in Main Street, a carpentry workshop, a place selling paint, a blacksmiths, a carriage works and an *ironmongers*. I had to look that up – it's a dealer in metal utensils, ironware and locks.

The *Strooidak Kerk* probably looked the same as it does now and I knew she wouldn't believe me so I didn't tell Aunt Frith I've been inside that church in a dream. I don't remember an organ but that's because I've never seen one before. An organ is bigger than a piano with three keyboards, one on top of the other, rows of long pipes, round knobs and shiny pedals where you put your feet. *Click...freeze.* If I have another dream of the church I'll see the organ Dirk Barnard used to play.

I was writing her name – *'Charlotte'* – with my finger in the dust on a door behind the altar in lovely looping letters when Aunt Frith yelled, *'Don't open that door!'* and I almost jumped out of my skin.

It was peaceful inside the church and I wanted to think of the spirit in this holy place but Aunt Frith was marching back down the aisle saying, "Quick-sticks, Plum! Time to go!"- like we had a train to catch.

FRITH

It was late when we got back to *North Wind*. Plum made me halt on the brow of the hill where the manor comes into view.
"Look," she breathed.

I suppose there is something magical in the way the house stands so squarely with four chimneys rising like spires and the windows gilded by the last of the sunlight.

Wills was crouched on the front steps. His eyes searched mine anxiously. Putting out feelers, I smiled. "We've had a lovely day!" I announced.
"Ah!" William nodded.

81

We sat on the stair, one on each side of William and Plum began chattering about what we'd done that morning.

"I met a lawyer today," I said.

He looked baffled. "A lawyer?"

"Mmm. You never know when you might need one."

Plum went on, "That's the man I'm telling you about, the one who said *North Wind* is called '*The Pride of Paarl*'…and there was this waitress whose name is Zoe…"

She was rambling. William gazed vaguely. I could tell he wasn't listening.

PLUM

After she went indoors, Dad made his voice hushed and asked what Aunt Frith and the lawyer spoke about.

I had to think. "Uh, he gave Aunt Frith a card with his name on it. That's all I remember."

Dad seemed puzzled. "I've no idea why she wants to see a lawyer. Or why she made a point of mentioning it." He made a half sighing, half groaning noise.

"Oh Plum…I *desperately* need your Aunt Frith to stay here with us."

"Why?"

"Well, if anything should happen to me, God forbid, your aunt will take care of you."

It was like I'd swallowed a boiled sweet whole and had a hard lump stuck in my throat.

"Are you sick, Dad?"

Dad gave a high laugh. "No, no! Nothing like that."

"Then *what?*"

Dad made twin arches with his eyebrows. "Don't go running away with something, darling. I'd like us to remain together as a family, that's all."

"That's all right then," I said and the lump in my throat started getting smaller.

But Dad looked a bit teary-eyed. "I just wish…"

"What?"

"I just wish the two of you weren't always at one another's throats."

"What's that mean?"

"You could try to stop arguing with her…putting up barriers and making it impossible for your aunt to get close."

I felt sick. "I can't believe you're taking *her* side!"

"Oh, Plum, do be reasonable!" Dad dropped his head in his hands and it got deathly quiet until all I could hear was my father's muffled breathing and Aunt Frith banging dishes in the kitchen.

I blurted, "Why can't it just be you and me?"

Dad blew a sigh that made his cheeks puff out like a hamster's.

"I can't do this on my own, Plum. I need help until I'm feeling stronger. You're at an age when you need a woman in your life and Frith is better at giving advice than I am. Please, Plum, don't make this more difficult than it already is."

I put on my dignified voice: "I know about periods if that's what you mean and Mom explained how you make a baby and where it comes out."

Dad's lips twitched like he wanted to smile but he kept running his fingers through his hair until it looked like mowed grass.

"I want you two to be friends but that's not going to happen unless you make more of an effort, Plum."

"All he wants is for you to be nice to her."

I'm always hearing voices like there's my voice and then there's the *'Other Plum'* voice that gives me a hard time but this was soft and calm like Mom's voice.

"Oh, darling, look how pale and exhausted he is. He hasn't been well since the day of the funeral. You can see he's not coping and who else can he turn to for help except Aunt Frith?"

It was like having a bucket of stones emptied into my stomach. I couldn't talk for the longest time and then, somewhere far away, I heard Dad saying, "Plum? What's up?"

"Okay, I'll do my best to be nicer to her," I said and it was like I was giving Dad a gift, something terribly, terribly precious.

Dad smiled and I saw a wobble in his chin and a shine of tears in his eyes.

FRITH

We're not immutable beings. Shit happens. We make different choices, change our minds, take the other fork in the road and end up in places we never expected to find ourselves. Like me being here in Paarl with Wills and Plum when Lily's the one who should be with them and I should be in France; skypeing, sending What's Apps and birthday cards and visiting every other Christmas.

After Lily was diagnosed with cancer, William pleaded with me to come to England. He was weeping inconsolably and I packed a bag after his call although I should have guessed it was he who needed me, not Lil. I got a fright the first time I saw her. Her skin was transparently sallow and she had purple shadows beneath her eyes and hollow cheeks. She walked cautiously towards me with short, tottering steps; her skinny arms wrapped around her midriff, barely holding herself together.

"I know I look a wreck but I'm feeling so much better." she smiled. "I'm going to make it, I swear I am." As I hugged her, her arms hung limply, too weak to hug me back.

I remember fighting tears as I gazed over her shoulder at William, white as stone. I had to close my eyes against the unspeakable grief in his face.

There was a time when Lil and I could read one another's thoughts, when we'd open our mouths and say the same thing at the same time. If she cut her finger, mine would sting. All this made sense. We came from the same egg, shared the same genetic blueprint and emerged from our mother's womb with the same features and expressions. And, up until the time Lily met William, we loved one another exclusively.

Our mother didn't hide her lack of love for us and though our father loved us, it was in an absent-minded, almost careless way – so we made do with one another to provide everything a child needs growing up – love, protection, friendship, thoughtfulness, comfort and consolation.

Until Wills, I was never jealous of Lily though she was more popular at school and better at academics and sport. As we became teenagers, she bloomed prettily while I broke out in angry spots and rough patches of ugly red eczema attacked my arms, legs and torso.

After that, we were never mistaken for identical twins until towards the end of Lily's life when, with our shaved heads and gaunt features, we laughed that we looked like Carmelite nuns doing penance on bread and water.

I had a breakdown after Lily's funeral. Drank bottles of J&B and dissolved into a crying jag that lasted weeks. Wills packed me off to stay with my father as far away from Plum as possible. I don't remember much about that time. I'd always wondered, on and off, what life would be like without Lily and though we'd lived apart for years, I'd always known she was there and we kept in touch faithfully. But when Lily died, I lost the best part of myself and what was left seemed flimsy and insubstantial, poisoned with regret and self-loathing.

Our sorrowful father pulled me through. He kept asking if I wanted to talk, get things off my chest but I couldn't admit to what I'd done to Lil because I knew it would hurt and confound him. "You can't give up," he kept urging. "There's Plum to consider. What's to become of her if you don't pull yourself together? She can't lose her mother and her aunt in one fell swoop. That would be unconscionably cruel."

Around that time, I watched an Italian documentary produced by researchers at the University of Padova. The film showed 3D ultrasound pictures of in-utero twins interacting with one another from fourteen weeks. You saw fetuses reaching out and touching.

By eighteen weeks, they were repeatedly stroking one another and I remember being in awe of how very careful they were when their fingers approached their twin's sensitive eye-areas.

The situation was radically different in cases where twins were forced to fight for space in the womb. One twin would kick or punch the other and the sibling attempting to move away, would curl up or hold tightly to its umbilical cord. When I saw this, I knew with absolute certainty that, if we'd been fighting, I'd have been the twin lashing out and Lily would've been the one folding into herself.

CHAPTER EIGHT

PLUM

Weird things keep happening. They might be important and I don't want to forget.

Number one…With my own two eyes I saw curtains blowing at the attic window where there are no curtains only grubby windowpanes and a sticky web with a fly dead in the middle. They were toothpaste green, the curtains, with white and yellow daisies and they were billowing though there wasn't a wind and then they were gone.

I think the dirty cloth wrapped around Charlotte Butler's diary all those years was once the toothpasty green of those blowy curtains.

Number two…I'm *almost* one hundred percent certain the spirit in the house is not Mom, she's Charlotte Butler because spirits are lost souls and Mom was never lost and after she died she'd have gone right to heaven which is where she is now.

She talks to me from Heaven though she doesn't sound the same, more whispery and so quiet I sometimes miss some of her words.

Number three…I didn't want our spirit to have her heart broken so I went up to the attic and explained how the house would *'have to die before it could be reborn'* – those are Dad's words. I told her builders would be making a din with drills and stuff and precious things like the wonky crystal chandeliers would be thrown in a skip as if they didn't matter.

I know she heard because after a few minutes there was a kind of vibrating from somewhere high in the roof and my whole body from the top of my head to my toes began buzzing with pin-pricks of electricity. I'm not making this up, it really truly happened – unless I had a blank and imagined the vibrations and the buzzing, but I don't think so.

Weird thing number four…I was looking out of the attic window wondering if my feet were in the same place where Charlotte stood once and if, like me, she'd breathed a whitish misty patch on the glass…and then I wasn't looking at the same view. I saw grass where there'd been paving, roses instead of the boxy green hedge and way off in the distance, a field where men were digging and best of all I saw a grey horse pulling a cart along a muddy track towards the house.

I must have closed my eyes because when I opened them the light in the attic was darker as if it was later – the paving stones and hedge were back and the men and horse were gone.

Aunt Frith keeps telling Dad I'm having more seizures and I am but they're not the same as they used to be. I don't have that sickish feeling before a blank comes over me or see whirly white lights or feel the room tilting on its axis. My brain switches off and it's like I'm in a world that's light and bright one minute and pitch black the next.

I wake with a woolly head thinking if I could just force my brain to think straight it will all come back, all the stuff I've seen and done or said or thought while I've been deep inside the smothering darkness of the rabbit hole.

FRITH

We had an argument this morning. He expects me to be all sweetness and light, but this is *me* we're talking about, not Lil.

I've been nagging him to take Plum to a doctor but he's insufferably pig-headed and keeps pooh-poohing my concerns over Plum's seizures, her not eating much and crying out at night from nightmares.

William's grasp of the situation is Plum misses Lily and needs more time to settle but that's too simplistic. Her moods have more to do with the ghost she's created than this move. She's like a dog with its ears pricked, listening, tense, jumpy and distracted – more so than usual. And, yes, of course Plum's still grieving for her mother but she's also deeply resentful of my being here, not that I blame her. I'm no substitute for Lily and never will be.

A book I ordered arrived, *'The Asperger's Child'*. I wrapped the cover in brown paper though this prompted them to ask what I was reading. "A murder mystery." I lied, which seemed safe since neither is remotely interested in this particular subject.

'Children with Asperger's syndrome need a very structured approach to living and learning. They do best in an environment in which there are regular, set routines rather than a fluid, evolving schedule which can make them anxious or hyperactive.

I scribbled in the margin…Fucking impossible to achieve a structured approach to living and regular set routines in a house about to be torn down!

They have a desire to finish every task they begin but also require regular periods of quiet time in which to 'decompress' by focusing on their own special interests and repetitive behaviours.

Plum's 'special interest' – the diary…not sure how helpful this is – and then there's the 'spirit'. She needs more distractions – get her into a good school, ASAP!

Try to break learning down into short steps. Give praise where it is due. It is typical of an Asperger's child to aspire to come first and always win. However, he or she will be highly frustrated by losing, dealing with personal imperfections or handling any form of criticism.

True enough…she hates being criticised. Must try to give more praise!

Along with firmly established routines, Asperger's children need love, care, infinite patience and understanding and, within this framework they will flourish.'

That was Lily's department…not sure I have the patience. This is going to be ***hard!***

89

I spread a rug on the grass and Plum lay in the shade while I paged through the diary.

I'm discovering Charlotte's handwriting is a good indication of her mental state.

When she's happy, her penmanship is beautiful, round and flowing, easy to decipher. But then one page of perfect copperplate leads to another crammed with violent crossings out and messy ink blots.

If she's feeling emotional, Charlotte's writing is cramped and the page is sometimes marked with bumpy, raised circles in which ink has bled into the paper. I'm guessing these bumps were made by tears.

I asked Plum, "Do you remember where we were?" She hoisted herself up on an elbow, looking into the distance. "Captain Butler was coming home to *North Wind Manor*…"

April 13th, 1905

"I woke in mortal dread, though the day was pleasant, the sun shining, birds warbling and the garden fresh after last evening's welcome shower. Despite this, I remained agitated and by the time a clattering of wheels announced Edward's carriage, my head was throbbing beyond endurance.

With a rapidly beating heart, I went to greet my husband. After surveying me critically, Edward dryly kissed my cheeks and commented I was looking quite well.

I returned the compliment though, truth to tell, my husband has grown ruddy and corpulent – the buttons of his frock-coat are fit to bursting and the new black Homburg perched precariously atop his dome was made for a much smaller head.

I was calling for young Thomas to bring in the luggage when Edward stiffly took my hand.

"I have a gift for you," he announced and, to my astonishment, led me to a magnificent bay gelding, a chestnut, rising five years.

"This is Pegasus. He is yours," Edward told me. "I find him to be a good jumper with the calm, steady temperament required for a buggy horse."

Pegasus looked upon me with an eye both brilliant and gentle and I loved him at once!

Edward's unexpected gift left me stunned. "My dear Edward!" I exclaimed. "I am touched by your generosity and kindness."

He bowed. "Ah, this is the least I can do for my faithful wife, left quite alone and longing for her absent husband these many months."

I heard mocking in Edward's smooth, measured tones yet he smiled pleasantly, seemingly resolved to preserve peace between us, whatever the cost.

After thorough inspection, Edward professed himself most satisfied with the new stables and servants' quarters although he made plain his regret they have been constructed, as per his father's wishes, in Cape Dutch rather than traditional Georgian style.

Personally, I far prefer these gabled dwellings with their steeply pitched thatched roofs and low ceilings prettily made from rows of young, green saplings but thought it wise to say nothing on this score.

April 14ᵗʰ, 1905

One of the happiest days shared with Edward and my early despair is now forgotten!

Declaring himself pleased to be restored to the comforts of home, Edward unpacked many gifts from his collection of bulging portmanteaus.

One gold-plate dinner service. One dozen beaten silver wine goblets. A ruby locket in a fine morocco case. A silver sword from Wilkinson's the esteemed London sword-makers. Two silken Indian shawls. Two French hair combs, one decorated with semi-precious stones, the other studded with exquisitely made enamel flowers.

I caught sight of a leather hatbox but Edward hurriedly secreted this away for another occasion. Since it was a lady's hatbox, I suspect this gift may also be for me.

My husband's gruff demeanor has all but vanished. I found him talkative and jovial and while at dinner, we sat companionably at the table with Edward relaying entertaining tales of his travels until the candles burned low.

April 15th, 1905

Our marital relations resumed last evening when, after midnight, Edward came to my bedroom naked beneath his smoking gown. He wore a manly-scented cologne and his breath had an odour of the tiny pink sweets called 'Otto of Rose' – sucked to mask a smoker's breath.

"It is evident you have missed your husband, Charlotte," he said. "And now here I am."

I am required to do little more than surrender to Edward, he asks for nothing more and the act is concluded within minutes. My husband is not a gentle lover. He does not kiss me, caress my body or utter words of affection. Indeed, there's almost something furtive in Edward's love-making and strangest of all is his manner after, when he appears to despise me for a time.

Is this, I wonder, how it is with all men?

I find yielding to Edward easier if I close my eyes and bring Dirk Barnard's handsome face to mind.

I imagine burying my fingers in his glossy hair, twisting his soft curls...so different from Edward's sparse, ginger tufts and so vivid are my thoughts, I can almost feel a silky lock falling forward, brushing my cheek.

April 17th, 1905

Of course it was all too good to last!

Life grows more constricted as Edward resorts to his true nature, subjecting me to scrutiny, censure and discipline. A sudden loss of liberty lies at the root of my increasing unhappiness – although there are other reasons. In addition to smoking far too strong, Turkish tobacco, Edward has a new habit of regularly sucking cocaine lozenges recommended as a curative for a painful throat. I find these make him particularly surly.

My husband has also been spending a great deal of money on himself.

A few of his more recent acquisitions include expensive guns for hunting, a camera and several leather-bound Conan Doyle mysteries with which he plans to stave off boredom.

It is no secret the best cure for boredom is industry but Edward considers it beneath him to soil his hands in physical exertion and prefers to meddle annoyingly in my daily habits.

How it sets my teeth on edge to have him watching my every move as I set about boiling fruit for jam, cutting flowers for the bowl or attending to the minor domestic chores I once enjoyed.

With nothing to do, time hangs heavily for Edward and I find, at the end of a long day, we have so little to say that a leaden silence hangs between us.

April 18th, 1905

After mustering the courage to voice my objections at being housebound, Edward has grudgingly permitted me to ride alone for a period each day.

Every afternoon, I don my grey and black riding habit and ride Pegasus through the rough countryside. The exercise and fresh air is beneficial for both me and my beloved horse.

This morning, Edward had business in town and, answering an impulse too strong to ignore, I rode to the Strooidak Kerk where I found Dirk Barnard practicing at the organ.

I sat, still as a mouse, in a pew at the back of the church, listening. The organist sensed my presence, ceased playing and came to me carrying an armful of music scores.

His dark eyes were searching. "You are early for choir practice, Mrs. Butler."

I replied without thinking. "It is you I have come to see, Mr. Barnard."

He dipped his head politely. "How may I be of assistance?"

With his eyes upon my face, my neck and cheeks began flushing turkey red. Oh, how I curse myself for this weakness! I uttered the first words that came into my mind.

"I should be grateful if you could have a word with Miss Kriel," I said. "I am a soprano yet she has me with the contraltos at the back of the choir where my voice is lost."

A smile formed upon his lips. "Oh, dear, I am afraid a lowly church organist has no influence on the indomitable Miss Kriel."

He went on, "I have a question, Mrs. Butler. How is it an Englishwoman has chosen to join a Dutch Reformed Church? Can you understand our Dominee's sermons and the words of our hymns?"

I told a half-truth. I said there were few English-speaking people in Paarl and unless I made an effort to learn Afrikaans, I should find myself alone and friendless.

Mr. Barnard smiled once more. "You are to be commended for your efforts."

Boldly, I touched his sleeve. "I have a new horse. Would you like to see him?"

We walked to where I had tethered my gelding. I did not know what to say to Mr Barnard and so I babbled of Pegasus being named for the mythical winged horse, son of Poseidon and the Gorgon Medusa. At least, that's what I think I said, I cannot truly remember.

I detected faint amusement and suspect the organist knew I was clumsily trying to fashion a friendship between us. I could see Mr Barnard was impressed with Pegasus but when I invited him to ride, he declined saying he was not a good horseman.

Before we parted, Dirk Barnard gently took my hand and as he did, my knees turned to water.

I could not meet his eyes. My throat closed. Stuck dumb, I could not even mutter, 'Goodbye.'

We galloped like the wind, Pegasus and I, and somewhere between the church and North Wind Manor, my little yellow straw bonnet flew away.

April 19th, 1905

Today a parcel was delivered from 'Morris, Marshall, Faulkner & Co.' in London. Inside were heavy rolls of wallpaper chosen by Edward for the downstairs drawing room. The paper is a William Morris – one of his most famous – the 'Vine' wallpaper, designed in 1873.

These papers are made in a variety of hues but Edward has chosen the most ostentatious with grapes and leaves in tones of olive and sage against a hard gold lacquer background.

"I take it you are pleased?" Edward enquired, draping a length against the wall.

I made a foolish mistake. I said I would have preferred a version with a paler background, cream perhaps.

"Too bland!" he snapped. "Why would you choose something so insipid?"

The answer is simple, we have different taste.

"You're right, of course," I said, making an attempt to mollify Edward but it was too late.

His face turned puce and, in a fit of pique, he flung the paper to the floor and stormed from the room. He is so querulous and perverse. These days nothing I do or say pleases him.

April 20th, 1905

Edward has been on a spending spree! We now own a large, comfortable buggy in which Pegasus takes us regularly into the town for shopping. Dozens of fruit trees have been delivered from the Cape including peach, pear, cherry and apricot and, with this order, a quantity of red and white grape vines. Edward has set the workers to clearing the fields where the trees and vines are to be planted.

Just yesterday, he placed an order for a dovecot and corn for four pairs of snow white mating doves due to arrive next week.

I meekly asked if it was wise to be so extravagant in an area in which there is still much poverty and want but Edward only snorted angrily at me. "This is no business of yours," he said.

I note whenever I am accompanied by Edward to town, trades-people are coolly distant in their manner towards us. How ashamed I am of the hauteur Edward displays when speaking to these honest, hard-working people – ordering them about in a lordly, overbearing way and even rudely snapping his fingers to command attention!

My husband is even more arrogant dealing with our servants despite their being mild and gentle-mannered, willing to do whatever we ask of them without complaint.

Lately, I observe a secretive fearfulness creeping into their faces whenever Edward approaches.

They never look directly, their eyes slew right or left, as if they dread facing him. This is because they know he erupts in violent rages for the smallest misdemeanor.

April 22ⁿᵈ, 1905

I assume Dirk Barnard had words with Miss Kriel for she allowed me to take my place amongst the sopranos and to prove myself their equal, I sang out loudly!

I've learned many hymns by heart though I cannot fathom all the words and am often guilty of mispronouncing them. When this happens, there are titters from other choristers though their laughter is not unkind and often I am taken aside and taught how to pronounce certain words.

Afrikaans is a strange language. I believe it originated from Dutch spoken by early settlers and I recognise a scattering of German. I am also told it has been influenced by the Khoikoi tribe and languages of the slaves from West Africa and Madagascar.

During our practice, I could not stop staring at the organist's long fingers upon the keys, the dark hair curling into the back of his neck, his slender shoulders.

As I rode away, I kept repeating his name to myself as if it were a lucky charm…

Dirk Barnard, Dirk Barnard…

Oh Lord, I am like a silly girl!

April 23ʳᵈ, 1905

The greater part of this day has been taken up by papering the walls of the drawing room with the Morris design. I admit the effect is striking though, in my humble opinion, too lavish for such a small room.

I invited Edward to join me in admiring the paper and we two sat together upon the chaise in a companionable fashion, sipping tea and talking of this and that, for once perfectly in agreement.

He seemed to gaze a little more fondly at me – how I wish it was always like this.

April 24ᵗʰ, 1905

I keep myself occupied while North Wind, according to my husband, is 'finally being put to rights'.

The vineyard has been dug and vines are being planted.

Edward has the men toiling twelve hours and longer – it does not occur to him that men work better after regular periods of rest.

Poor Moses, too old and decrepit for such work, looks thin and poorly. When I complained to Edward, he accused me of molly-coddling. He forgets how well we managed during his lengthy absence. Despite Edward's objections, I summoned Moses indoors and set him to cleaning silver in the kitchen.

This afternoon, Aletta Prinsloo's sons brought a hat filled with ripe tomatoes. Immediately cheered by the sight of these dear barefoot boys, I hurriedly filled a basket with figs, cheese, coffee and soap and gave the elder a jug of iced tea to carry home. Coming upon the boys as they were leaving, Edward bellowed after them, calling them filthy Boer brats and threatening to have them horse-whipped for trespassing.

Thank God the Prinsloo lads understood nothing of what Edward said though there was no mistaking his fury. These boys will tell their mother that Captain Butler is newly returned to North Wind.

I pray this does not affect our friendship.

April 25th, 1905

God! How I hate, loath and detest Edward – there, I've said it – the truth is out!

Today, he cruelly beat Thomas for what he said was 'insubordination' though, from what the others told me, this undeserved whipping was given because Thomas, who speaks barely any English, could not understand what Edward asked of him and my husband made no attempt to explain.

Thomas has just turned sixteen, too young to be lashed. He sat still and silent as I dressed his wounds with salve. I dosed him with Paine's Celery Compound and made a cup of beef tea – though none of these could subdue his evident pain and fear.

My head is aching. I have been searching my Bible yet find little comfort.

Marriage to Edward is torture, pure and simple. He has not harmed a hair upon my head but, even so, he has the power to crush my spirit and even my will to live!

97

April 28ᵗʰ, 1905

Edward attempts to control me in all things. Today he insisted upon accompanying me to church despite my saying that Dominee de Villiers conducts his sermon in Afrikaans.

Lately, this congregation has been very amiable towards me. All this changed at the sight of Edward as currents of dislike surfaced in the church once he was recognised as the notorious Captain Butler of the Imperial Yeomanry.

I cringed as we took our places and those already seated made a disgruntled show of removing themselves to another pew so that we two sat quite alone.

How ironic the Dominee's message should be one of forgiveness. He read from an English Bible, quoting a passage from Luke.

'Judge not and ye shall not be judged, condemn not, and ye shall not be condemned, forgive and ye shall be forgiven.'

I sat with strained nerves until the close of the sermon when I whispered to Edward to please remain seated until the last parishioner had departed. Of course, he would not listen and thrust his way down the aisle with pompous swaggering wearing an odious look of conceit.

I followed hesitantly and was comforted when tiny Mrs. Minnaar tapped me upon the shoulder and softly said, "Mrs. Butler – we know you are not accountable for your husband's deeds!"

What she spoke is true. I was a young girl during the Boer War and my only contribution lay in knitting comforters and scarves for British soldiers. How well I recall crocheting dozens of hideous Balaclava helmets with dreary grey thread.

Sadly, not everyone shares Mrs Minnaar's sympathy. There are many in this town who do not consider me blameless for, when all is said and done, I am Edward's wife.

April 30ᵗʰ, 1905

Thomas's wounds are not healing. I rode to Aletta Prinsloo to plead, in my execrable Afrikaans, for her help in this matter and she kindly offered a jar of smooth, green ointment made from the crushed leaves of the eucalyptus tree. Happily, my good-natured friend was as cordial as ever, despite Edward's contemptible behaviour towards her boys.

Riding home on Pegasus, I was consumed by the beauty of the morning – the peaks of the mountain draped in veils of mist – the sky a searing blue.

I rested my gaze fondly upon North Wind Manor with its twin chimneys gleaming whitely and with a row of doves roosting upon the roof.

Even Edward's hateful presence cannot dissuade me from believing this blessed house is a sanctuary and a solace. Pray the Lord I am permitted to remain within these sheltering walls until I draw my last breath."

FRITH

This poor, poor woman…my God, what a fucking awful life!

I've had to leave out chunks of her diary, eyes racing ahead, the stuff about marital relations with that bloody bastard. Why on earth didn't she pack her bags and leave the sod?

Where would she go, though? No money of her own. No friends except the woman down the road.

"You keep stopping," Plum complained.

"It's this handwriting. I think that's enough for now."

"I've seen that horse," she said. "Saw it in a dream, pulling a cart."

I shut the diary with a sigh. "Did you?"

She flapped her hands. "One more page, *please* Aunt Frith!"

"No." I made my voice firm. "I've a brochure I'd like you to read."

A look of suspicion. "What brochure?"

"I've been mailing schools, looking for one that might be suitable."

Her whiny voice: "I don't want to go back to school yet."

"You've already missed part of the term. You can't afford to fall behind. Besides, I like the look of this school. I think you'll fit right in."

She shook her head mournfully. "I never fit in."

PLUM

It's like listening to a play on BBC radio when my aunt reads the diary. We always had the radio tuned to 'Afternoon Drama' when Mom was sick. She said she loved being drawn into the theatre of other people's lives because it took her mind off other things.

I wish she could've read Charlotte Butler's story. I know she'd have loved knowing everything Charlotte wrote happened right here in this house. If I close my eyes, I can see Charlotte pouring tea from a silver teapot at the same table where my aunt in denims and muddy trainers was drinking coffee in a mug with a drawing of a brown bear on the front.

Aunt Frith was wearing two thick sweaters and long stripy socks to her knees.

"It's not cold." Dad tapped the side of his head with his pointing finger. "It's all up here. All psychological. You didn't want to come back to this country. You don't like this house and so it follows…"

She screwed her face at him. "Oh, don't talk such rot!"

My aunt had a shiny brochure in her hands. It landed smack on the table in front of me.

I read, *Paarl College for Girls* on the cover and my stomach flip-flopped.

"Go through this quietly, while I make an omelet. Think you can do that?"

I rolled my eyes. I hate it when she talks like I'm an idiot.

"Isn't it too early to eat?" Dad looked at his watch.

Aunt Frith frowned. "I'm trying to make our lives more…um… *structured*. We need regular, set routines. Lunch at noon…dinner at seven… bed at nine. The way we're living now is too…haphazard…not good for Plum."

Dad laughed. "That's ambitious! Aiming for structure while living in a tip with all this building going on around us."

Aunt Frith sent a cross look at Dad who said, "I'm going to have to shut up before I get reeled into another argument."

The brochure had a fancy name – *'Prospectus'* – but they're all the same, page after page of teeny-weeny print and boring photographs of girls with millions of merit badges pinned on their blazers. One girl could've been Lucy Atkins from my last school and another looked like Meena Banerjee who was in my music class. There were pictures of trophies with ribbons, hockey, swimming and netball teams, a science laboratory with a teacher bending over a Bunsen burner, a library, a music-centre and a stage set for a play…flip, flip, flip…I turned the pages to the end.

Aunt Frith put a plate in front of me. "Why that face?"

I shook my head because she's like on another planet and wouldn't understand.

Dad leaned across and sliced my omelet with a flashing knife and fork.

"Get some of that inside you," he smiled.

I never cry but a teeny tear overflowed onto my cheek and Dad pressed a napkin in my hand.

"This is *ridiculous!*" Aunt Frith burst out. "What did you think? That you were *never* going back to school?"

"I know how you feel," Dad said, "loathed school as a boy. Loathed university too. Never happier than the day I graduated. Like being released from prison."

Aunt Frith sighed. "Thanks a lot, William."

Nobody talked after that. All you could hear was the scratch and scrape of knives and forks on plates.

I wasn't hungry and the omelet was oozy so I pushed the plate away and closed my eyes and there was this picture behind my lids of old Moses polishing a mountain of silver while Charlotte arranged flowers in vases – crystal, like the glittery chandeliers in the sitting room – and Edward, fat and ugly, sucking cocaine lozenges and watching Charlotte like a spider with shiny pin-head eyes.

I heard Aunt Frith whispering, "What did I tell you? She's having another one."

My eyes flew open. "Another *what?*"

Dad lifted his finger to his mouth. "Don't," he said quietly to my aunt. "You've got it all wrong, she's like me – we're dreamers – at the drop of a hat, we find ourselves wandering off into our own mental landscape."

My aunt went 'Hmmm,' like she didn't believe him and he told her it's in my stars and I'm destined to be a Booker Prize-winning novelist or a poet or write unforgettable music lyrics.

I tuned out their voices like pressing the mute button on the remote and tried to move my mind back into Charlotte's world but he'd sewn a little brain seed that started me wondering if I could concentrate long enough to write an entire book with a plot and a beginning a middle and end and it made me sad to think I probably couldn't because my mind doesn't stay still in one place long enough.

CHAPTER NINE

FRITH

Living in Paarl is like throwing a switch and landing in another world. You're surrounded by seventeenth-century buildings emblazoned with ancient family crests, donkey carts creaking through side streets, needlepoint cushions on *riempie banks,* church bells tolling on the wind.

Afrikaans is spoken here, a smattering of English. Most street signs are in Afrikaans and there's a monument to the language, *Die Afrikaanse Taalmonument,* strangely beautiful curving obelisks rising from the harsh granite of Paarl Rock.

I'm trying to like Paarl for their sake though I've made it clear I'm leaving once the house is habitable, Plum's settled at school and William's coping as a single parent.

I care about them, they're the only family I have, but staying here and trying to make a life together would be an eternal penance and one I'm not prepared to make.

Not even for Lily.

Paarl Girls' College has a reputation of excellence in academic performance and, since Plum's precociously bright, she should thrive in this environment although allowances will have to be made for her... how would Lily phrase it... her *'specialness'*.

Wills insists I don't mention Asperger's for fear of prejudicing the teachers – but I wonder if that's fair to Plum?

"She's managed well enough until now," he told me, tetchily. "For God's sake don't go sticking a label on her when she's an ordinary kid with an inquiring mind."

Lily and William adopted Plum when she was just two weeks old. Lily begged to know something about her parents and the agency grudgingly allowed that the baby's mother was a Russian ballet dancer. The identity of the father, a married man, was unknown.

A year or so later, when Lily learned the dancer had flown home to Saint Petersburg, she stopped agonising over the threat of this woman banging on her door and demanding her baby back.

I went to visit Lily and Wills a few months after the adoption. Lily was glowing with joy as she took me to see the baby asleep in a Moses basket. I put my hand on Plum's chest and watched it rise and fall as she breathed. Her brow was furrowed in a tiny frown, her fists tightly clenched and even in sleep, she looked fiercely determined. I thought her name odd until Wills explained, "When the woman from the agency lifted the blanket, Lily said, 'Oh, do give me that little plum, I can't wait to hold her.'" He shrugged. "It seemed to fit."

They say you should never have a child to save a marriage but that's what Lily and William did and, in their case, Plum drew them together again. Wills was promoted to regional sales and marketing manager for the *Celeste Estate* and they moved into a bigger house. Lily started a herb garden and learned to weave on a loom.

Plum wasn't an easy baby. She was colicky and cried a lot. Lily used to calm her by laying her basket on a running washing machine and Wills' solution was to drive her in the car for hours. They both claimed she was soothed by gentle, repetitive rocking and swinging and I don't want to sound like a know-all but this is text-book Asperger's child.

There was a swing in our garden when we were kids. Our father made it. A smooth wooden platform threaded with two lengths of ship's rope knotted to the sturdy branch of a Jacaranda tree. We'd swing for hours, one sitting and the other standing with legs straddled, knees bent, the whole body moving forwards and backwards as the swing arched higher and higher and the bough groaned beneath our combined weight.

One day, the branch cracked with the noise of a bullet splintering the air. We screamed as we hit the ground. Lily, who'd been standing, came off worst with a chip in her front tooth and nine stitches in her chin – the faintly raised scar still visible until the last.

There was blood on Lily's face. Blood on my skinned palms and badly grazed knees. I sped to the house, screaming hysterically, *Mommy... Mommy...Mommy!*

The rooms were silent, empty. I ran next door. Our neighbour drove us to the hospital with a towel packed with ice wadded beneath Lil's leaking chin. Dad, shaky and pale, brought us home and put us to bed. Our mother returned late from playing bridge. "It's your own fault," she told us, surveying the train-track of neat black stitches across Lily's swollen chin. "I've told you about that swing before. You'll likely be scarred for life."

I can still see our mother's shadowy silhouette against the lamplight. She had her hands on her hips in a confrontational pose that was typical Julia. Incidents like these make us who we are. Fear brings the taste of dirt and gravel to my mouth.

PLUM

The college has a gate that slides open when you press a button and speak your name into a crackling box. A secretary took us down a corridor with all these photographs of principals from 1858 on the walls.

Something made me stop. "Hang on," I said and went back to have a good look at a picture with a square of brass that read, *'Miss Charity Cripps – School Principal, 1910.'*

I felt sorry for Miss Cripps whose parents named her 'Charity' and who had mad, staring eyes, a parrot's beak nose and tiny round glasses on a string around her neck.

Miss Cripps was holding a book exactly like Charlotte's diary – same size, same leather cover, same faded writing on the front. I can't read what it says on our diary because it's all scratched off with only little glimmers of gold where the letters used to be.

"Come *on,* Plum! We don't want to be late!"

The principal's name was Mrs van Wyk. She didn't look tidy like in her photo in the prospectus. Her bun was messy with bits of hair falling out and her face was covered with powdery white hair like a rabbit.

"So, you are Plum," she said. "Tell me about yourself."

"Can I ask you something first?"

I heard Aunt Frith whispering: "*May* I…"

The principal nodded. "Go ahead."

"There's a photograph of Miss Charity Cripps who was the school principal in 1910? Do you know the one?"

Behind me, I heard my aunt take a deep breath and her feet made a shuffling that sounded like she was hopping from one foot to the other.

"Not really, there are so many photographs."

"Can I…*may I* show it to you?"

Mrs van Wyk smiled. "Of course."

We both looked at the photograph. "Not flattering," the principal said. "What would you like to know about our Miss Cripps?"

"That book in her hand. Can you read what's on the cover?"

The principal rubbed the dusty glass with her sleeve and twisted her head. "I think it says *'Journal'.*"

"Is that like a diary?"

"It is. What makes you so interested?"

I told her I'd seen one exactly the same and asked where you'd have bought a journal like that in 1910. "Did they have book shops in Paarl then?"

"Oh, bound to. There may have been more than one. People were reading Dickens, Tolstoy…Chekov…Jane Austen…Mark Twain." She smiled again. "Did you see your journal in our local museum?"

A thought darted…if I told Mrs van Wyk I'd found the diary at *North Wind Manor* she might make me give it to the museum so I told her I couldn't say where I'd seen the journal because it was *a secret*.

She gave me a funny look and brushed feathery wisps of hair off her face and said, "Fair enough. Why don't we go back to my office and get to know one another?"

She made it sound like eating pudding.

I've been interviewed for heaps of schools and I know the drill. I rattled it off – my best subject is English and I adore reading and writing essays and history comes next and then geography and biology and drawing. My brain isn't wired for maths which is the only subject where my marks are below sixty percent.

My aunt interrupted. "If maths is a problem, we'll hire a tutor. She's extremely bright and absolutely *loves* school…"

Mom told me never to lie to a teacher so I said, "I don't actually *love* school. I don't even like it very much. I'm hopeless at sport except for swimming where I'm only fair and at my last school I was learning to play the violin but my music teacher said I don't have an ear."

Mrs van Wyk opened a book and scribbled on a page and then looked up. "You can start one week from today," she said. "Meet me in my office before assembly and I'll introduce you to a few of your classmates."

As she walked us back down the passage I heard the principal talking to Aunt Frith. "I like your niece. She seems interesting – intriguingly different, obviously bright."

"Well…," Aunt Frith looked to see if I was listening. "She's…um… she's…special."

Whatever that means!

FRITH

After the interview, I took Plum for lunch. She fiddled with her food, staring glumly into the distance. "Only one more week of freedom."

I used my reasonable voice. "Plum, let's enjoy lunch together. What shall we talk about? And, before you answer, two subjects are off-limits – how much you hate school and your ghost."

Well, right away, she was off. "I don't know why you call her *'my'* ghost. You can't *own* a ghost the way you own a dog or a cat. She doesn't *belong* to me, she's in our house and if you and Dad would only unblock your brain and try to *feel* her…"

Exasperated, I told Plum she was behaving like a dotty old lady with an Ouija board – "Listen to you…talking yourself into believing in a ghost that doesn't exist."

She blinked. "What's a *Ouija* board?"

I heard Lil's voice in my ear, mildly amused, *"Now you've done it! Let's see you wriggle your way out of this one."*

As we left the restaurant, a sudden breeze teased tablecloths and sent leaves scurrying into gutters. A hat, a straw-coloured Panama, tumbled across the street.

I ran after it as it wheeled nimbly, just out of reach, over cobblestones and across grass verges. I was panting by the time I trapped the brim under my foot and looked around for the owner. There was no one in sight. The hat was expensive, a real Panama with an embroidered *'Made in Ecuador'* label inside and the dusty shape of my footprint on the creamy woven brim.

I picked up a stone and anchored the hat on a pillar but seconds later the wind took it again. Plum grabbed it before it flew into a drain. There was a beef-coloured, jowly old man, walking towards us, leaning on a silver topped cane.

I brandished the hat. "Is this yours, by any chance?"

"It's yours," he replied.

Plum stepped forward. "No, it's not. She found it."

His smile showed snowy porcelain teeth. "Ancient common law… *finders keepers, losers weepers* – ever heard that?"

"Yes!" said Plum.

I nodded politely. "Only in the playground."

"Well, that's Paarl for you – one jolly playground. Keep the hat. It will suit you."

His heavily pouched eyes flitted between us. "You tourists? On holiday here?"

"We live here," Plum told him, gravely. "My Dad's bought *North Wind Manor*. He's going to restore the house to its former glory."

"Ah!" He gazed intently. "That explains all the coming and going at the old place. Good to see the manor being taken in hand at last. Hasn't been touched in…oh Lord knows how long? Decades, I should think. *North Wind* has a fascinating history." His chins quivered. "I suppose you've heard the stories people tell?"

I asked, "Are they to do with Charlotte and Edward Butler?"

"'Eh, sorry, what's that?" He cupped his hand behind an ear.

"Charlotte Butler!" Plum shouted.

"No, sorry, don't know any Butlers. Definitely not local. Lived in Paarl for nigh on forty years and know most locals hereabouts. Unless your Mrs. Butler was before my time, of course."

"She lived at *North Wind* in 1910," Plum said, eagerly.

"That explains it." The old man inched closer to Plum. "You must've heard the house is supposed to be haunted!"

Plum's eyes were saucers. *"Haunted!"*

I grabbed her sleeve. "No, we haven't."

"I'm surprised." The old man's brows bulged in concentration. "More people than I can shake a stick at swear they've seen a ghost at the manor. I don't know if it's urban legend but there's an extraordinary tale that bears repeating…"

I sent the old man a warning look. "She's only *eleven*, for God's sake." I barked. "We're *living* in that house. We don't need to hear a lot of silly nonsense."

His mouth dropped open.

"Look…sorry…I don't mean to be rude, but we're in a hurry."

I dragged Plum away.

She shook herself free. Her eyes sparkled. *"I told you!"*

"Oh, *please!* People are always talking tosh about ghosts and old houses. I don't believe a word of it."

I jammed the hat on my head and pulled the brim low over my forehead. "Why don't we visit the *Strooidak Kerk* again? Would you like that?"

Plum brightened. "Yes I would."

PLUM

There's a graveyard at the *Strooidak* with marble angels and cherubs with blank eyes and stone Bibles and crosses and what my aunt calls '*headstones*' because they stand at the head of the grave like a kind of marker with the name of the dead person. There are family *crypts* – that's another new word – it means an underground chamber where lots of bodies are buried.

I saw vases of dead flowers and sad black wreaths and on one grave a doll was leaning back against the headstone. I felt desperately sorry for that doll. Her dress was dirty and she had a crispy brown leaf trapped in her scraggly black hair. Worst of all, she was a cripple and I badly wanted to take her home, give her a bath and dress her in a long skirt to hide her lost leg.

"Put that doll back!" Aunt Frith said, digging me in the ribs with her pointy elbow. "She belonged to the child buried here. Look. Her name was Katie and she was only six when she died."

I asked how she'd like to be a doll in a creepy graveyard with only dead people for company but she wasn't listening. She patted a stone bench and told me in her quiet voice to sit.

Someone was playing the organ inside the church. The music was slow and deep.

Aunt Frith started singing softly, '*Holy, Holy, Holy, Lord God Almighty, early in the morning our song shall rise to Thee. Holy, Holy, Holy, Merciful and Mighty, God in Three Persons, blessed Trinity.*' I've never heard my aunt sing and her voice was high and sweet and I was going to tell her I loved her singing but before I could, another voice, big and booming shouted, 'Hello there!' and made me jump. I looked up and saw a giant with an orange pencil stuck behind one ear. He had a bushy beard and white hair tied back with a shredded ribbon. I thought he looked like somebody I knew and wondered if we'd met before and then I remembered a drawing in *Treasure Island*.

"Are you a pirate?"

He laughed. "I'd need a hook and eyepatch to pass as a pirate," he said. "Besides, these days there're only Somali pirates and their skins are generally a shade or two darker than mine."

He pointed to my aunt. "If I'm not mistaken, that's my hat you're wearing."

FRITH

This man was grinning down at me. Six-foot something with thick, greying hair and strong features, deep-set eyes, caterpillar brows, swarthy complexion.

"Sorry, I was miles away," I told him.

"Unless my hat has a double, that's my Panama on your head."

My face flushed hotly. I whipped off the hat and gave it to him. He fitted it with the brim pulled rakishly over one eye.

"You've an excellent voice," he said. "You should join our choir."

"Aunt Frith!" Plum said, dramatically. "Aunt Frith…that's what Dirk Barnard said to Charlotte!"

I shook my head at Plum. "Not now," I said.

I turned to the man in the hat. "Do you belong to the choir?"

He dropped beside me on the bench. "They won't have me. They say I bray like a donkey."

I opened my mouth and another bloody silly question popped out, "Are you the pastor?"

He threw his head back, laughing uproariously. "Do I look like a man of the cloth?"

I shrugged. "Who knows? They come in all shapes and sizes."

He leaned towards me. "I'm afraid there's nothing pious or saintly about me. You won't see the light of redemption shining from these wicked eyes.

People say I'm a reprobate, a sinner…a lost cause. Besides," he added, "look – no dog collar!"

He grinned. "I'm an artist. Theo Christianson." He wore that look people give when they expect you to react and when I didn't, he went on, sounding boastful, "You'll find my art in most of the better galleries in Paarl."

There was a disturbing intimacy in the man's nearness, in the faint residue of his expensive cologne. I edged away holding myself self-consciously erect with my treacherous cheeks flaming. "I'm Frith and this is Plum."

"Mother and daughter?"

His skin was grainy, pockmarked. A web of fine lines crisscrossed around his eyes. Not young, mid-fifties or thereabouts.

"Um, no, Plum is my…er…" for a few panicked seconds, I lost the word… "my *niece!*" He widened his eyes. Was he *laughing* at me? And then… "Are you married?" I asked, stunned at actually voicing the question uppermost in my mind.

Theo Christensen pulled a face of mock sorrow. "I am. Twenty years…a lifetime. And you?"

I shook my head. A missing shirt button offered a view of a muscular chest. He stood up, holding out his palm. I hesitated before giving him my hand. He touched it to his mouth, holding it there a second or two too long.

"Well, this has been a rare and unexpected pleasure. I hope we meet again."

As he passed through the iron gates, I had an almost visceral tug of disappointment at his leaving so soon. I kept my eyes on his hat as it bobbed above the church wall before disappearing behind a screen of trees. Organ music rolled into the churchyard. A different hymn this time, not one I knew.

"You've gone all red." Plum said, gazing curiously.

CHAPTER TEN

FRITH

I was emptying my suitcases when I came upon a bundle of Lily's letters. White, tissue-thin airmail envelopes edged with blue and red diagonal stripes, the *'Par Avon'* stamp and Lily's neat handwriting in black biro. Do they still make these airmail letters, I wonder?

I haven't seen one in years.

"...used to be so close but now it's habit keeps us together...habit and contempt and resentment and familiarity...and pity and friendship too, I suppose...all those things. Of course I love him, but do I like him, I wonder? Plum adores Will and you won't find a more loving and devoted father."

I flipped through the envelopes, hunting for the letter she had written about the wine bottles. *Christ...* my blood simmers whenever I think of it. Had he been completely out of his fucking mind?

"You'll have seen the UK stamp and, yes, we're in England, hiding like fugitives. Hard to believe but it's happened again – we've had to run away because of something unspeakable William's done.

I need to explain this properly, so you understand what happened and how I'm caught up in all of this.

It started when a vintage bottle of wine was found – not far from where we live – in a cellar owned by a wine farmer who'd died after a long illness. William went to see the wine and seemed excited by the find. The bottle was hand-blown with a label signed by Jacques Duval – one of the first French winemakers in the Cape. William thought the bottle might be worth a small fortune and asked the farmer's widow to let him show it to the owner of 'Celeste Estate', an avid collector of rare vintage wines. William took the wine to the owner but – and this detail only emerged much later – only after a week had passed.

Three vintage wine experts identified the wine as early nineteenth century. The 'Celeste Estate' sold the wine to the London-based 'Antique Wine Company' who, in turn, auctioned it to an American collector for a record seventy-five thousand dollars. Wills received a small commission for his trouble.

At the time, it seemed as if this was happening in the background of our lives. I wasn't particularly interested although I was pleased the Estate had profited from Wills' initiative, and hoped it would stand him in good stead. It did. After this, they thought the world of Wills. Bertram Lombard, the founder of Celeste, said he'd likely be offered full partnership before the end of the year. But that wasn't enough for Wills…nothing, it seems, is ever enough.

Without saying a word to me, Wills bought the widow's farm – a tumble-down house in the middle of ten hectares of barren land, choked with weeds. I hit the roof when he finally told me. I couldn't believe he'd acted so secretly…so recklessly and selfishly. We had the most terrible row.

I took Plum and stormed off to a friend who put me up for a week. Wills persuaded me to come home, saying he'd purposefully kept the purchase a secret because he'd planned to renovate the farmhouse over weekends, sell the property for a healthy profit and give me the money as a nest egg. Stupidly, I believed him. I even apologised for misjudging him.

A couple of months later, Wills was knocking down a wall at the farmhouse when he found a bricked-up pantry with a hidden cachet of wine – thirteen bottles, all identical to the original. Same hand blown glass. Same labels signed by Duval. He took me to see the collection.

"I can't believe our luck!" he told me. Nor could I. Something didn't feel right. I asked if he'd forged the bottles although I didn't really believe him capable –this kind of forgery is too skilled, even for William. He laughed

The wine experts certified the collection as genuine. "We're going to be rich!" Wills said.

But Wills didn't anticipate the flurry of publicity following his discovery.

Newspapers were full of the story. There were photographs of William and Lombard shaking hands…pictures of the two of them with representatives from the London Antique Wine Company. There was even a photograph of William, me and Plum. Wills seemed distinctly uncomfortable when these pictures were taken. In every picture, his eyes are looking away from the camera. That made me uneasy.

Wine connoisseurs from the world over bid in what was called the: 'Duval Heritage Wines Collection'.

All this time I knew something was wrong. Wills was tense, irritable, sleepless.

I've no idea the final sum deposited into one of his offshore accounts – a lot of money, in any event.

*In William's eyes, that's where it should've ended but, Murphy's Law, one of the buyers opened his bottle and had the contents tested. According to Wills, this **never** happens. Antique wines are bought for their historical value – not their drinkability. A complicated test involving an analysis of potassium content proved indisputably the wine in the bottle was only five years old.*

As the news was breaking, we left South Africa – just in time to escape William being arrested for fraud.

We've been under enormous strain. We hardly speak. Barely look at one another. We come and go like strangers leading separate lives. During one of our heated quarrels, I called Wills a ruthless con-artist (I've called him far worse).

"But, Lily, that's not who I am," he told me, deadly serious. "I'm an entrepreneur, an opportunist. The very rich are greedy and gullible. They get what they deserve."

What can I say? That's what he believes. I've been left as shocked as you must be now, reading this. Wills knows the difference between right and wrong and he's a good man in so many ways but, for him, cheating is as much an addiction as drink or drugs. He's too clever by far – always trying to overcome the odds however stacked they are against him. I've given up trying to change him.

I suppose divorce is inevitable although I dread it and I've no idea how I'll earn a living. Plum's the one I worry about most. She feels the tension between us and she's grown anxious.

God, Frith! I've never felt so frightened, so alone before. I miss you so much."

This was followed by Lil's scrawled signature and three x's scored deep into the paper.

Years later, I'd asked my sister how William managed to fool the wine experts.

"Easy," she'd answered. On his first visit, the widow had offered Wills a box of empty, labeled bottles, thick with dust. There were corks and a cracked block of sealing wax lying loose in the carton. 'Would this be of interest?' she'd asked innocently and it took just one split second for William's alpha brain to start scheming.

PLUM

Dad told my aunt he thought one of the builders recognised him.

"He kept giving sideways looks. 'Don't I know you?' he said. 'Weren't you in Cape Town two or three years ago?' I told him he was mistaken but I could see he was trying to work out when and where we might have met. Damn good electrician. I had to turn him down, couldn't risk it. Hope to Christ he doesn't remember."

"What if he does?" I asked Dad.

"Mmm. Well, nothing good can come from that."

"Is this about the man who jumped out of the window?"

Dad frowned. *"What?"*

I'd forgotten about Mom making me pinky-swear to keep it a secret.

My aunt butted in. "I told you," she said. "I told you this was dicey, but you never listen."

"You…" Dad pointed with a shaky finger. "You, of all people! You *know* why we came back here!"

"No need to get so excited!"

"Fuck off, Frith!" Dad yelled.

He hardly ever uses that word – you could tell he was really cross.

My aunt marched to the kitchen and banged the door hard behind her.

"Now you've done it," I said.

116

Dad pulled a face. "I shouldn't have shouted. We're all on edge."

"Don't worry about her. She's always on edge."

Dad sighed. "Don't be too hard on your aunt," he said and I could tell a lecture was coming. "Listen, Plum…" he said. "She is your Mom's sister. And Mom loved her very much."

"I don't know why. She's hard to love. She's nothing like Mom. Have you looked at her eyes?"

You could sink into Mom's eyes, that's how soft and warm they were. Hers are like fogged up glass and if you say the wrong thing her face shuts up tight but Mom showed *everything* on her face – all the love and all the hurt.

Dad rubbed his eyes.

I felt a bit scared. "You're not crying, are you, Dad?"

"Course not."

But his eyes were kind of wet and shiny and it's easy to see he misses Mom and thinks of her all the time and there's a big piece of him lost now which means he'll never be the way he was before. I wanted to tell him he still has me but then he said, "We're both going to have to be nicer to Frith," and I remembered something Granny used to say.

"I'll try," I said. "But I'm not a magician, you know. Not in the habit of pulling rabbits from hats."

He laughed and that made me feel better.

In the afternoon, Aunt Frith took me to town to buy school uniforms. She parked the car and we were walking down Main Street when she stopped and stared across the street at a shop with paintings in the window.

Then she breathed, *"Oh!"* like she'd just spotted a glittering diamond in the gutter but it was only him – the giant from the churchyard – coming out of the shop swinging a black bag.

Aunt Frith fluttered her fingers in a girly way and he walked to us and said, "Hello! What luck to bump into you two lovely ladies again!"

"Ha!" I said because he didn't mean me.

The giant waggled his eyebrows and it made me sick to watch them stretch like furry caterpillars right over his nose with just a tiny space between.

They looked at each other for the longest time like there was nobody except the two of them until I nudged her sandal with my shoe.

"Aunt Frith!"

She gave herself a little shake. "We're shopping for school uniforms," she told him.

He bowed and kissed her hand like a prince in a play and then said, "Until next time," and walked away with long steps and I got this funny feeling like I'd spied something I shouldn't have though I don't know for certain what it was except for my aunt being totally uncool.

We passed lots of shops – one with naked dummies waiting to be dressed – an *Astrology Centre* with silver stars and a half moon painted on the window, a pottery shop with baskets outside full of bright bowls. "*Cobalt and mustard,*" Aunt Frith said, though they looked ordinary blue and yellow to me. An African curio shop, the Tourist Information Bureau – and then – a white and green building with a sign, *'Stockists of school uniforms.'*

"Here it is!" I shouted. She was walking slowly with her silver earrings swaying like rain drops and she looked so happy that for just a few shivery seconds – I thought she was Mom.

FRITH

What *is it* with me and married men? A string of lovers in my past and all married, two with kids. My first proper affair was with Aubin, one of my Art lecturers at *Parson's Paris*.

I was naive enough to think he'd end his marriage but he didn't, they never do, not for me, anyway.

Next was Cheval, married to his second wife, one child and a flourishing landscaping business. That was the longest. We were together eighteen months before he got tired of me or I of him, I can't remember who walked away first. Didier came next and then, briefly, Jules and, after that, disillusioned, I entered a long winter of celibacy which, with one or two minor lapses, has lasted until now.

God knows why I'm never attracted to a man who's single and available. Lily's theory was that I'm terrified of commitment but that's not true, I'm as ready to commit as the next woman, I simply can't find the right man.

In the logical, clear-thinking part of my brain, I know Theo Christensen is wrong for me but, like all other men in my past, I find myself inexplicably drawn to him.

I woke this morning with a rumpled pillow crease down one side of my face and all I could think when I bumped into him was, thank God the crease had faded; I'd washed my hair in the shower and worn lipstick.

Plum was in a mood all afternoon. School looms – that's why she's so otherwise.

When we got home after buying school uniforms, I made tea and opened a packet of her favourite chokky biscuits. "No thanks," she said, sounding offish.

There's one thing guaranteed to jolt her out of a sulk. "Bring the diary and I'll read a few pages – but when I say 'that's enough,' I mean it. Promise you won't argue. Do we have a deal?"

She scooted upstairs. *"Deal!"* she yelled over her shoulder.

May 10th, 1905

This morning we received an invitation from Franklin Talbot (ex-officer of the Ninth Battalion of the Imperial Yeomanry), to visit the Talbot wine farm on the slopes of the Paarl. I have no desire to see Franklin and his wife Edwina again, though the countryside is truly lovely in May.

It was only a year ago the Talbots were our guests at North Wind and I cannot forget how they spent their time in games of cards and dice and excessive partaking of food and wine.

I wrote of my husband's advances upon Edwina in this journal though I must presume, since Franklin and Edward's friendship remains cordial, I was the only witness to this impropriety.

It appears I have no say in the matter – Edward has accepted Franklin's invitation – and we are to travel to their farm two days hence.

An assemblage of valises is packed. We are taking gifts of cured ham and a wooden crate filled with a staggering quantity of aged port. When I asked Edward why we were weighting the trap with so heavy a load, he replied it was common practice amongst the soldiers of the Ninth to begin each day by taking port with breakfast. Why, oh why is he reintroducing this hideous custom during our stay?

May 15th, 1905

The Talbot farm has been christened, 'Tortoise Mountain' – a name given to the Paarl mountain range by the Khoikhoi. This farm boasts twenty hectares of rich, fertile land under vines and the farmhouse has smooth cedar floors, as fine as any I have seen. There is also an imposing staircase leading below ground to cool cellars where wine vats are stored.

After our arrival, we were made welcome and offered tea on a shaded stoep with a splendid view of fields and mountains.

I am quietly amused at how the Talbots behave like landed gentry, posturing as experts in wine making.

They talked of purchasing and restoring an abandoned ruin although Mrs. Regina Fuller, Edwina's dear old mother, tells a rather different tale. She confided that this prosperous farm had, until quite recently, been owned by a family called Marais. Tragically, three sons were killed in battle and the ageing parents forced to auction the property after a plague of phylloxera devastated the vineyards.

I asked a farm worker to explain this plague and, most eloquently, he described an infestation of tiny yellow winged insects descending in their thousands, feeding upon root, leaf and stem and turning the entire crop a bright buttercup-yellow before the vines withered and died.

I was speaking to this worker in my halting Afrikaans when Edwina forcefully dragged me away saying, "God, keep me from believing you are speaking to a native in the rough, ugly tongue of our enemy!"

Calmly, I replied, "If you would like, I will teach you all I know of this language so you may make yourself more easily understood in your adopted country."

Mrs Talbot's face turned livid and she declared she found me 'caustic'.

I came close to accusing our hostess of gross stupidity but, to preserve harmony, bit my lip and answered meekly that my offer had been sincere and irony had not been intended.

May 16th, 1905

How astonishing to find the Talbots have feathered their Cape Dutch nest as if it were a traditional three-storey Victorian house in London. It is so densely crowded with furniture brought here from England by steamer, I suspect it has lost much of its former charm.

The sitting room alone is decorated with a velvet-draped grand piano, mahogany bureaus, marble busts of Greek ladies, gold framed paintings by Italian masters, Persian rugs and a forest of potted palms in blue and white Chinese urns.

When I asked what had become of the original furnishings, Edwina said most had been sold for a song at the local farmers' market and they'd made a bonfire of the rest.

That evening, a ball was staged and a small party of English ex-army men and their wives invited to attend. Edwina made a perfectly-timed, theatrical entrance with a young, tame cheetah named Caesar at her side. Professing the animal to be as 'sweet as a kitten', she held the cat upon a length of silken rope and fed him morsels from her plate. This performance ended badly after Caesar knocked a carafe of red wine on the carpet and clawed a velvet footstool to shreds. After mildly cuffing the animal's ears, Franklin ordered a servant to remove Caesar from the room but not before we all observed how the wild cat swung its tail, growling and baring dagger-sharp white teeth at our host. I would have laughed, had I not been so frightened of the ferocious animal.

May 18th, 1905

Truly, a bitter day!

At daylight, Franklin and Edward rode off with a hunting party. Finding myself alone, I went for a long walk with the Talbot's wolfhounds. When I returned to the farmhouse, I came upon Edwina preening at a glass. She wore a new hat of exquisite walnut silk trimmed with French lace and tied with grosgrain ribbons. I spotted a hatbox of distinctive design, crafted from leather with the milliner's name embossed upon the lid…one of the boxes Edward brought back from his travels. Naively, I assumed he'd set this aside to be given to me as a gift on the occasion of our anniversary.

Aware of my distress, Edwina turned from the mirror with an un-Christian expression of gloating that left me speechless. I have no great expectations of Edward but the knowledge he has given this intimate gift to another man's wife is hard to bear.

May 19th, 1905

More guests have arrived. I have counted twelve in residence at Tortoise Mountain as our visit deteriorates into what our hostess merrily describes as: 'an endless party'.

Personally, I find it all distasteful – this drunkenness and shameless flirting between married couples.

Last night's entertainment went on until after daybreak and many guests, my husband amongst them, were still smoking cigars and sipping brandy in glass bubbles when breakfast trays of kedgeree were served in the dining hall.

Later, I begged Edward to permit me to return home to North Wind but he erupted in rage, shaking his fist and bellowing that he will not be 'managed by an insipid, milk-coddled ninny of a wife'.

I pray no-one heard him.

I fled into the garden where Edwina's seventy-three-year old mother, Mrs. Regina Fuller, pressed a lawn handkerchief sprinkled with drops of eucalyptus into my hand, suggesting I inhale it for relief. From my red, swollen eyes, the sweet old dear believes I am suffering from a head cold!

How I ache to return home. If only I were brave enough to defy Edward.

Perhaps he's right and I am a milk-coddled ninny after all!

May 20th, 1905

Before dawn, Edward, too intoxicated to stand, was helped to our chambers by two servants, each gripping one of his slack arms.

I crept to the kitchen for a calming cup of tea and discovered Edwina looking an utter scarecrow, hair all anyhow, feet shoeless in filthy stockings, skirts torn and muddy.

She rambled incoherently and laughed in my face like a mad woman. Judging her to be as drunk as Edward, I helped her to a chair and, as she leaned back,

I spotted a chain around her neck hung with the gold ring Edward wears upon his little finger.

This ring, engraved with the intertwined letters E&C, is one I presented my husband on our wedding day! I would have snatched it away at once, had Edwina not been so witless with wine.

May 21st, 1905

This morning, pretending innocence, I asked Edward why he was not wearing his ring and, in a voice devoid of feeling, he said he'd lost it.

I left the house and rode beloved Pegasus to the foothills where the healthful climate is refreshed by light, cool breezes. There is nothing so restful as the solitary pleasure of riding my horse through this green and tranquil countryside.

Returning late, I claimed a headache and excused myself from dinner. I had heard Edwina telling everyone the evening would begin with sherry, with charades, music and duets in the drawing room.

I can imagine the rest – jewel-bedecked ladies in chiffon and lace; men in stiff collars and white ties; a meal of too many courses served with endless goblets of wine, followed with port, then brandy and cigars. There will be dancing while Franklin plays his fiddle and guests sing drunkenly until the hounds begin howling. Could anything be worse than socialising with these ghastly people?

May 22nd, 1905

Edward failed to return to our room last night and neither he nor Edwina were present for breakfast or luncheon next day. Witnessing my evident discomfort, dear Regina Fuller suggested we take apples and carrots to Pegasus who has been stabled with the Talbot's prized hunters.

Once we'd fed the horses, Regina ordered the pony chaise and we trotted to the vineyard to watch grapes being harvested. From there, we drove to the wine press where two buxom women and their children were treading out wine, all four merrily caroling church songs as they trampled grapes underfoot.

We did not speak of the unexplained absence of Edward and Edwina although Regina confided her daughter was both a trial and a grave disappointment to her.

A dramatic scene greeted our arrival at the house!

A gold cigarette box, presented by Queen Victoria to Franklin's father, had gone missing from the drawing room mantle! An immediate search of the servants' quarters had been ordered although I wonder why a servant would desire, of all things, an inscribed gold box decorated with royal coronets? I suspect this prize may have been stolen for its provenance by one of the Talbot's esteemed guests.

Coming upon Edward changing for dinner, I asked where he'd been all day. Speaking brusquely, he offered a poor apology, saying he'd collapsed from exhaustion and spent the night in the wine cellar. Another bare-faced lie! How smoothly they roll off his deceitful tongue.

May 23rd, 1905

I went riding before sunrise and as I turned Pegasus towards the town, a strong south-easterly began to blow, stirring shifting sand over the road and making it so impassable I was forced to return to the farm.

I could not face the Talbots or their guests and instead went into the garden, where I set about trimming a row of overgrown shrubs. How surprised I was to discover a shining row of enamel dishes shelved on wooden slats suspended between two trees. One of the servants told me this custom remains from the previous owners of the farm and later, when the lunch gong sounded, I saw workers each bringing one of these plates to the kitchen where a meal of lentil stew was served with baked bread. Each person also received a 'dop' of wine (one cup) to drink with their meal.

This is going to sound strange, but gazing from my concealed corner of the shrubbery, I felt a pang of something like envy mixed with regret. These people live such hard and hapless lives with little to call their own – no land nor house and scant possessions, yet I find them more content than those who claim to be rich. What a happy picture the farm workers made, enjoying their meal with chatter, laughter and a warm, shared kinship such as I have never known.

Just after midnight I was wakened by shouting.

I recognised Edward's voice followed by the sound of a woman screaming and soon after a gunshot rung out. At once I hurried to the drawing room where I found the most hideous scene.

Five or six haggard guests were kneeling over a man lying upon the floor. His face was chalky and a pool of dark blood spilled from a wound in his arm.

Despite her advanced age and frailty, Regina Fuller dashed from her chamber, still clad in a frilled muslin night cap and flannel nightdress. Dear Regina has the kindest heart God could fashion and the welcome sight of her brave, wrinkled, nut-brown face gave me the strength to assist with the examination of the man's wound. Fortunately, the bullet had only torn the upper arm and was not lodged in the flesh. Together, we two cleaned and bound the injury and medicated the patient with opium to induce a deep, restorative sleep.

Grim-faced, Franklin informed me that Edward had shot the guest after accusing him of cheating at poker. Laughingly, the man had denied this charge and his lips were still framed in a smile when Edward drew his pistol and fired.

May 24th, 1905

We left Tortoise Mountain at first light.

Edwina's complexion was ashen and Franklin appeared horribly bloated, as if too tightly stuffed into the seams of his worsted coat. They waited until we passed through the gate, standing stiffly and so distant from one another I suspect quarreling between the pair. Edward and I were also silent as Pegasus drew the trap briskly homewards.

During this tiring journey, I found my skittering thoughts straying to what manner of man my husband is.

Here is what I know to be true of Edward Butler:

1. He has cold-bloodedly murdered an innocent young man and, for minor provocation, shot at and wounded another.
2. He has been unfaithful – seducing a good friend's wife in his own home, beneath his very nose.
3. Edward is hated by many in Paarl for the notoriety of his war record.
4. His name – Captain Edward Butler of the Imperial Yeomanry – is listed amongst British soldiers accused of ransacking Boer farms before torching and burning them.
5. He has a violent temper and treats those he deems 'beneath him' with contempt and often cruelty.

So disgraced and tainted am I, not only by my husband's behavior but also his appalling character, I can barely look at him.

May 25th, 1905

The servants made a pleasing welcome. My maid, Pretty, had arranged garden flowers in every room and Cook had prepared a tea of almond cakes. The linen is freshly washed, the floors mopped until shining and all windows opened wide to sky and sunlight.

My heart is lighter for being home again.

May 26th, 1905

As I was unpacking Edward's valise, I came upon a shirt wrapped tightly around a weighty gold box decorated with coronets and delicately inscribed as follows: 'Awarded to Herbert Talbot for Services Rendered to the Queen.'

So, Edward is the thief!

I feel ill. Why, oh why must this man blight my life with such dishonour that I am, by association, demeaned, disgraced and made to feel utterly wretched?

Pray God, what am I to do now?"

Plum was transfixed. As I closed the diary, she reached for it.

"I want to put it under my pillow so I'll dream of Charlotte."

"You'll have nightmares," I said." I hesitated. "Don't you find this story...*disturbing*?"

Plum was silent a few seconds, preparing to say something but, after a quick glance at my face, she changed her mind. "I think we were meant to find this diary," she said solemnly, running her finger down the spine of the book.

Oddly, Plum seems unfazed by Charlotte's story. Unless she's pretending. Unless she thinks I'll stop reading, if she shows her true feelings. This diary always leaves me shaken. And then, after, I keep thinking about this tragic woman, her husband, their loveless, horrible marriage. I really must skip ahead and delete all frightening, shocking details before I read to Plum again.

I left the house early next morning and drove to Main Street.

Olympia's Gallery is the name of the art shop. There was a large painting in the window with Theo Christensen's signature spiking the bottom edge of the canvas. I studied the work carefully. An oil work of fishing boats anchored at a harbour wall before a storm breaks. Pewter sky, churning ocean, waves slapping boat hulls, a flurry of white gulls wheeling above a crayfish trap.

The painting brought a whoosh of relief, sudden and unexpected. It made me wonder if I would still be attracted to Theo Christensen if his work was only mediocre?

"Are you interested in Theo's paintings?"

Startled, I jumped back from the window. A woman blocked the doorway.

"I'm Olympia," she said, beckoning me into a cool interior. Tall, buxom and shapely, the woman had short bristling hair cut in a severe mannish style. Her mouth was thin-lipped and her nose a shade too sharp, but her dark eyes were deep-set and soulful. She wore dangling gold hoops in her ears and an expensive green linen sheath cinched with a metallic belt.

Olympia led me to where Theo's work was on display.

"His art is equally in demand by local and foreign collectors," she said, slipping into what was obviously a rehearsed speech.

Listening with half an ear, I counted seven artworks on view.

The largest was a self-portrait of Theo in a blinding white shirt open to the waist, exposing his torso. His style is impressionistic – the shadowed face was almost featureless and yet, from the grey, shoulder-length hair and brawny, matted chest, I'd have known the subject anywhere.

Olympia waved me to another oil painting, a shrouding mist lifting above a lake. This work was beyond good with an almost tactile dampness in an seeping patch of sodden moss at the water's edge. It would take a genius to paint this delicate a landscape in impasto, so thick it looked ridged. I had an overwhelming urge to run my fingers over the stiff peaks of paint but Olympia was on the move again.

"Now this…" She gestured at a pen and ink drawing of a barefoot woman pegging a sheet on a washing line. "This is one of Theo's *masterpieces*."

The work was freighted with eroticism. The woman's hair streamed across her face, her billowing skirt revealed a long length of thigh, a copse of phallic-shaped shrubs bloomed in the foreground.

I met Olympia's curious gaze. "So…do you two know each other? You and Theo?"

My instinct was to lie. I said we hadn't met though I'd heard the name.

"Do you paint?"

"Yes," I said. "Nothing like this though."

"Theo gives art lessons," Olympia declared. "Are you interested?"

The question took me aback. "Um, I don't know. I might be."

"You'll find all the information you need here," she said, passing a leaflet, "Do call, if you'd like to join our class. We've a few places left."

Our class!

"Sorry, I didn't catch your name."

"Olympia Christensen. Sorry, I thought you knew. I'm Theo's wife."

CHAPTER ELEVEN

PLUM

Whenever Aunt Frith reads Charlotte's diary it reminds me of Mom reading *Gone with the Wind* to me before the cancer stole her eyesight away and weirdly the stories of Charlotte and Scarlett are kind of similar because they both lived in manors with grand staircases and lost their hearts to tall dark handsome men and there were slaves at *North Wind* and slaves harvesting cotton on the plantation at *Tara*.

I'd watch Mom's face as she was reading and there was a lot going on. She'd wrinkle her nose, jiggle her eyebrows, make her eyes pop and then squeeze them half-shut until they were squinty. Mom had deep dimples like somebody had dug their thumbs into her cheeks and they'd come and go as she gave characters different voices – rough and deep, high and squeaky, sweet and hushed.

I like listening to my aunt when she reads but her face doesn't move like Mom's and she doesn't keep sending quick, smiley looks over the tops of her glasses to see what I'm thinking or feeling.

Before I go to sleep, I slide Charlotte's diary under my pillow so her words and the pictures they make filter up through duck feathers and stream into my dreams.

Last night I had a dream about Edward Butler shooting a man and shouted for Mom – I still do that sometimes – forget she's not here. She always used to come and sit on the edge of my bed and I'd keep opening my eyes to check if her shadow was pinned to the wall protecting me until I fell sleep. I still hurt deep inside from missing Mom but I never cry so I pinched the skin on my wrist and twisted with my fingernails until a drop of blood squeezed out and I felt better.

After that I had another dream but it wasn't about Charlotte or Edward… we were all together, Mom, Dad and me and I was running ahead swooping my butterfly net in the air and they were laughing with their voices going up and down but then Dad yelled, 'Come back, Lily!' and when I turned he was staring up at Mom spinning away like a butterfly sucked into the sky.

I woke with sadness heavy on my chest making it hard to breathe. Dad used to say we were *the Trinity* – mother, father and daughter and told me never to lose faith in the three of us because we'd stick together like crazy glue but it turns out Dad was wrong about lots of things and this was one.

I look like a total dork in my uniform with the skirt three centimeters below my knees and ugly leather lace-ups with thick rubbery soles that make my feet drag.

Even my new satchel is all wrong – hard and stiff with straps that aren't bendy and don't buckle properly because their holes are too small.

"Give that to me," Dad said and started stabbing holes with his biro leaving runny blue ink blots on the leather so I took it away.

"You're only making it worse," I said and used a fork instead.

I throw up when I'm nervous so I didn't eat breakfast. My aunt said "Try a banana," but it was greenish and sticky so I spat it out.

"I'm worn to fiddle strings," I said in my pretend-Charlotte voice. "I need a mixture of Phosphorus and *Nux Vomica* for nerves and exhaustion."

She laughed, "Charlotte Butler, if I'm not mistaken?"

Dad blotted a blob of egg yolk on his chin. "*Nux Vomica*…highly poisonous…comes from the strychnine tree…mostly used in medicines before World War II."

Aunt Frith picked up his empty plate. "Listen to you!" she said with a snarky look. "You should get onto one of those TV quiz shows and get rich without having to cheat someone out of their inheritance."

Dad didn't pay attention. "The first day is always the worst," he told me. "By the second or third you're starting to get the hang of things and before you know it the end of the week arrives and you're making friends, joining the netball team and everything's hunky dory."

Aunt Frith clicked her tongue. "Good grief, Wills. Do you ever listen to yourself?"

"What have I said?"

She shook her head. "You're making it sound like a walk in the park."

"We've all had to go to school, Frith."

"Yes, but we're not all like Plum…she's…"

What? I thought. *What am I?*

She looked at me. "It's not easy, is it Plum? Meeting new people, trying to make friends?"

Before I could answer, she went on, "I hope you don't mind but I've written a letter to your class teacher. I've explained you don't always relate to other students right away. You need time to settle and get to know your classmates. I've said you're bright – you love words and have an extraordinary vocabulary – but teachers will have to be patient because sometimes you daydream and get lost in your own world."

Dad's forehead was knotted. "I've no idea what you're going on about… Plum relates perfectly well to others."

I asked why they were talking like I wasn't in the same room.

"Sorry." She waved an envelope in my face. "This must be your decision, Plum. Last thing I want is to force you into doing something that will make you uncomfortable. Do you want to give this letter to your class teacher?"

"Okay" I said and asked if she'd cut the label off my blouse because I was coming up in itchy bumps at the back of my neck.

It's weird – the stuff about making friends and getting in trouble for daydreaming is all true but I've never told her so how does she know?

"Do you really think I've got a good vocab?" I asked.

Aunt Frith snipped at the scratchy label. "Your Mom said you were already talking in sentences at the age of two. When you were three, you were fascinated with dinosaurs. Lily took you to a museum to see an enormous skeleton and, right off the bat, you said: "That's a Diplodocus."

The way my aunt said this – with a smile in her voice – made my chest puff with pride.

FRITH

I've been reading *'The Asperger's Child'* in its brown paper wrapper. I wish I could talk to Lily about this – he won't listen to a word I say about Plum being 'different'.

"Though children with Asperger's are often highly intelligent, areas of their brain linked to social skills are limited which can result in an ongoing struggle to form lasting 'give and take' friendships.

Often they will have difficulty in picking up on non-verbal cues and interpreting facial expressions and body language which can be problematic for them.

This disorder also prevents them from seeing another's perspective or even noticing if a playmate loses interest. They are aware they're not popular with others but can't comprehend why and this makes them feel rejected, frustrated and unhappy.

Parents and teachers must work together to discover the best methods of increasing the social skills of the Asperger's child and his or her ability to interact with peers.

Parent/teacher interventions should begin when the child goes to primary school. By the time they're adolescents, these teenagers will need fully-developed coping skills to survive in an increasingly complex and sophisticated social environment."

All of this is mostly accurate except I find Plum is intuitive and sensitive to moods and feelings, more so than most kids her age. William and Lily have always believed Plum is gifted. Her way with words, her early sentences and the extent of her vocabulary made them think she was precociously bright.

And she was. But they missed a few cues. The way she'd suddenly blurt words out of context, mimic voices like a parrot, ask dozens of questions without listening to answers.

She was always OCD with a compulsion to organise books by their colours, line up crayons in neat rows, arrange dolls in a specific order, from oldest to newest or tallest to smallest. Then there was the food issue. Plum insisted on eating different foods from separate plates. That would've driven me mad. But Lily – patient as a saint – graduated slowly to saucers, closer together and then arranging food in groups on a bigger plate.

"One of Plum's quirks," she explained.

I suppose she'd have been about eight when Lily invited a 'friend' from school for a play-date. I'd given Plum a book – *The Man Who Walked Between Two Towers* – the true story of French aerialist, Philippe Petit who walked and danced on a tightrope thrown between the towers of the World Trade Centre, four hundred meters into the sky.

Lil said the book was too advanced but Plum loved it.

"Sit in that chair while I read to you," Plum told the friend.

The child sat obediently but it wasn't long before she got bored. "Stop reading now," she demanded. "Let's play a game." Seemingly deaf, Plum carried on reading.

The girl began whining, pleading with Plum to stop until, exasperated, she shouted: "*I don't like you, I'm going home!*" Even after the child had wandered off, Plum kept reading to an empty chair.

She was an only child and they didn't see it, Lily and Wills – didn't see she was different. Or perhaps they did and hoped she'd change as she grew older.

Whenever I tried to discuss it, they'd become defensive as if – because I was childless – I was jealous and trying to spoil something perfect.

She's better than she used to be, I admit. But still I have this nagging, ever-present feeling something is not quite right with Plum.

After William dropped Plum at school, I took the car into town to buy groceries.

I ordered toast and coffee at the courtyard café. I have no appetite inside the house. Probably something to do with the pervasive coldness, the sickening smell of decay or suffocating clouds of dust that rear up whenever a broom is moved about.

I tried not to look at the waiter bringing my breakfast. There's a kind of café etiquette that dictates you avoid eye contact if you wish to be left alone.

I was chewing toast when this bright, chirpy voice said, "Good morning!" The face looked familiar.

"Louis Venter. We met the other day. Mind if I join you?"

I stifled a sigh. "Please do," I said, gesturing politely at the empty chair opposite.

Venter asked for an Espresso and turned to me. "Still feeling displaced?" The question threw me. "Um…did I say I was feeling displaced?"

He smiled knowingly. "You have that fish-out-of-water look. It's not unusual. Most people feel lost at first. We may be famed for our hospitality in Paarl but we also have a tendency to treat newcomers as extra-terrestrials."

I faked a laugh. "You see me as an alien, do you?"

He rested his chin in his hands, leaning forward, sending a lazy smile. "A very lovely one, I have to say."

I flushed hotly.

It's been *years* since a man flirted with me and within a fortnight, there've been two – Theo Christensen and now this lawyer.

Venter was saying something. "…attend a wine tasting at Mont Benedict…great opportunity to meet and greet a few of our locals and ingratiate yourself into our good graces."

I hid an involuntary shudder, imagining people poking their noses in, asking questions. I drained my cup.

"Thanks for the offer but I'm afraid meeting people is not top of the list of things I want to do right now."

"Oh?" He looked mildly affronted. "We're not all farmers, you know. We've a few judges, politicos, authors, artists, doctors – not to mention a brilliant flock of legal eagles. We're worth getting to know, I assure you."

"Yes, yes." My mind was elsewhere. "Er, may I ask you something?"

When she was about forty or so, our mother, Julia, came into a lot of money from a family trust. Following the advice of our father, she invested this windfall in artworks and, before she died, Julia gave Lily and me a painting each.

"This is your inheritance," she told us, sternly. "Do not squander it."

Mine was a black ink sketch of three nude dancers by the Expressionist artist, Vivienne Vine. Julia had grown fonder of Lily who was kinder, more pliant and more forgiving than I was and she gave my sister a landscape in oils by the Flemish artist, Jan Berens. The painting was dark with a dull gleam to it – a scene of an estuary with birds gathering at the water's edge, an arched bridge curving in the distance. Appraised by Christie's, Lil's painting was worth a tidy fortune.

I sold my sketch and bought a teeny-weeny apartment in Paris with the proceeds.

Lily, more sentimental, kept her heavy, gold-framed oil hanging on a wall in their dining room, beneath a concealed spotlight.

Before she died, Lily whispered she'd left her painting to me. Tears welling, she'd said, "Ma's Berens is the most valuable thing I possess. I want you to have it. Promise you'll think of me whenever you look at it."

By then, Lily was slipping in and out of a coma with rare moments of lucidity.

Weeks after her funeral, I was given a copy of her will but there was no mention of the Berens. William flatly denied Lily had left it to me. I went to look for it in the dining room and discovered a grimy square in the space where it had been hanging.

I told this to Venter and added. "I think my brother-in-law tricked my sister into signing a will he'd altered. Her eyesight was failing. She couldn't read at the end. She'd never have known if he'd removed the clause leaving the painting to me."

"Mmm." Venter sipped his coffee, thoughtfully. "My field is divorce. You'll have to talk to an attorney specialising in probate, estate and trust law. However, to the best of my knowledge, if the will was signed by your sister and two witnesses, it'll be damned difficult to prove your brother-in-law purposely excluded you from inheriting this painting."

"I'm convinced that's what happened."

He nodded. "You'll need to provide irrefutable evidence of wrongdoing on your brother-in-law's part. Alternately, you'll need medical evidence your sister was sick and therefore incompetent when she signed her will."

"So what do I do? Ask her doctor for proof?"

His expression was serious. "I should warn you – challenging the validity of a will can be time-consuming and costly."

"So you're saying *what?* Let him get away with it?"

Venter shrugged. "I'm no expert in these matters. I'll introduce you to one of our senior partners who'll advise you better than I can."

I wasn't about to start running up a tab at Venter's law firm. "Let me think about it."

I pushed away from the table.

He seemed surprised. "You're leaving? Before we've had a chance to get to know one another properly?"

"Sorry…I have to be somewhere."

"Ah, well then," he smiled over his coffee cup. "If you have a *rendezvous…*" he said, making it sound salacious. "Do you still have my card?"

"I think so."

"Take another, just to be sure. And call me. Please. I'd like to see you again." My bag swung from my shoulder, my feet frisked lightly. The years seemed to fall away.

Louis Venter was too sharp, too ironic for my liking – but I couldn't help feeling flattered at his attempt to charm me.

A car drove past. The driver lifted her hand in simple acknowledgement. I waved back. Clean pavements, trimmed verges, cheerful flower pots, charming shops, wine bars. Paarl was starting to feel more like home. And yet, behind my oversized sunglasses, I was still thankful to be a stranger in this town, Miss Nobody, divested of the ballast of my shameful past.

PLUM

"You'll be in Grade Five A – the top class," the principal said. "You'll fit right in."

But how does a spotty giraffe fit into a herd of gazelles if the gazelles have been best friends since grade one which makes the giraffe the odd one out?

It was five weeks after start of term and Miss Everett, the class teacher, shook her head and said, "Oh, dear! What a lot of catching up you have to do!"

I gave her my aunt's letter and stared at my shoes while she read it and the rest of the class giggled. Miss Everett sent me a long worried look and pointed at a desk right in front of her table. "You'd better sit there," she said. "Where I can keep an eye on you."

The whole day was horrible but the last lesson – drama – was the worst.

Grade Seven A was rehearsing a play and all the parts had been taken so I was told to join the chorus line of dancers.

Miss van Reenan said, "No need to look so frightened, I'm sure you'll manage. This is pretty basic stuff." I wanted to say giraffes aren't the best dancers but before I could she'd asked a girl called Erica to run through the moves with me.

Erica's pin-straight flossy hair twirled like a ballerina's skirt as she started bending and dipping and spinning in circles that kept getting wider. My brain shut down the way it does when I know I'll never be able to do something like kicking my legs high and straight or extending my arms like Erica's.

When she'd finished I told Erica I'd have to practice a million times to learn the steps and she said, "It's easy. Let me show you again."

This time she moved in slow motion. "Basic step-tap, step to one side, like this, follow with the other foot, tapping as the shoe lands, got it? And then, left foot to the front, right foot to the…"

I tried my best but I'm two heads taller and all the swoops and turns made me dizzy. I stumbled and almost fell and Erica snorted through her nose like a pig and the class laughed.

The drama teacher got this look on her face like she was giving up and said, "Maybe you should watch the others until the bell rings" so that's what I did.

"So how was it?" Dad asked and I told him about the snooty, sly, superior girls in Grade Seven A who don't want a new girl with a weird name joining their stupid stuck-up little group.

"Don't rush to conclusions, darling. Hang in there and give it time."

"That's dumb – this isn't to do with time! It's about clever girls thinking they're better than everyone else and *why*, just for once, couldn't they have put me in the B class?"

Aunt Frith chipped in, "Oh, Plum! Your Mom was always so proud of you being an A-student!"

I wanted to tell her it wasn't being a clever clogs but having a kind heart and sharing and telling the truth that made Mom proud but Dad gave one of his slow winks which is code for, 'Don't say something you'll be sorry for later' – so I swallowed my words and Dad smiled.

"Right then, girls .What shall we have for tea?"

Aunt Frith looked at Dad. "Dancing." she said. "You'd think it would be in the genes."

CHAPTER TWELVE

FRITH

I heard Plum whispering fretfully to her father: "Sure you can do this, Dad?
Her sweeping arm took in the upstairs bedrooms of *North Wind*.

"Don't you worry your pretty head. I grew up on a building site!" He
flashed a grin, exaggerating as usual. "Spent weekends and school holidays
mucking about with cement mixers, scaffolding and bricks. Best time of my
life."

I watched Plum's brow furrow as she tried to imagine her father in an
industrial wasteland of sand and cement. He doesn't look the part – clean
fingernails, fawn jacket, not a hair out of place, even his parting, a narrow
vertical groove of pink scalp, is precise.

"If I'd had any sense, I'd have taken Grandpa's advice and studied
engineering or architecture," he told her. "I've a hunch if I'd followed a
different course, I'd have made fewer mistakes along the way."

Plum's face screwed into a frown. "But, Dad, if you'd been a builder…
would I have been born?"

He darted a look at me, momentarily confused. "Mmm…interesting
question. I'm not sure of the chronology, but, you're right, there's a chance
I wouldn't have met your mother and therefore, we wouldn't have had you."
He winced. "That doesn't bear thinking about."

Plum said nothing. Her eyes had glazed over. She seemed in a kind of
trance.

Here we go again. I wondered how long it would take for him to notice.

"Anyway, sweetheart, don't you worry about your old Dad. I'm confident I can handle this conversion. I'm not saying it won't be one hell of a challenge, but you bet your boots I'm up for it." He saw how still she was. "Plum?" He grabbed and shook her arm. *"Plum!"*

She blinked. "Huh?"

"Good Lord! You drifted off for a second or two. Thought you were having one of your…your *things*. Sure you're okay, darling? Anyway, as I was saying…" He shrugged. "Bugger me. Can't remember. Not important. Today the work begins. We're embarking on our mission to restore lost pride and dignity to this old house."

Plum lifted her face. "Lost pride and dignity," she repeated. "I like the sound of that."

She went upstairs to change for school. "So, what's the plan today?" I asked.

William shrugged on a jacket. "I'll drop Plum at school and, by the time I'm back, the workmen will be arriving." He assumed his puppy-dog look. "Any chance you could stay in today and help keep an eye on things? These men are reputed to be conversion specialists but they might be chancers. Another pair of eyes would help."

William's lost confidence. He told me he's praying the lessons he learned working alongside his father and grandfather will return from where they've been squirrelled away in some long-forgotten corner of his mind.

"But suppose they don't?" he asked, anxiously. "What if I create an unholy mess, throw good money after bad and end up making the place look worse than it does now?"

"It couldn't look worse if it tried."

He carried on glumly: "I should be raring to go. Excited at the prospect of bringing this old house into the twenty-first century. But my gut is clenching. And I feel…I feel…God dammit – I feel *guilty.*"

That wasn't what I expected. "Why?"

"Well, it's obvious, isn't it? I'll be tearing down parts of the original building. It seems *sacrilegious* somehow – like destroying a church."

"Except it's not a church. It's an old ruin. Besides, aren't you 'returning pride and dignity' to the house."

He looked pained. "I could do without the thinly veiled sarcasm, if you don't mind."

After William had left with Plum, I prowled the echoing house, steering clear of the attic. The room at the top of the second flight of stairs gives me the heebie-jeebies.

Plum, on the other hand, has an unhealthy preoccupation with both the attic and the diary.

Yesterday, I caught her ripping paper off the dining room walls, hunting for the William Morris grape-leaf design Charlotte wrote about. I led her to a room adjacent the hallway where I'd peeled away a patch exposing four different wallpapers, one pasted over the other. She knelt at the wall, rubbing her finger lightly over a faded olive and gold pattern.

"You found it," she said, disappointed. "You found it before I did. *She* touched this wallpaper. Charlotte. She left fingerprints here."

She expelled a long, husky breath. "I've been thinking," she said.

"Yes?"

"Do you think the feelings of people who've lived in this house before us, people like Charlotte, could be trapped under wallpaper or mixed with paint or locked in a cupboard?"

"No," I said, firmly. "You can't trap human emotions."

"But how do you know?"

"Common sense tells me."

Plum seemed not to have heard. "I think they're still here," she said quietly. "All the feelings Charlotte had when she was living in this house."

Tipping her head back, she gazed with narrowed eyes at glittery swirling dust motes suspended in the air.

"I feel them sometimes, swear to God."

I shuddered.

All this…Plum's unnerving behaviour, Charlotte's morbid story, the uncanny creepiness of this old house…lately, my mind's been playing tricks. At night I think I see flitting bats throwing witchy silhouettes against walls.

During the day, harmless noises like water rumbling through pipes sound disturbingly like low groans.

My hearing seems to have sharpened, attuned to faint sounds like those made by woodland creatures shuffling through undergrowth or dead branches scraping like fingernails against glass panes of windows.

Every morning, I find a new spider's web draped like bridal lace across the hallway mirror, yet I never see a spider.

And something else – in this heightened state of imagination – I'm starting to wonder if the interminable cold seeping into my bones is some kind of personal attack since I'm the only one of the three of us who feels it. It sounds absurd, but it's almost as if I've been singled out to be punished for something bad I've done.

A car drew up outside. I hurried downstairs and found a workman in blue overalls at the door. "I'm here to fix the windows," he mumbled. He carried a battered toolbox, plastic lunch box, flask and transistor radio.

As we made our way upstairs, I told the man William wanted window frames crafted to exactly resemble the originals. He gave a disparaging look, dumped his toolbox, rolled up his sleeves and tuned the radio to thumping Reggae.

"Get on with it, shall I?" he asked pointedly.

Downstairs, William was back and making nervous circuits of the hallway. Round and round he went, glancing at his watch, stopping every few seconds to stare through the window.

"The window man is upstairs," I told him.

He nodded. "Waiting for the joiner," he said. "Thomas Nyasulu. Expert in restoring flooring."

There was a loud rapping. "That'll be him!" Wills bounded to the door.

The man at the entrance was young, not yet twenty, with hair twisted into stiff horns hung with bright glass beads that gave off a musical tinkling as he moved.

His name, he said, was, Zaba Nyasulu and with youthful arrogance, he claimed to be as skilled as his father who'd been laid off with a bad back.

William bit his lip. "You've restored floors in this condition before?"

"Ja." Nyasulu dropped gracefully to his knees, running his hands over worm-eaten timbers, jabbing a thumb into wood with the texture of marshmallow.

"You seem very young," William said, doubtfully, but Nyasulu, tapping for decay, didn't answer.

Minutes later, a green mini-van disgorged four plasterers who carelessly hurled bags of cement to the paving before grabbing tools and marching to the door with ashy cigarettes hanging between their lips.

"Sorry. No smoking!" William barred the entrance.

They stood scowling.

William scowled back. "You can't smoke. This place is like a tinderbox."

Sparks flew as the men flung their cigarettes to the floor and stamped on them.

Looking surly, they flung a dusty tarpaulin over the floor of the master bedroom before pausing to silently gulp cooling cups of stewed tea.

William consulted his notes. "Try to save as much of the original plaster as you can." He tapped his file. "Says here… *'When you remove the original plasterwork, you change the historic appearance and the value of the dwelling.'*" He looked around the room. "We don't want that, do we?"

The men smirked as they rooted in a box for hammers and scrapers.

One spoke up. "Aish, Boss, no offence, but there's no need for all that twak! Leave it to us, okay? I bet you there's nothing you can tell us about plaster we don't already know."

Another van roared up the driveway with a *'Waterworks'* logo on the doors.

William introduced me to the father and son plumbers who were to install new copper piping and white enamelware in the bathrooms. The duo, Jan and Kleinjan, came with a team of burly men in orange overalls, carrying sledgehammers. Briskly, Jan told Wills his squad would set about taking out old baths, basins, toilets and tiling.

"I take it you'll be supervising?" William asked, but father and son were retreating downstairs. "Back later to check on things," Jan shouted.

It was obvious the orange overalls weren't familiar with the rules of restoration. There was nothing sensitive in the way they wielded sledgehammers to shatter porcelain tiles into flying shards, capable of removing an eye. Two hours later, one of the bathrooms was knee-deep in broken tiles and we both kept finding crumbly bits of cement in our hair.

There were damp blue circles under William's arms. He looked drawn.

"They're going at it like bloody bulls in china shops," he shouted. I had to lip-read – it was impossible to speak over the noise of the men singing a rousing marching song as they swung their hammers to the rhythm.

"This isn't how I imagined it." As William cupped his hand to yell into my ear, I saw a nasty bloody nick on his wrist. "I'd no idea it would be so... *violent.*"

By mid-day, Zaba, the floor expert, had ripped up a dozen or so planks to expose a dark space heaving with soft, black fungi.

A hill of shattered window frames lay uselessly at the feet of the carpenter. "Nothing salvageable?" William asked, hoarsely. Casually, the man shook his head. "Nothing."

After lunch, an electrician arrived and, at his heels, a small mixed-breed terrier with a wiry coat, wagging tail and bright eyes.

"This is George," the electrician said, "he goes everywhere with me. He won't be any trouble."

The man jogged upstairs to check the wiring and a little later, I saw the dog streaking downstairs, followed by his owner shouting, "George, wait... *wait boy!*"

"Whoa!" William called. "Where are you going?"

The electrician grabbed the dog's collar, struggling to hold him as the panting terrier pawed wildly at the floor, straining at his collar. A raised ridge of stiffened hair ran down the length of his back.

The electrician eyes were bulging. "*Shit!* Something in that room spooked my George. Look how terrified he is. He's never done anything like this before. Sorry, you'll have to find someone else to do this job."

The man returned after locking his dog in his van. "I can't go back up there," he said, abashed. "Ah...would you mind collecting my tools?"

I followed William who made a show of sauntering calmly into the room.

There was nothing there. Marble-topped fireplace, a gaping hole where Wills' foot had plunged through a beetle-bored panel, wildly scattered tools. I helped pick these up, dislodging scampering woodlice from my fingers.

"Bats in the belfry," William joked, returning the man's tools to him. "There's a family of bats in the roof, high in the rafters. That's what scared your dog."

Looking queasy, the electrician lowered his voice. "I've heard stories. People say there's a ghost at *North Wind*."

After he'd gone, I gripped William's arm. "That's the second person who's mentioned a ghost."

"C'mon Frith!" he snapped. "I can't believe this is you talking, you're usually so sensible. Bats put the wind up that dog. Simple as that."

A deafening hush fell after the workmen left. I found a discarded peak cap and zip-up jacket half buried in sediment. The second floor looked like a bomb site: gaping holes, an exposed skeleton of raw roof beams, a tide of rubble flooding into passages.

I heard Plum bolting up the stairs. She stood in the doorway, mouth open, dramatically clutching at her chest.

"Oh, Dad!" she wailed. "You've wiped her life away!"

"What?" William, picking plaster chips off his sweater, looked up, vaguely. "Whose life?"

"The author of the diary we found," I said. "I've told you before. Her name was Charlotte Butler. She lived at *North Wind* a hundred or so years ago. She's still here!" Plum declared earnestly. "You can't see her because she's a spirit. All this…" She gulped. "…it's going to break her heart, I swear."

PLUM

Miss Cooper, our English teacher, speaks so softly you have to strain your ears to pick up what she's saying.

I've heard them calling her '*fish eyes*' because her specs make her eyes seem huge and watery. She also has a baby's wobbly mouth and looks as if she's about to cry.

I feel desperately sorry for Miss Cooper. It hurts when people laugh at you which is why I won't unless she says something funny but that's a different kind of laugh and there's no spite in it.

This morning we had Poetry – we're learning one of Olive Schreiner's verses – and Miss Cooper nodded at me and said, quiet as a mouse: "Please read for us, Plum."

First, I read the poem to myself and saw it had a regular *dum-de-dum-de-dum* rhythm like a train clacking over tracks.

"The morning sun is shining on,
The green, green willow tree,
And sends a golden sunbeam,
To dance upon my knee…"

I read loudly the way Mom told me – *'pretend you're on a stage and project your voice to the back row of the audience'* – and I kind of flattened the lines so it didn't sound as if Olive Schreiner had written the poem for little kids and when I got to the last four lines, I made my voice sad and mysterious:

"There is a hand I never touch
And a face I never see;
Now what is sunshine, what is song?
Now what is light to me?"

Miss Cooper said, "Well done, Plum!' and blotted her eyes with a tissue that made her eye-shadow streaky.

I sat down with a bump but then she said, "One moment, my dear. I'd like you to give me a word – one word mind – to describe the tone of the first four lines of the verse?"

I read the lines to myself again and was going to say 'happy' but that was too easy so I thought a bit and said, "Um…what about…*joyful?*"

Miss Cooper bobbed her head. "Good! Now – can you think of one word to describe the tone of the next four lines?"

There'd been a word in Charlotte's journal – it took a while to remember but when I did I knew it was perfect. "Is the tone – *despairing?*"

"Oh!" Miss Cooper squashed her lips into a fat little circle as her eyes went swimming around the classroom so we could all see how pleased she was.

It got quiet. My skin started prickling. I could feel them – Annelie, Tanya, Roxy, Carla, Samantha, Zelda and the other girls – sending hateful thoughts in my direction.

It's not Miss Cooper's fault but teachers like her ruin everything when they make a fuss of you because nobody likes a smarty pants.

When I look down from a tall building a hand grips my throat and starts pressing and that's the feeling I got when I saw what the builders had done upstairs. I was choking and Aunt Frith was pounding my back and saying something in my ear, her voice coming from miles away, "You okay?"

"How can I be okay?" I shouted because a chunk of Charlotte's life had been wiped away. My stomach was making squelchy noises – another thing that happens when I look down from a high place – and then a terrible thought flew into my head so I ran to the attic taking the stairs three at a time.

The room was just as I'd left it that morning. I was so relieved I laughed out loud but instead of ha, ha, ha…*ahuh-ahuh-ahuh* came out of my mouth.

I looked up and she was there.

"Now, now," she said, rubbing circles on my back. "You're usually so brave. It's not the end of the world. Wait and see how lovely the house looks once Dad's restored it."

I ducked away from her hand. "You don't believe that," I told her. "You're just saying it to make me feel better."

It feels wrong to stare directly into a person's eyes, right into their tiny black dots, but I made myself do it and she wasn't telling the truth.

She ran a bath and washed my hair with chamomile shampoo and let me wear Mom's dressing gown. It's palest pink like inside a sea-shell with silky tufts that stand up when you rub them the wrong way. What I love most is it smells of Mom – Chanel Number Five and roses from the cream she smoothed on her hands and something like vanilla in a cake.

"Do you think she'll ever find it in her heart to forgive Dad?" I asked.

Her eyes got big. "Mom?" she said, in a quaky voice.

"No, the spirit."

That got me thinking. "And, if the spirit has a heart, does she also have kidneys and lungs and breathe and pee like we do?"

"Plum!" Her voice bounced off the walls.

"What?"

She shook her head in a way that's supposed to make you believe she's being forced to look after a baby chimpanzee.

"If you stop asking questions, I'll read a few pages from the diary."

CHAPTER THIRTEEN

FRITH

I like pressing my nose into the brittle, opened spine of the diary, inhaling the oddly comforting combination of dust, ink, antique linen and something gluey.

A thin strip of fraying ribbon keeps our place and when I turned to the yellowing page, Charlotte's handwriting was tightly cramped and she'd used green instead of her customary black ink. Not a good sign.

Plum peered at the page. "Uh-oh…she was crying when she wrote this."

She pointed to a blot where water – presumably tears – had dripped onto the page, soaking through the paper, dissolving the ink and distorting Charlotte's words so they were barely legible.

Plum was overwrought after William's bloody onslaught upstairs; hopefully reading the diary takes her mind off the destruction and stops her obsessing about the spirit being 'heartbroken'.

This child is so intense, God knows how Lily managed all this and cancer at the same time but maybe it's different if it's your own child.

May 30th, 1905

It pains me to write this but Edward has been intoxicated since our return home. He staggers about, befuddled and besotted. Alcohol inflames his temper – he is always in a fury, making hideous, shameful scenes in front of the servants, finding fault where there is none.

I hide from his awful rages by shutting myself in the upstairs attic where I am deaf to Edward's shouting. It is a fact that Edward will cease drinking only once he has consumed every last bottle in the house. With all the wine jugs and whiskey decanters drained, he's taken to drinking rum which makes him bilious and gives him scorched cheeks and a swollen bottle-nose. Pretty and I have taken the precaution of concealing supplies of port and sherry in the stables where I pray Edward does not find their hiding place.

June 2nd, 1905

Coming upon Pretty, distraught and weeping, I tried to coax my little maid into explaining the cause of her misery but she covered her face with her hands and refused to speak one word.

I am perplexed. What can the matter be? Have I carelessly said or done something to cause her pain?

Edward is still as drunk as a fiddler – it takes four strong men to carry him to his chamber where he lies in bed suffering shivering attacks of delirium tremens.

I find myself sinking deeper into darkness. Could my life be any worse?

June 3rd, 1905

Oh, Lord – Edward is beside himself, overturning furniture, breaking crockery and glass...accusing the servants of stealing his liquor. I have locked myself in the attic where I shall remain whilst Edward is on the rampage.

June 4th, 1905

Pretty brings regular supplies of food and water and I have books, paints, sewing and this journal. I escape to the bathroom when I must, but otherwise I am quiet and secure in my confinement.

The hours hang heavily. I have begun reading Charles Dickens' 'Great Expectations', one of the many books Edward brought from London. The book is not new but this copy is of excellent quality with a cover of Moroccan leather and inside, the papers are marbled and smooth as silk,

I hope Mr. Dickens, the most famous novelist of the day, fully engages my attention and keeps me from agonising over Edward.

When my spirits are equal to it, I take out my little box of Windsor and Newton watercolours and attempt to paint the row of lofty oaks seen from the window. This aspect of trees, grass and sky is soothing to the eye. How indifferent Nature is to my self-imposed imprisonment or Edward's shameful descent into drunkenness and possible madness.

June 5th, 1905

I woke to piercing screams and, flinging on my wrapper, ran outdoors where I found Edward in the servants' quarters, cracking his whip and bellowing like a bull as our terrified servants ran hither and thither.

Never before have I seen my husband in such a state, his face ugly and engorged, veins snaking across his brow, his clothing spotted and stained.

I tried to grasp his hand. "Edward, you are not yourself," I cried. "Come to the house, please."

He fumed the servants had stolen his liquor and swore he'd report this theft to the District Police. "They are innocent, this is all my doing!" I confessed.

Edward thrust me aside so roughly I fell to the ground, tearing my skirt and grazing my hands.

Old Moses helped me to my feet and would have received a lashing for his trouble had he not been so spry in ducking Edward's whip.

I dispatched Pretty to the stables for a bottle of port and sherry and held these up in shaking hands. "Here...I have your alcohol, Edward."

At once, his anger dissolved. He stood with unfocused eyes, ruddiness draining from his mottled cheeks. I held out my hand and though he did not take it, he followed me quietly into the house and took himself directly to his room where he remains, even now.

Poor Pretty...her pallor is turned to ash so frightened is she for my sake. I am not sorry for telling the truth. How could I allow Edward to punish our servants for something I had done?

June 6th, 1905

Early this morning, I was sifting flour when Moses' wife – Jina – our Xhosa kitchen maid called Moses into the kitchen and asked him to give me a message.

There ensued a noisy chattering between these two with Moses shaking his head and waving his arms in agitation and Jina pleading with him to tell me what it was she wanted me to know.

But Moses would not speak, no matter how she begged and the argument went on until, shrinking with shame, Moses scuttled into the garden.

I told Jina to call Pretty to translate whatever she wanted to tell me but when she heard mention of my maid's name, Jina threw up her hands and stormed away.

Clearly Jina is gravely anxious to report a matter of concern and since she will not speak to Pretty, I gather this information pertains to my maid. I've been closely observing Pretty. Her eyelids seem swollen from weeping and she is drooping from fatigue, illness or fearfulness.

"Will you tell me what ails you?" I asked. She fastened her eyes on me as if to speak but, at that moment Edward, entered the room and, with a strangled cry, Pretty darted away.

I asked directly, "Edward! Have you done anything to harm Pretty?"

He looked livid. His eyes bulged like two hard boiled eggs.

"How dare you humiliate me in front of the servants!"

"I apologise for hiding your drink," I told him. "I hope you know it was for your own good."

"Stupid...incompetent...imbecile of a wife!" he spat – his face a grotesque mask. "You must leave North Wind Manor. Go at once! I will notify your mother and arrange your passage to London."

"I will never leave!" I shouted. "You cannot force me to go. This is my rightful home!"

Edward raised an arm as if to strike and I ran to the attic, locking the door behind me.

How frightened I am. Frightened and ashamed. What a sickening shambles I have made of my life!

June 7th, 1905

Finally, Edward has ceased drinking although his temper is as hot as ever.

However much I may wish to, I cannot stay shut away forever. What must the servants think of me? It will cost drops of blood wrung from my heart but I must be strong and behave with propriety as Edward's wife and mistress of this house.

June 8th, 1905

I have eaten a galling dish of humble pie and begged for Edward's forgiveness.

"Please let us make peace." I said, giving him my hand. He held it limply.

At length, he spoke. His voice was cutting. "Am I to understand you have learned your lesson, Charlotte?"

Meekly, I replied that I had – although, truthfully I've no idea which lesson Edward refers to though I shall never hide his drink again.

"Very well," he replied. "Let us see if our marriage is salvageable. I strongly advise you show me greater love and loyalty."

"Yes, Edward," I answered. "For my part, I would like you to..."

He interrupted. "I also suggest you have less to say!"

After this, he allowed a small, mean smile. "Least said, soonest mended!"

We took a silent walk around the garden before I withdrew indoors leaving Edward motionless beneath a tree. I called feebly from the doorway, "Will you come inside, my dear?"

He might have been made from stone, so hard and cold was the look he gave me.

My hand trembles as I write these words...

This man is despicable. How I wish Edward would die and leave me in peace!

June 12th, 1905

I paid Aletta a visit and brought a head of cabbage, a leg of venison and spiced biscuits baked from a recipe I snipped from the 'Paarl Ladies' Paper'.

The boys had left before sunrise to walk to school but Aletta drew me inside where we sipped coffee and sampled the biscuits. Note to self – a little less ginger next time.

Since I am attempting to converse in her language, I find Aletta chatters naturally and easily. She tells me her sons pay twopence a week to attend St. Bartholomew's Church School. They earn this money collecting firewood and selling bundles in the town and, on Saturdays the eldest boy finds employment as a caddy at the golf course on Main Street, where golfers pay nine-pence a round.

Aletta takes in laundry, ironing and mending and, when there is work at 'De Bruin's Fruit Canning Factory', turns her hand to washing fruit and packing boxes. She told me this without rancour saying she was glad for an opportunity to earn money in these hard times.

I told Aletta that Pretty is ill and needs time to recover away from North Wind Manor. Kindly she offered a snug, dry barn where there is ample space now that the family can no longer afford to keep horses – only the small mule.

I promised to dispatch Thomas with the trap and a mattress, blankets, paraffin stove, food and such dishes and implements as Pretty might need and we agreed to a fair payment of half a crown a week for lodging and clean water from the well.

At the bridge, I turned to gaze back at the humble Prinsloo house basking in sunlight. Aletta was leaning over the gate waving as her grey mule cropped lazily at the long grass, surrounded by a brood of clucking hens. Cheered by this charming picture, I returned to North Wind lighter in spirit than when I had left a few hours previously.

June 15th, 1905

How glad I am that Pretty is installed in safe, commodious lodgings with the Prinsloo family

Despite this, there are still problems at North Wind Manor.

This morning I was greeted by cook in a flood of tears. She was dressed in her best, carrying bundled possessions and balancing a wobbling three-legged cooking pot atop her head. There was no mistaking cook's intention but she was sobbing so loudly, I could not understand why she was leaving.

I distinctly heard her use the Xhosa word 'inyoka' – which means snake – and called for Moses to interpret, but all he said was that Cook had accepted another position in the valley.

I suspect Cook's departure may, in some way, be linked to Edward although this may be unfair since, as far as I know, my husband has had nothing to do with our kitchen staff.

A niggling worry persists – could Cook have seen a snake inside our house? Has this frightened her away?

June 16ᵗʰ, 1905

I am training a new cook sent by – of all people! – Miss Kriel, choir mistress at Strooidak Church. Hearing of my troubles, she dispatched a young woman called Lena with a note testifying she had been employed by Miss Kriel's aged aunt – now deceased – and was considered hard-working, honest and capable of preparing basic meals. Lena is tall and striking and, according to Miss Kriel, has an agreeably placid temperament.

June 17ᵗʰ, 1905

Oh mercy!

I cannot imagine how Miss Kriel's old aunt reached her dotage! Lena can only boil potatoes and eggs, make pap and bake plain soda bread. She tells me she has never prepared meat, fowl, fish or vegetables or baked cake or pudding!

Today, I taught her to make clear soup, fillet a fish and boil a ham. Tomorrow I shall show Lena how to make a cake with farm butter and Worcester raisins and together, we will, by slow degrees, work our way, page by page, through the 'Common Sense Cook Book'.

How tediously life grinds on!

June 18ᵗʰ, 1905

Out of sorts and liverish, Edward has consulted a practicing physician who has warned him of the dire effects of excessive alcohol consumption. "Dead by the year end!" the doctor predicted. "That is your fate unless you seriously curb your liquor intake."

The physician's prognosis has done its work. Edward tells me our cellar will hold only a small store of red wine which, he professes, has health-giving properties when taken moderately with an evening meal.

June 21ˢᵗ 1905

For days Edward has been in the gloomiest of tempers, barely speaking. He spends most of his time listening to Caruso on his gramophone or supervising the workers planting vineyards, orchards and a vegetable garden.

Without a maid or competent cook, I occupy myself with dreary, repetitive domestic duties and my husband and I are like two ships passing on the stormiest of nights.

June 23rd, 1905

Edward's feelings for me have altered greatly. Even sober, he looks upon me with distaste and says I have grown too pale and pinched.

He has a signal I have come to know – a light touch in the small of my back signifies his desire for marital relations. Of late, however, his nightly visits to my bedchamber have grown scarce.

I am glad for I find no pleasure in intimacy – but I am also woefully aware this weakens my increasingly tenuous hold on Edward. At this rate, I shall never conceive a child and where will that leave me in his estimation?

As far as Edward is concerned, my present role is little more than that of housekeeper although at far greater cost and more aggravation than any paid domestic.

For myself, I am desperately lonely. I am like a starving mouse at a lump of cheese – a never ending yearning for love gnaws at my poor, starved heart!

June 26th, 1905

In setting the house to rights, I have found little time to read 'Great Expectations' but this afternoon I took my book to the church where I sat in the silent graveyard beneath a flowering laburnum and lost myself in the world of Pip Pirrip who never knew his father, mother or five infant brothers for, by the time he was born, they were all buried in a churchyard, a bleak place, overgrown with nettles.

I had reached a gripping place in the tale where Pip encounters a fearful man with a great iron on his leg and was shaken out of my wits when a hand touched my shoulder!

"We have all missed you, Mrs. Butler. Are you well?"

I have no words to describe how the sight of Dirk's handsome, gentle face filled me with joy.

I said we had been away visiting a wine farm, and since our return, our lives had been beset by hardship.

"It feels as though I am always pulling against the stream," I told him honestly. "Do you ever feel defeated by fate, Mr. Barnard?"

I knew at once I had misspoken for he withdrew, stepping a pace or two away from me.

"I can't say I do," he answered, politely tipping his hat and muttering about the lateness of the hour.

Oh Lord, I thought, I cannot do anything right!

I returned to my book and had reached the part where Pip smuggles a file and food to the chained convict when, hearing footsteps I looked up and, to my surprise, Dirk Barnard stood before me again.

He spoke quietly.

"It is true," he said. "Like you, I often find myself battered by fate, Mrs. Butler."

"Oh, thank you for saying that, Mr. Barnard," I replied. "I mean to say, I am not thankful that you are battered, but only…"

His lips curved. "I understand your meaning."

Then, to my delight, Dirk invited me to take tea with him next Wednesday afternoon. We are to meet at the Strooidak and walk a short distance to the boarding house where Dirk lives.

Light-headed, I galloped home, luxuriating in ecstatic thoughts of what next week may bring.

CHAPTER FOURTEEN

PLUM

Dad says he's happy to be back in South Africa but it doesn't feel like it 'cause he never stops grumbling about the president whose name is Jacob Zuma and who's done something bad called 'State Capture' – I don't know what that means but Dad gets red in the face about a family named the Guptas who own South Africa which is funny because I didn't know one family could own a whole country.

Every breakfast starts with Dad reading stuff on his laptop about protests, riots and demonstrations and saying things like: "The timing is perfect for anarchy and revolution and, I warn you, Frith, we're going to hell in a handbasket!"

"You're right," she says and gets this eager look. "Sell up. Get rid of this place. Let's get out of here, before it's too late."

"I like it here," I tell them. "I like the house. This is where we belong."

"And school?" she says, because she knows the answer.

"Not so much. But I love *North Wind*."

"Where would we go?" Dad asks Aunt Frith. "*Where?* Tell me? With the world in crisis? With Brexit and that idiot Trump. With global warming, swarms of homeless refugees, with terrorism and wars, the threat of a nuclear disaster?"

"I'll go to France," my aunt says in her sensible voice. "You two can go back to the UK. At least they don't have a water crisis like they do here."

"That's because it never stops raining."

On and on they go never getting anywhere.

This morning, my aunt interrupted Dad in the middle of a rant about Mr Trump saying his IQ is bigger than anyone else's when everyone knows he's a moron, or so Dad says.

"There's an excellent artist in town giving lessons," she said. "I'm taking his class on Friday."

Dad's mouth fell open. "You're not serious! You're an accomplished artist, for Christ's sake. All those years studying in France! That's bollocks when I need your help here."

"What do you want me to do?"

"Well, for one thing, I want you to go to town and check out those taps."

"You can do that yourself."

"There was this woman serving in that shop. She kept staring. Damn sure she knew my face."

"That's an excuse."

"I'm going to be forced to hide away. You said it yourself, 'What if someone recognises me?'"

"I'm not talking about this now. That's a risk you took."

"Please, Frith. Be reasonable. I need your help."

She pushed her plate away. "I'm not doing chores for you. Nor do I plan to be stuck here inhaling plaster dust into my lungs and turning deaf from drills and hammers going at it non-stop."

Her neck was coming up beetroot red and she jumped up from the table. "You didn't consult me on any of this. All your idea. Get on with it!"

When she'd left the room, Dad gave a dopey smile. "Sorry, Plum," he said. "Don't want you caught in the middle of all this. Isn't it time for school?"

"Maybe you could wear a disguise? A stick-on moustache. A hat pulled over your face. Nobody would recognise you then."

He gave me a pretend chuckle. "That's an idea!" he said, but didn't mean it.

She took me to school.

I didn't talk for half the way. Then I said. "You're *horrible* to Dad. You could check out those taps for him, you know you could."

"And I will, I'll go there now. But his hiding away is an excuse. He's going to have to face people in this town and he knows it."

"You want to take art lessons because you like that man."

"He's a talented artist. I can learn from him."

"How do you know he's not an axe murderer?"

"Oh, please, Plum, stop talking tosh. Why are you being difficult?"

"I don't like it when you're mean to Dad."

"I'm being honest. It was his idea to come back here and yet he does nothing but gripe about the politics, the economy, the lack of any change. I'm sick of it!"

"He's missing Mom. That's why he's sad and cranky."

"We're all missing Lily. It's not easy for any of us."

"You weren't always this mean to Dad."

FRITH

It was the way she said it. Plum's words were weighted with meaning.

I parked the car outside the school gates and turned to her.

"You want to tell me something, don't you?"

She looked out of the side window.

"Come on, out with it, then!"

She spoke slowly. "I saw you and Dad that night, when Mom was so sick. Afterwards she cried and cried. She couldn't stop, not for two days."

"Go on…"

She looked at me but the shutters were down. "You know," she mumbled.

I felt my throat clench. Could she have seen us? Oh, fuck, fuck, no!

"I don't. Mom cried all the time when she was sick."

Plum sighed heavily. Her eyes dropped. "I saw you and Dad. You were in your bed. You were kissing. And you weren't wearing clothes."

I closed my eyes. Bile at the back of my throat. The air sucked out of my lungs.

160

PLUM

She had her eyes closed tight. From nowhere, I had this lightness inside…
whoosh!…like letting go of a humungous rock I'd been lugging around for
the longest time.

My aunt sat still not saying anything. She kept her eyes shut like she
couldn't look at me and the minutes kept dragging by until I heard the
school bell.

"I've got to go." I said.

She sat up straight and opened her eyes.

I started biting my nails.

She gave me one of her no-blinking stares. Then she squished her
forehead into a jagged frown and said in her dead voice, "I see. So it was *you*
who told Lily."

FRITH

After Lily was diagnosed with stage four cancer it seemed to me that, of the
three of us, I was the one who suffered most from knowing she was terminal.

A tight knot of dread in my stomach put an end to sleeping or eating.
My body melted away until my hip bones turned into knife points and
raccoon rings darkened my eye sockets.

"Why are you doing this to yourself?" Lily asked although, deep down,
she would have known – I was becoming her.

When clumps of Lily's hair started falling out, we shaved our heads in
a sisterly ritual. I still have our shorn hair in a pillow slip; Lil's thick curly
tresses wound around my dull, straight locks.

We laughed at our grim images in the mirror until the laughter broke
and we held onto one another, weeping. "We're twins again, Lil," I told her.
"We're identical."

For Lily's sake, I tried to paint. She asked for a portrait of herself for Plum and I set up a table in her room.

Even now, I can see that table: the top strewn with pencils, flattened paint tubes, a smeared cloth, pallet knife, an art book opened to a colour plate of Blake's *The Ghost of a Flea*.

I was sketching Lily as she lay sleeping, numbed by pain-killers. Her skin was the pale blue of skimmed milk and though she was perilously thin, her cheeks were puffy from cortisone. My hair was growing back, a field of prickly dark bristles, but Lily stayed egg-bald without eyebrows, lashes or body hair. Even so, she was still, in my eyes, the prettier twin.

As I was drawing her, William crept silently into the room and leaned over the table to examine Blake's picture.

I recall being mesmerised by his hand on the page as I edged the book closer to him. I couldn't stop staring at the faint sheen of blond hair on his wrist, his clean, well-shaped fingernails. Not for the first time, I imagined his hand touching my body.

I pointed to the painting. "William Blake," I said. "Poet, painter, printer, prophet. Do you know his work?"

"No,' he answered, shortly. Wills took my hand and, in a gesture that seemed incredibly intimate, lightly scratched a dried blob of paint from my palm.

His nearness made me tremble.

"Like it?" I asked, nodding at the page.

He shuddered. "Why would anyone paint something so repellent?"

In those days, I thought of William as a man who knew everything and took pleasure in telling him Blake used to sketch his visions during séances with the dead and this was the painter's version of a flea in human form.

Wills peered at the figure with its gold and green overlapping scales, gristly spine and long muscular tongue flicking towards a cup of blood.

He looked deep into my eyes. "I'm not remotely interested in this odious Blake. Tell me what inspires *your* paintings?"

That night, we slept together.

Why did I do it?

God knows. I can't figure out why, after flirting openly with my sister's husband since our first meeting; I slept with him when my Lily was in the throes of dying.

Until my last day on earth, this will always be my greatest regret and deepest sorrow. I'm sick at my betrayal – but William's not completely innocent.

He couldn't have been blind to the fact I'd always been infatuated with him. He'd have known I was frightened, fragile and desperately lonely and took advantage of my weakness and misery.

At least, that's what I told myself. But now, with the passage of time, I think it was the other way around. I think I was the one who took advantage of Wills.

It's not easy to go over what happened, but I must.

I stayed up late – it was past midnight, when he came to my room. I was in bed reading when he put his head through the doorway. He whispered, "May I come in?"

I know what I should've done – acted affronted and shooed him away – but I didn't.

The sexual longing I'd had for William, suppressed for years, was too strong. I allowed the book to slide from my fingers and drew back the covers so William could climb in beside me. His arms were around me, his warm hands reaching beneath my pyjama top, his parted lips, tasting of wine, pressing down on my mouth. He removed my clothes and his own before stretching me out flat, leaning above me. I was intently aware of the flop of his hair, the dent of a dimple in his chin, the flat black mole beneath his right eye. A lamp was burning on the bedside table. He took off my glasses and the light fractured into sharp, golden splinters as shadows leapt and feathered on the walls.

But, when we started touching, sex was awkward and clumsy. We didn't allow our eyes to meet. My body was all bone. Penetration was painful. William couldn't climax.

At last, he rolled off me, sobbing like a child.

I pulled him close and he wept, soaking my breast.

When he could speak, he said, "Ah, Lily, don't leave me. Please don't leave me."

"Fuck!" I pushed him off in a quick, angry gesture. His face burned.

"I didn't mean that. Forgive me, Frith."

"What are we doing, William? This is *madness!*"

He hid his face in my shoulder. His body shook. "I think I'm losing my mind," he cried. "I can't live without her, Frith. I don't want to live without her."

"Go! Please leave now, William."

Stricken, he wiped his eyes with a corner of his unbuttoned shirt.

"This never happened," he said. "Swear, Frith."

"I swear."

Days later, Lily had a bad turn. Doctors increased her morphine and she started breathing oxygen through plastic tendrils in her nose. That's when she asked me to help William take care of Plum. I remember how carefully I'd answered. "I'll stay until William's well enough to cope alone. You can trust me, Lily. You know that, don't you?"

The look she gave shook me rigid! We've always been able to read one another like books. That's when I knew...she knew about me and William.

Immediately, I jumped to the conclusion that William had had one of his confessional crying jags and he'd admitted to sleeping with me to ease his conscience. I hoped he'd been honest and explained the sex had been crap and we'd reached for one another like two drowning sailors, grabbing the nearest body for comfort and nothing more.

When I accused him of telling Lily, he looked stunned and denied it. For days, he protested innocence, but I didn't believe him. Poor William, ever since I've treated him as my enemy.

The idea of Plum telling Lily turns me ice cold.

Lil believed I'd betrayed her as she lay dying, leading William astray when he was emotionally scraping rock bottom. She would have despised me for exposing Plum to the shocking sight of me and her father, naked in bed.

This hurts so badly. I can't bear that Lily died knowing only half the truth, the little Plum saw. I can't bear that I can never make this right between us.

And now it comes to me – *the painting!* Is this why Lily changed her mind about leaving the oil to me? Is that why she didn't include it in her will?

But no, Lily would never do that. She knew how much I needed money from the sale of the painting to survive. She knew I'd taken months off work to help her, William and Plum and I'd very little left in my bank account. It wasn't in Lily's nature to jeopardise my future because I'd made a stupid, reckless mistake and slept with Wills.

Was it?

PLUM

Dad picked me up from school. We didn't talk much.

"I'm feeling flat, darling," he said.

I knew what was coming. Dad's always saying things like this. *Flat as a pancake. Feeling blue. Got the morbs.* I know what this means.

"Flat as a tyre with the air let out. Punctured. Paralysed."

"You're depressed," I told him. "You can't help it. Mom said it's like a serious sickness."

"Your mother understood me very well."

"What's it feel like?"

"Mmm. Tricky to explain. You can't focus. Your mind flips and flops like a fish. You're tormented for no sound reason you can think of. You feel pain but it's invisible and can't be seen or explained. Your heart beats too fast. And you're always scared. It's hell, that's what it is, pure and simple."

"How can you make it go away?"

"I'll have to give myself the kind of good talking to your mother used to give me. That'll jolt me out of it."

I tried to do my homework but that thing Dad said about depression being like hell made me miserable so I lay on my sleeping bag with the diary on my chest and thought about Charlotte Butler. I must've fallen asleep. Aunt Frith came to wake me.

She was wearing Dad's duffle coat with sleeves so long she looked like she had no hands.

"If you've stopped sulking, come and have tea with us."

At that moment, I heard a noise coming from the rafters. It sounded like...*aaaah...uhah, aaaah...uhah.*

I pointed above our heads. "Listen."

Her eyebrows shot into her hair. "What?"

"It sounds like a baby crying."

"You can hear the wind blowing through the rafters. Probably going to rain. Go and tell your father to get plastic sheeting put up at the windows."

The *aaaah...uhah* noise got louder.

Now, this next bit is *vitally important* and every word is true, swear-to-God.

I was giving Aunt Frith one of my, 'Are you totally deaf?' looks but she went all soft and blurry like I was looking at her through coloured water and then she blew away like a scarf in the wind and there was a strange lady in the same spot where my aunt had stood.

She was younger than Aunt Frith, wearing a long green dress that floated and swirled around her legs as if she was paddling up to her ankles in the ocean.

The lady had a white, thin, pointy face, glowy like a pearl, and long black hair clipped in a knot with a silvery comb.

My words came out shaky, "Who are you?"

I don't think she heard me and she couldn't see me because she was looking down and muttering – not to me – it may have been to God because she was saying, *"Help me please, I beg you!"*

Then I heard, "Plum! Wake up, Plum!" and I blinked and my aunt was back in Dad's awful brown duffle-coat.

"Oh Lord," she said. "Have you had another of your...your...*blanks?*"

I told her right away. "Aunt Frith," I said, "I've just seen Charlotte Butler!"

CHAPTER FIFTEEN

FRITH

I pressed the bell at the gallery door. An arpeggio of chimes rang out and a woman came gliding towards me, arms outstretched wearing an expression of extravagant delight. "Frith…how *lovely!* Welcome, my dear. May I take your jacket? I think you'll find it quite warm in the courtyard."

I barely recognised Olympia with her head swathed in a flower-spattered turban and her figure concealed beneath a flowing muumuu, ropes of chunky wooden beads clunking at the neck. She smacked the air above my cheeks with flaming lips.

"Follow me, this way, my dear, oopsie…careful of that step."

Trailing in Olympia's expensively scented wake, I regretted not wearing the sexy, silky drawstring blouse I'd picked out that morning.

"I'm going to art class today," I'd told Plum, bending before a tiny mirror. As I'd dipped, the neckline of the blouse slid over my shoulder and Plum's reflection glowered in the glass.

"You can see your boobs!" she accused, crossly. Withering under her disapproval, I pulled on a plain t-shirt with my denims.

Behind an arty screen painted with flying cranes, a concealed door opened to a short flight of steps and a garden. A semi-circle of six women and two men were sitting at easels in an enclosed, dappled space brightened by yellow roses clambering over a rough wooden trellis.

Olympia clapped her hands. "Everyone – meet Frith!" I smiled self-consciously but no-one looked up, all intent on their canvases.

"Here's your perch." Olivia pointed to a narrow space between a doll-like woman with Oriental eyes and a stout, perspiring man in a gaudy sun-hat.

Looking around, I noticed most students were elderly, adorned in paint-spattered smocks with wide-brimmed hats clamped to their heads.

Olympia handed me a sketchbook and a box of sharpened pencils, gesturing at a table set with a single tiger lily and three twigs in a square glass vase.

"Begin by drawing this still-life," she instructed. "Use a F, 2H or 2B – whichever you prefer."

The other artists were using oils, acrylics and watercolours.

"I'd rather paint," I said, confidently withdrawing a box of watercolours from my hold-all.

She shook her head. "Sorry. Theo has a strict rule for newbies. A pencil drawing first, if you don't mind, Frith,"

I shrugged. "Where *is* Theo?"

At that moment, door chimes signaled a customer and without answering, Olympia swept away, leaving a heady scent of ambergris.

The chubby man grumbled under his breath. "Set your watch by Theo, you can. His Lordship generally makes an appearance half an hour after class starts. That's if you're lucky. Some days the bugger doesn't even pitch."

I began sketching. The still-life was deceptively simple: chunky vase, pendulous lily with an angular leaf, bent, and blackened twigs. But, when I looked closely, the thick, greenish glass had air bubbles trapped in its uneven surface and there was a rather tricky underwater refraction of the lily stalk and twigs to consider.

I sneaked a sideways glance at the Oriental woman's canvas. She'd laid down sure, natural strokes in a light pigment wash. "I *love* what you've done," I gushed, enviously.

She nodded briefly, her flat-lidded eyes sliding from the table to her painting.

"I'm Frith and you are…?"

"Chen," she answered, barely moving her lips.

"And I'm Donald," the portly man said, pressing crumpled tubes onto a messy pallet and rendering his twigs with demonic slashes of navy.

His work had nothing of Chen's delicate sensibility. His vase was a crude one-dimensional cube and his lily looked like an upturned trumpet. A choking fug of oil paint and turpentine rose from his corner. Seeing my expression, he grinned.

"Yeah, as you can see, I like a mess." His eyes trawled over me. "I happen to believe you need chaos in the soul to make art that speaks to people."

I tested his words carefully, not sure of his meaning. "Chaos in the soul?"

"You have it!" he declared, emphatically. "No mistaking it. Saw it the instant you walked in."

Startled, I did a double-take but I'd lost him. Donald was scraping away with a palette knife, cursing under his breath.

I'd produced three reasonably good sketches by the time Theo arrived. He greeted the class and then strode purposefully towards me.

"Frith – apologies for my tardiness. Something unexpected came up."

He flipped through my sketches. "Mmm, not bad. A little stiff, perhaps. You want your lines more fluid, more spontaneous, eh?"

Taking the pencil from my hand, Theo turned a page and began sketching.

"This is what I'm talking about." His pencil flew over the textured paper. "You want to create an individual style. Overall, your sketches are a touch bland. You need more vitality in your work."

He glanced my way. "You seem confused. Let me think of a simpler way to explain myself."

You arrogant shit!

"Ever heard of Chloe Cheese? Ralph Steadman? Lane Smith?"

Any artist worth her salt knows the work of all those artists, but he gave me no time to reply.

"Steadman's sketches are macabre, frenetic. Chloe Cheese does these charming drawings of domestic things like stripy cats and spindly-legged chairs. Then there's Lane Smith who illustrates children's books with dark, satirically funny drawings. What I'm getting at, Frith, is that each of these artists has a totally unique style that makes their work immediately recognisable. *Comprende vous?*"

Duh, yes! Oh God, what am I doing here, listening to this drivel?

Theo's voice droned on. "And then, of course, there's Marshal Arisman. I recommend stopping by his website. Arisman's tutorials taught me how to delve deep to find my artistic personality. If you don't do that, you face the danger of ending up all style without substance, a ship bobbing without a sail, if you catch my drift, eh?"

Oh, he is insufferable! What a stupid cow you are! What makes you think this man is attracted to you? And how could you find him attractive anyway?

Unkempt hair in need of a good cut. Pronounced bump on the bridge of a craggy Roman nose. Old acne scars pitting his cheeks. Unshaven whiskers. Frayed shirt collar and – *ugh!* – a tasteless, wide yellow-gold link chain slung around his neck.

On the pretext of reaching for a pencil sharpener, Theo moved closer until I could see every freckle and hair darkening his sallow skin. I found myself shrinking from the forced nearness of his bulky shoulder.

He's not remotely my type, too big, too fleshy, too hairy.

"Examine the flower as a child would," he was saying. "As if seeing it for the very first time." He smiled with a quirky lift of his mouth to one side and as the web of wrinkles around his eyes deepened and spread, my idiot heart started racing. "Over to you," he winked, returning my pad.

He'd drawn three separate sections of the still-life – the lily's drooping sepals, the curve of a leaf threaded with veins, an explosion of air bubbles trapped in a ledge of glass. His drawings were detailed, intricate – and perfect.

Theo moved on to another student and I caught myself stroking the wooden shaft of the pencil...*this is where his fingers gripped*...sliding my hand across the uneven, bumpy paper...*this is where his palm touched the page.*

Such schoolgirl silliness! How could I find a man who was too damned full of himself so arousing? I've never understood the sexual frisson between men and women – it's a total mystery. Something to do with brain circuitry releasing dopamine and serotonin – or is it pheromones?

I heard Theo's annoyingly loud laughter.

I don't like him – but I'd sleep with him in a heart-beat.

I did a page of show-off sketches for Theo, a wobbly Chloe Cheese and a bizarre Steadman…but there are only so many times one can keep drawing a lily and a few sticks in a vase and my pencil had ideas of its own.

On holiday visits to the beach, Lily and I used to draw one another's shadows with sticks in the sand. I was impatient and kept moving, hopping from foot to foot so her drawing of my shadow was never quite right. Lily would turn into a statue, standing quite still, arms arcing around her head with fingers knitted to form a circle and that's what I drew that morning, Lily's insubstantial, seven-year old shadow, hovering like a ghost above the grainy sand.

PLUM

Dad came home with a brand-new Raleigh.

"You're on the cusp of twelve," he said. "Old enough to ride to school and back."

I named the bike *'Pegasus'* and took it for a ride, pretending to be Charlotte racing against the wind on my horse. My school hat became a bonnet with flying ribbons and my uniform turned into the swirly green dress I saw in my vision.

The word *'blank'* describes what happens when the darkness comes but not when I see things so I'm using *'vision'* because we've been learning about Joan of Arc who was French and had her first vision when she was twelve and saw Saint Catherine, Saint Margaret, the Archangel Michael and a host of other saints and angels. People were horribly cruel to Joan of Arc. I try not to think of her burning to death on a blazing bonfire because they said she was a witch when she was only different like me.

Today at break a girl called Bronte came up and said, "Can we be friends?"

I couldn't answer because my mouth was full of a bite of one of Dad's goat's cheese with peppery ham sandwiches which took a long time to swallow and while I chewed I was thinking, *'Do I want this person to be my friend?'*

I honestly don't mind not having a friend. I read during breaks and don't have to swap my nice lunch for someone else's oozy jam sandwiches. Also I prefer riding home alone taking the long way and making the journey last for ages to give me time to think about stuff.

This girl, Bronte, has a bike and will probably want us to ride together like the others who break the rules riding side-by-side, four in a row, making cars hoot and drivers yell.

There's one good thing about having a friend though – it might make me fit in and stop girls staring like I'm a total freak.

Bronte asked, "Don't you *want* to be friends?"

I told her half of me did and the other half didn't and she said, "What's that mean?"

I tried to explain. "I'm not very good at being a friend. I don't play sports or games or watch TV. I don't go to parties. I'm not allowed sleep overs."

The last one is a lie but I don't want her visiting me at *North Wind* – I have to protect the spirit and make sure nobody but me sees her.

"I'd still like to be your friend," Bronte said.

I thought I should warn her. "My aunt says I'm pricklier than a hedgehog and Dad thinks I'm too intense and my Mom used to worry that I…" but I stopped because I didn't want to talk about Mom to a total stranger.

"I don't mind, really I don't," the girl said.

She wore me down so I said okay, I'd be her friend.

"*Cool!*" Bronte held up her palm.

"There has to be a rule – no high fives," I told her. "Real friends shake like grown-ups."

We sat in the quad and ate lunch. Bronte was reading: *The Princess Diaries* about a girl in New York who finds out her father's the prince of Genovia and she's a real princess.

"You can read it when I'm finished," Bronte said kindly but I told her I was reading a real diary, not a made-up one – a real diary written by…by a historical person.

Bronte asked, "You mean a king or queen?"

I said no, an ordinary person who lived long ago and she yelled, '*Boooring!*'

She made me cross. "That's not true. Reading a real diary is like creeping under the skin of the person who wrote it and after a while you start thinking and talking like that person."

"What kind of things do you say?"

"Oh, I dunno. Things like…um…like, '*North Wind Manor is beset by tempests'.*"

She pulled a face. "What's that mean?"

"It's a way of saying terrible things are happening."

But Bronte wasn't listening. She asked if she could have a sip of my strawberry juice to make her biscuit go down and then started laughing. "Hilarious!" She waved her book at me. "Listen to this, Mia's talking, she says, '*I can't be a princess – I'm waiting for my normal body parts to arrive!*'"

My aunt was out when I got home so I begged Dad to read the diary aloud because Aunt Frith won't read it again until I stop all the nonsense about seeing Charlotte.

Dad flipped through the diary, screwing up his eyes.

"Can't make out a word. Completely illegible. Might be Russian or Chinese for all I know. I've no idea how your aunt reads this. Sorry, Plum."

I asked Dad to try harder because we weren't even half-way through and it would be agony to stop at the place where Dirk invited Charlotte to tea and not know what happened.

Dad closed the book and said, "See, that's the problem, right there! Your aunt thinks your nightmares stem from this diary. She says it's very vivid and terrifying in places. She told me she thinks it over-stimulates your imagination and you've become obsessive about this Charlotte person. It's got to stop, Plum. I don't want you getting all worked up over a silly journal written a hundred years ago."

"You've got it all wrong," I said. "It's a sort of history of our house and the people who lived in it after the Boer War. I'm learning a lot from Mrs Butler's diary."

Dad's phone rang. "One minute," he said. But then he started scribbling on a scrap of paper and I knew I was wasting my time.

There's a place I hide when my mind gets too loud. It's a crumbly wall covered over with a saggy creeper that's thrown itself down a steep bank and put out roots in the grass.

I crawled into this green space and let my ears fill with the sounds of bees fussing in flowers and birds chirping.

I've been looking up local birds with enthralling names like – sugarbird, sunbird, whydah, hoopoe and francolin. There are hundreds in Dad's, *Birds of Southern Africa* and they're much more interesting than dull English birds like tits, thrushes, blackbirds and magpies.

I ran the tips of my fingers over Charlotte's handwriting. I can't read what she wrote but I remember a few lines from the first page. *"We passed beneath an avenue of tall trees, their branches curving overhead like a bridal bower."*

I know these trees – most are still standing in a wobbly line at the edge of driveway though some have toppled like soldiers with their heads cut off and their bodies rotting in the grass.

Dad's voice, "You in there, Plum?" Shiny brown lace-ups and trouser bottoms under a tangle of creeper.

"I came here to be by myself," I said very firmly.

He sounded thoughtful. "Yes, I guessed that might be the case. But we haven't had tea yet and I've fetched a bag of warm scones from the bakery. There's some really good jam – fig, strawberry and a jar of that creamed honey you love."

My tummy was rumbling but I wasn't ready to give up my snug little burrow so I said I wasn't hungry.

"What's making you unhappy, darling? Is it school?"

School! That's when I shouted, "Who cares about school? School is *nothing* compared to *never* finding out what happens to Charlotte and Dirk and *never* getting to the end of the diary. And I'm not *obsessing!* I'm just interested. You and Aunt Frith are being totally unfair!"

His shoes shuffled closer. "Why don't we talk about this indoors and see if we can find a solution?"

That sounded like a good idea so I tucked the diary in my waistband and crawled out on hands and knees and Dad helped me up.

"I'll do my best to change your aunt's mind about reading the diary to you, but I can't promise anything. It's damn nigh impossible to persuade that woman to do *anything.*"

Dad gave a creaky laugh.

I kicked a clump of spongy grass. "You feeling better, Dad?"

He jiggled his eyebrows at me. "Right as rain, thanks, Plum."

"You gave yourself a good talking to then?"

Dad was quiet for a bit. "I thought about what your Mom would say to me," he said and his voice sounded hoarse. He combed his hair with his fingers so it stuck out like wet hair on a dog that's been swimming.

"She'd have said, 'This is not all about you, Wills, there's also Plum to consider. You can't slide into another depression because I've gone, that's just selfish. Our daughter needs a strong parent and you're going to have to keep all that grief coiled down deep inside you. Plum can't deal with a depressed father on top of everything she's coping with now. You're going to have to pull yourself together, Wills, and do it quick-sticks'"

"That sounds like Mom," I said.

"Yes," Dad nodded. "I thought so too." and I saw the lump in his throat moving up and down.

After the scones stopped turning behind the little blue glass pane in the microwave, Dad passed me one.

He smiled. "I printed out a few pages from, *The Anglo-Boer War Diary of Private S. Hadfield.* I think you'll find this fascinating."

He cleared his throat.

"*We had marched some fifteen miles when we saw a quantity of smoking chimneys rising from what appeared to be a manufacturing town, some way in the distance. As we neared our destination, we saw we were approaching the famed great gold mines of the Rand.*

Our unit was halted behind a low ridge and our commanding officer ordered us to advance across an open plane. Our enemy had set fire to the veldt and we believed we should be burned alive as we lay shouldering our guns in the scorching grass. Bullets, thick as hailstones flew above our heads and, since our khaki made a splendid target against the blackened veldt, our comrades, vulnerable as lambs to wolves, fell on every side.'"

I tapped Dad's arm. "No!" I said. "No. I don't want you to read any old Boer War dairy – only Charlotte Butler's."

Dad looked surprised. "This diary was written at roughly the same time. I thought you'd appreciate Private Hadfield's point of view."

He went on about there being two sides to every war but I wasn't listening because through the window I spotted Aunt Frith with her sketchbook in her arms. Her mouth was droopy and she was walking slowly on tiptoes the way she does when she has a thundering head.

"I don't think Aunt Frith enjoyed her art class." I told Dad.

He hadn't seen her. "So you want me to stop reading then?"

"Yes, please."

Dad made a noise that sounded like, "That's that, then."

I felt sorry. "You know I love you, don't you, Dad?"

"Yes…yes, of course, never doubted it for a second."

"And you love me – and that's all that really matters, isn't it?" His forehead crinkled. "Um, yes, I suppose so. What are you getting at, Plum?"

It came out in a rush. "We don't need her, not really. She's never going to love us the way Mom did because Mom loved with her whole heart and there are lots of times I think Aunt Frith doesn't have a heart."

"That's unkind, Plum. She's doing her best. It can't be easy for Frith. She and Lily were as close as two sisters could be. She doesn't show much, but she's taking this as hard as we are."

See, I don't think that's true but I kept quiet because I could see Dad didn't want an argument and I felt guilty about asking him to stop reading Private Hadfield's diary.

Aunt Frith walked in.

"How was your class?" Dad asked.

She slumped in a chair. "Not what I expected," she said.

We waited for her to say more.

"I may have been wrong about Theo Christensen."

"He's not very nice, is he?" I said.

My aunt looked at me and her eyes were kind of hazy, like she wasn't seeing things properly because of her headache.

"Not nice at all," she nodded. "An idiot actually. Very full of himself."

A long sigh snaked out of my mouth. "That's what I thought."

CHAPTER SIXTEEN

FRITH

Plum's in a mood. This morning, staring straight ahead, not meeting my eyes, she blurted, "When are you going back to France?"

"I'm staying until Dad gets on his feet. That's what I promised Mom."

She stared above my head. "But what if Dad *never* gets on his feet?"

I made my voice calm. "Oh, he will, don't you worry. All your father needs is a little more time."

"He told me he's feeling flat."

"I'm not surprised. It's the house. He's bitten off more than he can chew. And he's not over Lily, not by a long shot. We're going to have to be patient with him, Plum – he's at a low ebb."

It's more than that, though. William believes he's made a mistake, coming back. He's appalled at finding South Africa another failed African tragedy run by a despicable despot with an economy reduced to junk status. He's scared of being recognised, arrested for fraud, tossed in jail.

And that frightens me too. I'd have to take care of Plum until she's an adult, another ten years!

I go cold, just thinking of it.

Plum grew quiet. Her eyes were downcast, her body stiff with tension. Puzzling over this, I saw she was summoning the courage to make some kind of a pronouncement.

Then she came out with it.

178

"Remember when Mom got so sick, right before the end?"

Oh, God, what now?

"Yes."

Swift intake of breath. "Mom wanted to die, didn't she?"

My first thought was, '*How does she know?* My second was how to reply. If I told the truth and said 'yes', Plum would think Lily hadn't cared enough about leaving her. If I said 'no', she'd sense I was lying. "Your Mom was in a lot of pain," I said, quietly.

At the end, Lily's pain was so excruciating, her oncologist had 'a drug pump' surgically inserted beneath the skin of her abdomen. The pump, a circular metal device, released liquid morphine through a catheter into the fluid around Lily's spinal cord, giving her periods of blessed relief.

At that stage, Lily was also attached to a urinary catheter and breathing oxygen from a tank.

She was restless, thrashing in bed, moaning, talking incessantly, even when seemingly asleep. One day, near the end, I leaned in close, catching mumbled snatches. When I could make out what she was saying, I'd write it down, in case it was important. I have my notebook still, but I can remember every word she uttered at the end.

'*Take care of my baby, promise you will, oh, God, my baby…*'

'*I've lost the car, Wills, left it outside the shopping mall, the one near the…I can't remember, is it near the sea?*'

'*Teeth, Plum…don't forget to brush your teeth.*'

'*Chanticleer's bowl is empty…water, canary seeds and…and peeled apple.*'

'*There are dishes in the sink and the fridge needs cleaning. I left a wilted lettuce in the crisper.*'

Poor little yellow canary. We bought him with our birthday money the day we turned twelve. Lily christened him *Chanticleer* after the rooster in Chaucer's fable and only when I learned French, did I discover *chanticleer* meant, 'to sing clearly'.

That birthday, after shopping, we were seized with tense, giggling excitement as Lily carefully carried the bird in a cardboard box punctured with holes, Father followed with a vintage Victorian cage and I brought up the rear with seeds, cuttlefish and bird's toys – the jangly silver bell, a long ladder, a bobbing blue plastic budgie swinging in a hoop.

We hadn't reckoned on our mother or perhaps we had, which would have explained our underlying sense of panic. Julia – who never stopped repeating how much she *loathed* dogs and cats – shrieked when she saw the cage in our father's arms.

It was exquisite. A miniature avian palace of glossy white-painted wood and silver wire standing twenty-eight inches high if you included the carved finial on a domed top attached to a gold-tasseled velvet cord for hanging.

"Over my *dead body* are you bringing that *hideous* contraption into this house," Julia barked. "Take it away! I won't have it and that's *final!*"

It was one of the only times we saw Dad get the better of our mother. He smiled evenly. "The cage will find a home in the girls' room, Jules," he said, firmly. "You barely go in there, do you, darling? And the bird will be no trouble. You won't even know the little chap is in the house."

I remember breaking out in a cold sweat as we shuffled past Julia and silently climbed the stairs to our room.

I kept waiting for her to make a scene but, oddly, she didn't say another word. There must have been something in our father's voice that silenced Julia that day.

Canaries can survive for ten years. *Chanticleer* lived just four. I was the one who killed him. I left a window open and he caught a chill and died. I sobbed for days.

Lily comforted me. I remember her motherly arms around my neck, her gentle voice in my ear. "These things happen, you can't blame yourself. This is not your fault, Frith."

But it was and we both knew it.

We never forgot *Chanticleer*. His rapturous singing, his lustrous, loving black eyes, the way he used to perch on our heads and softly tug our hair and nibble our ears. We'd let him fly around our room for daily exercise and, afterwards, take turns at touching a finger to the faint pulsing tremor in his feathered breast as his tiny heart beat with exertion.

At the end, Lily's thoughts were of Plum as a baby, Will, *Chanticleer* and random, seemingly unconnected things like whether the house was clean and where the car was parked.

She never mentioned my name in her ramblings but perhaps that's because she thought she didn't have to worry about me and, like a cat, I'd be the one to fall on my feet.

In the last week, Lily slipped into a semi-coma. She would wake for only a few minutes at a time before sliding back into oblivion. Her breathing grew harsh. Sometimes her eyes would open and we'd stare at one another in shock until I realised she saw nothing but a fragment of a dream or a distant, illusive memory.

There were rare moments of lucidity. "You're angry with Wills," she told me at the last, her voice clear and strong. "Don't be. Whatever he's done, forgive him. He's far from perfect – but then that's true of us, too, isn't it, Frith? And he has so many good qualities. I love him in spite of all the reckless, stupid things he's done. You know too much, that's your problem. I never should have sent you those angry letters, blaming him. After that, you turned against Wills. But, if I can still love him, surely you can forgive him?"

Lily kept a photograph under her pillow. Plum would've been about two in that picture, guileless little face, corkscrew curls, pudgy cheeks, sweet mouth, dark eyes.

I'd come into her room and seen Lily with the photograph held close to her eyes, tears sliding down a furrow from cheeks to chin.

"I've been holding on for Plum," she croaked. "But, it's too much. I can't anymore."

"Let go, Lily", I whispered. "You don't have to fight like this. It's okay to let go."

She gripped my fingers. Her eyes burned into mine. "Help me, Frith… *help me!*"

Seconds later, Lily closed her eyes and I sat trembling at her side, trying to match my breathing to hers, *in and out and in and out and in…and… out…*each ragged inhalation giving off a sound like fabric being roughly torn into strips.

Next day, she was coherent again. I brought clean sheets and, hearing William and Lily's voices, halted outside the bedroom door.

Lily's voice was rising, becoming agitated.

"You *have* to help me, Wills," she pleaded. "I can't keep waiting for my heart to stop. Look what it's doing to Plum! She's utterly terrified. You can see it in her face. Oh, please, Wills. Don't make me beg."

His voice was agonised. "I can't, *I can't!* Don't make me do this, darling! I couldn't live with myself."

And here was Plum, chewing her thumbnail, not looking at me, waiting for an answer -

'She wanted to die, didn't she?'

I touched her shoulder. "Your mother stayed alive as long as she could just to be with you. You were the one she dreaded leaving. She hated the idea of you having to grow up without her. The last weeks of holding on, that was for you, Plum."

Tearing at a half-moon of fingernail, Plum nodded sadly.

I cleared my throat. "The diary is in my trunk, under my blue sweater. Go and get it and we'll spend the next half-hour or so finding out what happens to Charlotte Butler."

June 27th, 1905

This morning, I found a slip of paper that had been posted beneath the front door.

"Please come at once! Aletta Prinsloo."

I found Aletta looking grave as an undertaker. She bade me sup a cup of strong coffee before she would impart her news.

Dear Lord, it pains me so to write this...

My maid Pretty informed Aletta that her master, my husband, made improper advances towards her on three occasions and not only beat her into submission when she protested, but threatened to kill her if she spoke of this to anyone.

Aletta relayed this information haltingly and when she could not find words, made do with awkwardly miming Edward's vile intentions lest I not grasp her meaning though I understood her so well I was hard-pressed to meet her honest eyes.

She whispered that if Edward ever found out what Pretty had confided, his wrath would know no bounds. So anxious was she, Aletta brought a Bible and made me swear to take this hideous secret into my coffin.

One thing is certain – Pretty must **never** return to North Wind Manor!

Aletta suggests my maid travels to the Cape to find employment. I am to prepare food and clothing and provide such money as I can spare – though it will not be much for Edward's grip on the purse is tighter than ever.

Before we said farewell, Aletta took my hand and spoke to me so urgently I could not fully comprehend everything she said though the gist, I gather, is that she believes my life may be in danger.

June 28ᵗʰ, 1905

I stayed awake all through the interminable night and now, as day is soon to break, everything falls into place with all the pieces in the puzzle made plain!

I remember the day when Jina begged Moses to give me an important message but he refused and ran from her, into the garden. Now I know Jina wanted Moses to tell me what Edward had done to Pretty.

I remember Pretty bolting in fear whenever Edward entered a room. I recall the day when, without explanation, our much prized cook left North Wind to work for less pay in the valley.

I am aghast at my stupidity and negligence. How could I not have guessed what lay directly beneath my nose?

At last, I fell asleep at dawn and my dreams were so choked with awful ghosts and bogies, I was grateful to wake from them next morning.

June 29ᵗʰ, 1905

These are the darkest days I have ever endured! I feel only disgust and contempt for Edward. To keep out of his way, I busy myself with domestic duties from morn 'till night, trimming lamps, putting up preserves, baking bread, making flannel petticoats and chemises for the maids.

When Jina and Lena laid their washing upon the grass to dry, I saw their only undergarments were ugly drawstring flannel drawers.

Cotton and flannel sell for one and eleven pence a yard at Main Street Haberdashery and these women cannot afford such luxuries. I took such pleasure in sewing petticoats and underskirts for them and they, in turn, were so grateful and happy for my consideration.

How long, I wonder, will Jina and Lena remain at North Wind? Soon I fear they too will depart from this house for their own safety.

June 30th, 1905

Edward has purchased the land adjoining North Wind. Now he boasts to all and sundry that he owns over eight hundred hectare, planted with the Pinot Noir grape of Burgundy, the Rhine Riesling and white Steen grape. The first I heard of this purchase was when the Provost brought the deed of sale to the manor to be signed.

This land is iron-hard, a mixture of flinty layers of granite and shale. If grapes are ever to grow in this soil, deep furrows must be dug and quantities of lime added to nourish the earth.

How sorry I feel for the men and beasts tasked with this back-breaking work.

As a caution, I have instructed Moses to warn the workers to behave obediently and even submissively for fear of paying a terrible price for provoking my husband's foul temper.

At night, in the silence of my room, I immerse myself in 'Great Expectations'.

I find this novel consoling. A comment from a character called Pip, resonated with me.

He says: "It is the most miserable thing to feel ashamed of home. There may be black ingratitude in the thing, and the punishment may be retributive and well deserved: but, that is a miserable thing, I can testify."

I also feel shame – not of beloved North Wind Manor – but of its cruel owner.

Edward Butler imprints his noxious character indelibly upon my life and the lives of those who live here – reducing us all to despair.

July 1st, 1905

Word has come at last. Tomorrow, Pretty will ride with the post-cart to Stellenbosch and from there, travel by train to the city of Cape Town. I packed a basket for her journey and sent a purse of money – all I can afford. I yearned to see Pretty one last time but could not find the courage to stand before her and bid this sweet girl a loving farewell knowing how despicably she has been treated in our home.

Aletta declares Pretty holds no blame against me, yet I can never forgive myself for not shielding my innocent and trusting maid from Edward's obscene intentions!

July 2nd, 1905

This is the day of our assignation! I am to meet Dirk Barnard at the Strooidak Kerk and from there we will walk to his boarding house to take tea together.

I imagined waking in a state of eager anticipation yet, sadly, this is not the case. I am in the doldrums, too occupied with regretful thoughts of Pretty and intense loathing of Edward.

My moods are increasingly morbid and I find myself preoccupied with thoughts of what destiny has in store for me. I also admit to being afraid of my dangerous depth of feeling for Mr. Barnard.

I pray my desire for romantic love does not make an utter fool of me!

Later...

Dirk was so properly circumspect, I was not in danger of swooning in his arms like a love-sick girl. Dirk refuses to call me Charlotte – it seems I am to remain 'Mrs. Butler' as if I were an elderly relative. Oh, I cannot write more – I am like the skeleton at the feast – my spirits are now more dejected than ever!

July 3rd, 1905

Waking with chest pains and a headache, I dosed myself with Lung Tonic, Beecham's Pills and a large tablespoonful of castor oil. I am not suffering from any recognised physical ailment – only a pathetic, self-pitying attack of 'Grievous Disappointment'.

The boarding house where Dirk lodges is named 'Strawberry Hill' and is not to my taste though it is worth describing. The property is owned by an eccentric German family and resembles a castle with Gothic chimneys and tall windows in which the glass has been painted with saints, birds and flowers. Inside are marble statues and dusty cases exhibiting stuffed birds, eggs and pinned butterflies.

There are hunting trophies – the worst a young doe's head with limpid, beseeching eyes, callously mounted above a fireplace.

The landlord, Mr. Jens Beck, portly, whiskered, wearing a tasseled red fez atop his head and a vivid green smoking jacket, invited us to take tea in the library. In this room, the sofas are covered in purple cretonne and the walls with crimson silk. I admired the many bookshelves lined with hide-bound books on German history, botany, poetry and philosophy, all particular interests of Mr. Beck who seems to be exceptionally well-read.

For me, the afternoon had a dreamlike quality. I found it extraordinary that Mr. Beck seems completely unaffected by the trials of war and the dire poverty that dogs this land. A life filled with extravagances is hard to bear in the midst of universal misery, deprivation and want.

Dirk and I were never alone for one moment. Mr Beck, proved an excellent chaperone though I believe he only followed Dirk's instruction for it was plain to see how much he pined to return to his books and pipe or whatever had happily occupied his attentions before our arrival.

After tea, Dirk walked with me to where I had tethered Pegasus. "Will I see you again?" I asked.

He bowed and replied, "I hope we shall meet in church on Sunday."

I had a lump in my throat so large I did not trust myself to speak. I mounted my horse and sped away before Dirk could see how my eyes were quickly blinded with tears.

July 6th, 1905

I have had neither the heart nor will to take up my pen for days but the time has come for me to write about what I have lately discovered.

With Edward away at an auction, bidding for a horse, I was tidying his rooms when I came upon two Bibles concealed at the back of a cupboard. When I opened these, both had Boer family records written in the frontispiece.

I have heard many reports of Bibles taken from Boer farms by British Officers as war souvenirs.

Unhappily, I conclude these two must have been stolen by Edward.

The finest, a large Bible artfully stamped in gold, belongs to a family by the name of Van Rooyan: Frans Willem Van Rooyan first wrote his name in this volume in March 1801 and thereafter follows a long list of recorded births, marriages and deaths.

The second Bible, a cracked older relic dating from 1760, belonged to Klaus Fischer who, from his name and others listed, must have numbered amongst the many German or Austrian settlers to this country. Three full pages, inscribed in perfect penmanship, document the history of the Fischer family.

Stealing precious family heirlooms would seem to be one of my husband's more contemptible pastimes. I presume he considers these Bibles as 'spoils of war'.

I have been wondering how to restore the Bibles to their rightful owners. If I bestow them to the church, the Dominee will accuse Edward of theft. Moreover, since these Bibles are repositories of family records, the minister may also see fit to denounce my husband for the destruction of church registers.

Alas, I am too much a coward to take this path. Edward will punish me for my treason – probably by banishing me from North Wind – and, as his spouse, I shall also be incriminated in his dishonor.

I have returned both Bibles to the cupboard where I found then, to hide once more in dust and darkness.

July 10th, 1905

I am heavy with grief! My image in the glass shows my face as thin and harrowed. Sadly, my dear and faithful old Moses is dead and tomorrow will be buried! This journal must act as testimony to the absolute truth of what occurred.

Two of our field-workers were struck down with weakness of the chest and coughing blood. Worried for Moses, I begged Edward to permit him to work quietly in the kitchen with me.

My husband scoffed at this request and forced the old man to take his turn at the plow, knowing full-well Moses is far too frail and decrepit for such strenuous work.

I am ashamed to say what happened as a consequence is partly my fault!

I had taken food to the pasture and called the men for lunch. Alerted by my shouting, Moses turned around and, in that instant, was struck upon the head by the plow handle and knocked senseless.

As he fell to the ground, Moses let go of the handle and the oxen bolted. Edward shouted to Moses to fetch the beasts and take up the plow again.

Moses staggered after the animals, struggling to perform Edward's bidding – but with my husband's cruel eye upon me, I was helpless to intervene. Half an hour later, Moses collapsed again and I was summoned to tend to him.

When I reached the old man, I saw how still he lay upon the ground. His eyes were vacant, his complexion turning paler and barely a breath issued from his mouth or nostrils. He died before nightfall.

July 12th, 1905

The simple grave where Moses is buried lies behind the servants' quarters, concealed from prying eyes. Dear Lord! How many innocent souls must be put to rest in this bitter, unyielding earth before our time here at North Wind Manor is done?

July 14th, 1905

Moses' sorrowing wife, Jina, has gone from North Wind Manor. She left late last night taking a quantity of silver cutlery, pewter goblets, French lace and two jeweled necklaces.

There may be more items missing, I do not know nor do I care. I cannot condemn this grieving woman for stealing. Between us, Edward and I killed her husband and all our possessions could never atone for her loss.

July 15th, 1905

We were eating dinner when two somber-faced policemen made a sudden appearance at the door. Though his manner was hearty, Edward paled at their sight, leading them to the sitting room where, before he closed the door, I overheard him cordially offering brandy.

Once the men had departed, I asked Edward the nature of their business.

"They were following an enquiry into the death of Moses," Edward replied. "I assured them our unfortunate servant died from being struck on the head by a plow. That is what happened, is it not, Charlotte?"

I gave no reply. I could not look at Edward's bloated face. Nothing, it seems, touches this man. He appears indestructible – one who openly kills, maims and steals – and yet remains unscathed by the law.

"We have work to do, my dear," Edward went on. "Between us, we must discover the identity of the man or woman who informed the authorities that I am responsible for the death of our servant."

He leaned closer. His breath was sour. "Who could this person be, I wonder?"

I pushed away from the table and made an attempt to get up, but he gripped my arm and held it firmly. "Was it you, Charlotte?"

"No! No!" I cried, as blood drained from my face. I would have fainted had Edward not tightened his hold upon my arm. "Are you lying to me, Charlotte?"

I opened my mouth to protest but he motioned to me to be silent.

"If I discover you have wronged me..." Edward did not complete this sentence but left no doubt as to his meaning.

He went upstairs to his room and I succumbed to an uncontrollable fit of shaking. Though I am innocent of this act, if Edward believes I am guilty, I may be in grave danger."

"There, that's it!" I snapped the diary shut. "Enough high drama for one day."

"What did Edward do to Pretty?"

My heart sank. Playing for time, I flipped back to the passage.

"My maid Pretty has informed Aletta that her master, my husband, had, upon three occasions, made improper advances..."

CHAPTER SEVENTEEN

PLUM

I'm going to read *Great Expectations* in the attic where Charlotte read it because if I do it might bring me closer to her. Dad thinks I'll never get through the book because Dickens is tricky and sometimes glum but Aunt Frith told him I'm brighter than most and she and Mom were whizzing through *Oliver Twist* at my age. I haven't explained *why* I want to read this book because I don't want them getting all worked up so I said I wanted to learn more about the eighteen hundreds and Aunt Frith said, "What a good idea!" It's called a *white* lie when you don't want someone getting upset by the truth so in a way it's a good lie.

Bronte asked why I wanted to read boring old Dickens who's been dead a hundred years but she's wrong because it's one hundred and forty-seven years and I know this because I Googled and Charles Dickens died in eighteen seventy from apoplexy.

Bronte asked what that was and I hadn't had time to look it up yet so I told her I thought it was mumps or maybe tuberculosis which is when you spit up blood.

"You're weird," she said and ate a whole *Kit Kat* without offering me a single bite. She does stuff like this sometimes and I'm starting to think of her as my *frenemy* – that's a word for a person who's your friend and enemy at the same time.

Great Expectations wasn't in the library so I asked our librarian Miss Hoekstra if I could reserve it but she said, "Our only copy has been missing for ages. Why don't you try *David Copperfield* instead?"

She must've seen my face because she said there's a second-hand book shop in town called *The Antiquarian* and why didn't I try looking for the book there?

I found the shop because it had a hanging sign that said: "*The Antiquarian. Over 2 000 volumes in stock. Fiction, Travel, Natural History, Art, South African History, Biography. Come in & browse!*"

There were all these very tall narrow book-cases touching the ceiling and long wooden tables stacked with an untidy jumble of books that my fingers twitched to neaten.

There were lots of Charles Dickens' books and they were all old, cracked hardcovers taking up three bottom shelves where *Great Expectations* was wedged between *Little Dorrit* and *The Old Curiosity Shop*.

The book's cover was coming away from its binding and when I touched my nose to the soft tissuey pages it had the same dusty nose-wrinkling smell as Charlotte's diary.

"How much is this book?" I asked the girl at the counter and went bananas when she said two hundred and fifty rands. "But it's falling apart – why is it so expensive?"

"*Expensive!*" She gave a little scream. "That's *dirt cheap* for a collector's item, which is what this book is and it's worth twice that, at least."

I asked if she'd keep it for me while I rode home for the money but she got a snooty look and said, "Put it back where you found it. It'll be *snatched up* if you leave it on the counter."

Ha ha I thought and was on my knees shoving *Great Expectations* into the space next to *Little Dorrit* when I heard a low gruff voice in my ear.

"Hello. It's Plum, isn't it?" The giant was squatting next to me and when I saw him my heart started thumping like a washing machine on spin cycle.

"You don't remember me, do you? I'm Theo Christensen. We met at the church."

He was smiling and his eyes were green like a snake and he hasn't done anything bad but I just know I don't want him in our lives.

The words flew out of my mouth before I had time to think. *"I don't like you!"*

He rocked backwards and would've fallen on his bum if he hadn't dug his fingers into the grungy carpet and I jumped up and ran out of the shop with the girl behind the counter yelling, "You coming back or what?"

Riding home, I made myself think about *Great Expectations* and that got me wondering about history starting with apes and then cavemen and dinosaurs and hairy mammoths and gigantic flying lizards then fast forward to Mary Queen of Scots losing her head and Victoria on the throne and the English fighting the Boers and men like Captain Edward Butler stealing family Bibles and this idea came into my head and I had to stop peddling and lean over my handlebars for a few minutes to take it all in.

This is the idea I had...

One day this time we're living in will be history and people will read about us on I-Pads and visit museums to stare at ancient relics like my red Raleigh and laugh their heads off because it's like nothing they've seen before.

I tried explaining this to Dad as he drove to *The Antiquarian* but he said he thought it rather obvious and went on a ramble about how places like *North Wind* are rooted in history because they've been lived in by generations of families and as these people have passed away the house has endured and stood still while time has marched steadily on.

That didn't make sense. "*North Wind* isn't standing still," I said. "You're knocking it down and soon it won't be the same house as the one we first moved into."

"Mmm, you've a point there," Dad mumbled and went on about change usually being a good thing and how we are all changing in different ways. "You, for instance, are becoming a young lady so fast it's making my head spin. You're going to be a beauty one of these days, just like your Mom, you mark my words."

I could feel tears popping up behind my eyes because that's not even a white lie it's just a lie and we both know deep in our hearts where it really matters I don't look the tiniest bit like Mom.

192

FRITH

This morning's still life is a pottery bowl of pomegranates. I'm in two minds about continuing with this class. I thought he'd have more imagination. I've learned nothing so far.

I laid everything out, neatly sharpened pencils, rubber, paints, water jar, brushes and clean pallet. As usual, Theo was annoyingly late and this made me tart with Donald who told an unfunny joke about women being like hurricanes: when they go they take your house and car with them, ha bloody ha.

I've grown used to Chen's silence which might be a language problem and bothers me less now I'm on first-name terms with three friendly 'girls' who always wave in welcome and invite me to *Nino's* for coffee afterwards. They tell me all the women in class are a little in love with Theo – even Chen – so perhaps she's not a porcelain figurine and there really is a heart beating beneath that smooth, glossy exterior.

Finally, Theo arrived, singing out a cheery: *'Good morning all!'* while striding directly towards me. My lips were curving into a smile as he swerved to Chen's easel.

"What have we here?" he asked, looking over her shoulder. Chen's pallor grew less waxy as he left his hand upon her shoulder for a few seconds. Gently, he lifted the brush from her fingers. "May I?" he asked, with a wink.

Theo daubed wide wet sweeps of purple over Chen's delicately rendered shadows and added a blur of royal blue to the translucent base of her pottery bowl. "This is what you want," he said, carried away. "More depth… enhanced lights and darks…greater *contrast!*"

He gave a sidelong glance in my direction. Showing off for my benefit, stupid arse!

He hasn't a clue how much of a turn-off that is.

Next, Theo tackled Donald's messy painting leaving Chen sitting rigidly, scowling at her canvas. *"Fuckwit!"* she said distinctly. Her brush clattered

193

furiously in her water jar as she wet the paint and blotted Theo's flagrant streaks with a wodge of paper towel.

I had to laugh – no language problem then.

At last, Theo stood beside me. "Stay after class," he whispered, adding in his normal voice, "Not too bad, Frith. Coming on quite nicely."

I waited half an hour, listening with half an ear to Theo conversing loudly with a prospective buyer in the gallery. Olympia was nowhere to be seen. On the counter was a little twirling display like the ones used to sell postcards.

The sign above read: *Olympia's Gems*.

The pieces were exquisite. Fine, twisted ropes of silver with hanging pendants of semi-precious stones – opals, garnets, topaz, jade, amethysts and some I couldn't identify.

I was admiring a bloodstone when Theo took it from my hand.

"Not this one," he spun the display. "Ah, here's what I'm looking for."

He led me to a mirror where he secured the chain around my neck.

"This is your stone," he declared, soberly.

I stared at our reflections in the glass. His head reared behind my right shoulder. Suspended at my throat was a gem of palest blue. I turned my head and as the light changed, the stone became transparent as glass.

"Moonstone." His voice was low, suggestive. "They call it the lovers' stone."

Theo adjusted the pendant and as his warm, paint-streaked fingers touched my throat, hair stood up at the back of my neck.

The doorbell chimed and Olympia burst in, laden with shopping bags and jingling a bunch of car keys. Prattling like a salesman, Theo hurriedly stepped to the jewelry display. "As far as I know, Olympia imports the gems from Sri Lanka or is it Brazil? Price depends on quality of course, but a rare specimen like the one you're wearing…"

He broke off in mock surprise. "Oh, sweetie, you're back! Frith was asking the price of that moonstone and I haven't the foggiest."

Olympia pulled off her hat and ran her fingers through her flattened hair.

"Excellent choice!" she gleamed, lifting a catalogue from a drawer and flipping through the plastic-sheathed pages. "Theo's got it all wrong. That's an Indian moonstone, not rare at all and most reasonably priced."

My cheeks blazed. "I'll take it." I said. She rang up the purchase and dropped the pendant into a silken pouch.

"I think I'll take one for my niece as well." I told her. "She needs cheering up."

"How old?"

"Almost twelve."

"Mmm. The Rose quartz is pretty."

Theo joined us. "Your niece," he said, with a glimmer of a smile. "Face like a flower as I recall…named after a fruit."

"Plum," I replied.

Theo snapped his fingers. "I have the very thing for your Plum," he said. "Hang on a sec."

Olympia lifted a tinted eyebrow. "When did Theo meet your niece?"

I heard myself stuttering. "Um…let me think…oh yes, we met outside the gallery when I was…er…showing Plum the paintings in your window."

Prickling heat raced from my cheeks to my neck. Bugger, bugger, *bugger!*

Olympia leaned forward, peering narrowly. "Are you taking oestrogen?" *Oestrogen?* Panicked, I tried to think. Oestrogen was…*what?* A hormone produced in the ovaries. A sex hormone. What in God's name was she implying? I stared into her frank, open face. "Sorry, *what?*"

"For your hot flushes?"

"For my…? Oh, I see!" I laughed, relieved. "No, no…I'm not meno-pausal, not yet anyway."

"HRT," Olympia nodded kindly. "I swear by it. You'll sail right through without feeling a thing!"

Theo came back unfurling a sheet of rolled paper. "Think this would cheer your Plum?"

A painting. Three clay pots on a patch of grass. Two pots standing upright, one fallen.

A dragonfly skimming above, a striped snail crawling through tufted grass.

The work was intricate and beautiful. The pots were faintly mottled with green verdigris. Curved water droplets clung to feathery grass stalks and a plume of glittery slime followed the snail.

Olympia tightened her mouth. "Sure about this, Theo?"

Unfazed, Theo rolled up the page and snapped on an elastic band. "Give this to Plum with my love."

Olympia's tight expression left me flustered. "Please let me pay for the painting."

"Wouldn't dream of it." With a lazy grin, he sauntered away.

Olympia wore her professional face. "Shall I wrap it?" she asked pleasantly.

I wasted a couple of hours in town and then ambled home.

It was dusk by the time I reached the manor. William and Plum were waiting on the front steps. Plum held a book in her lap. "*Great Expectations*," she announced. "I found it in *The Antiquarian*."

She saw the moonstone. "Who gave that to you?" she pointed.

I unclipped the pendant and handed it to her. "I bought it for myself…I was going to get one for you but found something else I think you'll like."

That wasn't strictly true. Plum would have loved the rose quartz but Theo had made such a magnanimous gesture with his painting, I hadn't known how to refuse without seeming rude.

PLUM

I love it when it's just Dad and the workmen have left and the house is quiet. We sat on the front steps, waiting for Aunt Frith and watching the sun dip below the horizon.

Dad promised he'd go out later for fish and chips at a shop where they make matchstick chips that don't taste oily and the fish falls off the bone in soft white flakes.

We usually have interesting conversations when it's just us but Dad was talking like a robot and didn't seem to hear half the things I said. "It's like you're not here, Dad," I told him.

"I'm a little worried." He looked at his watch. "Your aunt is taking an absolute age. It's getting late. Where on earth can she be at this time?"

"Dunno."

"Maybe we should take the car and see if we can find her?"

I let my eyes drift over the row of pine trees along the driveway with the mountain square and blue behind them and there was Aunt Frith tapping the twisted curly *North Wind Manor* sign, making it squeak and sway.

"There she is!" I said. "Can you see her?"

He made his eyes squinty. "I wonder if she knows how dangerous it is, walking around these parts, a woman alone, without protection?"

"Dunno."

She came up towards us.

"*Christ*! I thought we'd have to send out a search party!"

"But I told you I had an art class."

"You did…well, I think you did…but you've been gone an entire day. You can't have been painting all that time."

"No. I met friends for coffee. Did some shopping. The walk home takes an hour. Why, what's wrong? Have I missed something?"

"You do know this country has the highest murder rate in the world?"

She closed her eyes. "William, please." she said and I could tell she was trying to be calm."Don't start on this again."

Aunt Frith was wearing a silver chain with a beautiful pale stone around her neck. She unclipped it and gave it to me and the stone changed from milky blue to a kind of glassy nothingness.

"It's a moonstone," she said.

I rubbed the stone against my lips feeling its hard, cool smoothness and wishing I had a one just like it.

Aunt Frith held out a flat, square shape wrapped in black paper covered with gold squiggles. "I think you'll like this."

I dropped the chain into her hand and balanced the parcel on my knees.

It was too thin…too flat…too light and didn't feel like anything I wanted unless…unless it was a drawing she'd made especially for me. That thought made me happy.

"Oh," I said. "I think I know what this is!"

I ripped open the paper and inside was a painting of three pots on a patch of lawn. There was a dragonfly – you could see it was flying from the soft blurriness around its tiny beating wings. And a creeping snail with waxy tentacles, a long, damp, squishy body and a brown shell decorated with curling white circles. And a name in the bottom corner… *Theo Christensen!*

FRITH

She was bending over the painting, examining it minutely, tracing a realistic rendering of spiral helical ridges on the snail's shell with her finger – when I heard an intake of breath and, as she looked up, her startled eyes met mine for a shocked second.

I was mystified. *"What?"*

Her mouth dropped open. "But…I thought…I thought…" She leapt up and the painting fluttered to her feet. "You said I'd love it…but I don't, I don't…I *hate* it!"

Plum dashed indoors.

I was dumbstruck. "What was *that* about?" I asked William.

He gathered up the painting. "There must be something here." he muttered. "It's this painting. It's really upset her."

"You can look all you like," I snapped. "You won't find anything. Have you two been quarreling or something?"

He sent an indignant look. "Don't pin this on me. Plum was fine until you gave her this painting. Who's this… *Theo Christensen?*"

"That's my art teacher. He gave me this for Plum. Probably worth quite a bit. Extremely generous, I thought."

He shrugged. "Suppose."

Warily, I took the painting and started rolling it up. William sighed heavily. "I'd better check on her."

I sat on the doorstep, hugging myself. With my eyes shut, I saw him imprinted on the velvety back of my lids…his wild thatch of whitening hair…lazy seducer's smile…our eyes catching and holding in the mirror. Butterflies swarmed in my stomach.

"Oh, get a grip!" I told myself sternly.

CHAPTER EIGHTEEN

PLUM

Miss Cooper wrote the title of our English essay, *"Something strange happened…"* on the whiteboard and told us not to write more than three exercise-book pages and when in doubt refer to our dictionaries because there's simply no excuse for poor spelling.

The title was sort of like a command so I began writing…

"Something strange happened when we arrived from England to live at North Wind Manor and on the very first day I discovered a spirit in our house. I wasn't surprised or frightened because the manor is the kind of house that looks like it comes with a spirit – old, dark and spooky with cobwebs and stairs that creak even when nobody's walking on them.

I was exploring the attic when the spirit gave me a sort of greeting like fingers tapping gently against my spine and straight away I knew she was beside me. The attic is where I feel her most though I now know she floats through the house and she's also tapped me softly in the upstairs bedrooms, the bathroom and once in the sitting room that used to be known as a parlour.

I've never seen the spirit but always know when she's there because she throws an invisible shawl over me that's cozy and warm and makes the air seem lighter and brighter. I hear a kind of whispering but no words which might mean she's speaking spirit language and you probably have to be another spirit to understand what she's saying. To imagine this whispering, think of the flap of butterfly wings or the quiet hum of bees fussing in pollen.

I have a feeling deep inside the spirit is trying to tell me something vitally important and though I haven't worked out what it is yet it could be a warning that something bad is going to happen.

Dad started fixing up North Wind Manor to bring it into the twentieth century and says he's restoring the house to its former glory but never speaks about destroying lovely things Charlotte left behind like velvet drapes, wallpapers with drawings of flowers and birds, glittery chandeliers and marble fireplaces. Even the sweetish smell of damp and mice has vanished along with crops of shell-pink fairy mushrooms that used to sprout between broken tiles in the bathrooms.

When we first entered our house it welcomed us with comforting noises like creaking and sighing and a few tired groans but now the upstairs is silent and scrubbed clean like a hospital with a nose-pinching smell of wet paint and turps. I haven't told Dad how sad it makes me that soon there'll be nothing left of Charlotte Butler in all the boring boxy white rooms above the stairs.

Dad tells us he's fixing the house for me and Aunt Frith but I liked it the way it was and my aunt would rather not live here in South Africa. She says the manor is too big and blood-stoppingly cold and besides she has her own life to live and soon she'll be leaving for France where she has a pied-a-terre which means flat in French.

The real reason Dad's restoring the house is to keep himself so busy he doesn't have time to think about Mom and how he misses her so much he calls out in his sleep, "Lily...Lily...Lily...don't leave me!"

For a while, I thought our spirit might be the ghost of Mom who died from cancer at 88 St Stephen's Place in Shropshire which is in England. Before she died, Mom promised she'd always love and protect me cross her heart and hope to die which is why Dad and I both think Mom is safe in Heaven so it's more likely this is the spirit of Mrs. Charlotte Butler who lived at North Wind Manor long ago and left a journal in a locked cupboard in the attic for me to find.

The journal – that's a posh word for a diary – begins in 1904 when Charlotte moved into the manor after she married Captain Edward Butler. Charlotte died a long time ago – I can't say exactly when because I haven't reached that page yet and I'll be desperately sorry when I do because her story will end and it'll be like saying goodbye to an old friend who loves the house as much as I do.

201

Aunt Frith and Dad don't believe in spirits because they've never seen one but there are millions of things I've never seen like a Kangaroo or Stonehenge or Mars and that doesn't mean they don't exist and sometimes you've got to simply trust in yourself.

It's kind of hard to explain what a spirit is but I think it's the soul of a dead person who's got lost in a lonely place between earth and heaven with something or someone pulling them back so they don't go through the pearly gates of heaven until they have peace in their hearts.

Mom had peace and love in her heart enough for ten people but from reading her diary you can tell Mrs Butler had moods and depressions like Dad which is why I think there's a chance we're sharing our house with her spirit.

Before she got sick Mom used to sing a nursery rhyme that goes like this…

"If wishes were horses then beggars would ride and if turnips were watches I'd wear one by my side and if if's and and's were pots and pans there's be no work for tinkers' hands," and what I think that means is it's no good just wishing for something – you've got to do something to make whatever you wish for come true.

One of these days I'll work out what Charlotte Butler is trying to tell me and I've got to keep believing in her so she can find a way to send her message or warning or whatever it is before something happens. A person reading this might think I'm scared but I'm not because the spirit has chosen me and that makes me feel like I'm part of a magical miracle happening at North Wind Manor and how many other people can say that?"

Miss Cooper said, "Pens down, class."

I read over what I'd written and I got this feeling like my insides were being tied in knots and when Miss Cooper stopped at my desk to collect my essay I blurted, "Everything I wrote…it's not true."

"Excellent!" Her lips twitched. "That means you're using your imagination."

Bronte told me her essay is about the day her cat *Babushka* had five kittens and I said I'd written about a ghost and she laughed and said 'Cool beans!' and I told Bronte I hoped Miss Cooper didn't think my story was true but Bronte said old Fish-eyes only cares about commas and semi-colons and getting spelling right.

Dad was waiting when I got home. "I'm going out of my mind with noise and dust," he said. "Can't hear myself think. Why don't we get out of this place, eh?"

I thought Dad had to stay on site to supervise but he said he was being attacked by the Deadly Doldrums and if he didn't get out he might have to hurl himself from one of the upstairs windows – I couldn't tell if he was joking because he wasn't laughing but I think he must have been.

We took a drive in Dad's swishy new BMW that's shiny black with seats that smell of a new doll at Christmas and window wipers that don't make any noise even when it's thundering down. Dad says this car makes him feel like Neil Armstrong in the Apollo 11 Lunar Module blasting off for the moon but that's too thrilling and I'm happy we're just zooming along the roads in Paarl. We stopped for a walk around a park and I used Mom's soothing voice to say, "So, tell me what's wrong."

"It's getting to me, darling," Dad explained. "Builders arriving late, leaving early…their total ruddy incompetence…the way they take you for a tit and rob you blind."

He kicked a pile of dead leaves that flew into the air.

"Had this idea about turning this sprawl of stone into a Five Star guest house but your aunt is making it quite clear she won't be around for much longer. This is not something a man can do alone, certainly not a limited man, which is how I think of myself since…well, you know."

He was going to say 'since…Mom died.'

Dad held up three fingers wrapped in grubby sticking plasters. "My mouth is full of ulcers and I've got painful fissures on the tips of my fingers. It's either the blasted weather or I'm run-down and need a dose of vitamins."

I had a brainwave. "Why don't you send the workmen away and leave the rest of the house till you're feeling stronger?"

"If only it were that simple." Dad shook his head. "I'd put an end to all this in a jiffy if I could, but I can't turn back now. Papers have been signed and unless I'm prepared to face a barrage of summonses for reneging on lawful contracts, I've no choice but to press on until the bitter end."

I didn't know what 'reneging' meant but it didn't seem a good time to ask.

There was a slide in the park and I sat on it while Dad slumped on a bench with his head in his hands. The slide wasn't very slippery and I kept sticking and then this memory came back...a slide in a playground near our house in Shropshire where, when nobody was looking, Mom slid down first and then me and we kept taking turns until we landed in a heap at the bottom and couldn't stop laughing.

You think the ache inside isn't so bad anymore but then you're on an un-slippery slide and it all comes back and that's the trouble with memory – the bad stuff never stops hurting.

Dad pulled a pen and a wad of folded papers from his pocket and started doing sums. He looked gross – he hadn't shaved and his hair was standing straight up like he'd been plugged into an electric socket and his jersey was all snagged and sprinkled with sawdust and there was a raggedy tear in his trousers above the knee.

"Mom would have a fit if she saw you!" I said, but he didn't answer. "You look like one of those homeless people who push trolleys full of cardboard and live on a park bench."

Still nothing.

His lips were moving so I leaned in closer to hear better.

'Five thousand minus seventeen sixty equals...uh...seventeen fifty five...minus twelve hundred equals...er...five hundred and fifty five, shit, that can't be right, surely?'

Then Dad started singing, *'Half a pound of tuppenny rice, half a pound of treacle, that's the way the money goes, Pop goes the weasel!'*

It was the fierce explosion on the *'Pop'* that made me jump but Dad looked up with the sweetest smile and said, "Feeling hungry, Plum? What do you say to a nice steak and kidney pie? Or a few scoops of rum and raisin ice-cream in a sugar cone? What would tickle your fancy, sweetheart?"

On the way home I played a game – I do this sometimes – promised myself if I spotted three black cars and two dog-walkers before we reached our gate Dad would stop being weird and turn back into his normal self.

I counted one black car and a blue-haired lady with a Pekinese on a lead and when we turned into our driveway I had a thought that made me shiver – maybe Dad will never be normal again.

FRITH

Yesterday, after class, Theo took me to where he and Olympia live in a Victorian Gothic built in the 1870's, set back from the road in a leafy garden. Pitched slate roof, arched windows, stone turrets and a gingerbread trim along the gable edges with hideous gargoyles as rainwater spouts. I counted six grotesquely squat, open-mouthed frogs and toads with ogling eyes and long tongues. There were three leering dragon heads on the south side although, since these are permanently blocked with leaves, Theo says they serve little purpose other than embellishment.

"How can you live with all these disgusting dragons and frogs?" I asked and he laughed though I wasn't trying to be amusing. I found something disquieting about all those peeled and bulging eyes looking right at me.

Oddest of all was entering through the ivy-clad Gothic edifice to find Olympia had ruthlessly destroyed every vestige of the original Victorian interior except for a staircase and a few stained-glass panels.

Theo showed me these survivors of Olympia's barbarous attack. Glowing with pride, he admitted his wife had single-mindedly razed and discarded over a hundred years of history in a ruthless quest to create her private kingdom.

Inside, everything was space-age modern – an unfolding expanse of black granite and stainless steel with cement floors, minimal furniture and abstract canvases large enough to cover entire walls.

Theo has a studio on the north side. A tower with a door opening into a messy room reeking of cigarette smoke. He kicked a pair of woman's red shoes beneath a chair; bundled up a pile of newspapers and scraped the cold remains of a take-away pizza into an overflowing bin.

I found myself wiping my fingers on my skirt after touching anything.

Right away, Theo shrugged off his shirt and stepped out of his paint-streaked denims and baggy cotton underpants, letting them fall to the gritty floor. I was taken aback at how casual he was. I thought he'd at least make appropriate overtures – kissing and caressing me – before slowly stripping off my clothes and taking me to bed.

"Get undressed." he said, matter-of-factly. "We haven't long."

I couldn't take my eyes off his massive shoulders, his broad hairy chest. He had a hard flat belly, huge arms, thighs and legs and even his penis was oversized, swelling in its hairy pelt. As he reached for me, his gaze was steady and unsmiling.

"Come here," he demanded huskily and right on cue the room began to tilt.

"Christ," he sighed, when it was over. "That was fucking fantastic!" He waited for a few seconds before asking pointedly, "So, was it good for you?"

I didn't reply. I wish he hadn't asked. I came first, while he was still rocking above me and I saw stars – tiny flashing pinpricks of white light – but didn't feel inclined to tell him because I knew a self-satisfied smirk would settle on his face.

He reached for his jeans. "I want to paint you. Don't move. Stay as you are. No, don't fix your hair – it's perfect."

I couldn't help myself. As usual, I destroyed the mood. "Do you do this often?"

He blinked. "Do what?"

"Have carnal sex with a stranger in the afternoon?"

A muscle throbbed in his jaw. His frown deepened. "Ahh, Frith. Let's not do this, okay?"

"Do what?"

"Don't take me for an arse, Frith. I don't *do* postmortems. That means I'm not going to tell you how many women I've slept with, what they were like, whether my wife knows and, if she does, what she thinks about my infidelity. Got it?"

I was gasping at his rudeness as he propped a canvas on an easel and started daubing paint onto his pallet. His expression softened. "Shoulders back...that's right, now just relax. Release the tension in your face. If you could turn a little more towards the light, there...that's good, don't move, not one centimeter."

I'll never be able to explain my taste in men. Why am I attracted to yet another jackass?

"I want to paint a series of nudes," Theo said, self-absorbed, his eyes sliding between me and the canvas. "Chin up. Yeah, nice. Think you can hold that?"

I was pondering over 'series' when he went on, "I've been searching for the right model and it came to me yesterday – you're it! I'd like to paint you *dishabille* after sex. Say about five or six big canvases. You okay with that?"

I tried not to look self-conscious. "Um...I suppose so...as long as the work is abstract and nobody recognises me."

He nodded. "Yeah, that's the plan."

An hour later, stiff and cold, I got dressed. Theo draped the canvas with a filthy cloth and wagged a finger in my face. "All in good time," he grinned.

I asked if I could brush my teeth and he handed me a flattened tube without a cap and a shaggy, toothpaste-encrusted brush. I rubbed hardened paste over my teeth with a finger and spat delicately in the sink. "Where's Olympia?" I asked.

"It's our anniversary tomorrow. She's buying me a gift."

"Have you one for her?"

"Ha! In Olympia's eyes, forgetting an anniversary will get you thrown behind bars, defrocked or stoned in a public square."

"What did you buy her?"

"Twenty years we've been together. Platinum, I'm told, is what you give to celebrate this anniversary. I've chosen a bracelet. Now, drop the subject, okay?"

I couldn't let it go. Lacing my shoes, I asked. "So, tell me, Theo, do you love your wife?"

"Jesus Christ!" He winced. "What kind of question is that?"

I spoke in a small, injured tone. "I'm curious, that's all."

With a look of mingled resignation and boredom, Theo rested meaty hands on my shoulders.

"Look, when you've been married as long as we have, something gets lost…the excitement, passion, romance…it drains away over the years. You make the mistake of getting too comfortable. You start imagining yourself with other women. Younger, sexier women, like you. So, to answer your question, Frith, yes, I love my wife as my best friend and loyal companion. I'll never leave Olympia. Satisfied?"

I nodded and then, before I could stop myself, asked, "When do I see you again?"

"We'll have to wait for Olympia to decide that." He grinned crookedly. "I'll let you know next time she has an assignment out of town."

PLUM

I knew I'd get in trouble for writing about the spirit. Miss Cooper leaned over my desk and said, "Mrs. Van Wyk would like to see you, Plum."

My voice was wobbly. "Have I done something wrong?"

"No, nothing at all, Plum, " Miss Cooper answered.

"Is this to do with my essay, Miss?"

Her eyes went swimming off to the side and she took a deep breath. "Let's just say the principal has something she wants to discuss but there's *absolutely nothing to worry about.*"

Miss Cooper gave my arm a sad squeeze and I knew I was in hot water.

"Best not keep Mrs Van Wyk waiting," Miss Cooper smiled.

The Principal held up an exercise book with my name and the big smiley face I'd drawn in green koki on the cover.

"I've been looking over your compositions," she said. "I must commend you, Plum, you write very well. Miss Cooper tells me she's extremely pleased with your progress."

"Thank you, Miss."

I scuffed the carpet with my shoe and saw it wasn't a plain muddy green as I'd first thought but a pattern of light leaves on a dark background.

The principal tapped her fingers on her desk. "Your last essay is…um… most unusual. You've written it with, ah, let me see, how to put this… with…*extraordinary conviction.*"

She seemed to be waiting for me to say something so I told her I was sorry but I didn't really understand what she meant.

Tap, tap, tap on the desk with nice, clean fingernails painted in shiny clear varnish.

"Do you *believe* in this spirit, Plum?"

It was the way she said '*believe*' that told me this was a trick question so to give myself time to think carefully, I repeated, "Do I believe in the spirit I've written about?"

Her eyebrows hooked over her nose. "Yes. Do you really think there's a spirit in your house?"

I don't like looking into people's faces almost as much as I don't like it when people stare at me and it was torture to keep my eyes on her pointy nose but I did because if I looked away, she'd think I was hiding something.

"I'm reading *Great Expectations* which you probably know is a book written by Charles Dickens," I said. "It's about this boy called Pip and Magwitch who's a convict and then there's Jaggers and Wemmick, Pumblechook and Miss Havisham and Estella who's the girl Pip falls madly in love with."

Mrs Van Wyk bobbed her head. "Yes, Plum, I *have* read the book. What's your point?"

"Charles Dickens imagined all these people. Nobody thinks they're real."

"Go on."

"Well, Miss Cooper told us to write about something strange and I decided to make up a story about the spirit of a dead person living in our house because there can't be anything stranger than that but I never got to finish because Miss Cooper said *'pens down'* when I was only half-way through."

The principal had her head on one side like she wasn't sure if I was being truthful so I forced myself to stare right back.

"There are no ghosts," I said, firmly. "Dad says there's no evidence they exist."

"He's quite right," she said. "No solid empirical evidence, anyway."

She closed my book. "Miss Cooper was anxious I should speak to you. I'm glad we've cleared this up. Oh and, before it slips my mind, that journal you wrote about, is that real?"

I sighed. "It's just a made-up story, Mrs Van Wyk."

CHAPTER NINETEEN

FRITH

I've taken to wearing a floppy artist's smock in class. Chen makes these quaintly old-fashioned garments to protect her clothing from paint spills. "For you," she said, dropping a bundle of fabric in my lap. This was her first overture of friendship and though she shied from my thanks, an uncertain smile passed over her face. Unlike the no-nonsense navy and sage-green smocks Chen fashions for herself, mine was pretty – a soft pink and lilac floral cotton with pleated shoulders and a voluminous pocket at the front for artist's materials.

I told Theo his classes were sending us to sleep and as a result he's graduated to more ambitious creative projects. This week, we're *'Doing a Leo'* – Theo's description of painting our own Mona Lisa. We'd roughly mapped out a sketch of a seated female figure against a background and were set to paint our subject from a photograph taken for this purpose.

Theo started the class with one of his dreary lectures. He gestured at a tattered poster of the Mona Lisa taped to the wall. "Do you all see the classic pyramid shape in this art?"

We were silent, itching to get on with our paintings. Annoyed, Theo turned to face us.

"At the risk of sounding pedantic, I'll repeat the question. Does everyone see the underlying geometry in this painting? Well, *do you?*"

"Yes," we murmured in unison, obedient children.

Pretty damn obvious, I'd have thought. The head is the apex of the pyramid and the folded hands form one of the corners but seriously, who cares?

Moving from pyramids, Theo pointed out spheres and circles in the painting, showing off as usual, making the lesson more complex than it needed be.

As part of this tutorial, Theo stood with his back to the class drawing his own Leo and, from his first rough sketch, I recognised his female figure as his wife, Olympia.

I was painting Plum from a photograph I'd taken of her sitting upright with arms folded and hair falling like a cloud around her face. I showed Plum the famous Mona Lisa and asked for her most mysterious smile but in my photo, Plum's mouth is down-turned and sulky and her eyes, somewhere above the camera lens, are cold and unblinking.

"Could you try to smile lifting only the corners of your mouth?" I'd asked, but she'd thrown up her hands and shouted, "I don't want to do this. It's *stupid!*"

It's easy to forget how gifted Theo is. He had us all captivated as he brought Olympia to life in what he dubbed his 'Old Masters' pallet' of earthy browns, tans and neutral greys.

He demonstrated a technique called '*sfumato*' – basically shadowy areas where one shape blends into another. "The word comes from *fumo* – Italian for smoke," he said, sweeping back his hair with a bent wrist. "Leo used this technique to soften unflattering, hard edges."

He grinned wickedly as he blurred the sharp outline of Olympia's obstinate jaw with his thumb. "Works a charm."

Unlike the rest of us, Theo painted from memory. He drew Olympia in a russet velvet gown with deeply scooped neckline hinting at a pair of full, soft breasts. Her brutally shaved head was concealed beneath the flattering folds of a cowl. I watched enviously as he added a touch of light to his wife's glowing brown irises. Her eyes, large and set deep in hollow sockets, are Olympia's best feature and I couldn't help wondering if they'd follow the observer as the Mona Lisa's are said to do. God, how to bear this when Olympia's eyes are already everywhere?

Mid-way through the lesson, Theo laid down his brush and sauntered amongst the group, making comments, offering advice, showing how to lay the under-painting on canvas.

He dallied a while with Chen and then, jostling past on his way to Donald, dropped a folded square of paper at my feet. I bent to pick it up.

"This afternoon at three? Can you make it?" My heart quickened as I nodded.

Donald was painting a dog, his female Doberman named Monica.

"What the fuck is this?" Theo boomed.

Donald snorted indignantly. "This is my Mona Lisa. Thought it was obvious!"

"You're painting a...a *dog*!"

"Christ sake!" Donald spluttered. "I'm using your blasted palette... limiting myself to a vile range of muddy browns and tans. I'm painting my dearly beloved companion. And I've even got a bit of bloody fug going... my attempt at *sfumato* in case you're wondering. What more do you want?"

The class grew quiet. Theo smiled thinly. "So," he said, "I take it this is your way of saying the only woman in your life is a bitch?"

There was a spatter of uneasy laughter as Theo moved to Zelda, an artist in her late seventies who paints like a child. I heard Theo falsely praising "extremes of light and shade" in Zelda's ghastly painting.

I try so hard to impress yet he *never* comments on my work, barely glances at it, in fact.

Why, I wonder?

I was barely aware of time passing as I worked, engrossed in my portrait.

My thoughts drifted to the painting Lily had promised me, a chunky gold frame enclosing a dark, moody oil painted in 1870 by the Flemish artist Jan Berens who'd died impoverished two years later. When Julia was alive, Christie's valued the Old Master at over three hundred and fifty thousand pounds. By now it would probably be worth more.

Where was the painting? Had Lily altered her will after Plum told her about me and William? Or had William removed the bequest and sold or hidden the painting for himself? Or – my mind racing now – had he made sure I hadn't inherited the Berens because it offered independence and security at a time he wanted me cash-strapped and dependent?

I cast my mind back to when Lily had said she wanted me to have the painting. It would have been soon after her diagnosis when she'd first considered the possibility of dying.

I'd been living in Paris at the time which means she'd told me over the phone unless…*unless she'd written to me?* If Lil had sent a letter it would serve as proof she'd wanted me to inherit the painting. I could use the letter to threaten to take William to court. His fear of publicity would force him into giving me something that was rightfully mine anyway.

After Lily had told me about her cancer, it was like pressing a pause button – my life stopped. Day after day I'd walk miles like a mindless zombie through the drenched streets of Paris in order to sleep like a corpse at night. I couldn't paint. I had no appetite, no taste for wine or coffee.

Shutting up my life and moving to England, knowing Lily might die, was the hardest thing I've ever had to do. I gave my beloved Burmese, Columbine, to a cat-loving neighbour for safe-keeping and never told Lily how much I desperately missed holding her in my arms and taking consolation from her rumbling purr and the touch of her silky fur.

I gave away carefully tended hot-house orchids, lush ferns and aspidistras, draped furniture with dust sheets, emptied fridge and freezer and bolted the door.

Had I been thinking straight, I'd have rented out the flat and made some money but I had no idea how long I'd be away and, at that stage, couldn't face a stranger hibernating in my small, solitary nest.

When he collected me from the airport, William made it glaringly obvious he didn't want me there. He seemed distinctly 'off' and sounded curt when he asked how long I'd be staying.

"As long as it takes," I answered, unhelpfully.

"Two weeks…three…a month?"

"You don't get it!" I told him, sounding cranky. "She's my *sister*! I'm staying until she gets better or…or…she doesn't. Either way, I'm not budging. And don't fight me on this, Wills. My mind's made up and that's that."

Then there was Plum.

"Why have you come, Aunt Frith?" she asked in her odd, direct way.

"To help look after your Mom."

"But, that's what we're doing!" She sounded wounded. "Me and Dad are taking care of Mom."

"Good," I said, bluntly. "Now there are three of us doing that!"

We lived a lie, concealing our torment, pretending to be confident Lil would get better though we knew she hadn't a snowball's chance.

For the first couple of months, Lily played along. She devoted herself to Plum; helping with homework; reading to her; plaiting her hair; sewing dolls' clothes; planting daffodils for spring so Plum could see the first pale green shoots peeking through the earth.

She filled the freezer with comfort food and that Christmas, Lily wrapped gifts, made a gorgeous berry-studded wreath and trimmed the tree as always.

Two weeks after New Year, Lily's eyes lost their light as she succumbed to agonising pain. The doctor increased her meds but even so, she grew depressed and distracted.

I asked outright, "What troubles you most, Lil?"

She took a few moments to reply. "Plum growing up without me. Wills as a single parent. I tell myself he'll manage but I'm not certain." Tiredly, she rubbed her eyes. "I imagine Plum as a teenager…her first dance…being kissed for the first time…falling in love." Her face was empty of expression. "It hurts I won't be there."

I was stung she hadn't mentioned me. She read my face. "And you," she added, quickly. "You, in Paris, living like a spinster, without a good man to love you, without a child of your own."

I didn't want her to know how much I cared she'd forgotten me.

"Oh, Lil, you can scratch me off the list," I joked. "We know I'm destined for the shelf."

Her mouth was working. "I'll never see Plum in her wedding dress."

Cry, Lily, I thought. *Let go and cry, please…*but she shrugged her narrow shoulders and purposefully padded into the kitchen. Minutes later, I heard the busy whirr of electric egg beaters.

PLUM

All the Grade Seven girls and our history teacher, Miss Bloomberg, were in a long queue unwinding outside the Paarl Museum. We had notebooks and pens and a five rand coin to donate to the museum.

My ears were flapping as I tuned in to three conversations at once – two girls giggling about a boy called Herman; Miss Bloomberg on her mobile saying, "Oh, I shouldn't worry, I'll have them all back in about an hour, no later than that…"and a beggar sitting on the pavement rubbing his tummy, whining, "*Hungry, hungry, hungry…*"

I wanted to give my money to the poor starving man but then they wouldn't allow me into the museum and I absolutely adore history especially the Anglo Boer War which is what we're studying now.

From the corner of my eye I spotted Aunt Frith and the artist teacher across the street and from the bouncy way she was walking, she was happy – laughing in a stupid girly way.

He put his hand on her back and I felt sick and then they turned a corner and I heard panting in my ears like a dog that's been running hard and it was only when Miss Bloomberg hurried over I found out it was me making that awful gasping noise.

"Sit down and put your head between your legs, that's a good girl," Miss Bloomberg said.

I felt like a spare part with them all staring but I put my head down and she knelt and rubbed my back and waited with me while the others filed into the museum.

I didn't want to miss the video so I said, "I'm a bit dizzy, Miss, that's all," and Miss Bloomberg gave me her hand and said, "We don't want them starting without us, do we?"

A man from the museum was standing at a lectern. I watched his mouth moving but couldn't hear what he was saying because there were two voices jibber-jabbering rather loudly in my head.

What's wrong with you?

I feel scared when I see him.

But why when he hasn't done anything to you?

It feels like he could, though.

What's that mean?

It means maybe he could do something to me or Dad or Aunt Frith.

That's just silly. He's an artist. He likes Aunt Frith. He wouldn't hurt her.

How do you know?

I don't…but you don't either. You're just being a Drama Queen as usual.

You think?

Then the museum went dark and the video started and the voices got softer until I couldn't hear them anymore.

I love poring over pictures of people who lived years ago like General Koos De La Ray who led a commando of wild-looking Boers against the droopy-moustached Viscount Alfred Milner with his army of 'red-coats' which is what they called British soldiers back then.

The video showed grainy flickering photos of men fighting on horseback, farms burning and concentration camps filled with sad-faced women and crying children – skinny as insects.

I filed away a picture of a young Boer soldier in my brain. He was standing with four other men all wearing hats turned up at one side, gripping a rifle with both hands like it might go off if he didn't hold on tight. He looked more like a young boy playing dress-up than a soldier and if I'd been living then I could so easily have been him staring into the camera with terrified cow's eyes.

I didn't want the video to end and would have been happy to stay in the dark with my eyes glued to jumpy black and white war pictures and my mind going a million miles a minute but the lights came on and Miss Bloomberg said I was still looking washed-out and asked if she should call my mother but I couldn't tell her I don't have one because I didn't want her feeling sorry for me so I said, "No thank you, Miss. I'm feeling heaps better."

That video made the war seem terribly real and all the way home I made believe I was the young Boer soldier galloping along a track through the bush. I have this trick where if I press my eyes half-shut I can make buildings, fences, bridges and roads disappear and all I see is dry yellow grass and raggedy thorn trees and way off in the distance, a boxy farmhouse pressed against the side of the mountain.

When I got home I went up to the attic and buried my face in Dahlia's chest, breathing in her comforting smell of cotton sheets and pajamas and fabric softener and tears.

I've been worried because Dahlia's been crying lately and her eyes were watery so I whispered, "Everything's going to be okay. You don't have to be scared about anything, especially not that awful artist, he can't hurt us, swear to God."

Dahlia gets anxious about stuff like this and hates it when Dad acts all weird but her worst is when my aunt locks her in a suitcase and leaves her alone in the dark feeling frightened and unloved.

"Turn your mind into an empty bowl," I whispered. "Try not to think of anything but if that's too hard think of something that makes you smile inside."

I thought I'd read the diary to Dahlia – I haven't told her I can't make out Charlotte's sharp squiggly writing – so I pretended to read until I heard Dahlia's breathing get slower and then at last her eyes clicked shut.

FRITH

Theo's a good lover. He knows how to bring me to a climax, when to rock slowly and deeply and when to move urgently – something most lovers have never understood.

It's astonishing that such a narcissist should be sensitive during sex though, of course, Theo adores women and his is a skill acquired through years of practice.

I was aware of him studying my face as I tensed, my eyes tightly shut, clenching my body. His mouth at my ear, he whispered, *'Cleave unto me,'* just before I came.

Later, I erupted in giggles.

"Did you really say, *'Cleave unto me?'"*

He gave a sleepy smile. "Cleave – old English word meaning 'to adhere unwaveringly'. Know the quote? It's from the Bible. It goes something like, *'A man shall cleave to his wife and they twain shall be one flesh.'"*

That's all it took to ruin the moment.

Theo switched on a tinny transistor radio, set up his easel and silently painted me for over an hour. Finally, covered in goosebumps, I reached for my clothes.

Tenderly, he helped slide my arms into the sleeves of my blouse and, picking up my wrinkled skirt, knelt while I stepped into it, dressing me as attentively as if I were a child.

Securing the clasp of my moonstone, he kissed the nape of my neck.

"You smell of my cologne," he breathed. "And something else...something musky. God, Frith, you're a sexy woman."

With his arm around my waist, he walked me to the door. "Will I see you in class?"

I nodded, vaguely disappointed. "Yes, of course."

I waited for him to say more. He gave his slow grin.

I smiled back. "Well, um, bye, then."

He turned to retreat indoors.

A blaze swept my cheeks. "Theo!"

"Yeah?"

Do you feel anything for me? Anything at all – or is this just a game for you?

"Sorry...did I bring a bag with me?"

"I don't recall a bag. Got your sunglasses?"

"Yes, thanks. Okay, well, see you soon."

I found Plum sitting on the floor of the attic, cradling that wretched doll. The diary lay open on her lap and, looking down at the top of her head, I was suddenly swamped with guilt.

"What's the matter?"

Eyes downcast, she shook her head. She looked as miserable as I felt.

My knees creaked as I lowered myself to sit cross-legged beside her.

I picked up the diary. "Right, where were we?"

CHAPTER TWENTY

FRITH

Plum turned her serious, oval face to me. "Can I ask you something?"

She leaned forward, looking intent. "Have you sometimes heard Dad crying at night?"

I replied quickly, "No."

That's a lie. I'm deeply troubled by William's muffled weeping.

She looked right through me. "You must have," she said flatly.

"Well..." *What to say?* "We both know your father's been um... depressed, lately."

She nodded. "We have to try to make him better." Her eyes were almost transparent in the light.

"Yes," I said.

She bent to lightly kiss the doll in her arms. "Please read to me."

August 18th, 1905

I have been ill, confined to bed for many weeks. Today, a little of my waning strength has returned, permitting me to take up my pen and scratch a few words in this sadly neglected journal.

One of Edward's erstwhile colleagues, a grim-faced, ex-army surgeon, Dr. Thomas Clutterbuck has been treating me for pneumonia though I believe my illness stems more from nerves and unhappiness than an infection of the chest.

When he was first summoned, Dr. Clutterbuck gravely pronounced I was in failing health and, to my astonishment, Edward promised the doctor a generous purse if he could restore me to health.

Perhaps for this reason, though also in deference to their long-time friendship, Dr. Clutterbuck cycles every day from his surgery on Main Street to North Wind Manor.

The doctor is stern and makes little or no effort to be agreeable though he has proven exceedingly diligent in caring for me. Every few days, he changes the soft linseed poultice wrapped around my chest and tightly binds a fresh one with a length of oiled silk. I am dosed daily with ten grains of Dover's powder for pain and twenty grains of cream of tartar for evacuation of bowels.

The doctor has also prescribed a new diet. I am fed upon milk with brandy to stimulate my heart and beef broth to nourish my blood. These sensible treatments taken together with quiet days of bed-rest have led to Dr. Clutterbuck pronouncing I am truly cured and claim his purse.

I do not begrudge the doctor his money. My body seems stronger though my spirits are far from recovered.

August 20th, 1905

This morning, after a modest breakfast, I was assisted downstairs where Edward was waiting.

"Thank you, husband," I said, endeavouring to express my gratitude by laying my hand upon his arm. "You have been my dear, kind saviour these past few weeks."

Without replying, Edward withdrew to the window where he stood looking out at the drear, wintry day. "I have urgent business in London, Charlotte," he announced, stiffly. "I have been waiting for you to mend and now that you are restored to health, I am confident I may leave the manor in your care. My trunks are packed and I depart at first light."

I gasped in surprise. There was a time such news would have made me happy but, due to my husband's seemingly genuine concern for my well-being, I was struck mute by his dispassionate words. Perhaps this shock was visible for

Edward asked, with more consideration: "Is there anything I may bring you from London, Charlotte?"

"There is a book I should like to read," I told him, shakily. "It is called 'Bleak House' and is written by Mr. Charles Dickens."

Edward bowed. "I shall do my best to find it."

Later, when he came to bid farewell, Edward pressed several pages of written instructions into my hand saying, "Please be vigilant in the upkeep of my house and grounds. Do not allow my servants to slacken and become tardy. Stern discipline must be maintained and punishment extracted for laziness or rudeness. Do you understand, Charlotte?"

I said I did, whereupon, without another word, my husband turned upon his heel and departed.

'My house,' he had said, with deliberate phrasing. 'My servants'. I must presume Edward now considers me his housekeeper and – in his absence – substitute caretaker of North Wind Manor.

Well, well…this sets me in my proper place, does it not?

August 27th, 1905

Now that I am well again, I find North Wind Manor greatly changed though not for the better! From nine field-workers only four remain on the land. The rest have run away in fear or been banished for so-called 'misdemeanors'. Our cook, the comely, laughing Lena is no longer with us and, since none of our servants will say why she has left, I gather she flew like a frightened bird from my husband's hawkish intentions.

Without a cook, Edward has made do with Tuppence, a young Malay kitchen boy, barely fourteen, who has been taught rudimentary cooking and is able to prepare a limited menu of meat and potatoes, broth and bread. It is impossible to teach Tuppence from my, 'Common Sense Cookery Book' for he cannot read and is, besides, stone deaf.

I have placed an advertisement in the 'Paarl Chronicle' offering employment for five strong field-workers, a cook and lady's maid, all in good health with excellent references and a basic understanding of spoken English.

September 4th, 1905

To my dismay, the Chronicle has buried my advertisement amongst a great many others. I am astonished at the extraordinary number of items available for sale this week. Readers are compelled to purchase, 'Burdock's Blood Bitters' for stomach-cramps, casks of farm butter, Clark's 'Hygienic Boots', tallow candles, boxes of Huntley and Palmer's 'Marie' Biscuits, well-bred ponies, bottles of sweet sherry and tins of Indian and China Tea.

Will anyone see my call for workers amidst this higgledy-piggledy jumble?

September 7th, 1905

The weighty burden of caring for North Wind Manor without sufficient help has reduced me to a bundle of jangled nerves! Unable to sleep, I also suffer from lack of appetite though this latter symptom may have more to do with Tuppence's dire cooking than this bothersome anxiety that overcomes me.

September 10th, 1905

I found myself in a beastly temper at the sight of Dr. Clutterbuck cycling up to the house today. His eyes started at the picture I made in a stained apron with my hair disheveled and my cheeks flour streaked. "Why have you come, doctor?" I asked sharply. "As you see, I am up and about once more."

The doctor is stubborn. Without invitation, he entered the kitchen, asked for a jug of water and made himself comfortable at the table. He stared before gruffly pronouncing I was looking pallid, fatigued and thin as bone.

"What ails you, Mrs Butler?" he asked.

"Lack of sleep," I replied shortly, although I did not tell him that it is a troubled mind brimming with distorted fears that keeps me awake in the wee hours.

Dr. Clutterbuck suggested 'chloral hydrate' for sleeplessness.

Having heard horrid tales of this addictive potion, I turned upon the medic saying, "So you would drive me to madness? Is this your aim? Has Edward dispatched you expressly for this evil purpose?"

The doctor paled. "Good God!" he exclaimed, "What can you mean?"

I told him Edward's first wife had died from an overdose of laudanum and added spitefully, "I have sometimes wondered what wicked part my husband played in his wife's tragic demise."

"You are unwell," Dr. Clutterbuck prognosticated, giving me a cold look. "You would not speak such lies otherwise."

The frostiness in his eyes brought me to my senses. It is foolish to speak so openly to one of Edward's closest colleagues – a man who could so easily betray me to my husband.

Hastily, I collected myself. "Pray do not repeat what I have said," I begged. "My unjust accusation springs from nerves shredded with tension."

"I am perplexed, Mrs. Butler," the doctor mused. "Why do you speak of chloral hydrate and madness in the same breath?"

I said it was well-documented that the famous poet and painter, Gabriel Rossetti, had been prescribed chloral hydrate and thereafter his insatiable cravings for this hypnotic drug not only made him insane but, in the end, half paralyzed his brain and stopped his heart.

"I did not know that," was all the doctor replied though I saw a glimmering of respect dawn upon his face.

Clutterbuck fell silent as he quietly pondered, resting his whiskery chin upon his folded hands.

"As a young medical student I studied Culpepper's natural cures," he told me. "For sleeplessness, I suggest three flower heads of lavender steeped in a cup of boiling water and supped before bed."

This seems a mild cure for a serious condition, though I shall try it out of respect for the doctor.

September 16th, 1905

There are only six remaining at North Wind Manor, four field workers, Tuppence and myself.

In Edward's absence, my dear friend, Aletta is more inclined to visit and today she arrived with a scrap torn from the 'Paarl Chronicle' that I recognised as my advertisement.

"I have a cook for you!" she smiled and handed me a reference written in exquisite copperplate by a Mrs. Jonas Woodcock, the cook's previous employer.

Here follows an extract taken from that referral.

"Magdalena has served our family most attentively and obediently for seven years and is of excellent character, good tempered and honest. She is, besides, a capital cook and maid, pleats and irons well and can do housework in general and fine needlework as well."

"But why did this woman come to you?" I asked.

Dipping to conceal her face beneath her hat brim, Aletta answered that Magdalena had requested reassurance that Captain Butler was no longer residing at North Wind Manor. My good friend went on to tell me what I already know – my husband's reputation for cruelty has spread throughout Paarl and whilst employment is pitifully scarce, few have the courage to seek work at the manor.

September 30th, 1905

Fat, merry Magdalena has come to live with us and, with my permission has brought her two strong, able-bodied sons, Tobias and Joshua – and Rosa, her grown-up daughter. Now our field workers number six and, at last, I have my cook and maid.

Poor Tuppence has been demoted from cook to houseboy, yet he seems cheerful, partially, I suspect, because the taste and quality of our meals has greatly improved.

Last evening, we dined upon roast venison served with our own potatoes, carrots, shredded cabbage and a suet pudding studded with plump raisins and sultanas. I dined in pleasant solitude, immersed in my Dickens, more content than I have been for longer than I can remember.

October 5th, 1905

Pegasus has grown lazy from lack of exercise. Now that I am no longer housebound, I plan to celebrate my new-found freedom by riding my horse at a brisk trot to the Strooidak Kerk and home again. An outing in the fresh air will do us both good!

October 10th, 1905

Magdalena and Rosa have put North Wind to rights and the manor is shining clean and bright. Linens have been laundered and starched, floors scrubbed, windows sponged with vinegar, silver and brass polished, clocks wound and lamp wicks trimmed.

Neat piles of sawed logs for wood fires have been laid in the downstairs rooms and my bed chamber. The house is scented with soap and polish, baked bread and the peppercorns and spices cook uses to flavour her tempting stews.

Music pulses within and without the manor. Indoors, rousing hymns are sung by Rosa and Magdalena – the former in a piping soprano and her mother in deeper contralto. There is more singing outdoors in the fields, rolling laughter and the distant shouts of men calling to one another and their beasts. I also hear cheery birdsong, the deep lowing of oxen and a comforting drone of busy bees feasting at honeysuckle. Oh, that my life was always thus!

October 15th, 1905

My nightly brew of lavender tea has granted me the blessed gift of sleeping like a newborn, undisturbed by nightmares.

Of late, under the pretext of caring for my health, Thomas Clutterbuck has become a regular visitor to our house and I detect, beneath the disagreeable countenance of this lonely widower, a simple, unaffected manner and generous heart.

Often the doctor comes bearing gifts – a bag of chamomile tea, a brace of grouse, a hat filled with mushrooms. Yesterday, the doctor presented me with a sewing basket, a pretty thing adorned with velvet ribbons and glass beads, containing needles, bone buttons, thread and skeins of embroidery silks in every hue. He said the basket once belonged to his deceased wife and it was a shame not to put it to good use.

I find myself softening towards Thomas Clutterbuck as we grow more at ease with one another.

He is like an amiable uncle and I am ashamed to have so sorely misjudged a man whose only crime is befriending Edward.

October 19ᵗʰ, 1905

Before his departure, Edward bestowed an allowance for wages and such minor household purchases as I might deem necessary in his absence. With more wages to pay and mouths to feed, these funds are dwindling and, though I strive through small economies to make both ends meet, our daily struggle grows harder.

Despite this, I am perfectly at peace and today, as I caught myself singing hymns with Rosa and Magdalena, I decided to return to the church and take my place in the choir.

Later…

I rode Pegasus to the Kerk and tethered him in the graveyard.

Dominee De Villiers and Tante Katrina came out to admire my gelding and stroke his glossy coat.

We were all three gathered about my horse when Dirk Barnard joined us. As he tipped his hat, his eyes searched my face.

"I am sorry to hear you have been ill, Mrs. Butler," he said. "I hope you have recovered?"

"Oh, yes, thank you," I replied shortly.

I threaded my arm through Tante Katrina's. "I yearn for news!" I said, knowing what an inveterate gossip she is. "Please tell me what I have missed during my indisposition."

Side by side, we entered the the church where Katrina began snipping stems and arranging altar flowers and ferns. I helped her fill urns with blooms and branches and, throughout this task, grew conscious of the organist sending covert glances from the vestibule.

A throng of choristers gathered and, happily, I took my place.

"You have been missed," Miss Emmeline Kriel allowed, before lifting her hands and leading us into a rousing hymn.

Dirk followed when I left the church, half-running in his haste to catch up with me. Swiftly, I mounted Pegasus and made to ride away but, at the entrance, I was forced to halt and hold open the gate with my riding crop to allow a visiting group to pass through.

Dirk waited until we were alone. "I have heard rumours," he stammered. "People say your husband, Captain Butler, now lives in London. Can this be true?"

"What business is it of yours?" I demanded, rudely.

"Forgive me," he answered, abashed. "I have no wish to meddle in your private affairs."

I should have urged my horse homeward but, filled with desperate longing, I cried out involuntarily, "Yes! It is true...he has gone! My husband has left me!"

I saw expressions of disbelief followed by delight upon Dirk's face. He laid his hand briefly upon my riding boot before shyly pronouncing, "You have been much on my mind."

I answered boldly. "And you on mine!"

At once I dismounted and stood before him, gripped with the certainty that I should seize this chance for happiness. I swear I would have shamelessly flung myself into his arms were it not for the appearance of two old parishioners, tottering towards the gate.

I looked directly into his eyes. "Will you visit me at the manor?"

"When?"

"Tomorrow," I replied rashly. "Come for dinner. Please."

Dirk stepped politely aside to let the old couple hobble past.

"I shall look forward to it," he said quietly.

Riding home, my eyes were dazzled by sunlight and from the dim recesses of memory came the words of a hymn I used to sing regularly at our parish church when I lived in England.

'Amazing Grace,
how sweet the sound,
that sav'd a wretch like me,
I once was lost,
but now am found,
was blind, but now I see.'

I wonder if true love has the power to save me? I will not sleep tonight – no matter how many lavender flower-heads are drowned in hot water. Love has pierced my heart and I pray to God it does not also destroy it.

CHAPTER TWENTY ONE

FRITH

I found Lily's letter in a box crammed with saved birthday, Christmas and 'Get Well' cards.

I don't know why I'd forgotten it. Perhaps because it wasn't a letter – it was a postcard with a picture of Kew Gardens on the front.

"If I go – no, that's me being delusional – **when** *I go – I want you to have the painting Julia left me. I've never liked it. Too bleak and cold, like her. However, it's my most valuable possession, worth a king's ransom and it's yours. Christie's are interested. Ask them to sell it for you."*

I remember yelling over the phone. '*Christ* Lily! It's not the end you know. Cancer doesn't have to be a death sentence!'

Lily answered quietly she still had her faith and believed she'd be going to a better world.

"But what if there isn't one?" I asked. "What if it's only ash and dust?"

"Then what's the point of anything?"

"Suppose there isn't a point? Suppose this is all there is?"

I'm ashamed of the things I said. She'd have been clinging to the only shred of hope she had. What a stupid, thoughtless bitch I've been.

I try to get away often. It's colder indoors than out, almost gelid, and the constant head-bashing din from the builders makes me want to climb walls.

William is not good company. He's become more reclusive. He buys most of what he needs online but when he goes out for fittings or fixtures, he wears a wide-brimmed hat pulled low over his ears and dark sunglasses. "You look as if you're ailing from some hideous skin disease," I tell him, not that it makes any difference, he simply ignores me.

He's also grown darkly pessimistic about the future of this country. Never stops moaning about endemic corruption, lack of leadership, poverty – this bloody drought – joblessness.

On and on he goes and I've stopped reminding him he uprooted us all to come here, it only makes him worse.

"I want things to be normal," I say, but what's that? There's nothing 'normal' about William, Plum and I, tossed together like shells in the surf, rubbing up against one another every time another wave breaks. This friction will break us.

It started to rain mid-way to Main Street. Needle-sharp drops pricking my face. I hadn't thought to bring an umbrella and by the time I arrived at the lawyers' offices, I was soaked to the skin. Louis Venter was meeting a client. The receptionist asked if I'd like to leave a message.

"I want to talk to someone about a will."

"About making a will?"

"Contesting one, actually."

"Ah – you want our senior partner – Ms. Katrina Burger. She's the one dealing with estate, probate and family law. You're in luck. She has a gap in about fifteen minutes. Want me to slot you in?"

I sat huddled in drenched, slippery clothes until Ms. Burger appeared and waved me into her office. Immediately, I was struck by her familiarity.

"Hello!" I said, gawping. "You look like…like…hold on a sec, it's on the tip of my tongue. Help me here. People must have told you umpteen times. You look like an actress. Famous, blonde, oh you must know the one." In the nick of time, the name came to me, "That Russian film…Dr. Zhivago… *Julie Christie!*"

Impassively, the lawyer extended a hand. "Really? You don't say."

Somber, professorial clothes aside, her resemblance to a well-preserved Julie Christie was extraordinary. Bleached hair piled in a messily collapsing bee-hive. Great bones. Flawless skin. She'd have been stunning twenty years ago.

Ms. Burger had none of Julie Christie's seductive warmth. Right away she got down to business. "How can I help?"

I laid the postcard on her desk and explained the picture Lily mentioned had been excluded from her will.

"I suspect my brother-in-law changed the will. Lily would've been sick when she signed a new one. Too sick to notice the painting was missing from things she left me."

Ms. Burger sent a doubtful look across her desk. "Mmm. Can you provide *conclusive medical evidence* your sister didn't understand the will she made?"

I went blank. "How do you do that?" I asked, confused. "Lil had a doctor, an oncologist, who was treating her. I could get in touch with him and ask for medical records."

Impatiently, the lawyer scribbled on a yellow pad.

"Was your sister suffering from Alzheimer's or any other form of dementia?"

"No!" I interrupted, hastily. "God, no, nothing like that! But the constant pain she had to endure made her weak and tired and, towards the end, Lily kept drifting off and couldn't concentrate properly."

Katrina Burger chose her words carefully. "So are you suggesting your sister was *unduly influenced* into signing her will?"

'*Unduly influenced*?' I tried to think. "Um, I'm not sure what that means. All I know is the painting is worth a lot and it was in William's interest – he's my brother-in-law – to make sure I didn't inherit it."

Miss Burger shook her head. Her hair was not, as I'd first thought, loosely tousled but sprayed to helmet crispness.

"Help me here. I'm trying to understand your claim. Are you saying your brother-in-law exerted such extreme pressure as to *force* your sister to revise her will?"

I found myself sweating, damp circles spreading beneath my armpits.

"I don't know what to say, really. I'm not saying William *forced* Lil to do anything. I don't know if he even mentioned the painting to her. He

WHERE THE TRUTH LIES

wouldn't have wanted to bring it to Lily's attention, you see. He'd probably keep quiet and hope she'd forget about it."

Miss Burger frowned and drew a cube on her pad. I saw my chance slipping away. Desperately, I went on, "On the other hand, he may have nagged her into…"

She spoke sharply. "We're not talking about *nagging*! You can't get away with verbal threats. You'll need to provide *definite evidence of coercion* on the part of your brother-in-law. Can you?"

I was floundering. "I haven't a clue. How does one do that, anyway – *prove* coercion? I mean it all happened a year or so ago and I'm hazy on the details. Have I left it too late, do you think?"

"I feel I should warn you," Ms. Burger stared shrewdly. "From my experience, contesting a will is difficult and *very* expensive. Before you open a case against your sister's husband, you'd best get your ducks in a row."

I tried for flippancy. "So how do you suggest I line up my ducks then?"

Unamused, Ms. Burger rocked a pencil between thumb and forefinger. Her eyes bore unflinchingly into mine. "If you wish to challenge the validity of your sister's will, you can consider one of two options. You'll need *explicit* medical evidence to verify she was incompetent to sign her will. Or, you'll have to prove *blatant wrongdoing* on the part of your brother-in-law."

Before I left her office, Ms. Burger handed me a pamphlet. "Read the sections on: 'Proving a lack of testamentary capacity' and 'Demonstrating undue influence'."

In the dying seconds of our interview, I made a last-ditch effort to win her over.

"Did you see Julie Christie in that film about the woman with Alzheimer's?"

The lawyer's eyes dropped pointedly to the watch on her wrist.

"I don't think so. Do you have my card?"

"Yes, thanks." I patted my pocket. "You'd remember this film if you'd seen it. It was about getting old and sick and forgetful and the desperate strain that puts on a marriage."

She pinched her lips. "Sorry. I *definitely* didn't see it."

"Well, you missed something, then. There's this line Julie Christie's character says, *'I think I may be beginning to disappear.'* I've never forgotten it."

Katrina Burger cut me off. "Don't hesitate to get in touch if you decide to take this further."

"I think that's how Lily must've felt, at the end – like she was beginning to disappear."

Miss Burger's eyes glazed over. "I hope you don't mind…I have a client waiting."

"Sorry, sorry. Thanks for seeing me at such short notice."

PLUM

It stopped raining so I put on my Day-glo orange mac and pink Wellies and went into the garden to help with weeding. Weeds come up with a satisfying *plop* after rain and the plastic bag I gave the Oom was bulging with dandelion, sorrel and creeping clover – I know all the proper weed names now because the Oom is a good teacher.

The Oom showed his shiny gums and said, *'Baie dankie'* which means 'thank you' in Afrikaans. He's being especially nice to me because of the shoes. He doesn't have proper shoes – only slip-slops – so I gave him Dad's bright blue trainers only it turns out they'd hardly been worn and fat watery blisters popped up on the Oom's poor cracked heels and Dad got squinty-eyed and said, "That distinctive tick means those are *Nike* and cost an arm and a leg. At the very least, you could have asked!"

The sun came out and I went indoors for one of Aunt Frith's shady hats and my book, *Great Expectations*. Only six more chapters till the end and Aunt Frith says I should read her favourite Dickens, *The Old Curiosity Shop* next but it'll have to be *Bleak House* – the book Charlotte asked Edward to bring from London.

It's kind of weird knowing Charlotte must once have stood right where I'm standing now and if she'd turned her head she'd have seen the same totally awesome view of the mountains after the rain with a wishy-washy sky and raindrops like sprinklings of silver glitter in the grass.

I felt a vibrating on top of Aunt Frith's hat and got all trembly because I thought it might be the spirit trying to connect but it turned out to be a bee. I sat on the bench and laid the hat on my knees and watched the bee slowly bumping against a bunch of dusty silk flowers on the brim.

Dad's shadow fell over me. "What are you up to?"

I showed him the bee and said I thought it was blind or sleepy because it kept nudging the fake flowers and didn't seem to be able to fly.

Dad shook his head. "Sign of the times," he said. "Pesticides are to blame, of course. Deadly poisons invade the bee's microscopically-tiny immune system leaving it weak and so confused it can't tell the difference between nature's fresh flowers and those artificial ones on that hat. We're doomed, I'm afraid. Once bees finally disappear for good, the earth has only four years left to survive. And that's not me talking. That's Albert Einstein."

Dad sat down with a heavy thump.

This is how Dad talks these days and it makes me scared 'cause it's not like how he used to be – funny and smiley – so I asked if he was feeling blue again but for the longest time Dad just stared at the mountain like he wasn't seeing anything.

Then he blurted, "Not blue. I'm in a grey phase."

"Is that worse?"

"Yes, I believe it is. Ever wondered how many shades of grey there are? Iron-grey…steel grey…lead grey…battleship grey…cinder grey…gun-metal grey. Notice how dreary these names are? Well, that's the state of my mind right now."

"There's sludgy grey too," I said, helpfully.

"You're right. That's exactly my mood," and he sighed and said, "I'm dead tired, sweetheart."

"Yes," I said sadly because he did look tired with his eyes fallen back into his head and whiskers on his cheeks and his face all crumpled like it needed ironing but before I could cheer him up, he went on, "No good telling me to down tools, Plum. I'm in this for the long-haul, the entire up-hill journey and God knows how many more months it'll take before I finally stagger to the finish line with this house finally done."

If Mom had heard Dad talking like this she'd have rubbed comforting circles on his back and said, "Oh, do buck up, Wills, it's not the end of the world."

I was going to say that but didn't want him to start thinking about Mom and getting watery eyes so I tried to lift his spirits by telling a lie – not a small white one – a humungous one.

"You've done a really good job on the house so far, Dad!" I said.

"Think so?" His voice sounded thin and empty so I nodded furiously. "I do."

He pulled a Polaroid out of his pocket. "I asked one of the chaps to take this photo of me the other day," he said. "I think it makes me look like a real pro. What do you think?"

"What does a real pro, look like?"

"I'm talking about a professional restorer and, to my mind, he looks like the man in this picture."

The photo showed Dad leaning against a wall with building stuff all around him.

He stabbed the picture with a finger. "Wrinkled shirtsleeves rolled to the elbow; dust covering my shoes; electric sander at my feet. In the back there – just protruding into the frame – you can make out the blunt end of a pile of short-tongued oak panels."

I wasn't sure what I was supposed to say so I didn't say anything.

Dad brought the picture closer to his eyes. "I have an eerie disconnect with the man in this picture. It's like staring at a stranger. I keep asking myself – *who is this person?*"

"It's you!" I said but he wasn't listening.

"This man," he went on, "looks like someone I might enjoy meeting. I like the way his eyes are directed at the camera, not shying away from the lens as mine so often do. And there's something else appealing in this snapshot and that's this fellow's easy, honest smile. That's the smile of a contented man, wouldn't you say?"

I didn't like the way Dad was talking like the person in the picture was somebody else.

He rubbed his forehead. "Thing is, Plum, this photograph is a lie – a clever deception between the lens, the light and the person posing for the picture. This fellow is a consummate actor. Know why?" He stared like the photo was a puzzle. "Because there's nothing in this picture that even *hints* at this man's inner torment!"

I think 'torment' must be to do with suffering – I remember from history how Joan of Arc was tormented by demons.

I looked at the hat on my lap. "I think the bee died," I said. "It's not moving. It's wings have stopped fluttering, do you see?"

"That's life," Dad said. He took the hat and emptied the bee into the flower bed. "Or, in this case, that's death."

He jumped up. "I'm starving! I could eat a hot-dog with sharp English mustard or a roast beef sandwich with sliced onion rings. Let's put an end to wallowing in abject misery. Time waits for no man, darling." He grabbed my hand and pulled. "Ups-a-daisy, Plum. Ups-a-daisy, there's a good girl!"

FRITH

All the way home, I stewed over tough-as-rhino-hide lawyer, Ms. Burger, treating me like an ignoramus – lifting perfect eyebrows at my wet footprints on the carpet and the bum-shaped patch I'd left on the pale damask of the chair.

Back at *North Wind*, I dragged my easel outdoors and set it up in a feeble pool of sunlight.

I've been sketching the manor as Theo has suggested – face-on, with the front steps and side walls diminishing to a single point in the middle. "Practice, practice, practice," Theo keeps telling me. "That's the secret – that and developing a style all your own."

I started drawing the paneled front door with its lion's head knocker and opalescent fanlight and, above this, the edge of the roof and the base of the tall twin chimneys with two grey pigeons roosting there.

I was taking off my sweater when a convertible roared up the driveway. Unfolding his legs from the low-slung vehicle, Louis Venter got out and sauntered towards me.

"What are you doing here?" I said, startled.

He peered at my canvas and his face lit up. "You're an artist! Why didn't I guess? Now I think of it, you do have this delightfully Bohemian look about you."

God, was the stupid arse flirting again? I pulled a face.

"I met your Ms. Burger this morning. We discussed contesting my sister's will."

"What advice did she offer?"

"She told me to get my ducks in a row."

Venter looked rueful. "Yeah, that sounds like Hester. She can be a tad abrasive but she knows her stuff."

"Mmm."

"So, an artist! Now it all fits. Heard you're taking lessons with Theo Christensen."

"Yes." I pretended to be absorbed in my work, touching my paintbrush to a stained-glass panel in the door – a design of hummingbird, birch tree and rose.

"No flies on Theo, I'll say that for him. A beautiful, single woman arrives in Paarl and in no time he's got his hooks into you."

He broke off as William barged down the front steps, carrying a box of tiles.

Venter lowered his voice, "Your brother-in-law?"

"Hello there," William advanced, friendly as always, offering his free hand, "William Westwood."

Surprised, Venter blinked. "Have we met before? I know your face."

William recoiled, frowning. "Unlikely. We're new to the area. Haven't been here long."

Venter gazed frankly at William. "Yet, you seem familiar. I'm almost convinced we've met though I can't quite place you. Give it time. It'll come to me, I'm good with faces."

William widened his eyes. "You have the advantage over me, Mr...?"

"Louis Venter. I'm from Venter and Swart. A firm of attorneys."

William darted a look at me. "And your business here?"

"Just paying a social visit. Curious to know who's moved into the old manor. I tip my hat to you, Mr. Westwood, I really do. You've taken on a daunting task, remodeling this place. Cost a pretty penny, I'll bet."

Uncomfortably, William cleared his throat. "Er, well...you'll have to excuse me, Mr. er...Venter. I'm afraid I'm rather busy. Another time, perhaps?"

As William carried the box to his car, Venter whispered, "Listen...the real reason for my visit is to ask if you'll join me for lunch."

I was genuinely surprised. "Why? What's the occasion?"

"No occasion. No mariachi bands or dancing girls. A simple lunch for two. Any chance you can make it tomorrow?"

I shook my head. "Sorry. I've an art class."

"What about Friday? Does one o'clock suit? *De Kelder Restaurant*. Know the place?"

"I've seen it."

His face cracked in a grin. "Excellent. See you Friday."

As Venter's convertible glided away, I felt a twist of anxiety. *Shit!* What was that about?

William strode purposefully towards me. "Fuck, Frith! Who was that Nosy bloody Parker?"

"His name is Louis Venter."

William's brow beetled. "You visited his law firm. Did you invite him here?"

Flushing hotly, I turned on him. "No, I did not! But Venter *recognised* you, William. He hasn't put a name to your face, but there's a good chance he will."

I heard the tremor in William's voice. *"Christ*, Frith! I've made a God-awful mistake. You were right. We should never have come back. What happens to Plum if I get locked up?" His face looked drained. His pupils were wide and black. "The *shame*, Frith! I go cold. It's not me I care about, don't get me wrong. It's Plum living her life under a cloud. The daughter of another despicable Bernie Madoff! She'll grow to hate me, I know she will."

My jaw dropped. "Oh, come on! It's not that bad."

William laughed bitterly. "What do you know, Frith?"

"Let's pack up and leave." I saw myself eagerly boarding a plane for France. "You and Plum can be back in the UK in a fortnight."

He covered his face with both hands. His voice was muffled. "That's not a solution. I can't keep running. And it's not what Lily wanted for Plum."

"What then?"

William let his hands fall. "Truth is, I've sunk most of my money into *North Wind*. If it's not going to bring in an income as a guest house, I'll have to sell the property. But, first, I've got to complete this sodding restoration and that's another three to four months, at best."

I didn't believe him. Lily always said William had money squirreled away in dozens of off-shore accounts in places like Jersey, Bermuda, the Cayman Islands.

William stared defiantly, waiting for me to say something.

"Um, Louis Venter," I managed. "Don't worry about him. It's me he's after, not you."

CHAPTER TWENTY TWO

PLUM

I pulled the sheet over my head and hid in cottony dimness waiting for Dad to call me to breakfast. The problem with birthdays is everyone expects them to turn into a precious memory you can take out and look at when you want to remember a happy time but that hardly ever happens and I hate being fake and saying I love a present when it totally sucks and isn't what I really want.

There's what Dad calls 'an unbreakable tradition' to my birthday. It begins with French toast and a mug of hot chocolate and I should've told them ages ago how I *hate soggy* squelchy eggy toast and sick-making hot chocolate and I'd far prefer boiled egg and Rooibos tea, like the Oom makes, sweet and strong.

For my last birthday Mom gave me a gold locket in the shape of a heart and from Dad I got a musical jewelry box with a stiff ballerina in a pink tutu twirling to *Swan Lake* after I stuck up thousands of yellow sticky notes begging for a Chinchilla rabbit in a roomy wooden hutch.

If my birthday falls on a weekend or a holiday we visit the zoo or a museum or the planetarium but if it's a school-day there's a party that's small because I never have more than two friends so it's birthday cake with candles and Dad organises games and Mom…well anyway that's the kind of birthday I've had before – but this year's different.

Dad says this is my last year of childhood and next year when I turn thirteen a hormonal whirlwind will take hold of my body as I evolve into the person I'm going to be which sounds weird because who am I now if I'm not a tadpole of the frog I'm going to be?

I get a birthday wish when I blow out the candles and I've already decided to wish for Dad to be normal again – ha ha, what's that? – our family's never been normal but maybe more normal than he is now.

I got dressed and put my hair up to look older and then wasted time at the window watching a feather floating from where two rock pigeons live in the eaves and as it twisted to the ground I made a bet – '*If the feather falls on the grass I'll have a spectacular birthday but if it falls into the rockery it'll be craptacular!*'

I was cheating because there's miles of lawn and a tiny half-moon rockery but the feather dropped smack in a patch of pink and white busy lizzies and that's when I knew turning twelve wasn't going to be any fun.

Aunt Frith was frying disgusting eggy bread in butter and lifting a pan of bubbling milk off the hot plate. She blew a kiss and chirped, "Happy birthday, Plum! Goodness me, twelve years old and all grown up!"

Then she smiled at Dad and said, "Remember Wills? That day you and Lil saw her for the first time…that woman from the agency brought her all wrapped in a pink blanket like a gift you'd been waiting for so long and you said…"

Right then Dad burst out singing '*Happy Birthday*' but really loudly like he was trying to drown her out so I thought about what she'd said and asked, "What woman from the agency?"

A fiery whoosh scorched my aunt's neck. I turned to Dad. "You said you were in the delivery room when Mom had me."

"I was!" Dad stared daggers at Aunt Frith. "Your aunt is confused."

Aunt Frith's face was blazing and she didn't speak but her eyes were looking into Dad's and they were saying, "*Sorry, sorry, sorry!*"

I made my mind quiet so I could remember exactly what she'd said.

"*You and Lil saw her for the first time…that woman from the agency brought her wrapped up in a pink blanket like a gift you'd been waiting for so long…*"

242

FRITH

I'd been thinking about the day they'd got Plum from the agency and how twelve years had passed in a twinkling…and…and it just came out. William's face! *God!* I stood, helplessly, as William glared in disbelief, hands shaking in anger.

Then Plum said, 'What woman from the agency?'…and I wanted the floor to open up.

Plum's eyes moved from William to me and we knew her clever brain would be computing this information behind her flat, calm exterior.

We'd been going at one another, hammer and tongs, before she came down. I'd planned the entire day. A drive into Stellenbosch. Lunch at a swanky wine farm and a film in the evening – the romantic comedy with Sandra Bullock or the George Clooney thriller.

No party – her only friend is Bronte who's invited her out tomorrow.

I'd studied William as he came into the kitchen carrying two parcels. For once he wasn't wearing paint-spattered khakis and veldskoene. He'd showered and shaved with a tuft of bloody cotton wool on his chin to prove it.

"How are you?" I asked, cautiously.

"Fair to middling." He spoke through a clenched jaw.

I went on slowly. "I know you're doing your best to keep things together, Wills, but please think before you speak. I want this birthday to be special."

Ignoring me, he placed his boxes on the table and peered into the frying pan.

"She's gone off French toast. And she's not that partial to hot chocolate either." His nostrils pinched as if he were smelling something rotten. "Why don't you *ask* what she'd like to eat instead of assuming you know?"

Instantly, I got rattled. "Let's not do this today, Wills. I'm sick of this bickering back and forth. Can we be civil on her birthday?"

243

He sank into a chair and started fiddling with ribbons on a box. "How did we get to *civil?* What's happened, Frith? We used to be good friends when Lil was alive. You know how she'd have loved being here with us today. I can't believe our daughter's turning twelve and Lil isn't here to…"

I blocked his voice. Started thinking about Lily telling me about the day the woman from the agency had brought Plum and then…Plum walked in with her hair caught back in a sprouting twist secured with one of Lily's silver combs. She was wearing a yellow t-shirt tucked into denims and, with her long legs, slender neck and huge, unblinking eyes – she looked like a gorgeous giraffe.

I wanted to tell her how beautiful she was but then, despite my careful plans, I ruined everything in just a few seconds.

PLUM

She put a plate of French toast in front of me and dropped a marshmallow into a mug of hot chocolate.

Dad was fiddling with a bunch of ribbons on a box, trying to look like Aunt Frith hadn't just said the weirdest thing.

I heard my tummy somersaulting. "I'll be sick if I eat that," I told her.

Dad snorted through his nose. "What did I tell you?"

I could tell from the hard scratchy noise she made scraping the toast into the bin she was cross but Dad didn't care. He poured from the *cafetiere.* "Twelve is when you start enjoying coffee," he said. "Add a dollop of milk and a spoon of sugar and stir briskly. Which cereal would you like?"

I was deciding on Rice Crispies or Cornflakes when this thought leapfrogged into my mind. "I'm adopted!" I said. "That's why I don't look like anyone in our family."

Dad swallowed the wrong way and started coughing and when he could speak he said, *"No!"* – spitting toast crumbs. "Of course you're not adopted. It's not true…what your aunt said…she's mistaken…that came later…when we were getting ready to leave the hospital…the *nurses* brought you wrapped in a blanket. That's what you meant to say isn't it *Frith*?"

They looked like two like hissing cats with hair stiff and backs arching ready to pounce so I stored the adoption idea away to think about another time.

"Which present should I open first?" I asked.

Aunt Frith pressed a long box into my hand and I lifted the lid.

"It's a moonstone like mine," she said, holding up a green oval stone on a silver chain. "This one comes from Burma and has more green hues than blue so when it twists in the light it looks like water in a stream."

The stone was bigger and thicker than hers with a kind of ghostly glow trapped inside.

She put it around my neck and clasped it at the back.

"It's called 'Moonstone' because the Romans thought the stones were made from moonlight," she said.

I hated how heavy and cold it felt around my neck and the greeny-yellowness of the stone was nothing like moonlight and not much like water from a stream either.

"It's the same colour as a dandelion weed," I told her.

Dad gave me a flat square box and from the shape it was a laptop and I was sort of glad because girls at school have identical ones and I'll fit in better with the same Apple Mac.

I tore the paper and said, "Wow!" but it didn't come out right so I said it again, "**Wow!**" this time really loudly. "Thanks, Dad!"

Dad opened his mouth to say something but his words melted into a long, sad sigh and he forced out a tired smile and rubbed his eyes.

Her next present was the Mona Lisa she painted in her art class and the shock of my face staring back made me squawk like a parrot because she made me look like I was in a bad mood and I didn't have a mysterious smile only a sulky mouth turning down.

She'd painted me against a background that wasn't real – an ugly hump-backed mountain with a pile of crumbling stone supposed to be a ruined church. The colours in her painting were dark and dirty and even the sky was rainy-day-grey hanging with heavy purplish clouds.

Then I heard Dad saying, "God! This is beyond good! The likeness is remarkable! That's Plum to a T!"

Aunt Frith said, "You really think so?" in a little girl voice and Dad said he was no expert when it came to art but her portrait of me fairly took his breath away.

She gave a wobbly smile and said, "Plum?" with a question mark hanging off the end and I knew she was desperate for me to say how much I liked her painting but I didn't so I began unwrapping my last present like I hadn't heard her say my name in that hopeful way.

FRITH

Plum's expression didn't change one iota. She looked straight ahead, no eye-contact with either of us.

Then she said, matter-of-fact, *"I'm adopted, aren't I?"* That threw me.

She really is the strangest child.

What I'd said was stupid, cruel and thoughtless, but I'd unwittingly given William an opportunity to finally let Plum know the truth and, typically, he'd lost his nerve and started tap-dancing his way out of a painfully awkward moment.

I'm beginning to think Plum is *not* text-book Asperger's. These kids have an inability to read facial expressions, body gestures and shifting vocal tones, which is why they're usually socially inadequate. This isn't true in Plum's case. She's extremely perceptive when it comes to gauging other people's feelings. I may have made a mistake in labelling her with this diagnosis – no surprises there – I seem to be lurching from one blunder to another.

My gifts were flops. She didn't like the moonstone or the painting – or she was punishing me for what I'd said and I don't blame her if that's the case.

Plum reached for William's second gift. "I think you'll like this," he said, feebly.

She spilled the contents of the box on the table top. It took a few moments to work out what I was looking at…tiny, doll-size dresses, perfect miniatures of Victorian gowns, lacy chemises, flouncy silk petticoats, taffeta bonnets, tiny white boots with black buttons.

"Oh, Daddy!" Her face was alight. "These are for Dahlia! They're *beautiful!* Where did you find them?"

"I saw this shop in Main Street – *Tabitha's Couture.* The sign in the window grabbed my attention. *'Bridal fashions, formal gowns and custom-designed outfits made to order'.* I went inside and said, "I don't suppose you make dolls' clothes?" and this woman, Tabitha was her name, didn't even blink. She asked what style I wanted – period, high-fashion or funk. Well, I couldn't see your Dahlia in a rocker jacket and military boots, so I went for Victorian."

He leaned across the table to pick up a black and white plaid dress with a red velvet trim and pretty rose-pink satin gown with a pleated skirt and ruffles.

"These are what they used to call 'morning dresses'," he explained. "This one has 'leg-o'-mutton sleeves'. They're worn with a chemise and half-petticoat. The shoes are made from kid leather. I'm told by Tabitha the hats are Regency, high-brim spoon bonnets."

Her face glowed. "Why's it called *'leg-o'-mutton'* sleeve?"

He drew the shape with his hands. "Voluminous at the top, tapering to the elbow – looks like a lamb shank."

Plum laughed. "I'm going to get Dahlia," she said, whirling away.

"How much did you pay for those doll's clothes?" I asked, sourly.

Brushing toast crumbs off his sweater, William shrugged carelessly. "Just shy of what I shelled out for one of the world's most advanced laptops."

"William, this is *madness!* I thought we agreed to persuade Plum to put her dolls away when she turned twelve."

He frowned. "Don't drag me into this. That was your idea, not mine. I had a stuffed bear for years. His name was Theodore and I found him a great comfort right up until the day I left home for 'varsity."

I felt myself bridle. "You bought those clothes on purpose. You know how I feel about that wretched doll!"

William smiled. "Surprisingly, none of this is about you, my dear. I've never had much luck with birthday gifts but this one seems to have touched the spot. For once, I may have given Plum exactly what she wants."

We got ready for our outing to the wine farm. William scowled at my suggestion that I drive us there. "There's *nothing* wrong with me!" he hissed in my ear. "Don't make a mountain out of this, for Christ's sake!"

Totally absorbed, Plum sat in the back with Dahlia, buttoning the tiny kid boots onto her feet, murmuring quietly to the doll. I riffled through William's CDs and slid Vivaldi's *Four Seasons* into the player. The English Chamber Orchestra's rendering of *'Winter'* usually soothes me.

I have no ear for Baroque music. Lily was the one who loved it. She always thrilled at the part where the north wind blows, the shepherd weeps and – waving her hands, conductor-style – got carried away with the drama of crashing thunder in the final movement of *'Summer'*. I turned the volume up to drown a torrent of agitated thoughts that kept flooding my mind.

William was looking drawn and anxious. His deeply sunken eyes were bloodshot. I noticed his right eyelid twitching, very slightly. I nudged his arm. "I do wish you'd stop being so stubborn and let me drive." As if I hadn't spoken, he stared dully through the window at a view of endless undulating meadows sliced by rivers.

Paarl gave way to Wellington and then Malmsebury and from here the road curved through wine, sheep and grain farms. I must have nodded off. When I woke, the windscreen was spattered with the sticky corpses of crushed insects and William was still forging steadily along at the regulation one twenty kilometers an hour.

I glanced at the map. "You've missed it!" I said, irritated. "The farm where we're supposed to stop for lunch. It's back there."

He pulled onto the side of the road. I showed the map, my finger following the wavy blue line. "Look," I said, sounding sharp. "You should've turned at the ballpoint X."

William shuddered. His eyes were fixed on crops of feathery dandelions and clumps of delicately waving grass. Flocks of red-winged birds burst from a leafy tree.

"All this loveliness," he said, softly. "And all I see is my life collapsing around me."

"Buck up!" I hissed. "It's her birthday, for God's sake."

"I'm not myself," William said, gloomily.

"That's because you're swamped in self-pity. Try considering someone other than yourself for a change."

My tone and the words I'd spoken held a familiar ring. Ah yes. Julia, our mother, used to say the exact same thing to Lil and me.

After lunch, I took photographs of the farm house. I've decided to paint a collection of old houses and one, built in 1850, was a perfect specimen of its period. The front door had an architrave of molded plaster flowers and there were French windows with wooden shutters opening to a wide veranda scattered with comfy wicker chairs.

I waved at an old man shambling from a doorway with a newspaper folded beneath his arm. "Do you mind?" I called, lifting my Nikon to show what I was doing. He eased himself onto a cushion and determinedly opened his paper to shield himself from my camera.

A middle aged woman beckoned. "Don't mind Dad," she smiled. "I've made a pot of coffee. Come and have a cup." As I got closer, she did a double-take.

"Don't I know you?" she asked.

I shook my head. "I don't think so. I've been living in France for donkey's years."

The woman introduced herself as Catherine Montpellier and said her husband was a winemaker in the area.

William cheered as he told her about restoring *North Wind Manor* and she appeared genuinely interested, bowing towards him, drawing him out, listening closely, as if he were about to impart a wonderful secret.

They got on famously until Catherine announced, "I can't get rid of this feeling I've met the two of you before. You *are* married?"

William gasped. "No, no, we're not!"

I made my voice normal. "William is my brother-in-law. He was married to my twin sister, Lily. She's dead now but we…we were identical."

I petered out, feeling foolish. William got up quickly. "Thanks for coffee – and the chat. I'm afraid we've overstayed our welcome. Best be on our way before it gets dark."

Dragging me by an arm, almost stumbling in haste, Wills shouted for Plum who was stroking a tabby cat.

In the car, he dropped his head in his hands. *"Christ!"* he groaned. I had a shudder of disquiet. "The name – Montpellier – didn't ring any bells. She was Cathy Thorpe, back then. One of the weavers in Lil's class when we lived in Robertson. Her hair is darker and she's put on weight, but that's her, no shadow of a doubt."

As we sped towards the gate, Catherine cupped her hands around her mouth and shouted, "By the way…you ever live in Robertson?"

William waved wildly from the open window. He gave a sidelong glance in my direction.

"Fuck!" he said, beneath his breath. *"Fuckety-fuckety-fuck!"*

PLUM

The day after my birthday was Sunday and Bronte and her parents took me to lunch at her Dad's club. I like them, they're ordinary and nice and Mrs Ward is a whole head shorter than me with soft skin and she smells like flowers.

She gave me a kiss that left a red shape on my cheek. "So…*twelve!*" she said making it sound like I'd just climbed a mountain right to the very top.

Mr. Ward is tall and bony. "Ah ha!" He shook my hand. "Plum! We've heard so much. All good. Enchanted to be meeting Bronte's best friend!"

I made a face at Bronte because it's not true, we're not really best friends – all we do is eat lunch together at break and talk books.

Bronte handed me a skinny black box. "Open it!" They were all smiling as I lifted out a silver bracelet dangling with four charms – a heart with a chip of red glass in the middle, an angel with wings, a key and an open book.

Bronte fitted the bracelet on my wrist. "I've got one the same but with more charms," she said. "If I get over sixty-percent for maths, Mom's giving me a leaping dolphin."

Mr. Ward asked if I was good at maths and I said, "No, not very," but Mrs. Ward said I shouldn't worry and went on to tell a long story about a best friend from school, a girl called Marjorie Jamieson who was hopeless at maths and failed most exams but went on to become Minister for Information for a minor African country like Gambia or Burundi. Anyway, Mrs. Ward went on, Marjorie wrote a book, a rattling good yarn about an evil president, an illicit arms deal, a cargo of gold, devil worship and white slave traders and would you believe it, Marjorie's novel shot right to the top of the best-seller lists and after that they made a film about it called, *'Devil's Gold'* which made her very rich as well as famous.

I couldn't stop staring at the bracelet swinging from my arm and it didn't take me long to work out the charms are a secret code. The angel is the spirit at *North Wind*, the key is the one I used to unlock the attic cupboard, the book is Charlotte's secret journal and the heart, well, that's easy – the heart means love and that's Mom.

We piled into a long car Mr. Ward called an estate wagon and they were all talking and laughing at once and I felt kind of dizzy like I might have a 'vision' so I stared hard through the window at a blur of trees and hedges and fields and huge houses behind locked gates.

Mrs. Ward looked over her shoulder. "Do you ride, Plum?"

"I do." I said, thinking of my Raleigh.

"Oh, good!" Mrs. Ward clapped her hands. "Bronte has a pony. You must ride together. Have you joined the Pony Club yet? There's a junior show-jumping competition coming up. You mustn't miss that. It'll be enormous fun."

Bronte started giggling and rolled her eyes back until only the whites showed.

We sat in the club dining room at a table with a folded card in the middle that said: *'Reserved for N.C. Ward & Family.'*

The tablecloth was snowy with a vase of roses so red they were almost black and heavy silver cutlery with *Twin Hills Country Club* in curly handwriting like Charlotte's. For lunch we had pink roast beef with crispy potatoes and tiny sunken Yorkshire puddings and peas and I liked it all so much I had a second helping of everything.

Mr. Ward patted my hand. "Such a pleasure to meet a girl with an appetite. None of this pecking like a bird."

My trifle came with a flaming candle in a blob of cream and everyone sang, *'Happy Birthday'* – Bronte's parents and Bronte with two waiters joining in and then Bronte shouted, "Hip, hip, hurrah!' and Mrs. Ward blew a kiss and Mr. Ward lifted his glass and winked, "Chin, chin!"

We had a cheeseboard and then Mrs. Ward got up to go to what she called the 'powder room' which is really a toilet and Mr. Ward went off to use the credit card machine and me and Bronte waited at the entrance and I closed my eyes and wished the day would never end.

I shook my bracelet and the charms made a lovely tinkling and I told Bronte the last time I'd been this happy was the day we'd moved into *North Wind* when I'd felt the spirit in the upstairs attic the first time.

Bronte screwed up her face and asked, "What spirit?" and, without thinking I said, "I'm not one hundred percent sure if she's the spirit of Charlotte Butler who lived in the house a hundred years ago…or if she's my mother's spirit."

"*Holy smoke!*" Bronte shouted and Mrs. Ward heard and shook her head, saying "Where did you get that *dreadful* expression?"

Mr. Ward whispered his daughter was watching too many American cartoons and then said, "What say we take the long way home and enjoy a leisurely drive through the countryside on this fine afternoon?"

At home I wrote in my diary Bronte was a lucky fish and I wished I had nice, normal, happy parents like Mr. and Mrs. Ward but then I felt like Judas Iscariot and scribbled over what I'd written in thick black Koki so nobody would ever know.

CHAPTER TWENTY THREE

FRITH

I was waiting for Louis Venter as he sauntered towards the restaurant. His jaunty grin faded when I told him I wouldn't be joining him for lunch.

"That's a shame," he said. "They've an excellent wild mushroom and venison on the menu. Sure I can't twist your arm?"

"What is it you want?" I asked, bluntly.

He didn't blink. "A chance to get to know you. No hidden agenda. It's not often I get to spend an hour or two with a beautiful woman."

"Mmm. All that flattery. You must want something."

Louis drew a cigarette from a pack and put it between his lips. Struck a lighter.

"Ah, well, since you've brought it up, there is a small matter I should mention."

"Yes?"

"That day at the manor…after I left, I couldn't stop thinking about where and when I might have met your brother-in-law." He exhaled a cloud of smoke. "And then it came to me…" The plume spiraled lazily in the air.

"Go on."

"Right, well, I'm going back some years now. There was a William Westwood who was involved in a fraudulent antique wine auction that became a national scandal. You'll remember this, I'm sure." He smiled expectantly.

"No," I said flatly. "Some years back, I was living in France."

"Ah, I see. Permit me to enlighten you. A number of extremely wealthy and, I have to say, very gullible, wine connoisseurs, some from around these parts, were duped out of a great deal of money by your brother-in-law. Odd coincidence, I know, but one of these was my elder brother, Thys Venter. I find it constantly surprising how small the world is, don't you?"

My heart began drumming loudly. Slowly, disbelieving, I shook my head.

"I don't know what this has to do with me."

"I only mention it because, well, he is your brother-in-law."

I shrugged. "So what?"

He curled his lips. "I imagine there are a few people who'd be interested to hear William Westwood – wanted for fraud by the South African police – has returned to the Cape and taken up in residence at *North Wind Manor*. Obviously, I can't speak for other victims of this crime, but as far as my brother, Thys, is concerned, the mere mention of *Duval Heritage Wines* is like a red rag to a bull."

I spoke slowly. "I'm trying to work out what you're saying." I gave him a long, hard look.

"The fact you're telling *me* this instead of directly confronting William makes me suspect you're threatening to expose my brother-in-law and wondering how far I'll go to buy your silence."

His voice was lightly mocking. "Really? Is that how you see it?"

"You *shit!* You're *blackmailing* me, aren't you?"

Louis Venter hooted with derisive laughter.

I heard my voice getting louder. "Well, you're wasting your time. I've no money, not a bean. And I won't sleep with you if that's what you want to keep quiet about this."

Another bark of laughter. "*Lunch* was what I had in mind, actually. But if you can't or won't join me, I'll enjoy my venison alone."

Venter flung his cigarette on the pavement and ground it with a heel before striding into the restaurant.

I touched my fingers to my cheeks feeling their heat. All the way home, I kept going over what I'd say to William.

Fucking mess…what made you think you could get away with it? That you wouldn't be recognised? People never forget scandals like this! It'll be in all the papers. You'll be sent to rot in jail…and what about us, me and Plum, what's going to happen to the two of us now?

I found William crawling on hands and knees along the upstairs passage. Nervous fizzing bubbled up in my abdomen.

"What are you doing now?" I asked, shrilly.

He looked up, perplexed. "Checking the floor. What do you think I'm doing?"

"I don't know. You're behaving so…"

He frowned. "So…*what?*"

"Look, can we talk? There's something I must tell you. Downstairs, if you don't mind. I can't hear a damn thing up here." I jerked a thumb at two workmen banging nails into skirting boards.

I made tea and poured two cups. "You look like a tramp!" I burst out. "That shirt is filthy and your shoes belong in the bin. I don't understand. This isn't like you. You've always been so fastidious."

"I'm working," William said, mildly, rubbing his dusty hands on his jeans. He sat, elbows on the table, cheek resting in the palm of one hand. His eyelids looked heavy.

"What's the matter? Are you unwell?"

He straightened in the chair. When he spoke, his voice was husky.

"I had this dream. It woke me up. I didn't trust myself to sleep again for fear it would come back. I lost Lily. She was there, right beside me and we were laughing, walking somewhere together – and then she was gone. I stood on the edge of sheer cliffs, looking into rocks below. I roamed the banks of raging rivers that could have swept her away. I hunted smelly, dark caves, feeling the breath of wild animals inside. I remember scooping mud out of a pit, finding one of her shoes. I kept calling her name, over and over and woke myself, shouting 'Lily!', my pillow soaked. All day, I've had this feeling I've been punched in the gut."

"Oh, William." I didn't know what to say.

"The dream. I know what it means. I've lost Lily, that's obvious. But there's something else. A sign everything's going to get worse."

"It's just a dream, Wills."

"You say that, but it felt so real! I can't go through that again, not ever. I'll have to knock myself out with one of your sleeping pills tonight, Frith."

"Drink your tea," I said, quietly. "And have a nap. You need to rest. It'll do you good."

"You wanted to talk about something."

"It'll wait," I said. "It's not important right now."

William slept for three hours and got up just after Plum returned from school.

"I'm off to have a word with the Oom about planting a few fruit trees," he told me, with false enthusiasm. "I was thinking lemons, mulberries, olives."

PLUM

Dad came downstairs looking weird with a pillow crease across his cheek and his hair sticking up on his head so I followed him outside and asked if he was okay.

"Right as rain," he said.

"You sure – only you look a bit 'off'."

"You sound like your aunt. No, no, I'm fine."

"But you never sleep during the day."

"Ah, my little Inspector Jacques Clouseau! I can't hide anything from your prying eyes."

"You can talk to me, you know."

"There is a time to laugh and a time not to laugh and this is not one of them."

"That doesn't make sense."

"I'm quoting Inspector Clouseau. He has another memorable quote that goes: *'Life is not all shoot-shoot, bang-bang, you know.'*"

Dad laughed, like he'd said something very funny.

"You've been talking to yourself quite a lot," I said. "You have long conversations and ask questions and answer them too."

"Doesn't everyone?"

"I don't think so."

"I'll take your word for it, my darling." Dad knocked the side of his head three times with his knuckles. "There!" he said. "I'm clearing my mind. From now on, I shall make every attempt to behave like a sensible, rational human being with his head screwed on the right way."

The Oom was trimming a creeper very slowly with a gigantic pair of rusty old sheers.

Dad told him he wanted to plant fruit trees in the scrubby, overgrown patch behind the wine cellars. "You're the expert, naturally," Dad said. "You'll know whether this is the right site for trees. Failing that, we could plant vegetables. I've always said we should be self-sustaining. Potatoes, tomatoes, pumpkin, lettuce. I'm not over-fond of beetroot but I suppose we could give that a whirl and then there are onions, carrots and whatever else you suggest."

Oom Jacob stared at Dad. "Not there. Not that place."

Dad frowned. "What's the problem? You've got full sun and it's pretty sheltered from the wind."

The Oom shook his head. "There are graves."

Dad got this empty look and it took a while for what the Oom said to sink in. "Good God, man…are you saying there are *bodies* under there?"

Oom Jacob stuck out four fingers and Dad's eyebrows shot up. *"Four* bodies! Bugger me. That surely can't be true!"

The Oom waved for us to follow behind the cellars where the earth is cracked with anthills and there are stones, white as flour laid in patterns.

"I thought there were only two graves," I told the Oom.

Dad growled, "What have you been telling her?"

"It's not the Oom," I said quickly. "It's in her diary – Charlotte Butler wrote about two graves."

There were three stones, big, medium and small, balancing one on top of the other and the Oom dropped on his knees in front of these. "They say a man who died many years ago is buried here."

Dad looked grim. "This is altogether too much for an impressionable twelve-year old," he said in his firm, fatherly voice. "Let's go indoors, Plum."

But I couldn't go without seeing the other graves.

The Oom pointed to a chunk of stone with two letters – PR – scratched into the surface.

Then he took me to a wobbly, crumbly cross – and a little further on, to a circle of chalky stones.

"You're right," I told the Oom. "That's four graves – not two."

We walked back to the house and I used Mom's calm voice to say, "Dad, those graves have been there for over a hundred years – they can't hurt us."

We trooped inside. "You're coming down with something," Aunt Frith told Dad. "You've looking awfully pale."

"There are graves behind the cellar," he said. "Four, according to the Oom. No bloody wonder I have nightmares in this house."

My aunt shot a look at me. "I imagine there are a great many graves in the grounds of old houses like this," she said.

"Two of those dead people were murdered by Edward Butler," I told Dad.

"*Christ!*" Dad shook his head at my aunt. "Why don't you two play Scrabble or cards or something instead of reading that woman's gruesome diary?"

"It's history," I said.

Dad shrugged. "I'm going upstairs to check on the painters and make sure they're not sitting around on their fat arses."

At the stairs he turned and winked at me. "I've just remembered another one: *A woman is like an artichoke. You have to work hard to get at her heart.*'"

A frown was beginning between my aunt's eyebrows. "Don't worry – he's not talking about you," I said. "That's an Inspector Clouseau quote."

I told Aunt Frith that I had a lot of questions about the four graves the Oom had mentioned. "In that case, we should read on," she said and when

I saw she had the diary with the ribbon in our place, waiting, my heart gave a hop of happiness.

"Hang on a sec!" I said and for once she didn't pinch her lips when I ran to fetch Dahlia so she could listen to Charlotte's story.

I watched Aunt Frith's face as she was reading and it was kind of still and flat as if the crackling electricity that's always sparking out of her had been switched off and I couldn't work out if that was a good or a bad thing.

October 21st, 1905

Last evening Dirk and I dined happily at the manor. Magdalena was curious about our guest so I introduced him as a dear cousin from England – a mistake, I believe, since with his sunburned complexion and marked Dutch accent, Mr. Barnard is plainly of South African heritage.

Now that we've properly conversed together, I find the organist deeply sincere and very earnest.

He may also be Calvinistic as is the case with many members of the Strooidak congregation, although this is only speculation for we did not speak of our religious beliefs.

As usual, wine was served with our meal but when Dirk admitted to being a strict teetotaler, Magdalena replaced his goblet with a cup of water "For your next visit," she beamed, "I will make lemonade."

The meal ended and, with Magdalena and Rosa dispatched to their quarters, Dirk and I sat, as cosy as you please at the drawing room fireside. He pressed me to speak of my marriage to Edward and it all spilled out – the unequal years between us, the starved life I lead – starved of love, that is – my husband's aloofness, his infidelity and abominable mental cruelty.

After recounting Edward's acts of brutality to our staff, I dissolved in tears and Dirk gathered me into his arms and held me tight, whispering. "Praise God your husband has left you. You deserve better."

"Do I deserve a man like you?" I replied, gazing into his eyes.

At first, I saw how confounded Dirk was by my comment, but then, drawing me close, he kissed me deeply.

I wish with all my heart I had a sympathetic female friend to talk to for I could gabble for hours of my love for Dirk! I dare not confide in Aletta who is a staunch Christian and will sternly disapprove of an illicit liaison between an older married woman and the Strooidak's most respected young bachelor.

October 28th, 1905

Oh, I am so happy! I bless the day I first cast my eyes upon Dirk. I bless the day he opened his heart to me. I pray to God Edward never returns to North Wind Manor!

Last evening, after our meal, I persuaded Dirk to stay the night and he left at dawn before the servants were up and about.

I stood at the door to wave farewell but could not bear to see him go! I ran to him – a sight to behold in my wrapper and slippers with my hair unpinned – yet I did not care! Dirk jumped down from his gig to hold me one more time. At last he let me go and I waved to my lover until the last puff of dust from the retreating pony's hooves settled before I turned happily back to the house. Sun was breaking and it seemed as if my world was suddenly awash with pink and gold. Never before have I known such joy as this!

November 3rd, 1905

God forgive me, I have such dreams as make me blush!

Ravenous for Dirk, I kiss his cheeks, his mouth. I press my lips upon his eyelids and stroke his silky hair. As his hands touch me, I feel a quickening throughout my body. He calls me 'beloved'!

I wake in laughter and tears. The laughter is for the love and desire I have discovered at last. My salty tears are a foreshadowing of pain. We two are flirting with terrible danger. Our happiness cannot continue forever.

November 10th, 1905

I see in Dirk's doubtful expressions and his too frequent silences that my lover is troubled by his Christian conscience. He imagines critical eyes everywhere and warns me that, unless we are very cautious, the wicked tongues of village gossips will soon be wagging.

Magdalena and Rosa are no longer so warmly hospitable to 'my cousin'. During Dirk's last visit, both women cast sly, knowing glances and I caught

them nudging one another when Dirk touched my hand. They are not fools.
They know Dirk is my lover. I sense their withdrawal of kindness and sympathy.

This morning, as Dirk departed in inky darkness, I spotted a candle feebly
flickering and saw Tobias, Magdalena's eldest son, steadily staring from the
outhouse.

I agree with Dirk that we must protect our secret with careful discretion – yet
cannot pretend the love we share does not exist. Nor do I believe the Almighty
would cast us aside for our sin if he is, as Dirk insists, wise and just.

November 13th, 1905

Were two lovers ever so disparate, so set upon such divergent paths?

I am transported to Heaven while Dirk lives in fear of burning in Hell! Every
day he grows more frantic, tortured by our breaking God's commandments.

Last night he woke from nightmares, crying, "I have committed adultery;
God will punish me!"

Dirk prays to a grim, righteous God who offers salvation only to those who
follow the strict teachings of the Dutch church. Sadly, I sense my lover turning
from me as he leans more closely into the hard, cold bosom of his God. Religion,
I fear, not Edward, may be our ultimate undoing!

November 15th, 1905

I have not laid eyes upon Dr. Thomas Clutterbuck for many weeks and was
astonished to hear his hard rapping at the front door this morning.

After presenting me with gifts of canned tomatoes and a yellow flowering
cactus, the doctor explained his absence saying he had lately been confined to bed
feeling liverish and out-of-sorts.

Keenly, I searched the doctor's seamed face for signs he may have overheard
gossip of Dirk's nightly visits yet saw no obvious disapproval in his frank
expression.

I remained quietly composed and, after we had had tea together, I lied about
a sore throat and the need for bed-rest. The doctor did not hear a false note in
my voice and immediately prescribed linseed tea and liquorice for throat pain.

Before he bade me goodbye, Dr. Clutterbuck handed me a cloth-bound Bible.

"Thank you but I have one of my own," I told him. Nevertheless, the doctor placed the volume in my hand. "Now you have two," he replied in a low voice. "Do you read your Bible every day, Charlotte?"

"I do," I said uncomfortably, wondering if his words held a deeper meaning.

The doctor and Edward are long-time friends and, even now, I believe they are in communication.

It is unwise to consider Thomas Clutterbuck as a confidant or friend – but should I go so far as to suspect him of betrayal? I cannot stop puzzling over the reason for the doctor's unexpected visit.

Was it to spy upon me?

November 18th, 1905

I knew Dirk would come to me last night. I felt certain of it all day.

His first words to me were, "This is rash and dangerous and we both know I should not be here!"

My lover looked unwell – his black alpaca jacket contrasting markedly with his pallor. I held him as he wept upon my bosom. My heart cracks to see him suffer so.

Dirk refused either food or drink though he permitted me to lead him to my bed where we slept, hand in hand, like two innocent children. By morning, though his aspect was sober, Dirk seemed a little recovered. He breakfasted upon milk with bread and sugar, nursery food is all he can stomach.

We kissed goodbye and, as his cart bowled through the gate, I felt a little lighter.

Perhaps all is not yet lost?

November 20th, 1905

I have passed an interminable night of sleeplessness!

Yesterday, I received a letter from Dirk. He tells me he sought guidance from the Dominee who counsels he must atone for his sins through devout prayers, begging forgiveness.

Dirk is now in a fever of repentance. 'Dearest Charlotte, pray for mercy,' he writes. 'Otherwise you will never be included amongst God's chosen few.'

262

And here am I, naively believing that love has already anointed and placed the two of us amongst the chosen!

For many long hours I lay in bed listening to the hooting of the snowy White Owl perched upon the roof. I imagine this great bird priming his talons, sharpening his hooked beak as he watches and listens for scuttling in the undergrowth. I cringe to hear the terrified screams of creatures snatched from their nesting places. How little we know of what life holds in store for us.

November 23rd, 1905

So, my suspicions were correct! Dr. Clutterbuck did come to spy upon me! This man is like a mean-faced ferret, scrutinising me with watchful eyes whilst asking probing questions regarding my daily habits.

Today he quizzed me regarding my companions.

"I have few friends," I told him. "You are one and there is my kind neighbour, Mrs. Prinsloo."

To confound the doctor, I also mentioned Dirk's name in absent fashion, saying he visited, though not frequently. The doctor's eyes gleamed. "How is it you know this man?"

"We share an interest in church music," I replied, guilelessly. "He plays the organ and I am a member of the choir."

The doctor spoke his mind, "But you cannot permit a young man to visit whilst your husband is away! People will talk. You must stop this unseemly behavior until Edward is once more at your side."

An awkward moment followed. Unaccountably, I was gripped with an urge to laugh out loud at the doctor's po-faced expression. "You are right, of course," I replied, demurely. "Though there is nothing in it. We are merely friends with a similar taste in music, as I said."

November 29th, 1905

A parcel arrived from Edward. Opening it, I found a copy of Dickens' 'Bleak House' and a letter.

Here follows, word for word, what my husband wrote:

'Dear Charlotte,

*Suppose I were to divorce you for infidelity – imagine the scandal! Suppose I were to banish you from North Wind Manor and arrange for your speedy return to England? Suppose, I were to take another bride? A fairer, younger woman possessed of such desirable qualities as loyalty, humility, obedience and **gratitude** – gratitude most of all.*

I have it on trusted authority that you are regularly receiving unsuitable guests at the manor.

If this is indeed the case, you may wish to carefully consider the questions I have set out above.

I expect an immediate reply.

Respectfully,

Edward Butler.'

At once, I rode into town where I dispatched a telegram reading:

'Dear Edward,

North Wind Manor is closed to all visitors until your safe and welcome return.

Yours obediently,

Charlotte.'

November 30th, 1905

I heard loud knocking and from my window saw my husband's mendacious spy, Dr. Thomas Clutterbuck. Hastily, I instructed Magdalena to inform the doctor that Captain Butler had sent word his wife was not permitted to receive any visitors. Clutterbuck responded to this news with much blustering but, bless her, Magdalena stood resolute and the physician departed.

So, this is how things stand.

Dirk has abandoned me. The doctor has betrayed me. Edward threatens divorce and banishment from the manor. Could things be worse? Yes, upon reflection, perhaps they could. Thank God for North Wind – the single, unwavering constant in my life. Were it not for the sanctuary of this beloved house, I should be tempted to slash my wrists with a kitchen knife.

December 3rd, 1905

This morning, after a battle with my conscience, I rode to the Strooidak, intending to plead with Dirk to come back to me. I could not find him inside the church and was passing into the garden when the Dominee swiftly approached.

"You must turn away from sin, Mrs Butler," he said. "You must pray to be filled with the Holy Spirit and made whole again with your heart washed pure." His expression was contemptuous.

"You have a low opinion of me, Reverend," I remarked.

He scowled. "You know it is a sin to commit adultery, Mrs. Butler. You are surely aware that you are guilty of doing incalculable harm."

Just then we were interrupted by two chattering ladies and I used this distraction to hurriedly take my leave.

So, the Dominee believes I am a sinner – yet I do not feel wicked. I have been intimate with a man who is not my husband, but how can I pray for forgiveness when I desire nothing more than to be with Dirk even though no good can come from this? I am accused of doing harm though – had I kept my wits – I might have argued with the Dominee that, since my husband does not love me and Dirk is unmarried...who precisely are we harming?

December 10th, 1905

I received a message from Aletta telling me Pretty has returned to Paarl and is resting at the Prinsloo house after her journey from the Cape. I am confused. Why has she come back?

December 12th, 1905

This day finds me in a terrible state! I am overwhelmed with feelings...a passion of love and pity for Pretty. Seething, rancorous hatred for despicable Edward! Oh, how I hate him! And shame...shame for all of us!

I visited Aletta who immediately called for my maid and, as Pretty came near, I saw she was with child and was aghast...poor Pretty is but a child herself!

I made myself smile. "I see you have happy news."

Pretty shook her head and I observed how ill, weak and haggard she appeared. Oddly, she seemed to also wear an air of secretiveness, refusing to meet my eyes and looking everywhere but at me.

"What is the matter, Pretty?" I asked. When she would not answer, I turned to Aletta.

"Will you tell me?"

"Can you not guess?" Aletta cried out, uncharacteristically flustered.

Dreadful comprehension dawned.

Can it be true Pretty is carrying Edward's child?

CHAPTER TWENTY FOUR

FRITH

I've been examining two photographs. Each tells its own story. The first is of William aged fourteen or so. He's fishing at the edge of a lake and seems taken aback by the intrusion of the camera. His eyes are wide with surprise and there's the beginning of a smile on his lips. You can see when he fills out he'll be handsome in a way that will make even nice girls misbehave. There's something else you can see in this photograph, something written in the vulnerability of his clear, open, good-natured face…this is a boy who'll grow up to be a man with a breakable heart.

The other photograph is of Lily and me. We're about sixteen, dressed in peculiar clothes, old-fashioned – even for that time – twin-sets, longish pleated skirts, flat brogues.

Some would say we're identical – and at first glance we are – but there's a marked difference. Lily is softer, gentler, kinder. Her face is rounder, her eyes are trusting and her mouth curves up naturally. I'm the one with the frown knotting the brow of my serious, thin face.

This photograph is disturbing in a way that's difficult to articulate. The girl on the right is the one everyone will fall in love with. That's Lily. The other girl is less loveable and from the way she's standing with shoulders back and head held high, you can tell there's nothing fragile about the cone-shaped muscle pumping away behind her sternum. This is a heart that will keep issuing the normal thirty-eight million or so beats every year, come what may. There's another thing you can tell from this picture. This twin has the flame of a hungry fire in her eyes and a sense of purpose in her militant jaw and though she's too young to know what she wants from life, she already intends to be more than the loving wife and mother her sister is destined to be.

Growing up, I didn't like myself as much as I wanted to and admired Lily much more, and, as we got older, I began to actively dislike certain immutable qualities I possessed.

Qualities like selfishness, lack of empathy and a hardness that started creeping into my face as early as sixteen.

I've changed since Lily died. I'm not the same person. I can't say with certainty what caused the change. Maybe being back in this country is eating away at the core of who I am.

Maybe it's because I'm getting older. Then again, these changes might be the result of sharing the same sad space with Wills and Plum and all of us still grieving for our Lily.

I've lost my confidence. When I look in the mirror, I see a stranger with finger-nails chewed to the quick. This woman seems shadowy, insecure, vulnerable – and so thin-skinned you see her fear and anxiety swarming just beneath the surface.

I think I can explain the nervousness. It comes from the weight of responsibility for Plum with the added burden of having to deal with an oddly unhinged William.

I've never been prescient but lately I can't overcome a morbid sense we may be in some kind of danger. Logically, I suppose, this springs from a combination of Louis Venter's veiled threat, the woman on the wine farm recognising Lily in me, Plum going on about a spirit in the house. If you toss Charlotte Butler's disturbing diary into the mix, it's no wonder I'm seeing only dark clouds – no silver linings.

Our mother was one of those gloomy 'end-of-the-world-is-nigh' types, so this might be genetic. As she got older, Julia turned jittery as a cat and so scatter-brained she'd have to keep peering in the glass to remember what her face looked like. Wouldn't it be ironic if, instead of becoming more like Lily, I turned into Julia?

This morning, I found William leafing through a pile of invoices. He looked up and smiled.

"You okay?" I asked.

He nodded. "Never felt better!"

I got right to it. "Remember that lawyer…Louis Venter…the man who dropped in last week?"

He squinted vaguely. "What about him?"

"Well, I bumped into him in town. He made a point of telling me his brother was one of the bidders in the Duval antique wine auction."

William gave me a long, level look. "Is that true?"

This wasn't the answer I expected. "Why would I tell you if it wasn't?"

Shrugging, William turned to his invoices again.

"Anyway, I'm worried that he – not Venter, the brother – well, what if he reports you to the police?"

"Ah, I see where this is going." A ghost of a smile flickered.

"What that's supposed to mean?"

"You don't like this house. You've avoided any involvement in the restoration. You've made it clear you're simply biding your time, waiting for me to be done so you can pack your bags and leave with a clear conscience."

I gaped. "What's that got to do with Venter's brother going to the police?"

William's mouth lifted in an insincere smile. "Well, think about it. Your story plays rather well into the outcome you're hoping for, doesn't it?"

His tone was supercilious. I wanted to slap his smug face. "Now you've lost me. What outcome would that be?"

"Don't take me for a muggins, Frith, that's all I'm saying. You'd like nothing more than for me to bolt back to England in a panic, tail between my legs. Then you can say you were right all along and hive off to your cushy little flat in France."

Calmly, William stapled a receipt and started tapping buttons on a calculator.

Holding myself rigid, arms folded across my chest, I tried again.

"So, you're going to sit here and wait for the police to arrest you?"

William scribbled in a margin. At length he looked up.

He spoke politely. "I'm not sure what you suggest I do. Threaten this man? Turn myself in? Go into hiding? Don't answer please, it's all rhetorical. And now, if you have no objection, I'd prefer not to discuss this further."

Bands of iron tightened around my brow. Unchecked, this would tip into a migraine.

I shivered. That room…so frigidly cold it was *excruciating*.

I shook my head. "You've lost your mind! First, you're hiding away like a terrified rat. Then…after I've told you you've been recognised…you shrug it off as if it's…as if it's *nothing!*"

Humming now, William bowed over his invoices, blatantly ignoring me.

"*Stupid shit!*" I shouted.

His expression was pained. "I hope Plum can't hear you."

"There's none so blind as those who will not see," I said. Another of Julia's gems.

He didn't reply. "I'm going out," I blurted. Fighting an urge to slam the door, I shot down the stairs two at a time.

We were doing life-drawing. A young model was waiting – an ash-faced wraith wearing what looked like an old, slippery nightie with a moth-eaten shawl draped over her shoulders. She had white blond hair, dark at the roots and her eyes were light and glassy, like someone genetically blighted with transparent irises.

I stepped closer and saw her eyes were cerulean – it was the angle she was sitting at that made the light suck up the blue, giving her that mystifyingly empty look.

"Odd eyes," I said to Chen who frowned at me.

She'd sketched the figure in the chair with her hands tightly clenching the knot of the shawl; elbows lifted like wings; narrow toes pressing against the floor; heels in the air as if poised for flight. I felt a quick stab of envy. Chen had created a fine tension in her pencil drawing that was completely missing in mine.

"I love how you've made her seem…agitated," I whispered.

The brittle chinking Chen made tapping her paintbrush against a glass water jar suggested annoyance.

"Sorry," I murmured. "I'll shut up, shall I?"

Olympia arrived to apologise for Theo's lateness and the class tittered in a scoffing way. She's a chameleon, Theo's wife, different look every day. She'd masked her olive skin with pale foundation to complement a strawberry suit worn with a silk blouse as pink as the inside of a seashell.

It wasn't easy to gauge her mood. She was, as usual, playing the consummate professional, engaging in light banter and laughing in her ascending way but, behind the polished façade, she was as tense as a wire.

As I stared, Olympia glanced insidiously at the model who recoiled, changing her pose.

"Damn and blast!" Donald bellowed rudely. "Sit *still* will you!"

Olympia's eyes narrowed as she sent a searing sidelong look at the model.

Perturbed, the girl wiggled her bum to the edge of the chair.

There was an outburst from the class: "As you were!" "Please don't move!"

Then Theo walked in. Bewildered, he turned to Olympia. "What are you doing here? You said you were going to town."

I caught the sharp look from her glittering eyes to his uncanny green ones. Theo spun around to face the class. He spoke brusquely.

"Er…sorry, folks. There's been a change of plan. Nicole's not feeling well. Class is cancelled. That's all for today, I'm afraid."

There was a collective groan as the model hopped off the chair and flew into the gallery.

"Now what?" shouted Donald, clearly put-out. "Can't you find someone else?"

A light sweat dotted Theo's brow. "Yes, yes, no problem. Tomorrow I'll have another model to take Nicole's place."

Olympia bristled. "*Anyone* would be better than that…anorectic plucked hen!" she said shrilly.

The model must have heard her. She sprinted back towards the courtyard and, looking around frantically, grabbed an open jar of paint and hurled it at Olympia.

Cadmium red spattered like blood across the strawberry jacket, the silky blouse, the mid-calf skirt and tottering rose pumps.

"Fucking bitch!" Nicole screamed. "Fucking, *fat, ugly* bitch!"

"*OMG!*" exclaimed Donald, dramatically. He turned to me. "Quick, what do you see? Don't think about it. Tell me what comes *immediately* to mind."

I answered mechanically. "They've had an affair – Theo and that girl. Olympia knows."

He frowned. "No, not that, that's nothing – Theo's had *hundreds* of affairs! No, no…I'm thinking of November 22nd, 1963. The day Kennedy was assassinated in Dallas. Jackie in that classy pink suit drenched with the President's blood. See it now?" Donald smirked. "Acrylic paint can be a bugger. Olympia won't get that off in a hurry!"

I packed away my sketchbook and pencils. '*Theo's had hundreds of affairs…*'

Then he was at my elbow, sober-faced and contrite. He spoke in a whisper. "Can we meet for coffee in ten minutes? I need to talk."

Aware of Donald's keen glance in our direction, I kept my voice low.

"You should stay and make peace with Olympia."

He shook his head carelessly. "She's gone off in a huff."

On the way to the coffee shop, I kept replaying the scene in my mind: the model reaching for the paint; her awful shriek hanging in the air; Olympia, blotting the ruined suit with a wad of tissues, fingers visibly shaking; Theo, looking on with barely concealed amusement as the drama played out.

He ordered cappuccinos and reached for my hand. I snatched it away.

"You're a first class prick!"

"Me?" He pretended innocence.

"I saw you! Trying not to laugh at that shouting match between Olympia and your model."

Theo grinned idly. "You must admit…"

I went on accusingly. "You *slept* with that girl!"

His jaw dropped. "Whaa…?"

"You and that woman had an affair. Oh, don't insult me by denying it. You'd have to be a complete fool not to see what's going on. You're asking for trouble. Who uses their ex-lover to pose for a class with his wife hanging around? Talk about flinging your sex life in Olympia's face!"

Theo's nostrils flared. "*Jesus H. Christ!* Where do you get off being so fucking judgmental? Nicole needs the money. Olympia said she'd be out all morning. I was tricked, okay. Change the subject, 'eh?"

I heard a tight-edged warning in his voice. "What do you want to talk about?"

Theo spooned the frothy topping of the cappuccino into his mouth, playing for time, smiling in an abstracted way. "You know how much I'm attracted to you, don't you?"

I let the question lie. *Here it comes. He's tired of me.*

He cleared his throat. "I have a hunch she knows. Olympia mentions your name too often for my liking. That's a sure sign she's guessed something's up."

There was no hint of emotion in his voice. His expression was as smooth as blancmange.

Hurt, I spoke bluntly. "I knew this was coming. So it's over? Is that what you're saying?"

He licked a moustache of froth off his top lip. "Over?"

"You're breaking up with me."

Theo shook his head. "God, no! Last thing on my mind. All I'm suggesting is that we fly under the radar for a while."

"What's that mean?"

"Well, I've been thinking…Perhaps if you could drop out of art class we can put paid to any cheap gossip going around."

It wasn't what I'd expected to hear. "Oh."

He saw my expression lighten. Theo leaned in close. A whiff of tobacco on his breath.

"Surely you know how much I adore being with you? The sex between us is…"

I don't know why, I can't explain. I began giggling like a young girl, holding a finger to my lips. "*Shhh!* People will hear."

I cringe to think of it. Stupid cow I am!

PLUM

Mom used to ask if I had a blank when I was tired or too excited but a blank comes from nowhere like a blowy wind after a still day and there's nothing you can do to stop it.

Sometimes there are clues before it happens like black spots dancing in the jelly in my eyes then spit in my mouth dries up and lights switch off and noise gets sucked away and then…*nothing*.

I don't know how long a blank lasts but when it's over my tongue is big as a shoe in my mouth and my arms and legs are weak and watery like drooping flower stalks on a hot day.

I haven't told Dad or Aunt Frith I've been having more blanks because I don't want them thinking there's a tumour growing in my brain or anything creepy like that.

That's also why I haven't said anything about this weird dream I've been having like every night for a week or maybe more.

Soon as I fall asleep this baby pops up in my dream and I see her clear as anything – tiny with peach-fuzz skin and an open mouth like a hungry bird. The dream is always the same.

I'm in the cobwebby attic and the baby's in the cradle screaming her head off, kicking her legs, waving her arms…opening her mouth wide… wider…until it's a black hole big enough to swallow me and I'm going to fall in and want to yell but nothing comes out and that's when I make myself wake up.

After the dream I think of the spirit for comfort – imagining her floating through the window from the dark where clouds of sleepy moths bump against night lamps, circling through the house, passing like mist under locked doors, drifting up to touch the glassy drops on the chandelier.

She glides up the Queen's staircase sliding her hand along the banisters and there isn't even the faintest mouse-creak because she weighs nothing but I see her nose twitching at the earthly smell of us – our skin and hair and feet – Mom's Chanel Number Five behind my ears, a choking stink from paint drying on walls and the smell of Dad's miserableness.

I know in a way I can't explain that the spirit and the dream and the attic fit together like Lego but puzzling about this gives my mind fuzzy edges and makes everything soft and blurry and that's when I fall asleep again.

This morning Aunt Frith asked if I remembered crying in my sleep.

No, I said.

Are you all right? You were dreaming.

You sounded…frightened.

I wasn't.

Are you sure? You were saying something that sounded like…

Like what?

Um…I forget now.

She had a shifty look so I must've been talking about Mom. It never goes away, not really. You think everything's okay and you're getting used to living with Dad and Aunt Frith at *North Wind* and going to Paarl High and sharing breaks with Bronte but then you dream about Mom and it's like you've been dumped by a humungous wave with all the wind knocked out of you and salt stinging your eyes and your heart squeezed like an orange.

I don't blame Mom for wanting to die. I heard her tell my aunt cancer was like razor teeth nibbling away inside until the person she used to be started disappearing, little by little.

She began forgetting stuff and talking about long ago when she and my aunt were kids and this one time I helped her to the bathroom she said, "Where are we?" and after that I worried she might forget who I was.

When I told her I was scared about her dying Mom looked into my eyes and whispered, "I won't be far away, darling. You might not see me but I swear I'll be up there with the sun, the moon and stars, looking down on you from heaven and keeping you safe."

After Mom got really sick, Aunt Frith and Dad used to make up stuff for me to do so I wouldn't spend too much time with her but I had a hidey-hole behind the dusty blue curtains and I'd sneak in when she was sleeping and stay listening to her breathing until they started calling for me.

I know Mom wanted to die because I heard her tell Dad the pain was too much and she didn't want me to remember her like this and please would he help her but Dad shouted, "No, no my darling! Don't ask me. I could *never* do anything to harm you."

Then Mom begged Aunt Frith.

My aunt said quietly, "Sssh! Little jugs have big ears. Take your pills and let's not talk about this now. Later, okay?"

Early next morning, Aunt Frith crept into my bed and put her arms around me and that's when I knew for certain. I raced to her room where Mom was lying very still with her face like a candle that's blown out and Dad was bending over her crying, "Don't leave me, Lily!" with his words coming out all mangled and snotty.

"She's at peace now, Wills," my aunt said.

But Dad cried for the longest time and only stopped when I said Mom hadn't left us.

"A host of angels carried her to heaven but she can still love us and keep us safe from there, that's what she told me and when I asked, 'Are you sure?' she said "A promise is a promise.'"

CHAPTER TWENTY FIVE

FRITH

Theo touches me with a reverence shown only by men who truly love women and handle them as if they're infinitely precious.

I've come to know his hands almost as well as my own. Long artist's fingers with a faint sheen of silvery hair on the knuckles…a small valley in the nail of his right thumb where it was once trapped in a car door…rough, weathered, sun-spotted skin with the fingertips worn to silky smoothness.

At night, before sleep, I will myself to dream about sex with Theo. I float away imagining his hands stroking my neck, shoulders and breasts before slowly working their way to the shallow dip where my stomach drops beneath my ribs. From here, they slide down my thighs to my calves, ankles and the soles of my feet where they pause to slowly massage my heel, instep and toes before returning on their slow, purposeful journey. Always, as they're gently working back to the top of my thighs, the dream ends abruptly leaving me aroused and disappointed.

I never intended to become obsessed. A meaningless sexual fling, I thought. A chance to feel desirable again, that's it, nothing more. And yet I can't stop thinking about this egotistical, lazy, habitually philandering, middle-aged artist with a string of easy conquests behind him and an uncanny ability to charm birds from trees.

There's nothing in my face that hints I'm in thrall to this man aside from the occasional jolt of unexpected happiness bubbling to the surface or a feeble inclination to become tearful without reason. I've purposefully submerged my desire for Theo to a place where it lies undetected like an iceberg skulking in the deep. It would be fatal if Theo's sensitive receptors were to become attuned to my inexplicable yearning for him. He's made it plain he can't stand emotion or, God forbid, *neediness.*

We made love yesterday and, as he was painting me afterwards, I spotted a pewter statue of a cat on his workbench. "That's new," I said.

He didn't reply. "I'm guessing this is your anniversary gift from Olympia?"

Slowly, deliberately, he mixed paint before looking up. "Oh, that? Yes, it's from my wife." His voice changed. "It's an Abyssinian cat. Ever heard of the Goddess Bastet, eh?" He didn't wait for me to answer. "Well, the name means, *'She of Bast'* – named after the Egyptian cat temple in Bast, where thousands gathered every year to…"

Bored, I interrupted. "Do you mind? We're not in class now. All this lecturing…it gets a bit much, you know."

"Fair enough!" He snorted with laughter. "I'll say no more."

But I couldn't leave it there. After a second or two, I asked, "So…have you ever considered leaving Olympia?"

"No," he said, shortly. And then, "I'm parched. Whisky or tea?"

Running water into the kettle, he snatched a glance at his watch.

"Oh, am I keeping you?" I asked, offended. I flung aside the sheet and groped for my clothes. "You expecting Olympia soon?"

He gave a languid smile. "We've easily a good half an hour or so before she's due."

I heard myself sounding acerbic. "You always make me feel as if I'm being dismissed."

"That's rubbish!"

"Is it?"

"Yeah, it is. Is it milk and sugar?"

"Oh, don't worry! I'll skip the tea. That'll save time."

I splashed cold water over my face. A warning chirped: *Don't do this. Stay calm. Keep it together. Don't show how much you care…you'll ruin everything.*

Lightly, Theo touched my damp cheek. "Have tea before you go."

With a sigh, I pulled out a chair and accepted a cup.

He spoke levelly. "I'll never leave Olympia – there, I've said it. Now you know so don't ask again, please. But I do have feelings for you – very strong feelings – and the sex is fucking fantastic!"

I gulped a mouthful of tea. "It's hard to tell what you feel, if anything. You never say much."

His jaw clenched. "Are you listening? I've just told you how I feel. How much I want you."

I nodded miserably. "Yes – and it's like yanking teeth getting you to admit it."

He rolled his eyes. "Are we okay, Frith? Only you seem...annoyed."

Annoyed? You don't know the bloody half of it!

I stared dully at the pewter cat. She looked so dignified, upright, tall and lean with pointed ears erect and paws neatly together. Her slanted black-rimmed eyes, gold-flecked irises, exotic jeweled collar and the flattened diadem fitting her narrow head denotes her as Egyptian. Olympia has exquisite taste.

Theo's head was tilted, waiting for my answer.

I nodded at the statue. "Looks heavy. Solid pewter. Must've cost a bit."

He shrugged. "I suppose. So...you and me...we're okay, eh?"

It was getting late. I couldn't be bothered with an argument.

"Yes, of course."

Another slow smile. "Good. Glad that's over. More tea?"

"Why a cat? Is it symbolic?"

"Ah!" He grinned, amused. "Bastet is no ordinary feline. She's a 'Sacred Protector'."

"What's that mean?"

"She's here to guard me."

I looked into those slanted black-rimmed eyes, into Bastet's gold-flecked irises and, just for a moment, thought I saw a watchful gleam hiding there.

When I got home to *North Wind*, a team of four house painters were idly waiting for William to deliver a drum of white interior paint. "He's been gone since nine," one complained.

I called William's mobile. There was no reply so I left a message: "Where are you? The men are waiting for the paint!"

William's started doing this – vanishing for hours at a time. It's obvious he's depressed. There's nothing subtle about Will's misery – it's like the glutinous trail following a slug. He was like this after Lily died but I didn't expect his mood to continue for this long.

Not when he should be making a life for himself and Plum.

The day before, he'd been out from morning until late.

"Why do you keep disappearing?" I asked.

"I need a quiet place to think. All this dust and noise is making me ill."

"But, you have to stay on site, Wills. You said so yourself. These men need supervision."

He seemed confused. "I have to clear my head. There's too much chaos."

"You mean in the house?"

"No, I mean in my mind."

"Oh."

We've been talking about getting a housekeeper, someone responsible to help cook, clean and supervise Plum after school. William placed an advertisement in a 'Job Opportunities Group' on Facebook. I'm interviewing a candidate today and, fingers crossed, she turns out to be a competent, decent woman, reliable enough to take my place when I finally leave.

This woman is Zimbabwean. Her name is Tawanda Chikera. She's e-mailed excellent references attesting to cooking, child-care, cleaning and even gardening skills. Previous employers speak highly of her ability to deal with children and the elderly, painting a picture of someone who's patient and tolerant in the face of tantrums from young or old.

Miss Chikera arrived half an hour early. Opening the door, I gasped. One half of the woman's face was horribly scarred and disfigured. On the right side, the skin was shriveled and pulled taut. Both eyelids on this side were fused and the right half of her mouth sealed in a droop that made her seem sardonic, even when she smiled. Her right ear was turned in upon itself like a folded flower with petals tightly closed.

Then there was her right arm – the skin hideously twisted and marred – and she walked in a hop-and-skip style with an awkward gait, her right leg shorter than the left.

Discretely, Miss Chikera turned her good side to me. This half was pretty, the skin smooth, the eye clear and shining, this side of her mouth smilingly upturned.

It's impossible to guess her age – she could be anything from thirty-five to fifty – but she admitted to being twenty-five, unmarried and childless. She'd trained as a senior school teacher in Harare but, as an illegal immigrant in South Africa, her options have been sadly reduced to domestic work. She offered this information warily, her one good eye gazing sadly.

"What happened?" I asked. "To your face, I mean."

"A fire," she answered simply. "I am fortunate to be alive."

She drooled on the burned side of her mouth and kept dabbing the leaking moisture with a tissue.

"I need this job," she said, directly. "I would very much like to work for you."

I caught myself stammering. "The thing is…the house is very big." I gestured at her leg, "You may find it tricky managing the stairs. It's a lot of work for…someone with…um…your…" I closed my mouth before uttering the word, *'disabilities'*.

"It's not only cleaning and cooking," I added. "You'd have to care for my brother-in-law and his daughter…um…so you might find this position comes with more responsibility than you can handle."

"Me?" She laughed shortly. "I can handle anything."

"Well, if you'll follow me, I'll show you around."

Miss Chikera half-ran to keep up as I led her through the rooms of *North Wind*.

Striding ahead, I tried to imagine the house through a stranger's eyes.

The late afternoon sun was turning a layer of newly settled dust to gold as we moved between the upstairs rooms. William's decorated these spaces with expensive contemporary furniture upholstered in pale fabrics, light oak tables, chairs and cupboards.

I couldn't help thinking how different everything would have looked with Lily's signature touches – soft, plumped cushions…draped throws… vases of fresh flowers, walls of books, paintings, pottery and glass. Without Lil, these stark white rooms are as impersonal as an unfinished stage set.

Tawanda halted at Plum's portrait.

"This is good," she said with certainty.

"Think so? It's a painting I did of my niece, Plum."

She nodded solemnly. "I too come from a family of artists. My mother and I paint. My father sculpts in fruitwood. My brother is a carver in Rapoko stone."

I lifted my eyebrows in query. "Soapstone," she explained. "The oldest mineral in Africa – first found in the tombs of Pharaohs."

I found myself warming to her. "So, what do you paint?"

"I paint from nature but…please!" Urgently, she gripped my arm. "This house is not too big. I would be grateful for the work. I cannot return to Zimbabwe. There is nothing for me there, nothing for any of us."

I was touched by her pleading but, all the same, held back. "Before we make any final decisions, you must meet my brother-in-law and his daughter, Plum."

She smiled lopsidedly. "Thank you. I would like to meet the girl in the painting."

PLUM

"Our panel has chosen an essay written by one of the students in this class as our Grade Seven entry into the *National Book Day Short Story Competition*."

'Please, please, Miss Cooper, don't let it be me!'

I sent this message to my English teacher with my eyes but she showed her rabbit teeth in a big smile.

"Plum Westwood, stand up, please." Miss Cooper nodded kindly at me. "We found your story most unusual. It's sensitively written and very eloquent. Congratulations, my dear."

I looked around the classroom. Eyes staring back. Annelie Swart twirling her hair. Tanya sticking out her tongue. Roxy giving the finger.

"Plum?"

Miss Cooper was waiting for me to say something but I couldn't speak. Tanya started laughing like a hyena.

"Thanks, Miss Cooper," I said and sat with a bump.

At break Samantha, Zelda, Carika and Tanya crowded around Roxy as she walked on tiptoes, swaying her hips like Miss Cooper. She spotted me, cupped her hands around her mouth and shouted, "Breaking News! Our very own resident genius, Plum Westwood…recently voted 'National Suck-Up-To-Teachers Student of the Year'…has written a stupid, soppy story that's been entered into…"

The bell rang. They filed into class and I was left in the quadrangle breathing like I'd been running hard. I couldn't face them, so I got on my bike and rode home.

Dad and Aunt Frith were out and I was gulping cold milk from the carton and thinking how it would serve them all right if I won the competition when this terrifying person wearing what looked like an ugly Halloween mask walked into the kitchen and I jumped six feet into the air.

Her hand flew up. "Don't be frightened," she said. "My name is Tawanda. You are Plum, am I right?"

"Your poor, poor face. Does it hurt?"

"There is tightness and pulling…but it's been so long…I'm used to the pain."

She said Aunt Frith had gone out to fetch some paint. "I am looking for a position as a housekeeper here. Your aunt wishes that I meet with you and your father."

I had a feeling Dad would run a mile if he saw her.

"I have seen a painting of you," she said. "It is a very good likeness."

"I *hate* it!" I told her. "Have you been to the attic yet?"

She shook her head. I knew Aunt Frith would never have shown Tawanda the attic.

"The attic is my private space where I go to be quiet and think."

She gave a twisty smile. "Then I would like to see your attic."

The attic never gets cleaned so it's dusty like a forgotten place where family secrets are locked away forever. When she saw the cradle and rocking horse, Tawanda said, "Ahh...this was once a baby's room."

"That's what I think but my aunt says these things are just stored up here."

Tawanda moved to the window and a square of light fell over the good side of her face and made her seem beautiful. I sat cross-legged on the dusty floor and she sat beside me. After a few minutes I asked if she felt anything.

"What should I feel?"

"There's a spirit living in here."

She put her hand flat on the place where her heart is. "So you feel a spirit in this room?"

"Sometimes." It made me happy to have a proper conversation about the spirit. "Dad and Aunt Frith think I'm making it all up."

"I believe you. My mother is a spirit medium. My grandmother, on my mother's side, was also one but she died and crossed over."

"What's a spirit medium?"

"A person with the power to talk to our deceased ancestors."

That sounded thrilling. "Tell me more."

"I am from the Shona Tribe of Zimbabwe. Many of our women are bestowed with the gift of communicating with the dead."

"Can *you* talk to dead people?"

"Sadly, I have not been blessed."

"Oh."

"But, like you, I have felt the presence of the *mudzimu* – this is the name we give to wandering guardian spirits."

"So how do we feel spirits when other people can't?"

Tawanda shook her head. "I do not know the answer but I believe most people are fearful of the unknown. This may make them deaf and blind to the presence of ancestor spirits."

I heard Aunt Frith calling.

"My aunt's back," I said. "I want her to hear what you've just told me. She doesn't believe me when I talk about the spirit. Stay here while I fetch her."

"I've met Tawanda," I told my aunt.

She frowned. "Do you find her face…*off-putting?*"

"At first but you get used to it. She's from the Shona Tribe. She says she can feel the *mudzimu* – that's a new word I've just learned – it means…

"Where is she?"

"In the attic."

"Good grief! What's she doing there? It's *filthy!* Ask her to join us for tea. Your father should be back any minute. I'd like him to meet her and hear what he thinks."

I was going to climb the stairs when Tawanda came stumbling down. She tripped and saved herself falling to the bottom by holding onto the banisters. Her hands were shaking and her face was sweating.

"The spirit in this house is *evil!*" She stared with her good eye. "*Ngozi!*"

"What's that?"

"*Ngozi* are ancestors whose lives have ended with *the spilling of blood.*"

"You mean *murder?*" I breathed.

"You and your family must leave this place. It is not safe to stay here."

I watched her hobbling down the stairs then the door banged and she was gone.

I didn't want to forget the word so I said it to myself twice – '*Ngozi… ngozi*'.

"She's gone," I told Aunt Frith.

"What happened? Why did she leave without saying goodbye?"

"Dunno."

My aunt sighed. "Oh, Lord, I shouldn't say this – but I'm glad she's gone. Such a relief! I knew this house was too big for her with that leg. I thought we were stuck with her. It's bound to be illegal to turn someone down for a job just because her face is scarred."

I scooted upstairs. I don't know what evil looks or feels like but had to find out what had made Tawanda run away.

I couldn't feel the spirit at first but after a little while the white light began slowly to fill the room and my body tingled from head to toes. There was a smell – warm and spicy – and I knew she was with me and she wasn't evil.

Then the tingling stopped, the window clanged shut, the light got swallowed by shadows and the smell grew faint and went away.

We were eating dinner when I breathed in the same warm spicy smell again. I tried to work out where it was coming from. Not from Dad's beloved stinky blue cheese or garlic in the pasta or sweet peaches turning soft and brown in the fruit basket.

I ticked off smells…not roses or honeysuckle not vanilla not pillow spray or pine toilet cleaner or Cobra furniture polish or those little pink musk-scented sweets.

Then I remembered the orange and clove pomander balls Mom kept in her bedroom after she got sick.

They're easy to make. You stick an orange all over with cloves, wet it a bit and roll it in a bowl of spices and when the orange is dry, you tie it with a ribbon, red is best though you can also use green or blue.

"Long ago, people carried pomanders to ward off bad smells."

"What kind of bad smells?"

"You don't want to know."

"I do."

"Unwashed bodies…rotting teeth…bad breath…dirty linen…lack of sanitation. In those days they believed pomanders could ward off infections."

"So could these make you better, do you think?"

"You never know…maybe."

That's when we started telling lies, Mom and me…pretending a bowl of oranges stuck with prickly cloves could make her well again and all through dinner and late into the night I smelled oranges and cloves and ached for Mom.

CHAPTER TWENTY SIX

FRITH

Regular as clockwork, we make love once a week on Theo's rumpled bed or the sagging non-too-clean couch. A couple of times, we have become carried away and had sex like teenagers on the floor and once, memorably, on his hard, rickety table. I'm too old for this lark – now I've a splinter in my bum.

Theo's accumulated a dozen canvases – variously rendered in oil, acrylic and pastel – showing me semi-nude. These are turned to the wall – presumably to shield them from Olympia – though there's little danger of my being recognised since he paints me without a face. I can't help feeling hurt by this and the way he also obscures my identity by mutating my hair from straight chestnut to tousled blonde, dull frizzy mouse and a hideous shade of carroty orange.

His rendering of my body is unflatteringly accurate. He's faithfully captured my small, flattish breasts, long legs and bony hips down to the faint silvery striations weaving across the tops of my thighs. By reducing me to flat planes, gaunt lines and sharp edges, he's made me seem unsexy, even boyish.

The new bathrooms at *North Wind* have huge rectangular mirrors with beveled edges lit by tidily concealed spotlights. These mirrors reveal every flaw in exaggerated detail.

Whenever I timidly step from the shower into the blue-white glare of the glass; I'm struck anew by the hard shelf of my rib-cage, the spindly awkwardness of my elbows and knees and hollow depressions beneath each clavicle. God knows it's impossible to fathom how Theo finds this stringy, sinewy, angular woman desirable.

This morning, Olympia called and smoothly asked if I could visit her at the gallery.

"Yes, of course," I answered, slightly breathless. "What do you want to see me about?"

"A little chat, that's all."

My heart sank as I disconnected the call.

I waited a couple of hours to summon the strength to call at the gallery, prepared to face the worst.

Olympia extended a hand tipped with ice-blue nails.

"You've lost weight," she said crisply. "Not sure it suits you."

Stylishly dressed in slim-fitting black trousers and a scarlet silk shirt, she appeared, at first, to be wearing a dead animal on her shorn hair but it turned out to be a hairy black beret, probably Cashmere.

I accepted Olympia's offer of coffee and she disappeared to the kitchen leaving me with an undisturbed view of the courtyard. Theo was addressing a higgledy-piggledy group of artists in his pedagogical voice.

Returning with a tray, Olympia announced, "Theo's got them painting Egyptian mummy portraits."

How pretentious. I took a cup. "Sounds revolting!"

"Not at all – I think it's ingenious. You know about mummy portraits, of course? The Egyptians used to paint a likeness of the dead and bandage it over the face of the mummy."

I gave a sickly smile.

Sugaring her coffee, Olympia went on, "It's fascinating, once you get into it." Her expression was intense. "Hooks were used to pull the brain through the nose before it was thrown on a rubbish heap." She smiled, inappropriately. "The Egyptians had it all wrong. They turfed the brain and preserved the heart as the seat of intelligence."

Nauseated, I took a gulp of coffee, wondering how long it would take before she accused me of having an affair with her husband.

In the courtyard, Theo was talking to a young woman. They were standing too close. A private look passed between them and the intimacy of this glance made me gasp.

Olympia blinked. "Anything wrong?"

"Er…no. Who's that tall blonde? A new student?"

"I think so." Olympia was still intent upon edifying me. "Once the cadaver was dry, it was anointed with oils before being wrapped in layers of white linen glued with resin. Only at the end was the mummy mask placed over the head." Pointedly, she held my eye. "You know that quote? *'Behind every mask there is a face, and behind that a story'?*"

WTF? "I think so. Um, you wanted to see me about something?"

"Oh yes…" Olympia downed the last of her coffee.

"Theo's painted a series of nudes. Have you seen them?"

I watched her mouth moving. My ears were blocked with the *boom, boom, boom-diddy-boom* drumbeat of my heart.

Here it comes! What do I say?

"If you'll follow me, Frith."

I looked down, latching onto Olympia's sandals. Black leather, studded with circles of coloured glass that winked as she strode towards a wall displayed with Theo's abstracts. Eight nudes. I recognised every one.

Olympia stared at the wall and then at me.

"I don't know what you want me to say," I started out.

She shook her head. "Oh, I'm not asking for a critique," she stated, matter-of-fact. "Theo's received rave reviews from all quarters. No, it's not that. It's your brother-in-law I want to talk about."

Like a beached fish, I opened and closed my mouth. "My brother-in-law?"

"Yes. He visited the gallery yesterday."

"Oh."

What the fuck was William doing at the gallery?

"Your brother-in-law studied these nudes for a long time. Then he summoned me. Seemed convinced the canvases were paintings of the same woman. I told him he was mistaken and, as far as I know, Theo had used different models." Olympia paused. "He seemed upset, your brother-in-law. He was sweating, a little short of breath. He insisted it was the same woman in all of the canvases."

Shit, shit, shit!

"He pointed out similarities – wide shoulders, small breasts, narrow waist, jutting hips, tapered legs. And then, for no reason I can think of, your brother-in-law..."

"William," I interrupted, testily. "His name is *William.*"

"Yes, well, William turned on me. He was furious. His eyes were blazing. He shouted the model in Theo's paintings was his wife's twin sister. Unless I'm mistaken – that's *you!*"

My stomach flip-flopped. I touched her arm. "Oh, Lord! William hasn't been well, he's..."

"Wait!" Olympia held her palm open in a silencing gesture.

"He was distraught. Then something seemed to break. He began sobbing and said...wait, let me think, I want to get this straight. He said, 'God help me! Your husband has painted my sister-in-law stark naked and put her on show for everyone to see!'"

Olympia stared. "I thought I should tell you."

"Thank you." My knees buckled. Sandpaper in my mouth. "Let me explain. William's wife, Lily, died not long ago. He hasn't got over her. He's still grieving."

"Yes?"

"Well, we were identical twins, Lily and me. He sees her everywhere but, now she's dead, it's me he sees and, well, of course I'm not the model in the painting, but..."

But...what?

She peered closely. "I'm afraid, that's not the worst of it."

"Oh." I waited in dread.

"Your William suddenly bent over, groaning, clutching his chest. It looked as if he was having a heart attack. I asked him to sit down but he wouldn't listen."

A long look. She knew, of course she did. She had to know about me and Theo. Olympia wasn't stupid.

"I have to say I'm worried. Has he seen a doctor, your brother-in-law?"

PLUM

Last night they were shouting and that woke me up so I got out of bed and crept to the top of the stairs where I could hear properly.

"You're shameless! Your naked body all over the gallery. Lily would be humiliated for your sake. Sleeping with a married man!"

"Don't exaggerate…naked body, my foot! Those are abstracts."

"Bullshit! Have you no pride? You know people will talk. You've always been reckless as far as men are concerned. Never had any sense, Lily used to say."

I tiptoed downstairs holding onto the banisters with sweaty slippery-slidey hands. A window was open and blowy curtains were making shadowy shapes dance on the wall.

"I had to…you don't understand. I had to sleep with him…I did it…I did it to protect you."

"What do you mean?"

"He knows. Knows your name. Knows about the wine auction. He and Venter are friends. He threatened to expose you if I didn't…"

"What? What are you saying? If you didn't have sex with him?"

"Yes."

"Christ! So, he's blackmailing you? That bastard is blackmailing you?"

My aunt's voice – high and panicky. *"Yes, yes! I didn't have a choice, I swear. You do believe me, don't you?"*

The moon was pressed flat against the window and tiny brass beads on the curtain ties were hitting the wall with a *ting-ting-ting*.

"How long has this been going on? Why didn't you tell me?"

"I didn't want to make things worse for you. You've been...well, you haven't been yourself."

I took one step down and then another and then there was only space under my feet and I was falling in slow motion like a comic person with eyes popping and mouth open and a scream too deep down in my throat to come out.

Two hands slammed me in the chest and I flew back onto the landing and I must have yelled because Dad and Aunt Frith came rushing upstairs and suddenly I was in my aunt's arms – too shocked to push her away.

"Are you hurt?" She was feeling my arms and legs. "No broken bones, thank God."

Dad switched on the light. "You're just shaken, I think. I can't see any damage."

"It was her...the spirit saved me!"

I was going to tell them about her hands catching me when Dad said, "*This* is what saved you, darling. The curve of this banister broke your fall."

I touched the bone in my chest. "It was the spirit! I *know* it was her."

Aunt Frith unbuttoned my pajama top. "There's a red mark where you fell against the newel post." She turned to Dad. "The stairwell's too dark. It's dangerous. We must leave a light on. Plum could've been seriously hurt, coming down in the dark."

Dad carried me to my room though I'm quite heavy now I'm twelve.

"I thought you were sleeping, Plum."

"I was," I told him. "Something woke me up."

He pulled the blanket under my chin and the mattress made a creaking when he sat on the bed. "Did we wake you, Plum? Did you hear us?"

"I didn't hear anything," I lied. "I was getting a drink of water."

Aunt Frith tapped at the door with the diary in her hand.

"Why don't I read until you fall asleep?" she said in her quiet kind voice. "William, please fetch Plum a glass of cold water."

December 13th, 1905

I calculate Pretty must be seven months with child. She is emaciated and suffering from nervous exhaustion after days of rough travel by ox-wagon from

Cape Town. I said I would immediately summon a doctor but Aletta gave me a stern warning. "Tell no-one of this," she cautioned. "My advice is tend your maid yourself, until her child is born."

December 14th, 1905

We have made a bedroom in the attic where Pretty can hide away from prying eyes. I have informed our servants my maid is with child and unwell after a long and difficult journey.

I see how they despise me for my half-truths. Magdalena, in particular, gives sharp looks as make me wince in shame. How is it that everyone knows of this but me?

December 15th, 1905

Pretty grows weaker, refusing food and taking only small sips of water. I tried to coax her with spoons of giblet broth. "Please take some nourishment," I begged. "If not for yourself then for your unborn babe!" Feverishly, she thrust the spoon away and mumbled a stream of unintelligible words.

"She is praying for death for herself and the child," Magdalena translated.

Aletta visited, bringing a jug of peach cordial and a bowl of apples baked with raisins and sugar. Sadly, Pretty was not the slightest tempted by these delicacies. She took one look and turned her face to the wall.

December 16th, 1905

Today Pretty suffers from a headache so atrocious she cannot lift her head from the pillow.

Carefully, I followed a recipe for a headache cure, snipped from 'The Paarl Ladies' Almanac'.

The recipe calls for a fine powder potion made up of one gram each of white magnesia, rhubarb powder, cinnamon and ginger. Pretty has swallowed a teaspoonful of this in a half a cup of chamomile tea.

Later – Pretty declares her head a little easier.

December 18th, 1905

Magdalena says my little maid has lost the will to live. What am I to do? I cannot force her to eat and, without sustenance, Pretty grows feeble as a kitten.

Prayers offer no comfort. I am filled with hopelessness and despair. How I wish I could have spared Pretty this cruel and undeserved suffering!

December 19th, 1905

Pretty has fallen into a delirium!

Ignoring Aletta's warning, I sent a note requesting Dr. Clutterbuck's assistance. To his credit the doctor arrived within an hour and made no mention of my curt dismissal at his last visit.

I stood at his side, observing his consternation as he drew back the bedclothes to reveal Pretty, heavily swollen with child, shaking from fever, her once glowing complexion turned yellow and dry as a withered leaf.

"Will you leave us?" he asked and I did as he said.

Emerging, at last from his examination, the doctor probed me with questions. I admitted my former maid had come seeking help and I had pledged to care for her until her infant was delivered and her health restored.

Dr Clutterbuck asked for the name of the father of the child and, though I pleaded ignorance, he would not desist. "She's no more than a girl! Was she ravished? Seduced by false promises of betrothal or marriage? Can the man be found and made accountable?"

"I know nothing!" I protested.

From his bag, Dr. Clutterbuck withdrew a flask of lemon balm and yarrow. He has prescribed thirty drops in hot water to be taken twice daily together with two grams of herbal powder dissolved in half a cupful of peppermint tea. "And she must eat!" he insisted.

I felt tearful. "But she will not take any food. What am I to give her?"

The doctor told Magdalena to prepare an egg-custard sweetened with rose water and sugar – a dish soft enough to be slowly supped from a cup.

Before he left, Dr Clutterbuck urged me to find a seasoned midwife to attend at the birth.

December 20th, 1905

Magdalena and I took turns pouring custard from a kettle spout down Pretty's throat. Despite our efforts, she swallowed only two or three mouthfuls.

Pretty is in torment. Without the will to live, all the lemon balm and custard in the world cannot save her.

Magdalena has resorted to witchcraft. She has tied a variety of leather pouches, charms and amulets around Pretty's neck. I also watched my house-keeper making a strange ceremony of burning fowl feathers and pinning a bloody foot to Pretty's pillow. It looks to be a rabbit paw – I cannot bear to examine the thing too closely.

December 21st, 1905

With barely days to Christmas, wretchedness lies heavily upon us all.

Once more I summoned Dr. Clutterbuck and watched from the attic window as he proceeded on his bicycle up the path. He rides with feet firmly upon the pedals, bony knees apart, elbows akimbo and a large black hat falling over his face. When he dismounted at the front door, the good doctor was bright crimson from exertion. Had I been lighter in spirit, I might have laughed at the sight!

When he found breath to speak, Clutterbuck told me he had located an excellent midwife who lives barely five miles away. He has also secured a wet nurse to feed the newborn until the mother is strong enough to take care of her baby.

After his examination of Pretty, he predicted the infant will be born within the next few days.

"But Pretty is too feeble to deliver a child!" I cried.

"That is not for us to say," he replied. "Only the Almighty in his infinite mercy and wisdom may decide the fate of this woman."

December 22nd, 1905

With Edward absent for so long, money is desperately scarce and though I have – as the saying goes – been taking care of the pence – the pounds are not taking care of themselves.

Our servants have not yet received their wages and nor have I settled the doctor's steadily mounting accounts. We have no funds available to replenish our dwindling supplies of meal, granulated sugar, rice, pea-flour and tea. We make what economies we can. Clean our teeth with kitchen salt, boil our own soap and, without oil for lamps, resort to candles. I dare not complain for we are blessed with vegetables, eggs and fruit and will not go hungry.

All through the night I prayed for Pretty and her baby. I prayed for myself too, for the courage to remain strong until the end of this confinement, when, if God is merciful and forgiving, a healthy baby will be born.

December 23rd, 1905

This morning I sent a note to Dirk Barnard, care of The Strooidak Kerk. This is what I wrote:

"My best beloved, I beg you – please come to me. I carry a weighty burden and the sight of your dear face will make my intolerable load easier to endure. God bless you for your sympathetic understanding of this dilemma I find myself in."

Magdalena's eldest son rode Pegasus into town to deliver my note and while he was there, I asked him to purchase a length of flannel so I might sew nightdresses for the newborn.

No sooner had man and horse passed beyond the gate than I was filled with regret for my selfishness in considering my own needs when Pretty is far more deserving of comfort and kindness.

I sat through the night with Pretty, making a poor attempt to read 'Bleak House'. This book has been poisoned for me by Edward's spiteful note but, in any event, from the first chapters, I find it a dreary, tale with little of the mysterious sense of wonder captured in the glowing chapters of 'Great Expectations'. This dry, cheerless novel cannot provide the distraction I need at this painful time.

December 24th, 1905

Christmas Eve. Aletta came with a dear wooden cradle made by her husband for their first-born.

She has also sewn blankets and made a chaste white baby's gown. What will this be, I wonder – a Christening robe or funeral shroud?

It is past midnight. Carols are being sung by our servants and the ringing of their pure, pitched voices pierces me with sadness and whips hot tears into my eyes.

I had planned to dress North Wind with paper lanterns, crimson balls and streamers of holly and mistletoe. I had hoped to serve jugs of elderberry wine and spiced ale to our workers.

None of this will happen now.

December 25th, 1905

I ordered a pig slaughtered and roasted with new potatoes and provided wine and stewed plums for everyone – yet our hearts are heavy this Christmas Day.

All night long, I sat with a candle at the window, waiting. Why, when we loved each other so deeply, has Dirk abandoned me? What kind of man could be so heartless as to ignore my desperate cry for help?

December 26th, 1905

I woke to Pretty screaming in agony, as if she were being torn, limb from limb...

Aunt Frith closed the diary. "Oh, Plum..."

"Don't stop!" I said. "You can't stop now!"

"I shouldn't be reading this to you, I really shouldn't. Your mother would..."

"I know about babies being born – you don't have to worry, really you don't, Mom explained everything."

"It's nothing like as gruesome as this, honestly. This was written over a hundred years ago..."

"I know all that. Please go on, Aunt Frith. I *have* to find out what happens to Pretty and the baby."

My aunt found the page.

"I am alone. Magdalena has left to fetch the midwife. I am going out of my mind in the face of my little maid's terrible anguish.

Where is God in this hour of tragedy?"

She gave a long sigh and closed the book. "I can't go on, Plum, it's all too much. I'm sorry. Besides, it's late. After twelve. Shall I stay till you fall asleep?"

She sat for a bit so I closed my eyes and made my breathing deep and then she tiptoed out and left the light on though I wasn't scared, not really, I just wanted Pretty and the baby safe so I pulled the duvet over my face and said a little prayer. "Please don't let them die," I said. "Oh, God, *please* don't let them die," and it was only next morning that I thought stupid, stupid, stupid…they've been dead for years and years.

I showed my aunt a bruise on my chest like a perfect heart.

"This is where the spirit caught me when I fell."

She shook her head. "That's where you hit the banister. I've a tube of Arnica, somewhere."

"See the shape?"

She peered. "What of it?"

"What do you think it is?"

Aunt Frith sighed. "I'm not playing games, Plum. I've a lot on my mind."

I wanted to tell her about the invisible hands on my chest and the little pinky-purple heart the spirit left as a mark of love but I knew she wouldn't understand and it's times like these I really miss Mom who never said she wasn't playing games when I was trying to have a proper serious conversation with her.

CHAPTER TWENTY SEVEN

FRITH

I lied to William about Theo. It wasn't planned, it just came out. It was the way he said Lil would've been humiliated. There was truth in that and it stung. I know she wouldn't have approved of my having sex with another woman's husband – she knows I've done this before. I needed to justify the sex, to make it more than random shagging, so I hinted at Theo blackmailing me. Worst thing I could've said. Wills was incensed, for my sake.

Now, of course, guilt is eating me. I could stop this now, right away. I could tell him I lied, but it's gone too far and all I can do is promise him I'll break it off with Theo though that, of course, increases Will's concern about the danger of his being reported to the police.

I wish to God I hadn't said anything. Wish I could stop going over and over this conversation with him and yet…

Why the fuck does it matter so much what William thinks? I'm a grown woman. I can shag whoever I like!

The weight of this guilt took me back to Lily dying. I've suppressed this memory somewhere subterranean but it's back. Our last night together. Our last conversation. Last touch.

Her lips, I remember, were cold, her cheeks were cold, her hands were ice. I rubbed them in my own to warm them and she winced and said, "Don't, please, everything hurts."

And then next morning…William's wracking sobs, Plum, curled like a foetus and me, white-faced, grimly silent, sick to my stomach.

She'd been saving pills for months. Hiding them in a plastic pouch under her mattress cover. I crushed them to a fine powder with the back of a teaspoon and mixed the grains into a cup of strawberry yogurt.

The hardest part was getting her to sit up in bed. She weighed nothing but, without any strength, her arms were too limp to grip me and her body kept falling backwards.

I banked the pillows, heaved her forward and then gently pushed her back until she was in a half-sitting position.

I made her say the words again.

"You're sure, my darling…quite sure? You have to tell me, one last time."

Her lips were dry, the skin cracked and peeling. She spoke in a rough croak.

"I'm sure, Frith. I've never been surer of anything."

I touched my lips to her cheek. She pressed my fingers lightly.

"I have no words to thank you, Frith. You're a life-saver." We laughed at the irony. We've always had the same sense of humour.

She swallowed the first spoonful. "I saw Julia, last night," she said.

This was a surprise. "You saw our mother?"

Lily spoke slowly. "I felt someone watching me and there she was, in that corner over there, in the blue chair. Staring as if we'd just met. I smelled cigarettes. Lemon from her gin. I heard ice chinking and the sharp clicking she used to make with her fingernails on the chair arm, remember?"

I lifted another spoonful to her mouth. "Why do you think you saw Julia?"

She kept gagging. The yogurt took forever to slide down her throat. "Because she's dead and I'm dying. It's what happens, so people say. They cross over from the other side before you go. What other reason could there be?"

"She say anything?"

"No. Just sat there, sipping neat gin, dragging on a ciggy and staring in that bloody critical way of hers." Lily coughed and spluttered. "*Fuck!* I pray to God she's not up there waiting for me."

We laughed again – me hysterically, she weakly. When the cup was empty, I rinsed it carefully.

"Love you, Frith." She closed her eyes.

"Love you, Lily."

She fell into a drugged sleep and her breathing grew slower and more laboured. Her mouth hung open and, with each harsh breath, a soft rattling issued from her throat.

At quarter past two that morning, my sister stopped breathing. I climbed onto the bed and lay numbly, both arms wrapped around her. "You're my anchor, Lil," I whispered. "I'm lost without you."

Only as dawn broke, did I wake William.

She was cold when he touched her.

"She's gone, Wills."

"But…I wasn't there…wasn't with her…how could you let me sleep when Lily was dying?"

"I was sleeping myself, Wills. I've only just…"

She lay with hands upturned, bony fingers curled inwards, already stiffening. Her face was slack, her body a husk. There was nothing left of our Lily.

William laid his head upon her chest and howled. "She can't be dead… she can't! We didn't say goodbye!"

I touched his shoulder. "She didn't know anything, Wills. She was in a deep coma at the end."

"I'm sorry, darling," William sobbed. "I'll never forgive myself for sleeping when you were…" He stopped. "It's cold in this room, Frith!" Even thick with tears, his voice sounded accusing. "Get another blanket. Lil's frozen."

I used to think if Lily died before me I'd take a fatal dose or slit my wrists but never in a million years did I imagine myself at my sister's bedside, feeding her crushed Ambien as her life leaked away.

Oddly, I'm not haunted by what I did. Helping Lily – that's how I think of it…*helping*.

It seemed the right thing – the *only* thing to do.

After her funeral, William confided what I already knew. He told me Lil had begged him to help end her life. "But I couldn't, Frith," he whimpered, tears streaming down his face. "I loved her too much."

Or not enough, I thought.

He doesn't know what I did and I'll never tell.

PLUM

Yesterday I asked the Grade Seven C girls if I could join their game of hopscotch in the quadrangle. They'd chalked lines on the paving and numbered squares with the 'safe' arc at the top. Jana Schmidt said I could have a go so they threw the bottle cap they were using as a marker.

I haven't played for ages but when I tossed the cap it fell slap in the middle of a square without touching a chalked line or bouncing out so I hopped the single squares on one foot and landed with both feet in the side-by-side squares, left foot in the left square, right in the right one. I'm good at hopscotch and started jumping faster using my legs like springs and before the bell rang I'd hopped the grid eight times without a mistake.

Jana gave me a high five and Bronte said, "Wow! That was totally awesome, Plum!"

I pretended I hadn't seen Miss Cooper but Bronte yanked my sleeve, "Old Fish Eyes wants to talk to you."

Miss Cooper was smiley and bubbly. "Oh Plum, I've such happy news! You're among the semi-finalists in the short story competition! I do believe you've a good chance of winning."

Through the corner of my eye I saw Bronte staring at our English teacher. "What could she win, Miss?"

"A book voucher and a certificate."

Bronte pulled a face. "That all?"

Miss Cooper clicked her tongue. "The prize is unimportant, Bronte. One enters a competition like this for national recognition...for being singled out amongst one's peers...for the honour of winning."

Bronte giggled as we ran to class.

"What's so funny?"

"Who wants to win a stupid certificate?"

"I get a book voucher too!"

"You better not get a big fat head."

Dad was waiting after school. "Let's go for a drive," he said.

We've been driving a lot and Aunt Frith made me pinky-swear to keep a watchful eye on Dad though he says there's nothing wrong with his driving it's only his head that sometimes gets muddled.

"What's on your mind today, Dad?" I asked and then right away wished I hadn't.

"Syria," Dad said. "That monster, Bashar al-Assad dropped chemical barrel bombs on hundreds of women and children. There are all these graphic photographs, babies foaming at their lips…and what's the world doing about this horrific situation, *nothing,* that's what!"

He can go on like this forever so I looked at the view which was all green, lights and darks melting together and a long line of pine trees that turned into one tree when you squinted.

The needle on the speed-thingie was moving to one fifty so I nudged his arm.

"You have to stay on one-twenty," I reminded him.

"I never stop thinking of her," Dad said. "I wake up with her on my mind and at night she's in my dreams, large as life. She seldom leaves my side."

He means Mom. The needle started creeping up again.

"Dad!" I pointed at the *'Arrive Alive!'* sign. "There's a camera near!"

Dad stamped on the brake. "Good grief, Plum! I know what I'm doing! Visibility good. Tarmac smooth. Traffic light with only one or two long-distance haulage trucks on the road. Why are you getting yourself so worked up?"

We stopped at a Café & Wine Bar and sat in the garden where Dad asked for a glass of their finest Cabernet and a lime milkshake for me.

I told Dad he wasn't supposed to drink and drive with his head being so cotton-woolly but he said, "You're too on-edge. Relax, Plum. Feel the sun on your shoulders. Listen to the doves cooing. Are those ripe granadillas hanging from those vines? Why don't you pick a few?"

But then Dad went quiet and sipped his drink very slowly and I got fidgety and told him I had to revise photosynthesis but he pointed above our heads and said, "Look at that raptor, scanning the grass for a snack."

"You're not listening," I whined. "If we don't get home soon, I'll be toast."

He smiled sadly. "That's not a word I've heard you use in that context before. I do believe that's Lil's father's expression. I'd almost forgotten."

I thought of another of grandpa's sayings. "You're not supposed to drink before the sun hits the yardarm."

Dad laughed and said I was one hundred percent correct but it didn't stop him walking back across the spongy grass for another wine and a bowl of salt and vinegar crisps.

At last we got back in the car.

"Your eyelids are droopy." I said. "Are you feeling sleepy?"

Dad winked. "I'm done-for if we get stopped for a breathalyser test. Why don't you take the wheel?"

I got cross and said that wasn't funny but Dad only laughed. "Poor Plum! You're turning into a young version of your paranoid aunt. Lie down in the back and get a little shut-eye."

The car was warm with a trapped smell of Dad's Aramis and through the window I saw looping power-lines against the blue sky and then this memory came back.

Mom and Dad driving home from a party late at night with me half asleep in the back…low humming voices…sparkly lights…swishing tyres. The memory made me happy and I must've fallen asleep because when I opened my eyes Dad had pulled over to the side of the road and was bent over the steering wheel with his head in his hands and his shoulders heaving and right away I knew something terrible had happened.

"Dad?"

His voice was shaky. "Saw this tanker coming over the rise...one of those branded blue and white jobs with a cow on the side. The driver was speeding, weaving over the white line and with just seconds to spare, I spun the wheel and we skidded to safety. *Christ!* You might've been killed, Plum."

"You too, Dad."

"It slipped my mind you were in the back."

I climbed into the front seat. Dad started the engine and I opened my eyes wide so I could shout a warning if another tanker came over the rise.

Dad fiddled with the radio switching from sports to news to cookery to country music and then opera and there was too much jangly noise so I asked him please to turn it off.

He screwed his eyes. "See those mountains in the distance?"

"Yes."

"What do they look like to you?"

"Is this a game?"

"Yes. Use your imagination."

I saw a sheep with its head over a wooden fence...cows with their mouths moving together chewing grass...a little red farmhouse...puffy clouds hanging low in the sky...the mountains looked like...mountains.

"You go first."

"Well, there's a kind of sinister bulkiness to this range. If you half close your eyes...like this...the hills disappear and in their place you see four horny, squatting toads."

"Oh."

"Keep your eyes on them. The more you look, the more the craggy folds and creases in the rock become damp, granular, warty, toady skin. Do you see?"

"No," I said. "I see rock and stone and tufty grass and way up near the top there's a house."

Then Dad started singing. "*There is a house, Down in New Orleans, They call the rising sun, It's been the ruin of many a good girl And oh God, you know I'm one...*" He turned to me. "C'mon Plum, join in. Let's have a sing-along."

FRITH

I've been painting a series of watercolours, four so far. There's one of *North Wind*, another of the Strooidak Kerk and the farmhouse where we stopped for lunch on Plum's birthday. I've also finished a painting of a Cape Dutch restaurant shielded by two oaks on Main Street – an almost perfect composition of light and shade.

The Strooidak is my best work so far. I love how I've captured the gracefulness of the curving end-gables and the white dove soaring above the invocation, *'Light of Justice Enlighten Us'*.

I'm less satisfied with my painting of *North Wind*. I wanted to imitate the delicate touch of the artwork Plum found in the attic. I have managed to mix the exact translucent shades Charlotte has used in her painting and can't explain how I've ended up with a dark, menacing Edwardian manor fronting a stretch of sour grass. It's almost as if someone took my vision of a light, bright picture and replaced it with an archetypal gloomy haunted house.

I took the canvases to one of Paarl's bigger art galleries where a famous local artist who's now living in New York, had his work on show. I found the exhibition pretentious – raw, unframed canvases covered with a mish-mash of oil, acrylic, stencil and silkscreen. Shockingly overpriced, I thought, yet most pieces bore 'sold' stickers.

A lanky, pale-faced assistant crept up and enquired politely if he could help.

"I'd like to speak to the manager, please."

"That would be me."

I held up my portfolio and asked if he'd be kind enough to look at my work.

His Adam's apple bobbed as he swallowed a sigh. "It will be my pleasure."

I propped four canvases on the counter. "I'm painting a series of historical houses in this style. Would they sell, do you think?"

"Mmm." He looked inscrutable. "They might."

I lifted a flake of paint from the church roof with my fingernail. "Um…I suppose what I'm asking is whether you'd be prepared to sell my paintings?"

He shrugged carelessly. "I can't rightly say. I'll be in a better position to provide an answer once I've viewed the entire collection."

"I see."

The young man nodded stiffly and it seemed we'd reached an impasse. Reluctantly, I slid the canvases back into my bag.

He escorted me to the door and said mechanically, "Thank you for considering our gallery."

I turned to him. "I hate asking but I need to know and can't seem to get anyone to say…do you think I have talent or…am I wasting my time?"

The manager gave a pitying glance. "Let me put it this way – based upon what sells in this particular gallery, it's likely your art will find a market."

Confused, I asked, "So, you're saying…um…what exactly?"

"I think your work is good."

"You do!" I took a deep breath. My spirits lifted. "Thank you."

Across the polished counter with its tubular glass vase of black and white painted twigs, we smiled at one another.

I stopped at Olympia's. She wasn't there but Theo was reading a newspaper. He grinned. "This is unexpected."

"Did she tell you about William and his reaction to your nudes?"

He rubbed a hand over his face. "She mentioned something. Said she was worried he'd have a heart attack."

"You gave me your word no one would ever see those paintings."

"Did I?" His face twitched. "Well, I changed my mind. Decided they were too good to hide." He sent a smarmy smile. "There's a collector in London interested. Good chance I could make a packet."

"Good!" I exhaled. "Send them to London or Timbuktu – as far away as possible. I don't want anyone else recognising me."

He snorted. "Seriously, Frith, tell me how your brother-in-law saw you in these nudes?"

Theo had used a painterly technique, a series of rough-hewn shapes distinguished by colour rather than outline. Crude brushstrokes of saturated paint against swathes of untouched white canvas. At first glance, the subjects appeared to be different women. One had an aureole of light around her face and in another, the tip of a dry brush created a stippled effect over her head, like a shaved pate. The only quality the nudes had in common was their boyish angular shape, their provocative sensuality. How *had* William recognised me? Mystified, I shrugged.

Theo smiled smugly. "My point exactly."

CHAPTER TWENTY EIGHT

PLUM

I'm glad I don't live in Dad's world it's like being in a film – a horror –
with poison gas turning people yellow and Isis chopping heads off and boat
people drowning with their babies and nobody in the whole world caring
one bit.

Dad says he hates me growing up in a world where everything's gone
pear shaped and people have forgotten how to be kind and we've stopped
using our brains and allow computers and robots to tell us what to do
but this is the only world I know and it seems pretty good to me if you
aren't always watching the news and sucking up scary stuff about wars and
President Donald Trump taking the world backwards to a dark place.

I wish Dad had a normal human to talk to instead of me or my aunt
or builders who only care about how many hours on the job and smoke
breaks. My aunt thinks she's normal but she's wrong because she's quite
old with no husband or children only a cat left behind in France that she
couldn't have loved very much otherwise she'd have brought it with her in a
box punched with holes.

FRITH

No matter how you shield yourself, *North Wind* has a way of burrowing into you. The house remains an igloo but that's really my only objection to living here now.

Give him his due, William's turned this place into a lovely home and it would've been a tricky balancing act, respecting traditions while, at the same time, shaping airy, practical living spaces.

Mercifully, he hasn't gone the whole Georgian hog with antique finishes and damask papered walls. Will's style tends to the Quakerish-modest and clean with white painted walls, bare wooden floors and classic fittings. Lily would've been surprised at what he's achieved. Even Charlotte would've been pleased.

I've turned my bedroom into a chaste nun's cell with a single bed, narrow cupboard, armchair, table and bookcase with an easel near the window where the light is best.

It's oddly liberating being unencumbered by material things and when I return to my flat in France, the first thing I'll do is parcel up and give away the clutter of my life – all the endless bits collected over time and gathering dust.

I was at the kitchen table sorting through a glossy stack of photographs of heritage houses when William pulled out a chair. Tilting his head, he studied an upside-down picture of an old cottage with a twisting pebbled path, a bed of woody rhododendrons, a smoking chimney.

He sounded morose. "So, what's happening with you and that prick?"

"I told you. I'm going to break it off with him. I just hope…"

A contractor's truck rolled up the driveway. A door slammed. The truck's tailgate was unbolted.

"You hope, *what*?"

"Hadn't you better go and see who's arrived?"

"I'm expecting a delivery of a door. Are you going to answer me?"

310

"I just hope he doesn't follow through with his threat to report you." William picked up the picture of the cottage and stared at it.

"That's a photograph of a house I want to paint."

"There's always going to be someone," he said.

"What do you mean?"

"Someone recognising me. Threatening, bullying, trying to intimidate. It's dawned on me, finally, I'm not getting away with this. My chickens are coming home to roost."

I couldn't help myself. "We can always leave. Nothing keeping us here, except a promise you made to Lil."

"I promise I intend to keep."

"You *have* kept it! This is not what she expected. She didn't think this through properly. She imagined you'd be safe. If she knew the circumstances, she'd want you to leave to protect yourself and Plum."

"She wanted Plum to grow up here. She wanted you here too. She made that very clear."

I didn't like the way the conversation was leading. *Let's not go down that path again.*

"I visited a gallery yesterday. Not Olympia's. The manager thinks there's a market for my paintings in Paarl."

William shook his head. "You can't earn a living as an artist."

"Funny you should say that. I've always managed before."

"Barely scraping by."

His lofty expression made me angry. "Don't be so fucking sanctimonious! If you'd give me the painting Lily left me…the one that's rightfully mine… I'd be set for life!"

William leaned back in the chair, considering me judiciously.

"Thing is…" he said, slowly and deliberately. "Thing is, Frith, Lil changed her mind. She didn't want you to have that painting and decided against leaving it to you."

My response was automatic. "That's a barefaced lie!"

"I'm afraid it's not."

Bottled anger hurtled to the surface.

"You *forced* Lil to change her will when she was too ill to know better. You're a shit, that's what you are! Cold, manipulative, greedy shit! I don't know how you live with yourself!"

His eyebrows lifted. "You give me too much credit. I could never force my wife to do anything she didn't want to do."

"Come off it William! Don't take me for an idiot! We both know Lily left the painting to me. She told me to get Christie's to appraise and sell it. She knew I needed the money."

"You're dead wrong there. I haven't wanted to tell you because I knew it would hurt like hell." He paused.

"Go on!"

"She said…she said you didn't deserve it. Said you'd betrayed her."

My jaw dropped. "*Betrayed her*? In what way? You mean that time we had sex?"

"She didn't explain. Said you'd hurt her badly."

"When did she say this?"

"Couple of weeks before she died."

"Well it has to be the sex! Why didn't you tell her it was meaningless? We slept together for comfort more than anything else. Why didn't you stand up for me? It's the least you could've done."

"We never spoke of it. She say anything to you?"

"Plum saw you coming out of my room. She told Lily."

"*Christ.*" He covered his face with his hands.

"Where is the painting, anyway?"

William spoke through his fingers. "In a bank vault in England. A trustee's been appointed to give it to Plum when she turns twenty-one."

I exhaled loudly. "You could have explained this to me long ago. Why keep it a secret?"

William looked into my eyes. "You always jump to conclusions. Think the worst of me. I was waiting for you to consider maybe Lil was the one who didn't want you to have the painting."

'She said you didn't deserve it. Said you'd betrayed her.'

312

It had to be the sex. Yet, Lil would've known William's turning to me was nothing more than a desperate need for a warm body to cling to as his beloved wife lay dying.

"I'm sorry," William murmured, looking contrite.

I shrugged. "And I apologise for always thinking the worst of you – you're right, I do."

"Ah well, no surprises there. I haven't given anyone in this family a reason to have faith in me – have I now?"

Plum came in, dressed for school, hair still damp from the shower. William opened his eyes wide, pretending surprise. "Who are you?" he joked. "I don't believe we've met."

Anxiously, she searched his face.

"Are you a javelin thrower? A climber of mountains? One who swims icy channels?"

Plum sounded tentative. "You okay, Dad?"

He smiled. "Here you are my lovely daughter, morphing into a beautiful bronzed athlete while I look mortally ill. And here is your aunt, furiously painting while Rome burns."

After Plum left for school, William asked if I'd come with him to collect a brass bird bath he'd ordered.

"She'd have loved it," he said. "Two elegant, long-beaked cranes balancing a lily pad on their lovely bent necks." He'd had the piece inscribed with: *'In memory of our beloved Lily.'*

I'd have preferred to stay home and paint but there was something about William that set off a shudder of anxiety down my spine, so I hung my camera around my neck and joined him for the drive to Robertson.

His ventriloquist's dummy face behind the wheel – it was impossible to relax knowing his mind was not on the road. I kept my right foot hovering above an invisible brake.

What are you thinking William? Why...now? Now...when it's too late, are you so haunted by Lily?

All the things you did and said, regrets keeping you awake in the small hours. What's going on in that ticking brain of yours?

My mobile rang. A woman's voice, "You still looking?"

"Sorry, what's that?"

"This ad says you're looking for a housekeeper. Found one yet?"

"Um…no."

"Glad to hear it. Any chance we could meet?"

The disembodied voice was faintly irritating.

"Who are you? Have you done this kind of work before?"

"Can't tell a lie so, no, I haven't. Been wife and mother for thirty years and grandmother for ten though. Does that count?"

"I suppose so," I answered, grudgingly.

"Oh, and it's Mrs Partridge, only people call me Birdie. When can we get together?"

"I'm not sure."

What I wanted to tell the voice was: "*Look, our life is a mess right now. I'm stressed to hell. My brother-in-law is falling apart. I'm not sure whether you'll cope with my niece Plum, she's different.*"

A bright chirp in my ear. "You were saying?"

"Just that it's not an ideal time with everything…um…rather up in the air."

"We could chat, though, couldn't we? No harm in that. I could pop in after lunch, if you're free?"

"I really don't want to waste your time, Mrs Partridge."

"Birdie. I've a pencil handy, if you'll tell me where you live?"

"Who was that?" William asked, vacantly.

"A Mrs Partridge. Wants the job of housekeeper. Popping in after lunch."

It started to rain. Mindful of the slippery road, I suggested William drop his speed.

"Do you need to look at the map?"

From the way he spoke, his teeth were clenched. "*Jesus!* I know these roads like the back of my hand. I'm taking the N1 to Rawsonville, catching up with the N15 at the Nuy Valley, switching to the R60 to Robertson."

Mollified, I leaned back, soothed by the monotonous rhythm of slapping wipers.

The road unwound ahead – smooth and wetly shining.

We passed drowning canola fields bordered by bending palms and windswept bougainvillea. A rainbow arched across the sky. A drenched cat bolting across the road missed the car by centimeters.

By the time we had reached Robertson, the rain had stopped. William parked outside *Druids Lodge* – a museum with a sprawling rose garden.

"Let me show you this place," he smiled, opening the car door. "This building will interest you. You might want to paint it for that collection of yours."

"I thought you were afraid of being recognised in Robertson? Aren't you rather tempting fate?"

"Nothing to lose, really," he replied, carelessly. "It's inevitable, I'm afraid."

That day, we were the only visitors to the rectangular house, two rooms deep with a flat-roofed annex in which, William told me, a priceless archive is stored. We met the curator who said an eccentric family by the name of 'English' had owned Druids Lodge from 1883. Unmarried, Violet English, the last surviving member, had expired alone in the house in 1976. One year later, the Lodge had been declared a National Monument. William seemed captivated by the idea of the elderly spinster, Violet English, dying of old age in the house she'd grown up in.

"No sticky-end for old Vi," he chortled. "That's how we should all go – breathing our last at home in bed with our boots on!"

We wasted over an hour wandering through rooms furnished from the late nineteenth century. William told the curator about restoring *North Wind*.

And then, holding me in an icy blue stare, he said, "There was a time, not long ago, when I lived in Robertson."

The curator seemed interested. "Oh, yes? When would that have been?"

"Ah, well, roughly around the time of the *Duval Antique Wine Auction*. Remember that?"

The curator frowned. "Pardon?"

"You must've heard of this fraudster – can't recall his name – made a tidy fortune auctioning fake bottles of antique wine. It was in all the papers at the time."

"Sorry. Not ringing any bells. You've lost me there, I'm afraid."

"That was stupid and reckless," I snapped as we climbed into the car. William had the audacity to laugh.

I fell silent. We collected Lily's bird bath and, as we turned back along Route 62, I heard William cheerfully humming.

PLUM

Nobody was home when I got back from school which meant Aunt Frith had been talked into driving around the countryside with Dad so I made a sandwich and took it upstairs to my aunt's room. I like it there – it's clean and neat and light from the window falls like melted buttery toffee on the floor.

I sat on the bed my aunt makes with what she calls 'hospital corners' so it's always tight and smooth and as I bit into my sarmie a burst of pinprick stars blinked on and off in front of my eyes and I thought it was the spirit trying to make contact but then the black bag slipped over my head and the darkness came.

When I opened my eyes again there was a noise like water swirling down a plughole and I was still on my aunt's bed with my sarmie open and the peanut butter side on the floor.

I thought of making another one but my legs were dead-fish floppy so I just lay there and stared for ages at her painting of *North Wind* she's propped on an easel.

She's made the house spooky with a thundery sky and bony trees lifting crooked arms. There's the broken statue I found the day we arrived – the one with the missing head – half-hiding in long feathery grass and in her painting *North Wind* is wrapped in bluey shadows so everything's dark with only a patch of light from a glow in the attic window and as I looked at this an awesome idea popped into my head.

I picked up one of my aunt's thinnest brushes that she hadn't washed properly so the point was stiff. I dipped it in water before mixing it into the palest shade on her palette – a kind of porridge colour – just right for what I wanted.

I was painting on her canvas when I heard the doorbell so I ran downstairs and behind the door stood a skinny wrinkly old lady with curly white hair and wishy-washy blue eyes.

The lady rushed indoors shaking a flowery umbrella saying her name was 'Birdie' and calling me 'pet' like I was a kitten or a puppy. Her cheeks made dimples when she smiled. "I'm that parched I'd kill for a cuppa," she said.

"Does that mean you'd like some tea?"

She nodded so I took her to the kitchen and switched on the kettle. "Who are you?"

"I'm hoping to be your new housekeeper." Her dimples kept coming and going. "Is your mother in by any chance?"

I told her Mom was in heaven and Aunt Frith and Dad were both out and then I asked if she believed in ghosts.

Birdie made her voice very firm. "I'm not one for ghosts, I'm afraid. Also don't put much stock in UFO's, Abominable Snowmen or monsters – Loch Ness or any other kind – unless I've seen them with my own two eyes, and so far, I haven't. Why do you ask?"

I explained there'd been one other person who'd come for the housekeeper job and she'd said our house was haunted by *ngozi* which means bad spirits and Birdie said, "Oh dear," and tapped the side of her head. "Bit touched, was she?"

"She was funny looking if that's what you mean because she was burned in a fire that left her with a squiffy face and one shorter leg."

Birdie opened her eyes wide. "Gracious me! That would turn your mind, wouldn't it?"

I took down Mom's pretty teacups with the blue violets around the rim and emptied chokkie biscuits on a plate and Birdie told me I was quite the hostess and we sat at the table talking like grown-ups until I heard Dad's car.

A door banged and the car started up and roared away again and Dad came in with cheeks so red they looked like they'd been slapped. "Your

Aunt's gone to town to do a spot of shopping," he said which is code for they've had another fight and she's driven off in a temper.

Dad stuck out his hand. "Hello! You must be Mrs Partridge. My sister-in-law said you'd be dropping in."

Birdie started scrabbling under the table for her shoes but Dad said, "Oh, don't bother. I'm just about to take mine off. No need to stand on ceremony. Is there tea in that pot?"

She poured a cup for Dad and said her husband used to call her Birdie when he was alive.

"Right you are then, Birdie it is!" Dad helped himself to a biscuit. "I see you're using the Spode. They were always my wife's favourite."

Birdie said quietly she was sorry to hear about Mom and Dad nodded.

"Do you know, when I walked in and saw the two of you with Plum's books on the table, your handbag hooked to a chair, your shoes under there…cups, teapot and biscuits…you and Plum chatting away like magpies, it took me back to when I was a boy at my Gran's house."

"That's nice," Birdie said, biting into a biscuit.

"The house was nothing like this, of course, more small and homey. They had a cat and a fireplace, couple of chickens in the yard, noisy rooster. But there's a touch of Gran's sweetness in your face and I thought to myself, probably for the first time, *North Wind* feels just like home."

Birdie gave a funny shy smile and Dad said, "Tell me about yourself."

"Not much to tell except I don't mind admitting this job would be a right Godsend. I'm on my beam ends, surviving on cheese-parings since my husband, bless his cotton socks, passed last year."

"Oh, I know what that's like!" Dad combed his hair with his fingers till it stood up all higgledy piggeldy. "You become unmoored when the love of your life dies, don't you? You've lost your purpose. You find yourself floating listlessly, without direction. You think it's impossible to keep going and, frankly, you don't want to, not without her, but you can't do anything foolish because, of course, there's your daughter to consider."

Birdie jumped up. "I'll clear the table. Any idea when your sister-in-law will be back?"

Dad showed his teeth in a fake smile. "Oh, we don't need to wait for her. You've got the job, Birdie. I can see you're good with Plum. And my daughter desperately needs a warm, loving, motherly figure in her life. You'll do very nicely."

"Really?" Mrs Partridge said, not sounding very sure.

Dad went on, "How much should I pay you? Will it be weekly or monthly? I've no idea how these things work. It's all new to me. When she was alive, this was always my wife Lily's department."

Birdie was getting ready to leave when Aunt Frith opened the front door and right away Mrs Partridge bent her knees in a curtsy like my aunt was the Queen of England and said she was just nipping off but would be in tomorrow at eight-thirty sharp and not a minute later. I waited as she jiggled a key in her rusty yellow Mini which made a rude burping noise and then jerked down the driveway with black smoke trailing behind like a long snake.

I heard them before I got indoors. Aunt Frith was yelling at Dad. "I can't believe you've engaged that woman without giving me an opportunity to talk to her!"

Dad sounded cross. "If it's Plum you're worried about, this woman will do perfectly well. I like her. She's warm, loving and honest. No-nonsense. Anyway, this fits into your plan, if I'm not mistaken? Won't take long for Birdie to learn the ropes leaving you free to scuttle off to France."

They were looking daggers so I jiggled her arm. "Aunt Frith...can you help me with my homework...I've a really hard geometry question...and when we're done will you read Charlotte's diary so I'm not left worrying and not knowing what happened. *Pleeease.*"

FRITH

I kept going over an unfathomable geometry question asking if ABC is an isosceles triangle with AB equal to AC and the angle BAC equal to sixty degrees...but my mind couldn't take it in.

"Let's leave it till later," I suggested to Plum. "I'll start with the diary."

She held Dahlia in her lap. The doll was dressed in a chemise and petticoat for her 'afternoon nap'. It was on the tip of my tongue to tell Plum to put the doll away but Dahlia is proving both a comfort and a distraction, so I didn't.

I opened the diary. Words swam before my eyes. *"December the twenty seventh, nineteen hundred and five."*

Plum was watching my face and the doll's bottomless blue eyes seemed to pierce right through me. From where I was sitting, it looked as if Dahlia had opened her mouth very slightly. I gave an inward shudder.

"The midwife, Tante Hester, found me gibbering in terror…"

I've just realised what Lily meant. Oh God, how deeply we bury the things we can't bear thinking of!

There was a day towards the end when Plum knocked a Dresden figurine to the floor. I was upset for Lily's sake, knowing how much she treasured the delicate shepherdess with her frothy porcelain dress. I sent Plum to fetch a dustpan and brush to sweep up the china chips. "God, that child is clumsy!" I grumbled.

"It was an accident." Lily defended her. "Besides, I've learned *things* don't matter. Can't take it with you, can you?"

I bent to pick up the larger pieces. "Didn't you say her birth mother was a dancer? With those genes she shouldn't always be tripping over her feet."

Lily's face turned to stone.

"You never talk about it, Lil. Why?" I asked. "It's not natural."

I heard a movement behind me. Plum stood there. A flush of body heat. My face turning beetroot.

Lily beckoned Plum. "Will you bring me one of those little pots of fruity yogurt from the fridge, darling?"

Plum darted away. I looked at Lily, agonised. "I didn't know she was there, I swear."

Her expression was intense. "You do it on purpose. You're always dropping clues."

WHERE THE TRUTH LIES

"But that makes no sense. Why would I do that? It was an honest mistake."

"Was it? Listen, Frith – for the umpteenth time – it's my decision…no *ours*, Wills' and mine. I've told you repeatedly, we don't want Plum to know she's adopted. But you can't help yourself, can you? You're always hinting at her history when she can hear what you're saying. You're *cruel*, Frith, no other word for it."

In vain, I tried to excuse myself. "No, no, you've got it all wrong."

Lily carried on. "Another thing. I hate you always finding fault with Plum. All your fabricated theories. Saying she's ADD or autistic or has Asperger's or whatever. What's your problem, Frith? Are you *jealous* of Plum? Jealous because you don't have a child? And, face it, at the rate you're going, you'll never have one. Is that it?"

"No…no…"

"Every time you hurt my daughter, it's like a *betrayal!*" Her eyes were shining with tears.

Was I jealous? We were twins. We were dissimilar in nature yet also telepathic and empathetic. We understood one another. No words were necessary. We always knew what the other was thinking or feeling.

Lily belonged wholly to me until she met William and then she belonged to him.

When Plum came along, she grabbed the biggest slice of Lily's heart and left me third in the succession of those my sister loved best and this rankled and made me bitter.

Was I jealous of Plum? Yes, I suppose I was. If that's the case, perhaps, subconsciously, I wanted Plum to know she was adopted so she'd have less claim on Lily.

I don't deny I've always found fault with Plum. From the time she was a baby, I never considered her completely normal. I was always going on about the way she'd stare at nothing for ages or wave her hands frantically for no apparent reason. I'd comment on how long it took for her to learn to crawl and then to walk. How could I? What does a childless spinster know about a child's development?

My fault-finding begs the question – was I consciously making Plum out to be deficient in some way, exaggerating her differences from other children her age, so Lily would see her as imperfect and love her less?

I lost my twin when she became William's wife and Plum's mother and, over time, my unreasonable resentment created a chasm between us too wide for me to jump. Lily would've known this – she knew everything about me. She'd have been troubled about leaving her beloved Plum in the care of an imperfect husband and unloving sister.

My nasty comment over the broken Dresden shepherdess was probably the last straw. No wonder she'd changed her mind about giving me the painting.

"Aunt Frith! You've stopped reading! Please go on."

CHAPTER TWENTY NINE

December 27th, 1905

The midwife, Tante Hester, found me gibbering in terror after harrowing hours spent witnessing Pretty enduring a kind of pain no living being should have to bear.

The midwife lifted Pretty's nightdress and, laying strong hands upon her distended belly, pressed and prodded, muttering: "Too soon…this one's come too soon!"

Craven coward, I fled the attic leaving Pretty to Tante Hester and Magdalena. As I write, I hear Pretty's tormented pleas for mercy growing ever fainter.

Later…

Falling upon my knees, I prayed fervently to God. Is it a sin to bargain with the Almighty?

I have given the Lord my faithful word if He finds it in His heart to save Pretty, I shall willingly renounce Dirk and never, in this lifetime, meet with him again! I also pledge to attend church regularly, engage in worthy and charitable deeds and find it within myself to behave as a devoted, loyal and faithful wife to my odious husband, Edward.

December 28th, 1905

Three days past Christmas, at ten minutes past noon – Pretty gave birth to a baby girl. Sadly, this event is neither cause for joy or celebration.

Depleted and spent after thirty-five hours of relentless, racking pain, poor Pretty has lapsed into a deep sleep from which she cannot be stirred. Her bleeding will not stop. Tante Hester says she fears the worst. Never before have I seen so much blood! It soaks through the bed linens and mattress, dripping into a bucket placed on the floor.

In a frightened panic, I have sent Magdalena's eldest boy to urgently summon Dr. Clutterbuck.

The midwife ordered Magdalena to boil a large kettle and showed me how to bathe the baby in warm water. I did so clumsily, my fingers trembling for fear of dropping the unbearably tiny mite.

Swaddled in my softest shawl, I was shown how to feed the baby a few drops of scalded and cooled water. From tomorrow, until the wet-nurse arrives, this infant must regularly receive small quantities of boiled cows' milk. Tante Hester says I am to purchase a glass feeding bottle with a rubber nipple but, until then, we shall make do with a bottle stuffed with a clean length of milk-soaked flannel from which the baby should suckle.

December 29th, 1905

The doctor did not come!

I sat with Pretty through an agonising night, stroking her clammy brow until she breathed her last. In her final hour, Tante Hester laid the mewling infant upon her breast but, too far gone, Pretty succumbed to death without ever setting eyes upon her child.

Where was God when this young girl slipped silently away?

"You are too late!" I shouted at Clutterbuck when he arrived to discover the patient a corpse.

I asked the doctor to examine the health of the newborn and took myself to my room after locking the door against intruders. This is where I proposed to remain until I regained some semblance of composure. No sooner had I hidden in a dark tent beneath the bedclothes than Tante Hester banged at the door. She said she would be leaving at first light and demanded payment.

As I gave her the last of our money, I asked, "What hope do you have for this baby?"

"You'd do best to baptise her soon," the Tante replied. "She will not live long."

December 31ˢᵗ, 1905

Magdalena and I bathed and wrapped Pretty in a clean white binding sheet, ready for burial. With pain erased from her face, she appeared youthful, tranquil and lovely – just as I knew her when she was still alive. Pretty's baby is a violent shade of red and so very small she might be a chick fallen from the nest.

Today is the last day of 1905. And so concludes the cruelest, most sorrowful year of my life!

January 1ˢᵗ, 1906

I am half mad with worry! A wet nurse cannot be found and the baby will not stop crying!

Aletta has boiled water with seeds of dill to soothe the baby's gripes, though, disappointingly, I find this remedy has no effect. The infant's unstoppable shrieks are making me light-headed.

I have been taking solitary walks, abandoning the howling baby to Magdalena or her daughter.

Within the shelter of trees, I weep and rail aloud at God for taking Pretty instead of Edward.

What kind of justice is this?

Dr Clutterbuck delivered a glass bottle with a nipple. He warned me gravely our cows' milk may be contaminated and insisted that the milk, bottle and teat are well boiled before being given to the infant. I begged him to tell me if the baby had even the smallest chance of surviving.

He looked sorrowful. "This child entered the world before her time. She has only the slimmest chance of living through the next few days."

Poor little girl – no bigger than my cupped hands – yet I am gravely touched by her plucky strength and the way she curls her teeny fingers around my thumb, holding on with brave tenacity.

This evening, after the baby had sobbed herself to sleep in my arms, I searched her little face for evidence of Edward and happily found none. She is the very image of her beautiful mother, Pretty.

January 2nd, 1906

 Grief sits heavy upon North Wind Manor.

 Aletta came to pay condolences and brought a posy for Pretty's grave.

 Tomorrow my little maid will be laid to eternal rest in the ground behind the servants' quarters where two other bodies have also been buried. How fast this desolate land has become a graveyard!

 All is made ready. Without the funds to purchase a fine casket, the men have knocked together a humble pinewood coffin and dug a burial pit in our harsh, flinty soil.

 I washed a smooth white oval stone and scored it deeply with Pretty's initials and the words: 'RIP, requiescat in pace.'

 Once I have money to spare, I shall seek out a tall, carved marble angel with spreading wings as a fitting shrine for Pretty.

January 3rd, 1906

 This day we buried Pretty. Never have I known such bleakness. Even clouds above wept from morn till night.

 Those attending the funeral included Aletta, Thomas Clutterbuck, our servants and a few workers from neighbouring farms who came more from courtesy and respect than friendship with the deceased.

 The doctor brought a young minister newly arrived from Glasgow who spoke the prayers. I placed a wreath of Cyprus boughs and Aletta's posy on the coffin before it was carried and lowered into the earth.

 Every single person at that graveside had a heart overflowing with sympathy for a young woman taken long before her time and there were also tears for Pretty's ailing, orphaned baby.

 Silence was observed for a few minutes before the mourners silently departed.

 As I bid them goodbye, I could not help but wonder how many of those assembled knew the part my husband had played in Pretty's untimely death? Truth be told – if Pretty had never found employment at North Wind, she would be alive and in the bloom of health today. How this haunts me!

January 4th, 1906

Aletta gave me a beribboned basket filled with gifts donated by Strooidak parishioners who've heard of the tragedy that has befallen us.

"What precisely do they know?" I asked anxiously. My good friend laid a consoling hand upon my arm. "Only that your dear maid has passed away and you are left to care for her sickly newborn."

Humbly, I list the contents of the gift basket to illustrate the generosity of the charitable women of the church who, despite their own hardship, have thoughtfully donated useful gifts to help an orphaned infant left in the care of an undeserving English woman.

Two long flannel nightdresses.

A knitted crib blanket.

Six flannel squares.

Six Turkish toweling napkins.

Celluloid rattle and felt-covered ball.

A bottle of Lever's Glycerine to ease earache.

Fuller's Earth, for powdering infant bottoms.

Vaseline Salve.

Camphorated oil.

Mrs. Winslow's Soothing Syrup for Wind.

Whilst we were taking tea together, Aletta confided Dirk has been ill with diphtheria caught from a young choir boy who has died from this epidemic. She believes Dirk is gradually improving in health, though he is to remain quarantined until he is no longer contagious.

This news of Dirk's illness brought with it a faint reprieve, lightening the hour.

Did the unexpected onset of this illness keep Dirk from answering my call for help? Or had my letter arrived before the disease took hold and was it guilt made him resist my pleas for help?

Shall I ever know?

January 6th, 1906

This tiny scrap makes me tremble with fretfulness. She struggles to swallow and can only consume a few drops at a time, not enough to keep a mouse alive.

Today a wet nurse came but – contemptible, hideous, mean creature – she demanded to be paid immediately and when I explained we were waiting for money from London, she left at once.

I have sent a wire begging Edward to send money urgently.

January 7th, 1906

Night and day the baby screams – dragging me down to the bedrock of despair.

Magdalena says whatever comes to pass is God's will.

I despise my helplessness in the face of this baby's distress – surely there must be something I can do!

January 9th, 1906

I have set up a bed in the attic where I can tend the baby. In silence and darkness, with moonlight playing at the window, I rock the infant in my arms, crooning softly.

She weighs less than feathers and seems to shrink with each passing hour. A light is missing from her eyes and her tiny fingers are now too feeble to grip my thumb.

Tomorrow, Thomas Clutterbuck will bring the minister from Glasgow to baptise this baby girl.

January 10th, 1906

On the tenth day of January in the year of Our Lord, 1906, Pretty's daughter, a child of the angels, not yet two weeks of age, was christened, Angela Faith Butler.

"No! No!" Dr. Clutterbuck interjected when I made my choice known. "The infant must be baptised by her mother's name, not yours!"

Pressing my lips to the doctor's ear, I whispered, "I believe it right and proper this child takes the father's surname."

328

Hearing these words, the doctor's complexion blanched.

Unwillingly, I entrusted Baby Angela to the minister, bereft without her in my arms.

Wearing Aletta's firstborn's christening robe, pinned like a shawl to fit her impossibly tiny frame, the baby, pale as snow, seemed barely to draw breath as the minister intoned a prayer.

"May God, who has received you into His Church this day, pour upon you the riches of His grace…"

Never will I forget the moments between life and death when it seemed as if the world ceased spinning upon its axis. I observed Aletta caught mid-sigh, the doctor staring with glittering eyes,

Magdalena's head bowed in prayer. The sky grew black and clouds broke as our baby made her last soft whimpers and drops of water fell like tears upon her tiny brow.

January 11ᵗʰ, 1906

I barred the attic door and sat in the dark, without even a candle for light.

I would not allow them to take her from me. I held Baby Angela long after her body turned cold and stiff. My mind grew addled with hallucinations. I saw Pretty smiling, holding out her arms for the child. I thought she nodded in forgiveness and touched my cheek. I thought Baby Angela opened her eyes and waved her hands. And then I woke to the harsh brightness of day and knew that what I had seen was nothing more than a mocking dream.

January 12ᵗʰ, 1906

Magdalena shouted through the door that a visitor had come to North Wind Manor and, when she heard no reply, she called again.

"Madam, Mr. Barnard is here! Mr. Barnard from the church has come to see you."

I opened the door. Dirk gently took Angela from my arms and gave her to Magdalena and then held me to his chest.

He told me when I had sent my letter he had been delirious with fever and quarantined to prevent the spread of contagion amongst the townsfolk. In all that time, alone, with only books for company, Dirk said he had never stopped thinking of me.

I drew apart from him. "Hopelessness is easier to bear than hope," I said. "Hope, if it is false, if it comes to nothing, if it leaves one broken, is harder to endure."

He shook his head. "God forgive me – there is one thing I know to be true and that is that I love you."

Dirk had brought an object, clumsily wrapped in sacking, propped in the doorway.

Opening this, Dirk drew out a wooden rocking horse. "This was mine as a boy," he said. "It was all I had to give the baby. Forgive me, Charlotte. I did not know the child had been taken from you."

I set the wooden horse upon the floor and the sight of that gaily painted toy steed with its shiny mane and thick jaunty tail, bravely rocking, brought tears; my eyes grew blurred as the horse dipped forward and back.

"Will you stay tonight?" I begged.

"My dear Charlotte," Dirk replied, "if you will have me, I will remain at your side until death parts us."

January 13th, 1906

I heard a tremor in the young voice of the Scots minister as he prayed over Angela's miniature pine coffin. His eyes shone. Was the breeze whipping up these tears – or was it the pitiful sight of our tiny, newly baptised infant, ready to be laid to rest?

Dirk's firm arm kept me steady. Without it, I should have crumpled to the ground.

January 20th, 1906

Unbearable grief has made me unwell.

Dr. Clutterbuck has prescribed Chlorodyne, a cure he believes induces rest. Liberally dosed with this medication, I have slept like the dead for three days. This cure brought nightmares and filled the rooms of North Wind with bogies sent to terrify.

Pretty and Baby Angela and even dead Moses appeared before me, rags loosely hanging from scrawny limbs. And also in my dream, dressed for a funeral in black tail-coat and towering hat, an undertaker come for me!

January 21st, 1906

True to his word, Dirk remains at my side although this troubled journeying between nightmares and sad wakefulness has made me blind to his dear presence.

"'Tis the medication, mixed with fever in your blood, that gives you nightmares," he said.

Dirk believes Clutterbuck's chlorodyne contains liberal quantities of morphine and cannabis and may, if taken regularly, prove highly addictive.

With my permission, he has poured the medicine into the sink and asked Magdalena to prepare a mild diet of coddled eggs and milk pudding to build my strength.

I should be so happy with Dirk – how desperately I wish to be happy! – yet I am heavily burdened by my sorrows.

January 25th, 1906

I took the trap to town to send a telegram to Edward.

Here is what I wrote:

'Ruin stares us in the face! I beg you – send money urgently!

Your desperate wife, Charlotte.'

January 28th, 1906

All my life, or so it seems, I have waited for Dirk...for the love of a man who is honest and true.

How strange that now he has come, I am disturbed by doubt and despair. I keep asking how it can be possible that young, handsome Dirk loves a scarecrow? Illness has ravaged my looks making me thin and pinched with hollow cheeks and sunken eyes.

My hair falls out in handfuls. Added to this, is my troubled history and penurious future.

What do I have to offer Dirk? "You do not see me at my best," I said.

Dirk answered with compassion. "I see the woman I love."

Like many men of tender years, Dirk is a romantic who believes the power of his devotion will cure and make me whole again. Oh that this were possible!

February 2nd, 1906

My strength is slowly returning. Without word from Edward, I have taken to selling our fruit and vegetables to the canning factory and surplus eggs to the baker. I have also sent three dozen bottles of wine, all we had in our cellar, to be sold in town.

An inventory of the larder reveals the following – half a sack of flour, two sacks of potatoes, one crock of butter, five pounds of cheese, a side of salted bacon and one plucked fowl. We have sufficient milk to last a week or so though, sadly, six urns soured after being carelessly left in the sun.

February 3rd, 1906

This morning I informed our hard-working servants I could no longer pay their wages for the past month. Three good men left right away with signed promissory notes guaranteeing their salaries once funds have been dispatched from London. Magdalena's daughter has found occupation at the Adamson's farm and her two sons will work at the flourishing Noord Paarl Wagon Builders.

Dirk has provided a small loan – all he can afford from his humble organist's salary.

With this, I have barely enough to pay our remaining workers, purchase horse feed and replenish dwindling stocks of candles, meal, salt, tea, sugar and lard.

February 10th, 1906

I have packed trunks with a few of Edward's suits and coats and many of my own tucked capes, jackets, ostrich feather boas, parasols and hats. I no longer need such a frivolous wardrobe and these items will be sold for cash at Saturday's market.

Next week, there is an auction in town where stock will be traded, mainly cows and sheep, though we are told furnishings and artworks will also be for sale.

I have taken down two of Edward's prized oil paintings; his phonograph with its mock gold trumpet horn; a much-prized looking-glass embellished with Art Nouveau butterflies on a beaten silver frame; a Turkish tapestry and a beautiful marble mantel clock.

Dirk loaded these valuables carefully onto the wagonette to be transported to town although he did so reluctantly and only after many attempts to dissuade me from taking this path. He pleaded with me to consider what Edward will do when he discovers I have sold his treasured possessions. But I am neither amenable to reason nor am I afraid. All I care is that these items are sold to the highest bidder.

February 16th, 1906

With money collected from various sales of produce, clothing and furnishings, I have repaid our debts – including Dirk's loan – and we are free and clear with sufficient funds, by my reckoning, to last a full half-year, if we are frugal.

My heart is lighter, my footsteps less heavy. Today I heard happy laughter – my own – pealing in my unaccustomed ears.

February 17th, 1906

Alerted to news of our improved fortunes, two of our men have returned home.

Gladly, I welcomed them and set them to mucking out the stables and working the fields. After a late budding, our grapes are slowly growing though the globes are still small with thick skin.

It is too soon to taste if the fruit is bitter but, within a month, we shall be able to judge the quality of this year's harvest.

March 12th, 1906

Weeks have flown since my last entry. How life has altered since then. I catch myself singing as I perform the sweet trivialities of daily life. I am making cheese and butter; punishing the dusty rugs with bamboo carpet beaters; darning Dirk's stockings; arranging bowls of fresh flowers from our garden. Dirk practices at the piano and gives music lessons at the Strooidak Kerk.

We two are as content as an old married couple. Our past, present and future seem as tightly interlinked as fibers woven into a carpet, yet, I am not so innocent as to imagine it is impossible to separate one skein from the other. For this reason, I cherish each precious moment and, whenever I am tempted to dwell upon the past, purposefully fill my head with happy visions of our future together.

March 26th, 1906

    My fingers tremble as I write…

Dear God…I am five days past my monthly time!

CHAPTER THIRTY

PLUM

It's like jigsaw pieces fitting together – the baby crying – *uhug, uhug, uhug, uhugg* – it's not a cat because cats don't hiccup and then there's the attic and anyone can see it used to be a nursery not a storeroom for stuff nobody wanted. That cradle was made by Aletta's husband for their own baby and she gave it to Charlotte for Pretty's Angela and the rocking horse came from Dirk.

Pretty and her baby are buried out back behind the wine cellar under a stone scratched with PR and the baby's grave is covered with a blanket of dirty pebbles with weeds poking up between stones.

One thing I didn't understand.

"What does *'Five days past my monthly time'* mean?"

"Oh, Plum!" She gets this suffering face that says, 'Oh, for goodness sake, what now?' and you can tell she wishes she were somewhere else like in France wearing a beret and painting on a bridge.

Her eyes moved left and right, not looking at me.

"Um…so, you know what a period is?"

"Duh!" Everyone knows a period is when blood comes out of your uterus and you have to wear a tampon.

"Okay, so Charlotte calls her period her 'monthly time' and 'five days past' means she's late, so…if she and Dirk had…um…sex…she was probably pregnant with his baby."

She closed her eyes. "Do you think you could be quiet for a bit? Stop asking questions?"

"Can I bring your headache pills?"

"Oh, would you?"

When I got back, her eyes were still closed so I made my voice soft and quiet, "Why don't you lie down till you feel better?"

She had wonky ragdoll legs so I stuck out my arm. "I'll help you up the stairs."

I was proud I let her hold onto me because I don't like being touched especially by a hand like an iced lolly. The way she was leaning made me think of Mom and sadness whooshed through me and she must've felt it because she said, "What?"

"Mom," I mumbled and she nodded and we both sighed at the same time.

"You were good with your Mom when she was sick," she said. "You were helpful and loving and *so* brave," and it was like she'd pinned a shiny gold badge on my chest and I stood straighter the way Mom used to tell me with shoulders back and head high because nobody has ever said that to me before.

"Mom was the brave one," I told her.

Mom got so sick she couldn't do anything for herself. She had to wear big cottony pads like nappies and my aunt used to wash her with a warm soapy facecloth and give her teeny teaspoons of jelly or ice-cream but as she got sicker she could only suck bashed-up bits of ice and sip water through a bendy plastic straw. Dad got scared and I had to pretend I didn't know he was crying all the time and didn't really have a cold or sinuses playing up from pollen like he said.

Talking got hard for Mom and her words sometimes stuck together with slurry edges so you couldn't understand and then you'd hear soft popping snores as the medicine sent her to sleep in the middle of a sentence and all you could do was hold her hand and wait for her to squeeze though it was more a butterfly squeeze than the bear paw grip she used to give before she had cancer.

I don't like remembering that time so I make myself think of a photo of us picnicking on Bomere Heath and Mom's laughing in that picture with head back and hair blowing and I'm staring at Dad's camera with my dead face but you can see from my eyes I'm happy inside.

I heard voices the night Mom died. Mom and Aunt Frith were giggling and Mom said the word I'm not allowed – *"Fuck!"* – and laughed till tears came and then sobbed for a while. Through a crack in the door I watched Aunt Frith feeding Mom with a teaspoon and Mom was smiling and forcing herself to swallow and tiny bubbles started fizzing inside because I thought maybe she was turning a corner the way Dad had promised she would.

I fell asleep hugging myself but this scary noise barged into my dream – Dad moaning like a dog that's been knocked over by a car. I got this weird sick feeling in my stomach and dug my fingers in my ears but Aunt Frith came and crawled into my bed and touched my head and whispered, "Plum…Mom's gone, darling. She died peacefully in her sleep. Last thing she said was how much she loved you." I know people are always saying stuff like '*that was the day my life changed*' but for me it was true, swear to God.

Aunt Frith asked me to draw the curtains in her room because her headache made her eyes see light as shards of sparkling broken glass and I don't know what a shard is but I think it's something thin and sharp like a splinter. I smashed my aunt's feather pillow a couple of times to make it comfy but she said, "Shush…no noise, please Plum, it hurts."

"So, the night Mom died…" I started.

She groaned. "Oh, no, Plum! Not now. I can't."

"It's not a question. You don't have to answer. I want to *tell* you something."

"I'm not in the mood for this, sorry." She pressed her hand to her mouth. "Later, please. I can't talk. This head is killing me."

But I *had* to tell her.

"The night Mom died I was peeking through the crack in the door and it looked like she was getting better because she was laughing and eating – I saw you feeding her – and that's why I couldn't believe it when you said she'd died."

Aunt Frith's mouth started moving like she wanted to cry. "I don't understand. What are you saying?"

"Something I've been meaning to tell you but haven't because I've been so cross with you for the longest time."

A tear plopped on her chin. "What?"

I stared at the wetness. "Is it this headache making you cry?" She nodded.

"Oh. Me and Dad were sleeping which means if you hadn't been feeding Mom pudding and telling stories to make her laugh she'd have been by herself and would've been terribly lost and scared and it makes me feel better knowing she didn't die alone."

My aunt's mouth started trembling and then tears were spilling and her shoulders were heaving and the noise coming out of her mouth was the same knocked-over-dog howl Dad had made after Mom died.

FRITH

I've been lying on my bed under a quilt, shivering with cold, despite the weighty warmth of William's heavy fisherman's sweater.

Plum was implying something. She had that knowing look. Did she see me crushing Lil's sleeping tablets? Has she guessed I gave her mother drugs to help her die? Has she said anything to William?

I slept like the dead all that afternoon and through the night. Next morning, Mrs Partridge tiptoed in with a tray of tea and egg salad sandwiches, quartered and sprinkled with a green drift of parsley. I wolfed the sandwiches and scalded my mouth with boiling tea.

"This is kind of you," I said, surprised and grateful.

She gave a little bob. "My pleasure," she said. "Feeling better?"

"I am. Thank you. I get migraines."

"You relax. I'll be back later for the tray."

Minutes later, I heard her scrubbing the toilet in the en-suite bathroom and a reek of bleach and pine-scented cleaner filtered through the air.

I suppose this is Mrs Partridge's 'new broom' stage, likely to dissipate as time passes.

What worries me is the woman's bird-like frailty. I can't see her managing William, if he continues to deteriorate mentally. And she's soft. Plum will twist her around her little finger.

Next morning, Mrs Partridge arrived late and breathless after an athletic gallop from the bus stop. "Sorry! Car trouble!" she sang out. I looked up from arranging a vase of hydrangeas.

"Morning, Mrs Partridge."

She wasted no time. "Good to see you up and about. I've been wanting a word, if you don't mind."

Hurriedly, she sloughed off a pair of trainers and buttoned a navy overall.

"There's no easy way to say this but I'm not one for beating about the bush so here goes."

I stood stiffly, preparing myself. *What now?*

She took a breath. "Your Plum said something about a ghost in the attic that day I came for the interview. I didn't think anything of it at the time… but…"

I exhaled. "Oh, that. Nothing to worry about. I think you'll find my niece has an overdeveloped imagination."

Mrs Partridge nodded. "She's clever, bright as a button I will say. But this ghost she's always going on about – you do know about it, I suppose? She calls it a *'spirit'*. I think it may be affecting her and not in a good way."

She broke off, flustered.

"Thank you." I felt myself bridle. "I know *all* about the ghost, Mrs Partridge," I said, crisply.

"Yes, thought you might. And it's Birdie, please. Thing is, Plum had a bit of a turn yesterday afternoon. Your door was shut. I didn't want to disturb."

I nodded. "My niece suffers from…"

She rattled on as if I hadn't spoken.

"So, anyway, she was telling me about a cot in the attic and how sometimes she hears a baby crying and then she stopped and went deathly quiet. I said, 'Carry on with your story, pet,' but it was like she was in some kind of trance, staring into space, face white, eyes blank. This lasted for, oh, goodness, a few minutes, I suppose. Then, it was like somebody snapping fingers and back she came. Shaken to the bone I was. Never seen anything like it before."

I made my voice neutral. "I'm sorry, Mrs Partridge, I should have explained. Plum has *petit mal* seizures. A form of mild epilepsy. The episodes are usually over quickly. Since her mother's died, they seem more frequent, but they're not harmful. She has no recollection. No lingering after-effects or anything like that."

Mrs Partridge looked doubtful. "Well, that's as may be. It's just, you know – Plum talking about this baby crying and then going off like that. It made me wonder if there's a link between her...*seizure*...and the ghost she talks about."

"I'm not with you. Are you saying the ghost is the reason for Plum's seizures?"

"I'm just trying to fathom..."

Indignantly, I spun to face her. "There's no ghost, Mrs Partridge."

"Well, of course I know that."

"Plum's different. She believes her doll is alive despite having a fabric body of sawdust, eyes of glass and a head of porcelain bisque!"

She smiled weakly. "Sweet, the way she talks to it."

"This thing with the ghost, it's part of a pattern. As a toddler Plum had imaginary friends. A boy who lived in the pantry, a dog that followed her from school, even a herd of fairies she said flew into her bedroom every night, attracted by the night light."

I jabbed the last hydrangea into the sodden oasis and broke the stem. *Damn, damn!*

"Is there anything else, Mrs...Birdie?"

She shook her head. "Best get on with things..." she replied, warily.

My hands were shaking as Mrs Partridge trudged up the stairs with the vacuum cleaner.

I've no idea why I get so uncontrollably angry about Plum, that fatuous doll and the bloody ghost. The woman has a point though. She *is* having more lapses since we've been in this house. That's when she started seeing the ghost. Same time I started reading the diary which has only made things a million times worse. The diary seems to trigger Plum's imagination until she's consumed by what she thinks is the spirit of Charlotte Butler. I suppose I'm angry because Plum is my responsibility now, not Lily's and not William's – he couldn't care for a kitten in his present state – and the idea of protecting my odd, vulnerable niece from the world makes me want to run and hide.

I was in my bedroom, painting, when Plum came home from school.

She dropped her satchel on my bed. "What are you doing?" she asked, though it was obvious.

I've painted a house on a tree-lined street and made it look as it did in the early nineteen hundreds. At least that's what I've tried to do. Using one of my photographs as a reference I've blanked out a car, a fire hydrant and a neatly clipped French poodle and replaced these with dark rhododendrons and a spreading oak that's truer to the era.

Plum's plaits were coming undone and she had a streak of oil from her bicycle chain on her skirt. She leaned over my painting, almost knocking over the jar of water.

"Birdie said to tell you she's sorry and her husband, bless his heart, used to say she had the tact of an elephant in a bun shop – whatever that means."

"That's nice of her. How was school?"

She shrugged. "Same old same old. Where's Dad?"

"Out."

I could tell she wanted to ask if William was okay but didn't want to know if he wasn't. "He's fair to middling," I offered.

"I've a test on micro-organisms tomorrow."

"You'd best do your revision then."

"I'll be in the kitchen – Birdie's polishing silver and I like the smell."

I mixed bluey-purple for shadows and took a mental walk to the churchyard.

I haven't been there in over a month. The Azaleas and Cape Hawthorn will be blooming. Tightly pleated buds will be shooting on rose bushes and a squad of gardeners coaxing leaves into shuddery piles to gather into black plastic bags.

The church organist will be practicing, sounding a flat note, going back, the music echoing hollowly in the church. All I have to do is close my eyes and I can see Theo's slow smile. His thick thatch of whitened hair. The warm, muscular, reassuring bulkiness of his body. The dark, silky furrow of hair winding down his stomach. It's been weeks since we've been together. I suppose I'm rationing myself in preparation for the end. I've read somewhere that grieving over the loss of a loved one diminishes after a year or so. It's not happening in Lily's case and though my feelings for Theo are *nothing* like those I have for my sister, I'm beginning to wonder how long it will take for me to get over him.

PLUM

I tipped my head to one side, listening. "Hear that?" I asked.

Birdie looked up from polishing a soup ladle. "That bird?"

"What bird?"

"I don't know. I'm not good with bird names."

Uh-huh, uh-huh, uh-huh, uh-huh…a tiny baby crying, thin, bleating from the attic…how could she think it's a bird?

"You're a wee bit pale, love," Birdie said. "Feeling alright?"

When she cries, this baby makes me feel jittery in my chest and a bit sick. I was thinking, '*I wish I knew what was going to happen and if everything's going to be okay. It's the not knowing that makes me worry*' but it turned out I'd said this aloud.

Birdie winked. "That's what intuition is for, lamb."

"What do you mean?"

"Intuition tells you something's in the air." Birdie licked the tip of her finger and held it up and I wondered if it left the taste of silver polish in her mouth.

"Know how you can tell when there's a thunderstorm brewing?"

I shook my head.

"Well, there are clues. First the air gets softer. Then the sky grows darker. And then there's this stillness when everything falls silent and even birds stop singing. Nobody tells you there's a storm coming – you just know it, here." Birdie thumped her chest hard.

"I have good intuition and there's something in the air." Birdie rubbed at a silver tea-pot with a duster. "I wouldn't be the least surprised if it wasn't a bit of well-deserved happiness on its way to you."

That didn't sound right. "You really think so?"

"I do, my pet. I really do."

And then the baby stopped crying and my whole body went saggy and I could breathe properly again so I pulled my science books out of my satchel.

"Best get your nose into those," Birdie smiled.

After Birdie went home, Aunt Frith came downstairs. She pulled Dad's jersey tighter and opened her mouth in a yawn so wide I could see the dark fillings in her back teeth.

"Want me to quiz you on your…what was it?"

"Micro-organisms and I know everything by heart – bet I get a hundred percent for this test."

She looked at me sideways. "Wish I'd had your confidence at your age."

I made myself stare directly into the black spots in her eyes. "Aunt Frith, aren't you even a tiny bit curious? Don't you want to know if Charlotte Butler is going to have Dirk's baby?"

Her lips quivered like she wanted to laugh. "I've left the diary on the table beside my bed. Go and fetch it while I put the kettle on for tea."

April 14th, 1906

Today I impart to my journal – the sacred repository of my heart and mind – information which is both disastrous and yet also miraculously wonderful. I am pregnant with Dirk's child!

There can be no doubt of this since I am now twenty-four days past my monthly time.

April 15th, 1906

My joy has drained away. I find myself unable to do anything beyond fret over what fate holds in store for us and our child. What good outcome can there be from an illicit union between a married woman and a bachelor, many years her junior? My emotions swerve madly from feeling helpless to feeling a sense of being blessed that I have conceived a child in the heat of passion with a man I dearly love.

I have not yet told Dirk of my condition. I cannot bring myself to spoil everything when we two are, upon the surface, so happy and content. With Pretty's death still sadly fresh in our memory, Dirk will be frightened for me. Like me, he will dread Edward's reaction if my husband discovers I am with child! I cannot write more. My trembling makes my handwriting barely legible.

April 16th, 1906

I am feeling bilious. Hiding this secret has made me ill. Intense emotions continue to storm inside.

I've been considering whether I should uproot myself and escape to a secret place for the duration of my confinement. They have such places for women in my state, I believe.

It would be foolish to risk Edward's fury should he return and discover Dirk and I, living together as man and wife with a child on the way.

He would kill us both, I am convinced of that! Yet, how can I leave North Wind Manor in the knowledge that I would never again be able to return to my home?

April 20th, 1906

I had to speak or go insane. I chose to confess to Aletta but when I told her, she became silent and then, minutes later, shouted loudly at my lying with a man who is not my lawful husband.

I was surprised at the intensity of her anger and when I tried to explain, Aletta shook her head and hurried away without another word.

I am heart-sore at such uncharacteristic behaviour from my kind neighbour who has made it quite plain she is deeply disappointed in the weakness of my character.

Later…

I have received no word from Edward since his hateful note in which he threatened divorce.

This afternoon, I wrote asking when he proposes to return to North Wind Manor and offering lack of funds as a reason for my letter. It is vital I know Edward's future plans so I may formulate my own.

I pray he replies by post and does not shock me with an unannounced return.

April 22ⁿᵈ, 1906

Food makes me retch. Small sips of water and dry bread or hard biscuit are all I can endure.

Praise the Lord – Aletta has forgiven me as I hoped she would. She made me drink a cup of strong nettle tea for stomach sickness though the taste of it is so horrid, I'd rather swallow nails.

I have become thin and my dear friend cautions I may require a skilled physician if I am to deliver a healthy child. She refers, of course, to Dr. Clutterbuck but doesn't know the man is a spy and the last person on this earth I would make aware of my condition! Aletta recommends greens and bloody red meat for strength though the thought of this makes me dreadfully queasy.

April 24ᵗʰ, 1906

Is Clutterbuck a wizard? No sooner had I written his name upon the page when he was banging at the door. I opened it and reluctantly accepted his bags of pigs' trotters and freshly gathered gooseberries. Thankfully, Dirk had ridden early to the church to spend the day peacefully engaged in organ practice.

"How is it with you, Charlotte?" the doctor enquired. I observed his gaze taking in my pale aspect, and before he could grope in his bag for a cure, I asked if he had heard from Edward.

"Not for some time," Clutterbuck replied though, from the furtive manner in which his eyes swerved from mine, I believe he spoke a lie.

I had a sudden hunger for the gooseberries and served a portion for each of us, inviting the doctor to sit with me. We made dull conversation before, impatiently, I turned to the topic of Pretty and the dangers of childbirth. The doctor grudgingly admitted mortality is high and from his air of annoyance, could tell he thought I was setting the blame of Pretty's death at his feet.

He glared with eyes as hard as boot buttons. "Had I not been summoned too late, I might have been able to give your maid belladonna to calm her contractions."

I reassured Clutterbuck, saying the fault was not his and added I had long desired a child but, in witnessing Pretty's agony, was now in fearful dread of childbirth.

His relief was visible as he went on to assure me that many healthy women are able to give birth without a particle of pain. We spoke upon this matter for some time. I asked the doctor to explain the growth of the seed within the womb and recall his words exactly.

'By the twentieth day, the embryo takes on the appearance of an ant or a lettuce seed. By the thirtieth day, it has enlarged to the size of a common horse fly. When the fortieth day is reached, the embryo looks more human and by the fourth month it possesses active limbs and human characteristics like small, perfectly formed ears.'

So...our baby is no bigger than a horse fly!

April 27th, 1906

Three days later, and Clutterbuck has visited again. This time he tipped his hat and offered a bottle of port wine and a twist of Cayenne pepper. I sent silent thanks that Dirk was safely concealed, reading in the library.

We took tea in the garden where Clutterbuck told an appalling tale. He spoke of a young, unmarried woman, a prosperous farmer's daughter, not yet nineteen, who'd come to him many months prior, complaining of vomiting. He'd prescribed medicine and she'd returned, two days later, requesting more.

"I put direct questions to her," the doctor said, "and determined from her replies that she was pregnant although she strongly denied this."

He said he'd thought no more about the matter until he received a visit from the Chief Constable who presented him with the body of a newborn infant. The baby was a boy with a woman's yellow kerchief twisted around its neck.

"After examination, I concluded the baby had been strangulated after birth," the doctor told me. "The little mite's face was purple with tongue protruding."

The Constable said the newborn had been discovered in a field by a farmer whose dog had dug up a shallow grave covered over with sods of earth. Clutterbuck gave the policeman the name of the pregnant young girl he had attended.

A day later, the doctor was summoned for the purpose of examining the girl and, finding her distraught, he had asked her mother to be present during a medical examination which concluded that she bore the symptoms of a recent delivery.

"At first, the poor wretch denied the birth had occurred," Clutterbuck said, "But, with irrefutable evidence at hand, she broke down and confessed to tying a kerchief around her baby's throat and twisting until the infant stopped breathing."

This tale has left me agitated. I cannot imagine how the daughter of a well-known and respected family could be capable of murdering her own baby!

Clutterbuck says she committed the deed out of panic and shame. "I know the father to be a hard, puritanical Calvinist – a God-fearing man who would never condone his daughter's pregnancy out of wedlock." The girl has been confined to the infirmary in the Paarl Gaol until a trial date is set.

I will pray for her soul.

April 29th, 1906

I have excruciating nightmares...dead babies in shallow graves...Pretty with a river of blood flowing from her body...baby Angela, like a tiny, slippery fish dragged from the water, her sweet mouth gasping for breath. Shame and guilt bring these troubled dreams.

Oh, God help me, I am so unhappy!

May 3rd, 1906

"Are you unwell, Charlotte?" Dirk asked this morning.

"I am tired," I replied. I kissed his lips and waved merrily as he set off for the church.

My thoughts are like wild birds trapped in a cage. Has Dr. Clutterbuck guessed my condition?

Has he sent word to Edward? Could my husband, even now, be making his way home by steamer? Should Dirk and I pack our belongings and run away together?

But, where will we go? How will we survive? And what will the good people of Paarl make of our sudden and unexplained disappearance?

May 4th, 1906

One thing I know for certain – my life with Dirk, such as it is, cannot continue. We are living a lie, pretending to play at man and wife. A strange malaise has overtaken me. My common sense has fled leaving me timid as a young child. I cannot find the courage to tell Dirk I carry his child.

Over and over, I keep asking myself – what is the worst that could happen if I told my beloved the truth? My answer is simple – I am afraid Dirk will abandon me.

May 5th, 1906

I am well-disposed to prayer and welcome the blessing of our Lord but everything has altered with the knowledge I no longer feel worthy of God's kindness and charity.

This pathetic shilly-shallying must stop. I cannot keep staving off the inevitable!

Tonight, I swear, I will tell Dirk!

Later…

He laid his cheek upon my swelling belly.

"Oh, Charlotte!" Dirk cried. "If we were married in the eyes of God our joy would now be made complete!"

"What are we to do?" I asked.

I saw alarm bloom upon his sweet face.

Miserably, he shook his head. "I do not know," he answered.

CHAPTER THIRTY ONE

FRITH

Plum came to breakfast in tatty denims and a t-shirt with a gaping hole in the sleeve. "You're **not** wearing that to school," I said, firmly.

"We're allowed to wear anything," she shot back. "It's civvies day."

"Go upstairs and put on your new black skirt and white blouse – the one with puff sleeves."

She opened her mouth to object but I silenced her with a look. Pulling a face, she stamped upstairs.

William seemed more disorientated than usual. He poured a cup of tea and stared at it.

I set a plate of sliced fruit before him. "Eat something. You're wasting away."

He sighed. "No appetite." He raked his hair with his fingers.

"You seem out of it again," I said. "What's the matter?"

"Nothing. Everything. I don't know."

"Try to explain."

"There's this constant pain hardwired into my body. And there's mental agony. Neither is visible. I've no scabs or scars – it's all buried deep inside like a dark force. On top of that my brain is fogged and I have a sensation of falling even when I'm standing upright. Ever feel like that?"

"No."

349

"I'm disconnected – viewing the world from a different planet." He sighed. "And I hate, myself, Frith. I'm a bastard. A total arse. I have this urge to step out of my skin and become someone else. But I can't because…I'm paralysed."

He clutched at his chest dramatically and, in a rush of annoyance, I said the cruellest thing. "Lily would've been so disappointed…the way you're behaving."

I peeled an apple, watching the skin unfurl in an unending strip of smooth, shiny green.

Plum came in, squinting at her father. "How are you, Dad?" She asks this question every morning, tentative and wary, dreading his answer.

William makes no effort to hide his depression from her – almost revelling in the melodrama like some morbid character in a Jacobean play.

"Oh, bearing up, my darling," he sighed. "Setting one foot in front of the other, doing my utmost to hold on tight." He blinked. "Isn't it a school day? Why are you dressed like that?"

"Civvies." She spoke through a mouthful of banana. "Aunt Frith wants me wearing this but it's all wrong and I won't fit in."

William frowned, trying to concentrate. "What do the others wear?" She waved a hand, dismissively. "It doesn't matter. I've a flat tyre on my bike. Can you give me a lift?"

William's hand shook visibly as he carried the teacup to his mouth.

"I'll take you, Plum," I blurted. "I'm going into town. Mrs Partridge's given me a grocery list and I need a tube of Chinese White."

William interrupted. He sounded accusing: "It's *him* you're going to see. Am I right?"

"*What?*"

"You're meeting that effing Theo Christensen."

Plum's head swung back and forth between us.

I answered levelly. "I'm going shopping. Have you finished, Plum? We really must be off."

Remorse swamped as I drove into the school parking. Casting around, it was obvious Plum was the odd one out in a bobbing sea of casually dressed girls. She'd have blended in perfectly in her none-too-clean denims and washed out t-shirt with threads unravelling in the sleeve. She was also the only girl not wearing makeup – her clean, shiny face making her look innocent, as if playing at dress-up in her mother's clothes.

My heart welled with pity. A last glance in my rear-view mirror showed Plum talking to a girl with spiky gelled hair in a cropped leather jacket and skin tight jeans.

I sent a silent message. "*Oh, Christ, Lil, I've screwed up again, I never seem to get it right. I'm sorry, Lil, I really am.*"

I listened for my twin and thought I heard her whisper but it was probably only the swish of tyres on tarmac.

But then I did hear her "*…Love set you going like a fat gold watch,*" she said.

Words from a poem she used to read to Plum in her quiet, steady voice, slowing for the part Plum loved most.

"*Love set you going like a fat gold watch.*
The midwife slapped your footsoles,
And your bald cry took its place among the elements."

"Is that me?" Plum always asked, the beginning of a smile playing on her mouth. "Am I the baby?"

Lily would nod, gravely. "It's from a poem called *Morning Song* by Sylvia Plath who wrote about the precious time when her newly born child came into the world."

It was Lily who had told me Sylvia Plath had gassed herself one bitter winter in her London flat near Primrose Hill with her two children, three-year old Frieda and Nicholas, almost one, asleep in a nearby room. Plath was only thirty-one when she'd inhaled deadly fumes from her gas oven after leaving out cups of milk for the children and a pile of newly completed poems, ready for publication.

"Such a waste," Lily had once said, sounding bleak. "Such a shocking waste of a young life."

I still have Lil's copy of Sylvia Plath's poems. Sometimes I look at the sepia picture of the poet on the back cover, short curly hair, arching brows, open, smiling face.

"Stupid cow," I say out loud. "Stupid cow for killing yourself without good cause."

Often I'd ask Lily to recite *Morning Song* and I'll never forget her voice intoning Plath's beautifully strung words. I'd do anything to bring back one of those times when we used to sit up until dawn, sipping cold tea and talking. I wish I could remember what we'd spoken about so earnestly and for so long but all details of our conversations have long-since fled and it terrifies me just how much of Lily I've let go during this past year.

PLUM

I had to wear a straight cardboardy skirt and puffy-sleeved blouse for civvies day and Bronte said I'd look less weird if I had blush on the apples of my cheeks so she fixed my face with her pinkie crooked in the air and her fingernails shiny with blue glitter.

"There!" she said but her tiny mirror showed me looking like a stupid clown with round red cheeks so I scrubbed off the blush and gave her a slice of Birdie's jammy Victoria sponge to make it up to her.

Bronte asked if she could come to my house for a sleepover.

"My aunt has unbreakable rules," I said. "One of them is not having friends to stay."

I can lie with a straight face which is useful sometimes.

"What's wrong with friends staying over?"

What's wrong is I can't have Bronte seeing Dad's gone funny with still missing and longing for my dead Mom.

"Dunno," I said.

"Your aunt is a wicked witch."

"She's strict, that's all."

"She the one made you wear that skirt and stupid blouse?"

"Mmmm."

"She should be burnt at the stake like Joan of Arc."

Bronte can go on like this forever so I told her Dad's set up a humungous jigsaw puzzle on the coffee table. This puzzle has five hundred pieces making up a picture of snow and leafless trees huddled together. It's hard because the jigsaw pieces look almost identical except for bits of grey sky which fit at the top. I didn't tell Bronte we've been working on the puzzle for simply ages but we're not getting very far because I'm slotting together bits of frozen snow while Dad – who's supposed to do sky and trees – keeps staring at the cold, blindingly white picture on the lid of the puzzle box.

Last night, he told me about when he and Mom were trapped in a farm cottage during a snowstorm and the snow fell as high as the windows so they couldn't open the front door until the farmer brought a snow plough to rescue them.

"Was I there?" I asked.

"No, my darling. It was before you came along. We were young and so much in love with our whole lives waiting. It seems so very, very long ago."

"Life is still waiting," Aunt Frith said, and the way she said it made me think she was cross.

"Not for me," Dad pulled a face. "I'm stuck."

"That won't last. Nothing lasts forever."

"You've no idea what this feels like, have you? If I could just go back and start over. I wouldn't mess up. Everything would be perfect. I wouldn't go off the rails. She wouldn't get sick."

"Lord help us!" my aunt said. "Another whine fest. Do you ever listen to yourself, William?"

But then Dad was crying and my aunt was holding him and saying, "Okay, okay. Just hold on, everything's going to be okay."

"My arms have gone numb. No feeling in my fingers."

"You're having another panic attack. Breathe, slowly."

I don't want Bronte seeing Dad crumple which is why I lied about my aunt's unbreakable rules.

I was in the middle of telling Bronte about our snowy jigsaw puzzle and thinking about Dad crying when black dots started swimming through the jelly in my eyes like tadpoles doing a wiggly dance with curly tails moving fast like comets.

I heard Bronte say, "What's up, Plum?" but my mouth was glued and hot prickles of sweat popped up in my hair and on my face and the sky began slowly moving to one side and voices swirled into the far distance and then the bag was over my head.

When I came round, Miss Nell gave me a glass of sugary water to drink and said I'd fainted and if I held onto her arm she'd help me to the infirmary where I could have a quiet lie down until my mother came to take me home.

Bronte commented I didn't have a mother only an aunt who was a witch and wouldn't let me have friends over and Miss Nell told her to quick march back to class and said, "Lean on me Plum, that's right, are you still dizzy, my dear?"

Aunt Frith didn't answer her mobile so Miss Nell left a message.

"I have papers to mark," she said. "Back in half an hour."

I like the infirmary because it's cool and clean with a smell of Dettol and spotted curtains at the window. It is next door to Seven C, which is Mrs van Rooyen's room and clear as anything I could hear her voice and the mousy squeak of her Koki on the white board. She was talking Greek. "When we *multiply* fractions we times the top with the top and the bottom with the bottom,"…*squeak, squeak, squeak.* "Now, who remembers how to *divide* fractions? Anyone? No? Well, we invert the second fraction and then we change the divide symbol into a multiply symbol…who remembers now?" *Squeak, squeak, squeak.*

Clunky footsteps in the passage and then more footsteps, lighter, with tapping heels.

"Angelica de Witt! What are you doing outside your classroom?"

Mumble, mumble, mumble.

"We've just had small break. Why didn't you go then?"

Mumble, mumble, mumble.

"Well, hurry up and don't make a habit of this, Angelica!"

"No, Miss. Thank you Miss."

Singing from the music room with Mrs Robbins banging on the piano keys.

"When the night has come
And the land is dark
And the moon is the only light we'll see
No I won't be afraid
Oh, I won't be afraid
Just as long as you stand, stand by me."

I love that song and when I hear it I remember how I used to feel when Mom was with me and it makes me sad that I've almost forgotten that feeling.

I must've fallen asleep because when I woke I heard Dad telling Miss Nell, "I've come for Plum. I'm her father."

Miss Nell explained I'd fainted. "Doesn't sound right," Dad said. "Plum has *petit mal* seizures, had them since she was about two or three, I think. The details are a tad sketchy but my Lily would've known when the problem started. This would've been one of those."

Miss Nell gave me a kind look. "She's a lot better now."

"She misses her mother," Dad said. "We all do."

Birdie came up to my room with lemonade and a dish of something pink and wobbly called blancmange that tasted smooth and powdery and then Aunt Frith pushed my legs to one side and curled on my bed with the diary and I told her I'd faint every day if it meant getting spoiled like this.

May 7th, 1906

Dirk has answered a post for an organist and choir master at a Dutch Reformed Church in Beaufort West. There is a small cottage on the parsonage grounds that may be available in return for a modest rental. Dirk has urgently dispatched a wire to the church minister professing keen interest in the position.

I know nothing of Beaufort West. Dirk says the town is far away and reached only by traveling a great many weary, dust-laden miles across the burning hot platteland towards the Central Karoo.

Situated at the foot of a long blue ridge of mountains, the area thrives with prosperous sheep farms set amongst vast, open plains. Aletta tells me the town was named after Henry Somerset, Fifth Duke of Beaufort and is well-known for its avenues of pear trees and irrigation furrows, built in every street to channel water into fruit and vegetable gardens.

I have told Aletta that I am torn by indecision. I should be willing to follow Dirk to the relative safety of this distant Karoo town and yet find it almost impossible to even think of leaving North Wind Manor. My friend looked upon me with tender solicitude. "You must pray and trust in the good Lord to show you the way."

I have been on my knees praying every day throughout this perilous year. Sadly the Lord appears stone deaf to the pleas of this unworthy sinner.

May 8th, 1906

Observing me taking down the valises, Magdalena asked if I were planning a journey and, in a panic, I told a lie, claiming I proposed to visit a relative living some distance away.

She did not believe me. Her gaze lingered purposefully upon my belly with a look so forbidding I could not meet her eyes.

Magdalena and her daughter have altered towards me. They wear expressions of disdain and, by degrees, I see how their respect diminishes. I do not blame them. I know what Dirk and I are doing is wrong – yet I am powerless to stop.

May 9th, 1906

I have set aside my corset and taken to wearing looser garments to accommodate my swelling belly and breasts. Even my cheeks are now plump as peaches.

I pray this child grows strong and healthy and I am able to hold onto my baby until its rightful time. I pray I can overcome my terror of delivering a stillborn babe or having my life extinguished in the throes of childbirth.

It has been raining heavily today. The rain whips beneath the roof tiles and drips into the upstairs rooms. I have set out buckets and basins to catch the rainwater but the house is bitterly cold and damp. Winter will be upon us soon.

May 12th, 1906

My nerves are bad today. Dirk also seems increasingly anxious. Receiving no reply from the Dominee in Fort Beaufort, he has sent a second telegraph, begging an immediate answer.

This morning the trial of the poor, wretched farmer's daughter accused of murdering her newborn son has opened in court. She has pleaded not guilty by reason of insanity.

May 14th, 1906

Dominee Willem Steyn has agreed to meet Dirk in a fortnight. There is only one other candidate for this post and, since this person is a middle-aged woman, Dirk believes he has a good chance of being awarded the position.

My beloved uncorked a bottle of wine to celebrate 'our good fortune'. He urged me to pack clothing and only a few possessions. Pegasus will draw the cart with our luggage. All else must remain here.

I am in turmoil! My heart aches. Can I find the strength to tear myself from North Wind Manor, the first real home I have ever known?

May 15th, 1906

The farmer's daughter has been found guilty of willfully murdering her baby and condemned to twenty years in prison. I am appalled at such a hard, merciless verdict.

There are a great many like me who believe this misguided girl must have been in terrible fear of her stern father and therefore not in full possession of her faculties at the time of giving birth.

I cannot help thinking…there but for the grace of God go I!

May 16th, 1906

Lately, I have been engaged in introspection of my life. This is how it lies…

My marriage to Edward is the worst of it and from our bitterly divided union I have benefited nothing and an excess of mental suffering, shame, fear and hatred.

In balance, Edward has blessed me with North Wind Manor and this grace-filled house has offered a blessed sanctuary. Only within these walls have I come to know precious moments of happiness and peace. Despite all that's happened here, my feelings for the manor have never altered. I treasure this house with the devotion I would give a lover.

Then there is Dirk, the man to whom my heart belongs and whose child I carry. Our love feels honest and good, as natural as breathing. Yet, since I am older and already married, our relationship is not only immoral but also rash, selfish and dangerous. In the end, this may prove to be our undoing.

Dirk's plan sees us living as man and wife in a Dominee's cottage in Beaufort West. But my lover does not have the nature for deceit and could do far better for himself than settle for me.

I know how many young, pretty, marriageable women in this parish would be glad to be the wife of a man universally respected and admired by the community.

If we were to run away together, the people of Paarl would rapidly alter their good opinion of Dirk.

What possible happiness could we derive from such great personal sacrifice?

May 18th, 1906

I have been weeping which is why tears have obliterated this first sentence, causing me to begin again.

Dirk and I have been quarrelling, exchanging harsh words. I have begged him to forget me, return to his boarding house and resume his simpler, honest life. I have told him what I believe to be true – if we remain together, we shall be in jeopardy not only from Edward but from a crisis of our own conscience. In time, I promised, he would forget me and meet a young woman, closer to his own age to take as his lawful bride and the mother of his children.

If Edward returns before the birth, I shall have to deal with the consequences of my actions and submit to my husband's fury – though I will never reveal the name of my baby's father.

WHERE THE TRUTH LIES

But if luck is on my side and Edward comes later, once the baby and I have survived our confinement, I shall tell Edward I adopted the infant after its mother died.

Dirk laughed bitterly. "You think he will believe you?"

I do not know the answer to that question but this is what I must make Edward believe, if I am to save Dirk.

FRITH

After her seizure, I allowed Plum a day off school. Mrs Partridge packed a basket and we walked to an open field near *North Wind* for a picnic. Plum brought a book and I set up an easel.

"We didn't have a proper family, growing up," I told Plum. "Our mother was a neurotic, selfish bitch and our poor father used to spend his life hiding away in his antique shop. Lily and I took care of one another. That's why I'm so crap at this."

She looked uncomprehending. "At *what?*"

"Being the motherly type. Taking care of you and your Dad."

She thought for a while before answering gravely, "Mom was the best in the world even if she didn't have a proper family growing up."

"True, but we were different." I shrugged, helplessly. "Even as a little girl, Lily was maternal. This mothering thing doesn't come naturally to me. You may have noticed."

It's a long shot, but I suppose I could've been a good mother if I'd had a child with a man I'd loved. I was the one who suggested they adopt a baby although I could never have taken another woman's child as my own and when I looked at Plum it wasn't Lily I saw, but a Russian dancer who'd had an affair with a married man and flown back to St Petersburg after delivering her baby.

If she looked anything like her daughter, that woman would have been tall and slender with thick, wiry hair, widely spaced eyes and double-jointed thumbs. I've been watching Plum turn into this dancer and it's most likely

359

her Soviet DNA that sparks Plum's seizures in the intricate coils of her busy brain. I suppose there must be some genetic link but, hey, what do I know?

I tell myself I've tried to love Plum but I wonder how true that is. Aside from Lily, I've never wholly loved another person. There was that early, dizzying infatuation with William – and now this thing with Theo – but these are shallow compared to the depth of feeling I always had for my twin.

"You're thinking of Mom, aren't you?"

Her question caught me off guard. "How do you know?"

"You get this look."

"Do I?" She's perceptive for a kid with Asperger's.

"It's like…you want to be happy but you're still stuck in sadness."

I nodded. "Is it the same for you?"

She pondered and said, thoughtfully, "Mom's still with me, most of the time. I can talk to her if I want to."

"And do you? Talk to her?"

"Sometimes."

"And does she answer?"

"When it's important."

I spoke in a light, neutral tone. "So this spirit, is she Mom?"

"No." Plum answered unhesitatingly, "She's the spirit of Charlotte. I told you before and, anyway, it's kind of obvious."

"How so?"

"Mom went to heaven after she died. Charlotte died at *North Wind* and she's still there."

"Why didn't she enter into heaven?"

"Dunno yet. The diary will tell us."

She seemed so convinced. "But, how do you know Charlotte died in the house? We've just read her entry about travelling with Dirk to Beaufort West."

Plum affected a look of strained patience. "We found Charlotte's diary in the attic cupboard. How could it be locked inside if she'd gone to Beaufort West with Dirk?"

"I can think of two reasons. Perhaps she didn't take it with her. Or maybe she came back."

360

Plum tossed her head. "She didn't go."

I was painting Plum as she leaned against a tree-stump in a dazzle of sunlight, a book propped open against her knees. She was twirling her hair between the fingers of her right hand and her lips were moving as she read.

I can see the finished portrait hanging in a light, generous space in my flat in France – the hallway opposite the mirrored hall-stand with its hats and umbrellas and bundled winter coats.

It was a lovely morning – silent but for the occasional flap and twitch of birds in the trees above our heads. And then I heard the *Dancing Queen* ringtone on my mobile.

His voice, "Frith…it's been forever. I miss you."

I'd been waiting for his call. I'd planned to sound chilly, instead I answered with a simpering, "Me too."

There was an urgency in his tone. "What are you doing tomorrow afternoon?"

Tell him you're busy!

"Um…nothing I can think of."

"Good. Any chance we could get together?"

Say no! Tell him you've had time to think and…

"Where? What time"

Stupid cow!

"My place. Half-two? That okay?"

No…no…no…tell him no…say you can't make it, you've just remem-bered…"See you then."

You stupid, stupid, stupid…

Plum looked up. "Who was that?"

"Nobody important."

PLUM

When Mom and my aunt used to tell stories about growing up it was like listening to people from different families because their memories were never the same. They argued a lot-Aunt Frith was always yelling at Mom

361

about being a martyr and wearing a hairy shirt and bottling stuff instead of exploding and letting it all out and Mom would smile and say, "You do quite enough of that for both of us, darling."

Mom's stories were never scary like my aunt's and when Aunt Frith tells about how she learned to swim she says they visited friends with a pool in the yard and everyone wore full bathing suits with rubber caps and their mother had too many gin and tonics.

The way she tells it the pool had dirty green water floating with slimy leaves and cloudy shapes at the bottom like dead fish and crocodiles though she thinks these were probably bits of branches and drowned balls.

Mom and my aunt didn't know how to swim and were shivering at the edge of the pool when their mother pushed Aunt Frith into the water.

She says she remembers Lily's screams over the noise she made kicking and thrashing and then she went under with bubbles lifting in front of her face as she sank to the cloudy shapes at the bottom waiting to snatch her feet and hold her down. Arms reached and gripped and pulled her up and she was sobbing and coughing and couldn't breathe for the longest time.

My aunt smiles at the part where her father wrapped her in a towel and held her tight as he shouted in front of everyone, "That was a damned stupid thing to do, Julia!" and her mother answered, "Well, somebody has to teach her!"

When Mom tells this story she says Aunt Frith tripped and fell into the pool and their mother screamed as their father dived into the oily water and dragged my aunt out.

It's hard to know whose story to believe but I think I'm going with Aunt Frith's.

Before Aunt Frith came to live with us, we used to draw together, Mom and me.

Mom's drawings were funny and cartoony and sometimes weird and always made me laugh. Dad said Mom hid her light under a bushel because being an artist was my aunt's claim to fame and when I asked if a bushel was like a bush Dad told me it measures the same as four pecks – ha, ha, ha…I think he was making a joke.

Mom stopped drawing after she got sick and made me pinky-swear I wouldn't show Aunt Frith her sketches in case they hurt my aunt's feelings but I couldn't work out how they could do that because Mom hardly ever drew pictures of my aunt.

Aunt Frith doesn't draw – she paints with mostly dark colours and her pictures are of places that are shadowy or misty or waiting for a thunderstorm and when you look at them you feel sad and imagine getting lost in the place and never finding your way out and that gives you a hollow feeling inside.

You won't find the teeny hedgehog with soft prickles that sits in the right hand corner of Mom's pictures in any of my aunt's paintings. Mom used to say there was nothing as cute as a baby hedgehog and always added one to her paintings and though it takes a while to find, when you do you wonder why you couldn't see it in the first place.

There's a hedgehog riding in a leaf boat and another paddling in a rain puddle with tiny Wellingtons on its feet and one dozing in an empty bird's nest and a really dear mother hedgehog knitting a Beanie with a curly grape vine.

When her eyes started going, Mom gave me a cardboard box with notebooks and sketchpads and told me to store it someplace safe so when I'm older I can take it out and look at her drawings.

I'm proud Mom trusted me with her precious stuff but I'm not waiting till I'm older because you can die in a split second so I'm always going through Mom's sketches and now I know them by heart. There are drawings of me as a baby in a cot and learning to crawl and walk and she's drawn Dad in a million poses like laughing and sleeping and bending over his laptop, flipping a pancake and fixing my three-wheeler bike with his hair flopping and an oil smudge on his cheek.

Mom had a little round mirror on a stand she used to stare into so there are tons of pictures of her smiling or laughing or frowning or wiping away a tear. Her pencil was always moving and she could draw anything – coffee mugs, pens, shells, feathers, stones, teaspoons, her left hand, her feet, my feet – there's even a picture of a torn packet of chocolate digestives that's so real you can almost pick it up. One of my favourites is a drawing of a princess doll I had when I was little with a plastic, glittery tiara on her curly hair and long white silky gloves up to her elbows so she could wave gracefully at her subjects like ER – which stands for Elizabeth Regina and means her Majesty Queen Elizabeth the Second.

Mom loved all my paintings even ones that turned out a bit messy but when I'm drawing or painting my aunt says things like, "Are you quite sure that's the best colour to use?" or, "Proportions are important – the average person is usually seven and a half heads tall – including the head – so make sure the head fits into the body six and a half times."

She makes me nervous because I don't get proportions and I'm not very good at colours so sometimes I ask which to use and she says in her disappointed voice, "It's your drawing. You must be the one to decide."

This morning Aunt Frith took me for a picnic even though it's a school day and I carried the basket with Birdie's cheddar and pickle sandwiches and the crunchy, sugary shortbread she makes for teatime.

My aunt asked me to pose and I did because she was being nice though I hate sitting still. The sun was hot and my eyelids kept drooping and from the corner of my eye I saw this long thin shadow slinking between the trees. I opened my eyes and between my lashes the shadowy thing seemed to be flowing towards me and I saw it was a stringy black cat with a swishing tail and if you know anything about cats that tail means the cat is in a temper.

The cat crept closer until I could count each sharp silvery whisker on its furry pointed face and then I heard Aunt Frith saying in her jolly voice, "Come on, sleepy-head! Wake up! It's time we made our way home."

I looked around but the cat was gone and when I asked my aunt she said, "What cat?"

FRITH

Back at *North Wind*, William was wearing his uneasy, disgruntled face. "You two have been gone for ever. I've been beside myself with worry."

"We had a picnic, in that field with the stream." I spoke in the sensible tones I use with William to keep him on an even keel.

He pressed his hand to his chest, as if in pain.

"The thing is back," he said. "It's been watching me."

I gave Plum the basket and told her to take it to the kitchen. "Ask Mrs Partridge for a tray of tea, will you?"

Abstracted, Plum nodded. At the doorway she turned. "What thing, Daddy?"

He shut his eyes. "Even with my eyes closed, I can still see it."

"Plum...please...the tea."

After she'd gone, I said, "You've never mentioned a *thing* before. What are you talking about?"

He seemed bewildered. "I can't tell you the name of the creature, never seen anything like it. Roughly the size of an obese hamster...clammy skin covered with thorns – no, that's too mild – with dagger-sharp quills. Eyes rotating in sockets like a chameleon, backwards, sideways, forwards...always following me. Long forked tongue, fleshy lips"

"A porcupine?"

"*Christ!* Have you been listening? Does it sound like a fucking porcupine? This thing's been sent from hell to tell me that's where I'm headed, I know it!"

"You're not headed anywhere, Wills. Calm down. You don't want Plum to hear you talking like this."

He dropped his voice. "I'm scared. This thing...it's got a raspy voice like an old smoker with clogged tobacco lungs. Keeps saying things like, '*You are fucked, William Westwood. Well and truly fucked!*'"

I touched his shoulder. "It's not real – it's all in your head."

He grabbed my arm. "*Shit!* I almost forgot...he called this morning. Brother of that friend of yours...the architect...no...lawyer, wasn't he? Anyway, he says he's reporting me to the police. Opening a case of fraud."

Speechless, I opened and closed my mouth.

"Right off the bat, I said, 'Sir, please go ahead with your suit. Don't give a thought to any damaging repercussions. I've cooked my goose, good and proper. There's not much more anyone can do to harm me now.'"

I muttered all the way to Theo's house furious with myself at being so reckless as to initiate a relationship with that interfering son-of-a-bitch, Louis Venter, who'd told his brother that William Westwood, wanted for fraud by the South African police, was living at *North Wind*.

I bruised my fist, slamming it against the steering wheel.

"Christ, Lil! William will be arrested. There'll be a trial. He'll be sent to prison."

It was in this state that I met Theo.

He opened the door, grinning. His shirt was half unbuttoned. I caught a glimpse of brawny chest frosted with silver hair. His smile froze. "What's wrong?"

I shook my head. "Nothing."

"You're upset. Spill the beans."

"William's depressed. Has been for some time now. Oh God, Theo – I think he may be losing his mind."

Theo led me inside and picked up a bottle of Scotch. "You look like you could do with one of these." He poured a couple of fingers of liquid into a glass sticky with fingerprints. "Down the hatch, good girl!"

"Cheers." I sipped the filmy glass. I wanted to talk about William but Theo was clearly not interested. "So…how are you?"

He looked smug. "You know that buyer in London? The one Olympia found? Well, I've sold the nudes – the whole shebang…made a tidy packet."

"Is there a commission for your model?"

He choked on his drink.

I barked a laugh. "Just joking."

Arsehole!

Theo's easiness returned as he stepped towards me, stroking my cheek with a finger spattered in olive paint. "You're looking as desirable as always, Frith."

I flinched, taking a step back. "Mind if I finish my drink before you make your move?"

His eyebrows soared. "Look, if you're not in the mood."

I blurted, "Why haven't you called?"

"Ha! You might recall, we didn't end on the best terms. And besides, it's been a crazy couple of weeks. Been working my fingers to the bone."

"You're seeing someone else, aren't you?"

He scowled. "*Jesus*, Frith! Olympia's no fool – she's been sniffing the air. I've had to lie low."

I snorted. "Let me get this straight. You not calling me has nothing to do with that curvy blonde in your class?"

He stiffened. "What blonde?"

That's when I knew for certain. "Oh, come off it! You've slept with her, haven't you?"

It cost him an effort to rearrange his expression. "Now you're being absurd!"

"There's guilt written all over your face!"

Theo tossed back his drink, playing for time. "We had a coffee a couple of times, that's it."

Theo stroked my forearm. "What say you cut this out, Frith? Don't spoil things. Can we enjoy a pleasant afternoon together, eh?"

His green finger moved down my cheek to my throat, lingering there.

He leaned in until his face was a few inches from mine. I caught a whiff of expensive cologne and, beneath this, the sharp tang of turpentine and perspiration. Gently, Theo's fingers trailed to the top of my breasts. I felt giddy with rising excitement.

Then this voice in my head. *What do you see in him? His skin...shining with grease...pitted with open pores...scratchy white stubble...bags under his eyes...flecks of dandruff...Seriously, are you that desperate Frith du Buisson?*

He pressed his mouth to my jawbone and his lips, dry and chapped, grazed my skin as he worked his way down my throat.

You're the consolation prize...the blonde doesn't want him...and here's you jumping at an opportunity to make an utter fool of yourself again.

He opened the buttons of my blouse, reached to unzip my skirt, tugging the fabric over my hips. I heard myself groan and it was too late to stop because my skirt was on the floor and he was scooping me up in his arms, carrying me to the bed.

The mean little voice went on for a while: *This is un-fucking-believable… you don't even like him yet here you are having…* But then I shut it out.

Theo made tea afterwards and rooted out a packet of stale Lemon Creams.

"I'm not coming again," I said, nibbling at the biscuit and then spitting the soft crumbs into a tissue. "Ugh. *Years* old."

He smiled slowly. "Here we go again."

"Oh, I admit, the sex is great. But you and me…it's pointless. I'll never understand why I have affairs with married men. Must be something to do with commitment issues or a serious lack of self-esteem. You'd think I'd be past all this. I'm too old to be skulking around like a guilty teenager!"

"Why do you feel guilty?"

"Because there's a Mrs Christensen in the picture and I'm not doing her any favours."

"Olympia doesn't care what goes on outside her patch."

"Ah, you're wrong there. I think she does. You're the one who doesn't care about anyone and anything except yourself."

Theo laughed. "Is there a reason why you're always bad tempered after sex?"

I beeped at William's car with the remote. Theo bowed into the open window. "So, this is goodbye then?"

I nodded.

He grinned, not taking me seriously. "Good luck with your exhibition. What was it you said? A series of old houses?"

"Mmm."

"Hope I'm invited. Keen to see what progress you've made."

Arsehole!

Winding up the window, I inserted the key into the ignition.

With dusk falling, I switched the lights on: one light at the end of the curving driveway shining on a bicycle propped against the gate post. I braked to take a closer look. A bright red Raleigh – Plum's bike!

Reaching for my mobile, I called home.

"*North Wind Manor*…Plum speaking."

"What's your bike doing here?"

"Where?"

"Outside a house in Main Street."

"Dunno. I left it in the garage. Maybe it's not mine."

"It's yours. There's a silver scratch on the rear mudguard."

She sounded excited. "Somebody must've stolen it!"

I had a chilling thought. "Where's Dad?"

A momentary pause. "Out, I think. Which house?"

A cold hand on my heart. "I'd better leave it here," I said, heavily. "He'll need it to ride home."

I pounced as he walked in and drew him swiftly into the parlour.

"What the fuck are you playing at?"

He looked as if I'd tossed a bucket of cold water over him.

"I saw Plum's bicycle at the gate. You've been following me!"

He scanned my face. "That bastard is still blackmailing you! Don't deny it."

I stared, stunned. "You're *spying* on me?"

"What are you doing, Frith? You don't have to *prostitute* yourself to protect me for Christ's sake. Let him tell the police. Who cares? I told you, I'm done for anyway."

"Look, Wills…"

"You've got to stop! Please. Lily would be…"

His eyes were glazed, his mouth working. He gave a groan, pushed past me and took the stairs.

I allowed myself a good cry. I've made it all worse by lying. He'd never believe me if I told the truth now. I look at my life and think…*what happened?* How did I get here? Will I ever return to France to my small, neat apartment, my painting, my tidy, uneventful life?

Or…oh God!…am I trapped watching William slowly unravel…terrified about shouldering responsibility for Plum, with every sodding new day a mountain to climb?

There's a saying we used to have, Lil and me, though, come to think of it, it was more my saying than hers. It popped into my head, *'Not my circus – not my monkeys.'*

That's how I felt. Except, of course, it **is** my circus – **and** my monkeys.

CHAPTER THIRTY TWO

PLUM

There's this picture of Charlotte in a long blue dress frozen in my brain like a strawberry in a block of ice. It's the first thing I see every morning and the last thing in the cushiony space behind my eyelids before I fall sleep. It feels like she's a part of me and when I peddle like mad along the pedestrian footpath to school one minute I'm Plum Westwood and next I'm Charlotte Butler riding Pegasus and I hear thudding hooves and imagine clods of dirt kicking up behind us.

Sentences written in her diary come to me and I say her words out loud because I like the way they take me deeper into her world.

'I am torn by mortifying indecision'… 'The rain assaults the roof'… 'We shall be in jeopardy from a crisis of our own conscience.'

I'm good at pretending to be Charlotte and I know her life wasn't a bed of roses as Birdie would say but it was a whole lot more exciting than mine which is all school and homework, worrying about Dad and carrying this big empty crater in my heart where Mom used to be.

This morning Dad asked if I was happy at school and I said, "Were *you*?" and he said that was a good point and the saying that, *'schooldays are the happiest days of one's life'* is bollocks. Then he recited a poem that didn't rhyme about a whining schoolboy with his shining morning face creeping like a snail unwillingly to school.

371

The verse is from Shakespeare and Dad asked me to repeat the lines a few times until they were locked inside my brain because they might come in useful one day though I can't think how.

All the talk about school – I knew Dad was up to something – and when he asked if I missed my last school and I nodded- that's when he dropped a bombshell.

"In that case, how do you feel about going back there?"

I didn't answer because I needed time to think but I'll bet it's Aunt Frith who's sewn this seed.

Do I want to go back to my old school?

It's like being an apple sliced down the middle – one half can't bear thinking about leaving *North Wind* and Charlotte's spirit but the other half hasn't forgotten how I loved my last school which was over two hundred years old and surrounded by miles of wet foggy boggy countryside and rambling houses with meadows where girls kept ponies.

That's where I learned skipping and hopscotch, singing in the choir and scratching at a violin. There were more girls like me at *Upper Heath Academy*, and I fitted in better than at this stupid school where most girls think I'm a total freak.

I pretended to be revising for a spelling test while I ate my egg though I was really listening to them whispering. You could tell they were upset because her cheeks were hot and Dad's eyes pushed back in his head like olives in pizza dough.

"You need a plan. You can't sit waiting for the axe to fall."

"What do you propose?"

"Go back to the UK. It's safer there."

"Mmmm."

"Put the house on the market. Get it listed with a few good agents."

"Mmmm."

"Are you even listening?"

"Question is – am I safe anywhere with my history? Or is it time to pay the piper?"

"A court case…shameful publicity…incarceration! What about…?"

I didn't look up but I knew she was jiggling her eyebrows at me.

"It was Lily's last wish she grow up here."

"At what cost?"

"I can't keep running. There's nowhere left to hide."

"Lie low then."

"Two know about me already. It's all inevitable."

"The lawyer and his brother, they're the problem."

"Aah! You're forgetting Theo Christensen!"

"He won't say anything."

"Not as long as you…Christ! It doesn't bear thinking about!"

"Look, William…it's not true. I made it up."

"Now you're lying and that's beneath you!"

"I'm not, swear to God I'm not!"

"Stop it, Frith!"

They were quiet a long while then Dad said, "So, to your plan. Sell the house. Plum and I hive back to the UK. What happens to you?"

"There's my flat in France. It's been standing empty since Lily got sick. I'm going to have to go back sometime. I can't stay forever. I've my own life to live."

"So you keep saying."

She saw me looking.

"Plum! For goodness sake, you'll be late for school?"

I was flying through the air on Pegasus with my long riding skirt flapping in the wind and my hair coming undone. My left hand gripped the bridle and my right hand rested on the horse's rubbery muzzle but then I skidded over the edge of the footpath and a car hooted crossly and I turned back into ordinary Plum on my bike thinking if the police found Dad he'd be locked up for years and I'd be an orphan.

In assembly the principal read the daily prayer and talked about *never* forgetting we are ambassadors of our school which was not the case with two students who'd behaved so badly in the bus that no less than three people had phoned in to report that these girls – no names mentioned they know perfectly well who they are – had written disgusting words in red lipstick on the back window of the bus.

Miss Walker, the sports teacher, announced netball fixtures and Gutty short for Miss Gutridge told Grade Fives they'd better not be late for the after-school rehearsal of *Under the Baobab Tree* beginning at two thirty on the dot.

Mrs van Wyk stepped back to the podium and behind her specs her eyes were zooming up and down the rows. I felt desperately sorry for the girls she was searching for and my heart started booming when her eyes stopped on me and she gave a twisty smile and said, "I'd like to extend congratulations to Plum Westwood who's been selected as the winner of the first prize in the *National Book Day* short story competition."

The principal waved an envelope and asked me to come up and collect my prize and the hall was deathly quiet with nobody breathing but then one girl started clapping and others joined in and the clapping grew louder until I was carried along on an ear-splitting wave of noise.

I climbed the stairs praying I wouldn't trip and wishing my cheeks weren't blazing like fried tomatoes. Mrs van Wyk patted my shoulder and said, "I'm going to read what the competition judges had to say about your essay… *A beautifully written example of creative and imaginative storytelling from a gifted young writer.*' Well done, Plum. You've made us all very proud."

I mumbled 'Thank you' and took the envelope and didn't look right or left as I was stumbling down the stairs with everyone clapping and cheering and my face so hot I thought my fingers would sizzle if I touched my cheeks.

After assembly Miss Cooper said she was simply thrilled one of her girls had scooped the first prize and then the whole class gathered around me in a circle, Annelie, Tanya, Roxy, Carla, Carika, Antjie, Samantha, Zelda and the rest of the Grade Seven A girls.

Bronte told me to show them my book voucher and the certificate with: *National Book Day Short Story Competition. First Prize – Plum Westwood* in curly gold lettering on thick creamy paper.

Miss Cooper's eyes turned misty. "This is a first for our school! We've never had a student win this competition before."

Then the bell rang for first lesson and they started talking about last night's, *'So you think you can dance?'* and Zelda showed a picture of her kitten on her smartphone and Roxy said her sister had had her boyfriend's name tattooed on her bum a week ago and they'd already broken up.

They were all still talking when we walked into maths class and the teacher whacked her desk with a ruler and shouted, "Quiet! You sound like a pace of braying donkeys!"

Carla asked what a pace was and I said it's the collective noun for a group of donkeys though you can also use 'herd' if you prefer and the maths teacher said it was a pity I wasn't half as good at maths as English.

I felt happy. The sick feeling about Dad went away and I kept touching my bulky blazer pocket listening for the crackle of the envelope inside and it was like I was in a soap bubble floating high above the grubby floors of all the classrooms we passed through that magical Thursday.

FRITH

That afternoon, I heard a loud rapping and when I opened the door, a tall, middle-aged woman with a camera slung over her shoulder, barged in.

"I'd never have recognised the place in a million years," she said. "You've done wonders!"

Bewildered, I asked, "Are you an estate agent?"

She nodded vigorously. "Your brother-in-law called. Said he wanted a valuation on the house. I was in the area and thought I'd drop in right away. You don't mind, I hope?"

I hesitated, stepping aside. "Of course not. William didn't say anything, that's all."

The woman's boisterous energy was overwhelming – even her wiry hair seemed to spark with static. She started fiddling with the camera lens. "Mind if I take a few shots?"

I heard myself sounding edgy. "Don't photograph anything too personal. William wants our privacy respected."

"Understood." She framed the hallway in her camera lens, clicking away.

"You've got it exactly right, I must say. Not easy refurbing these old places." She grinned. "Quite a conundrum, I should think – dragging an Edwardian relic into the twenty-first century."

I began to relax. "William says the house has beautiful bones which made the restoration simpler."

" 'Beautiful bones' – I must use that." She kept snapping as she strode ahead, climbing the stairs, two at a time.

"Of course it's all in the details, isn't it? And your decorator has a light touch," she smiled. "Clean, elegant, very tasteful. Does it come fully furnished? All fittings and fixtures?"

"I think so."

"Nice."

"I'm surprised William called you," I said. "We were just talking about it. He didn't give any indication he was thinking of selling. In fact, I thought he had dismissed the idea."

"Changed his mind, I guess. Fetch a pretty penny. I've a few clients who'll be most interested."

I felt a surge of pride on his behalf. "William managed the entire project from start to finish. Did all the decorating himself."

In my bedroom, the agent halted at the canvas of *North Wind Manor*. "Oh, I do like this!" she said. "Interesting interpretation." She positioned her nose inches from the canvas. "Not how I see the house at all. Dark. Oddly disturbing. And, do tell, what's in the window? That one there?"

I leaned forward. "That's the attic window."

She laughed. "Are you having us on?"

"Sorry?" I gaped. "You've lost me?"

"There, at the window. Is it meant to be a ghost?"

I peered closely. Behind the glass of the attic window – a pale, featureless face the size of a fingernail.

The woman stared curiously. Feebly, I attempted a smile. "It's um…a private joke. You're perceptive. Most people don't notice."

That open grin again. "I *adore* this painting – ghost and all! If you can't find a buyer, I'm interested."

"Really?"

"Yes. This would be just the job, hanging in my study."

The minute the agent left, I went upstairs. Plum must have painted the face at the window. It couldn't be anyone else. The paint was dry. I began scratching lightly with a palette knife until the ghostly image faded.

William was still out so I borrowed Birdie's car and headed to town to pick up a stretched, medium-grain, cotton canvas I'd ordered from an art supply shop.

I couldn't stop thinking about the face in the attic as I drove the jerking, smoking rattletrap into Main Street. What would make Plum take up a brush and deliberately alter my painting? Was she trying to annoy me? To make the point that, despite what I believe, ghosts do exist? Or did she want me to think it was the spirit who'd painted that face?

I slotted into a parking space. The canvas was waiting, triple-acrylic primed, tacked and fitted with small wooden wedges to allow for adjusting tension.

I paid and stored the parcel in the boot. My watch beeped the hour. The thought of returning home gave me indigestion.

It was the most perfect afternoon. Above my head, an infinite blue sky floated with delicate streamers of cloud and beneath my feet, thick, tufty grass exploded in vibrant green.

A street market offered a reason to dawdle. I grew conscious of glimmers of recognition from passers-by, a smile here, a wave there, a cheery, "Hello!"

Main Street was thronging with every creed and colour, a reassuring example of the multicultural, multi-ethnic, heterogeneously cosmopolitan community democratic South Africa purports to be. Banishing William from my thoughts, I made an effort to conceal my anxiety behind a safe, blank face.

I bought a few things. A cone of furled pink roses to thank Birdie for the use of her car – a French loaf, still warm, a slab of goat's cheese, a punnet of cherry tomatoes. Idly, I examined vintage stalls laden with tarnished silverware, framed prints, china plates, pointy dancing shoes…a lovely marquetry table.

I was hunting for a price tag on the table when, from the corner of my eye, I saw a man approaching.

Louis bloody sodding Venter.

I spun to face him. "Go away! I've nothing to say to you."

"Wait!" He blocked my way, holding out his briefcase like a matador's cape. "I have to talk to you."

I heard the urgency in his voice. "What is it?" I asked, curtly.

He looked sheepish. "It's my brother, Thys…he's had a change of heart. He said to tell you he's prepared to let bygones be bygones."

It took a few moments to sink in. "So…he's *not* reporting William to the police?"

"No." Venter's bony shoulders lifted and fell. "When they spoke on the phone, Thys said your brother-in-law sounded…*beaten*. Said he got the impression he'd learned his lesson and didn't need his nose rubbed into the carpet."

"That's generous of him." This came out sounding harsher than intended so I tried to soften my tone. "William will be so grateful. He's not been well. A police enquiry is the last thing he needs right now."

Venter half smiled. "Yes, well…glad we've cleared that up."

"Please tell your brother we appreciate his thoughtfulness." I strode away, head held high.

A wind came up and kindly nudged Birdie's car all the way home. I should have been elated at Venter's revelation, but the pressure in my chest had settled into a leaden weight and, by the time I reached home, I had another bloody headache.

Birdie offered aspirin. "Fat lot of good that'll do," I grumbled, groping for my pills.

The stove bleated as Birdie took out a steaming apple pie. The rich waft of buttery pastry and apples made me nauseous. "I'm going upstairs to lie down," I told her.

"Oh, before you go…" She looked fidgety and jumpy. Her eyes glittery, her face, flushed from the oven, covered in a sheen of perspiration.

"I've had a real shocker of a day," she stated, puffing out her cheeks.

I held myself rigidly. *What now?*

Agitated, Birdie fanned herself with a tea-towel. "As you can see, I'm in a right old state."

I sighed. "You'd better tell me what the matter is."

"Well, I was in the kitchen making pastry when I heard this crash. I went upstairs and you know that blue and white pot, the one with birds and flowers that sits on your bookshelf?"

I nodded.

"Shattered in pieces all over the floor!"

Fuck!

I love that Chinese urn. I bought it in France with money from the sale of my first painting.

Birdie flapped the towel in front of her steaming face again.

"From that look, you think it was me who broke that pot. Well, I didn't. And it didn't leap off the bookshelf by itself. And no windows were open in your room so you can't blame the wind."

"What are you saying?"

Birdie shrugged. "It was just me in the house. Mr William out. Plum at school. You off somewhere, as usual."

I listened to the clicking of the cooling oven. Then it dawned.

"Oh, I get it! You want me to believe Plum's spirit chucked my urn on the floor, is that it?"

"All I'm saying is, I don't know how it broke."

"You must have knocked it off the shelf when you were tidying up."

"I didn't!"

"Look, the urn's broken and that's that. Frankly, there's nothing more to discuss."

I flung my pillows on the floor and lay flat on my bed. The pain intensified and grew shark's teeth. Walls warped and collapsed inwards. The sunlit window fractured into searing blades. I swallowed another pill that stuck in my gullet and left a taste of aloes.

Misery swamped. My urn…one of my few cherished treasures…that clumsy woman!

And then, distinct as anything, I heard Lily's voice, sympathetic and comforting, *"Take a pillow and lie on the tiles in the bathroom. That's what you used to do when it got bad, remember?"*

Obediently, I staggered with my pillow to the bathroom. I lay upon the hard, cool tiles until the pain burned itself out and afternoon faded into evening.

That's where Birdie found me. "I'm off. Let me help you to your room before I go."

Taking her hand, I hauled myself to my feet. "Maybe it was the cat," I told her, kindly.

She blinked.

"There's a cat been roaming outside. You must've heard it crying. Maybe it came in through an open window. It would've been prowling the bookshelf when it knocked the urn over."

Birdie gave a disbelieving grunt and I thought I heard her say: 'In a pig's eye!'

I shook my head. "Sorry, but I'm not buying your story. If you didn't do it – the cat is the only logical explanation. Oh, by the way, those roses in your car are for you, though they've probably wilted by now."

PLUM

Aunt Frith shuffled downstairs wearing Dad's green jumper with his striped woolly socks on her feet.

She was walking all hunched over like her bones were soft and bendy and from the far-away look in her eyes she'd had one of her headaches.

I held up the diary. "Can you read or is your head too awful for words?"

May 20th, 1906

For safety sake, I have secreted my journal in the attic, where it cannot be read by prying eyes.

The weather has altered with my mood. This morning brought banks of cloud, drenched lawns and storm-beaten roses with their petals blown adrift.

Two days have passed since my last entry. Dirk and I have devoted this time to discussion and, though we have had many disagreements, happily we remain perfectly calm.

Dirk is intractable and refuses to be swayed from his course. He insists we must take this chance for the two of us with our unborn child to make a contented life together.

He is so hopeful, I am almost persuaded the blissful life he envisages may even be possible!

On the morning of May 22nd, my best beloved departs from North Wind Manor at sunrise to set off upon the journey to Beaufort West where he will present his credentials for the position of church organist. Dirk has agreed to travel alone and summon me to join him once he has received notification the post is his.

Later…

I have spent a great many hours sitting quietly at the table in the vestibule, imagining my life away from North Wind Manor – a preoccupation that fills me with sorrow.

My only consolation is that the manor will never fade from my memory. I have only to close my eyes to imagine myself moving between rooms, climbing the staircase with my hand sliding smoothly upon the burnished surface of the banisters, entering my own room where silken drapes waft a welcome at the open window.

I picture the view from this window – blooming shrubs, lily pond, sundial, stables and beyond this, the meadow where Pegasus crops acres of tall grass made all the sweeter by early rains.

Dirk claims we can be happy in more modest lodgings and insists the Karoo, for all its suffocating heat and dust, has its own stark beauty. There will come a time, he promises, when I will gratefully accept this harsh desert as our home.

May 21st, 1906

On the eve of his departure, Dirk has been loading a few meager provisions into the cart.

I have given him one of Edward's wide-brimmed hats to shield him from the sun. Sensibly, he has made no public farewells for fear of jeopardising our secret.

Only his landlord has been entrusted with details of his plans and it was he who encouraged Dirk to request a leave of absence from the church to put an end to the suspicions of snooping townsfolk.

I spent an interminable day unable to settle to anything, consumed with unexplained foreboding weighing at my heart. We plan to retire early to bed this evening so Dirk may be fresh for his journey.

Oh God! What day is this?

Many hours or even days have passed, I cannot tell how many. I am a prisoner in the attic.

Edward is my jailer! Edward has killed Dirk!

I must find the strength to commit all details of Dirk's cruel murder to this journal for, if I do not, no other living soul will ever know the truth of what happened that hideous night.

It seems I cannot write. My hand trembles so much it is impossible to grip my pen. And my mind is incapable of finding words to describe the unspeakable horror of what has happened in this house.

More time has passed…God knows how long I have spent in a fit of weeping, babbling incoherently and longing to die.

Has another day passed? Is it more? Can it be two or three days later? I have lost all track of time.

I must pull myself together – I am the only living witness to Dirk's murder and he deserves an honest accounting of how his life has been so brutally, so tragically, cut short.

I woke shortly after midnight on the 22nd of May to see the figure of a man framed in the doorway of my bedchamber. Lighting a candle, I recognised my husband, Edward Butler, advancing with a pistol in his right hand. I screamed and tried to shake Dirk awake.

Dirk stirred but was not yet fully conscious when Edward aimed three bullets into his body.

The first entered Dirk's chest, the other two his head. Dirk's blood splattered upon my nightgown, my hair, face and hands. Even now smears of blood remain caked upon my hand. I press this fading stain to my lips. This is all I have left of my dearly beloved.

What took place next?

It's almost impossible to marshal my thoughts coherently with my brain still addled with the terrors of that night.

Yes, yes…now I remember! I screamed as Edward directed the muzzle of the pistol at my head.

Then the room began to tilt and blackness descended.

I awoke to find myself in a dark, confined, airless space. Stumbling about, I discovered I was in the attic. I tried the door and found it locked; the windows barred tight.

Like a child, I scrabbled beneath the bed to hide in ghastly, trembling wakefulness until the room grew light and morning came.

Time passed. I cannot guess the number of hours I paced the attic and banged my fists upon the door, crying out for help. I shouted until my throat became painful and my voice hoarse.

The house is silent as a grave. From the window, the fields are empty of menfolk.

Has Edward banished our servants? Am I alone at the mercy of my murderous husband?

Edward will kill me, of that I am convinced. I am praying the Lord makes my end swift with a bullet aimed with mortal accuracy into my heart. I keep calling for my husband – loathsome executioner – to come and end my life. I have no will to go on without Dirk.

A raging thirst overcomes me. I have been at the keyhole, begging for water, but to no avail. My voice is thin and weak and will soon fade, leaving me speechless.

Such terrible dreams I have when I fall asleep! I find myself falling upon Dirk's stiffened corpse, staring into blank, sightless eyes, kissing cold, blue lips. Oh, God, these nightmares defy the worst imagination!

Has Edward left me in the attic to starve and die alone? North Wind Manor is deserted. Straining my ears, I hear only an awful silence: no voices, no footsteps – even the birds are quite silent.

I keep a steady vigil at the window. We have no visitors. The absence of Edward's spy, the cunning Clutterbuck, proves his guilt as an accomplice to Dirk's murder.

The doctor has betrayed me though I have no-one to blame but myself. I suspected Clutterbuck might be passing information to Edward. Why was I not more cautious?

My hands are shaking too much to allow me to properly shape my letters. Ink blots spill upon the paper. So many questions in my mind. Has Edward taken Dirk's body from my chamber? Have his earthly remains been cast unsanctified into the ground? Or is his corpse still sprawled upon my bloodied bed?

Has Edward fled to London to escape conviction for murder? What will happen to me? Will isolation drive me mad or shall I first perish from thirst and starvation?

One question haunts more than the others. What is the fate of this poor, innocent child I carry?

I have slept, I think. I cannot say how long. I am confused. The chronology required to keep this record honest and true grows more taxing by the hour.

Here is some of what has recently happened, though not the exact sequence.

I woke in turmoil to hear Edward bellowing drunkenly from behind the locked attic door.

Whore he called me, whore, harlot and worse.

"Bring water!" I croaked.

He kicked the door and staggered away. I heard his boots, unsteady on the stairs, then nothing more.

Edward returned later. He drummed drunkenly upon the paneling, spewing a stream of vile abuse. Three words I understood; bawdy, lewd and sluttish. I heard the clanking of the key chain and hid beneath the bed while Edward cursed, too drunk to insert the key in the lock.

It was close to morning when I heard faint mouse-scratchings at the door. The key struggled in the lock. My head whirled with hideous fantasies. I was near fainting when the door burst open and there stood Magdalena. I fell into her arms, sobbing like a baby. She held me to her bosom and, once my weeping had ceased, pressed a jug of water upon me, urging me to sip slowly. I drank until the jug was emptied.

"Where is Dirk's body?" I asked at last. She could not look at me. 'Buried' was all she would say.

Magdalena relayed that Captain Butler had sent her away with the others but, anxious for my safety, she'd returned that night to find the master unconscious from drink.

Motioning for me to remove my blood-stained garments, she slipped away, returning with a petticoat and tea-gown. Numbly, I stepped into the dress.

Magdalena took my hand. "The horse and cart are ready. You must leave at once!"

"No!" I cried. "I will not leave whilst Edward still lives."

Magdalena beckoned for me to follow and led me to Edward's chamber.

I paused at the doorway of my own room where the bed had been stripped bare, the Turkish carpet taken up, walls washed clean and all evidence of the murder committed there carefully erased.

In his own room, Edward lay upon the floor, stinking from wine and vomit. I touched his sprawled leg with my naked foot and saw he was dead to the world.

I found his pistol on the chiffonier and as I held it in my hand, a wave of calmness fell upon me.

In that moment, I understood with clarity that, as his legal wife, it falls to me to ensure that justice is served. I am the one to punish Edward Butler for killing Dirk in cold blood. Not only Dirk, Edward has murdered others and committed a multitude of other crimes. The Bible demands retribution equal to the crime, eye for eye and tooth for tooth.

As I took up the pistol, Magdalena ran from the room. "You have nothing to fear," I said quietly, though, since she had gone, I offered this small comfort to myself.

Standing above Edward's figure, I pointed the pistol at his breast where his heart – if indeed he had one – was beating. As I shot, the pistol jumped wildly in my hand and, missing its mark, the bullet penetrated Edward's throat. Bright blood bubbled from the open wound.

I saw my husband's eyelids weakly fluttering and knew he was still alive. My nerves left me and the pistol slid to the floor.

How my blood ran cold to see Edward's mouth gaping wide. I heard a hiss of air, a gurgling like water in a drain. His hand reached out, his fingers shook. I stood rooted to the spot. I could not move.

CHAPTER THIRTY THREE

FRITH

She was chewing her thumb nail. Her eyes were enormous. I slammed the diary shut.

Plum gasped. "You can't stop now!"

"You won't sleep…and neither will I."

"I *have* to know what happens."

"Listen Plum, something I've been meaning to say. You know, don't you, that all this took place in nineteen hundred and six so that's um…well, it's over a hundred and nine…no-eleven years ago? These people – if they ever existed – are long dead, which means there's nothing to be afraid of."

She stared at a spot above my head. "What do you mean, '*if they ever existed*'?"

I did my best to sound chatty. "Well, I've been thinking about this diary for a quite a while. Mrs Butler certainly had a way with words. Her entries read like trashy Victorian melodrama and I'm beginning to wonder if *any* of what's written in this diary is true."

I stopped her as she opened her mouth to object.

"Let me have my say, please. It's true, the diary looks authentic, but you can fake anything these days. Just suppose someone wrote the diary as a prank and left it here to be found by unsuspecting new owners of the manor?"

She scowled. "Why would they bother?"

"You have a point. It does seem an awful lot of work if you never get to see a reaction. My other thought is that Charlotte might have been a novelist like Jane Austen or Emily Bronte. Let's say she had a wild imagination like yours. Suppose all this…" I flipped through the pages, "is simply the product of that imagination. Suppose it's a manuscript for a novel."

Plum's eyes were dark and shining. For a second, she looked directly at me.

"Charlotte Butler was a real person and every word she wrote is true." I swallowed a sigh. I've never been able to convince Plum to change her mind about anything. I glanced at my watch, smothering a yawn. "Your father will be home soon. I'm going to have a soak in the tub before dinner."

I lay in a deep bath, explaining things to Lily.

"Okay, I know what you're thinking. I should've gone through the diary before reading it to her. You're right, but it's too late to stop with only a few pages left. You can tell it's going to end badly. Charlotte's shot her husband in the throat. That's prison for life unless she's hanged.

Plum will say that's why her spirit haunts this house – seeking vengeance or forgiveness or some such thing. God, Lil! I've made a shitload of mistakes. I've absolutely no idea what I'm doing.

I think it's because I've lost you, Lil…lost my compass. Can you hear me? Lil, are you there?"

If I expected sympathy, I was disappointed. Lily said nothing at all.

They're called *'twinless twins'* – survivors left behind after their twin has died. That's who I am now and, unless you're also a twin who's lost a twin, you can't begin to know how I feel.

It's a documented fact that *identical* twins feel the loss of a brother or sister more strongly than fraternal twins. You've lost your mirror image and so, in a way, you've lost yourself.

I can't stop memories coming back. That day we were playing hide and seek, I remember it so clearly. We must have been about six or seven. We were in the antique shop. Our father was buried in accounts. Helen, his assistant, was paging through newspapers for notices of deceased estates. It was Lily's turn to hide and I turned the whole place upside down searching for her. I was better at the game than she was and knew all the best hidey-holes.

I looked in our usual places, the deep Rococo cabinet, the enormous oak wine barrels and the mildewed, salty-smelling, leather ship's kist.

I didn't find her rolled up in a dusty, sneeze-inducing Persian or crouched behind the walnut stand-up mirror with the glass turned foggy and speckled with green and black like a bird's egg.

Eventually, I had a full-blown tantrum. "You're a cheat, Lily du Buisson!" I yelled. "If you don't come out now, I'm never playing with you again."

She didn't answer. I sat cross-legged on a dusty sofa with ball and claw legs, waiting for my twin to emerge. After a while, I began whimpering, "Lily…Lily…Lily!" Before long, I was sobbing uncontrollably.

Helen summoned Dad who pottered over with a handkerchief.

"I have to find Lily," I told him desperately. *I can't be me without her."*

My father took my hand and we searched together. After a while, we found her asleep in a cast iron bathtub beneath a blue striped mattress.

I flung myself upon Lily, weeping. As our father peeled me off, I shouted hysterically, "You can't leave me ever again, Lily! Promise you won't."

So that's how it was with me. Not so much with Lily though. I know she loved me, but not with the intensity I had for her. Maybe it was different for Lil because she got the biggest share of everyone's love. What little love our mother had was eked out in mean thimblefuls to Lily. Our father adored us both, but Lily was his clear favourite. All our friends liked Lily more than they liked me. Even teachers, all the way from primary to secondary school, preferred my sister.

It's never easy being the one following, but I knew why everyone loved Lily more because that's how I loved her too.

These thoughts swirled as I lay in the tub staring up at the starkly white, newly painted ceiling.

Plum tapped on the door. "You've been in there for ages." She sounded tired and whiny.

I nodded. "I'll get out and you hop in."

I towelled myself dry. Plum stood motionless. "Get in," I repeated.

Fastidiously, she wrinkled her nose. "Using somebody's bathwater is like putting your head in a dent on a pillow that's not yours."

The bathwater was an unreal blue from the bubble bath I'd used – the surface still lacy with popping soapsuds. I sighed. "Pull the plug and fill the tub again."

I went off to get dressed and when I got back, Plum lay in clean water, soaping herself.

She waggled a finger at me. "See that shadow on the tiles?"

I studied a shadow cast by a silver ring bolted to the wall. The ring held a tooth mug with a half-squeezed tube of toothpaste and my toothbrush. I glanced at my watch. It was time to start dinner before William returned home. "What about it?"

"It's shaped like a cat."

The shadow clinging to the tiles was a blob. "I can't see a cat."

She twisted her head awkwardly. "Turn your head like this. See it now?"

"No."

"You're not trying. Turn your head to the left."

I dipped my head and, from another angle, saw a vague shape created by the blending of two shadows, one from the tooth mug, the other from the stainless steel holder.

"No cat. Sorry."

She blinked. "I don't know why you can't see it."

I was too tired to argue. "Does it matter what shape this shadow is?"

But she wasn't done yet. "What if it's a message from the spirit?"

"The shadow?"

"Yes. What do you think she's saying?"

I bit down on my back molars. *Here we go again!* "This is too far–fetched, sorry. I'm going to make supper. You okay with pasta?"

We waited an hour for William. I called his mobile and when he didn't answer, sent a text, *'When will you be home?'*

Dinner was a quiet affair. Plum sat hunched over a book, her fringe hanging over her forehead, pensively silent.

The Puttanesca sauce, made from memory, had an overpoweringly fishy taste from too many anchovies. Plum ate around the sauce, winding cooling strands of linguini on her fork and nibbling without appetite. I pushed my plate away. "There's bread and cheese with pickle, if you'd prefer."

She spat into her hand. "Yuck! I hate these horrible hairy things!"

"Anchovies," I corrected, mechanically.

"Where's Dad? Why isn't he home?"

I cleared the plates. "I'm guessing he went off on one of his long drives into the countryside."

"But it's pitch dark. He should've been back long ago."

I peered through the window at densely massed silhouettes of trees. Where *was* William?

I stepped outdoors. It was warmer out than in. A beam thrown from a garden lamp, illuminated the water in the fishpond, driving the helpless fish to the depths where they nervously circled and swarmed. Taking pity, I switched off the lamp and leaned back against the moist stone ledge of the fountain.

Last time I'd seen William was after breakfast. We'd been discussing his going back to the UK to escape the police. This was before I'd bumped into Louise Venter at the market. Before I knew Venter's brother had changed his mind about opening a case of fraud against William.

William's last words to me had been…*what?*

I wracked my brain. I'd been talking about getting my life back. *"There's my flat in France. It's been standing empty since Lily got sick. I'm going to have to go back sometime. I can't stay forever. I've my own life to live."*

His face had been expressionless. *"So you keep saying."*

No clue there.

Winking white lights floated above my head. If Plum had been with me she'd have interpreted this as some sort of a sign from the spirit instead of simply seeing a beautiful trail of fireflies on the wing.

I dialed and reached voice mail. *"Christ sake!* What are you playing at?" I snapped. "Where the hell are you? It's late. Plum's in a tizzy! Call me!"

Indoors, Plum was rocking back and forth in William's chair.

"No need to worry," I held up my mobile. "Dad's driven too far from home, got lost and decided to spend the night in a B&B. He'll be back first thing tomorrow. Okay?"

Plum smiled wanly, expelling a breath of relief. "Thanks Aunt Frith."

I tucked her into bed. There was a torn envelope on her desk. A certificate of some kind.

I picked it up. *National Book Day Short Story Competition. First Prize –* *Plum Westwood.* There was also an Exclusive Books voucher for a thousand rands.

"You won the competition!"

"Huh?"

"That's incredible! Congratulations! I'm so proud of you. Why didn't you tell me?"

"I'm waiting to show Dad."

I felt as if I'd been slapped.

Leave it. Let it go. Don't make it worse than it already is.

"I don't understand. Why did you feel it wasn't important to tell me?"

"I didn't think you'd care that much."

Something broke inside me. I had to swallow hard to stop from crying.

PLUM

She kept sending scissory-sharp looks so I made my face still because I didn't want her to know I was excited and scared at the same time with everything happening – Edward murdering Dirk and Charlotte shooting Edward with blood bubbling out of his neck.

I couldn't believe it when Aunt Frith closed the diary at the most thrilling part and started rabbiting on that maybe it's not true – just a made-up story like *Wuthering Heights* – which means she's probably thinking Mom would be mad at her reading gory stuff and I wanted to say Mom believed reading opens your world but didn't want her to know I could read her mind.

I was lying in the bath when I felt her fingers – soft like flower petals – tickling the back of my neck and pulling my hair sockets tight to make them tingle all over my head.

I feel her when she's in my head and Aunt Frith would say I make myself believe she's there but I don't think that's true and when I saw the shadow on the tiles, I knew she was with me and maybe even close enough to touch.

She made the shadow the shape of a bony cat with pointy ears and two front paws together and when I showed Aunt Frith she blew her lips in a rude rubbery noise and marched to the bathroom door. "Look at your shadow from here," she said.

I got out of the bath and stood right next to my aunt and the shadow looked like a tooth-mug with a brush and squashed tube of paste inside. It was funny – not ha ha – funny peculiar and the spirit changed the shape because she wanted to put my aunt off the scent. She doesn't much like Aunt Frith or Dad which is why she only sends messages to me.

Aunt Frith says I see and feel things that aren't there but that's because my brain is wired differently to hers and she never looks or listens properly so she misses pretty much everything. Here's an example. My aunt sees Dad every day but what she doesn't see is how he's shrinking little by little and soon he'll be like the Cheshire Cat in Alice with only his sad smile left hanging in the air.

This morning Dad told me a 'Remember-When' story and gave me a hug and whispered in my ear – low like a housefly buzzing.

I wriggled away because his jacket was prickling and he didn't look the same with his face droopy and all the light gone from his eyes and then I felt sorry so I kissed him – not on the cheek like I usually do, right on his mouth. *"I love you, Dad!"* I put every bit of feeling into those words but he just stood there not saying anything and his eyes got watery and that left me hollow inside.

In geography class I let myself think about Dad's 'Remember-When' story.

"Remember your school in Shropshire? Remember the day you had a music lesson and I was waiting outside the door while you practiced ascending and

descending scales in C major? Impossible to forget your teacher, no-nonsense Miss Longhorn, with those beady badger eyes? She was saying something like, 'Start with the third finger on the lowest string, C – then play open string D, first finger E.'

You made a hideous scratching on your violin and Miss Longhorn closed her eyes and said, "Our aim, Plum, is to produce a smooth, even tone. Try again."

Your scratching turned into a parrot shriek and Miss Longhorn shouted, "No! No! What is that little finger doing on that string, may I ask?" I always laugh at your reply, "I honestly have no idea what any of my fingers are doing, Miss," you said.

Oh, Plum, darling. I couldn't take my eyes off you. You had your instrument on your collarbone, held in place by your jaw, your head bent over exposing your vulnerable stalk of a neck. That sweet, tender image will stay with me forever."

I don't remember the lesson the way Dad does but I can still bring back a dry smell of dust and rosin and the piano covered in slippery music sheets that kept floating to the floor and a cork-board stabbed with red and blue drawing pins and my father behind the half-open door, smiling at me.

After telling me this, Dad leaned in close and whispered in my ear… buzz, buzz, buzz like a big fly rubbing wings together. It took me a while to work out what he'd said, *"Oh forgive me, my darling Plum, please forgive me."*

It bothers me I don't know what I'm supposed to forgive Dad for.

FRITH

I couldn't sleep a wink thanks to a combination of that terrifying diary and the onset of another headache brought on by bloody William. Nobody knows the agony of these headaches. It's indescribable. Akin to having the top of your head sliced off like a boiled egg, leaving your delicate brain exposed to violent currents of electric light and brittle fragments of dust and dirt.

Fucking William! Where is he? What's he playing at now?

I made tea and sat at the kitchen table, watching it turn cold. Most women would die for a kitchen like this. William's gone above and beyond with his design of a central island surrounded by seamless white cupboards and counters of smooth, pale grey stone. This kitchen could be a film set for a famous foodie, Nigella or Jamie.

I've just noticed Lily's recipe books on one of the shelves. William must have lugged these half way across the world. I knelt at the shelf and went through each one slowly.

The oil-spattered James Beard, the well-thumbed Julia Child. The Robert Carrier left in the rain with pages thickened and stuck together. One serious heavyweight – *The World Atlas of Great Food*. Pretentious French, Italian and Greek gastronomy bibles together with glossy TV celebrity books, Galloping Graham, Gordon, Rick, Delia and Two Fat Ladies.

Her name, *Lily Westwood,* scrawled in black biro on all the front pages.

I can still picture my sister's Shropshire kitchen with these books slotted cozily together in a tall, narrow, blue-painted bookcase. I don't know why he brought them here.

It would have been far easier to have left them behind, like hurling ballast overboard and feeling lighter for it. A slip of paper fell from one of the books. Lily's handwriting, *'Espresso maker? Pasta machine? Breadmaker? Handbag?'*

A Christmas or birthday list? Trust Lil to put a fucking Espresso maker at the top.

I make myself ill thinking of precious years Lily wasted cooking, serving, eating and washing up after an interminable routine of never-ending family meals.

"I heard you in here." Plum crept in with the diary in the pocket of her dressing-gown. "We can't sleep because we don't know what's going to happen so our brains can't stop whirring."

I started – was she was talking about William? Then I remembered, she thought her father was sleeping at a B&B.

"I'm enjoying a little peace and quiet." I lied.

"No, you're not." She pulled out a chair and sat down firmly. "You can't sleep because you don't know if Edward's really dead. Suppose he suddenly rears up like Captain Jack Harkness in *Doctor Who* after he was killed by the *Daleks*?"

I laughed weakly. "That's highly unlikely."

Plum placed the diary on the table. "Please," she said, plaintively.

We both looked at it. Plum hooked her hair behind her ear. "I'm not going to bed until we've read to the end." she said. "I've looked and there are only few pages left."

I cleared my throat.

"The act of shooting Edward rendered me immobile and though he cried out most awfully in torment and pain, I could do nothing but shake as I stared down upon his body.

My limbs were locked, my feet stuck fast. My mind kept reeling in fear.

But then I began thinking of all Edward's cruel, heartless deeds. Was it God, I wonder, who sent these images to spur me on? One after the other, Edward's innocent victims passed through my mind – Thomas, Moses, Pretty, Angela, my dearly beloved, Dirk.

Was it God's voice chiding? Reminding me of these untimely deaths at Edward's hand?

Was it God who gifted me with fortitude and courage, sufficient to lift and aim the pistol at Edward's frozen heart?

The bullet pierced, finding its target. Edward's body shuddered and then grew quite still.

I collapsed to the floor and prayed for my soul. I also prayed for the sweet, unblemished soul of my unborn child and all those dear departed with whom, if the Lord is merciful, I shall soon be reunited.

A still calmness has descended upon me.

I have written a letter to Aletta in which I have bequeathed my precious Pegasus to her loving care.

I have further instructed Aletta take from this house those of my possessions she might wish to have as keepsakes. The letter bears my signature and a clause verifying that I have written this in sound mind to legally serve as my last will and testament.

I added a postscript as follows:

"Please send for the Magistrate. Accompany him to North Wind Manor where two murders have taken place. In the attic, you will find my journal in which, at the end, I reveal the truth of how Dirk Barnard and Edward Butler died and why."

I gave this letter to shaken, tearful Magdalena and watched from the attic window as my loyal housekeeper set out stoically upon the path towards the Prinsloo house.

So little time remains…

I have said my farewells to North Wind Manor.

My hands have touched random, cherished objects: the curved oak chest; the great black kettle on the kitchen range; a china vase made bright with peacocks; the brass fender at the fireplace and pretty samplers nailed upon the walls.

Beyond the window, the grass has grown tall for want of mowing. The vineyards are untended, the roses dying. Too late now…too late.

Here follows my last entry.

There are some will say the devil entered my spirit and caused me, in a rash moment to commit an unpardonable crime. My prayer is there are others who believe, as I do, that God Himself gave me the resolution to punish Edward for his evil deeds and send him screaming to the gates of Hell.

I am prepared and ready for death. I have bathed, pinned my hair and put on my finest walnut silk. When, at last, I set down this pen, I shall take up Edward's pistol, press it to my head and squeeze the trigger. I have only one regret – our unborn child will not live beyond this fateful day.

Pray God our mutual end is swift and painless and my child is not punished for my sins.

My last wish is the sacred tether between this house and my heart will never be severed.

I comfort myself in these final moments with the hope my spirit will forever remain within this blessed sanctuary.

Farewell.

Charlotte Butler."

We sat wordlessly as I blinked away tears. Plum didn't cry. I've never seen her cry properly, not even after Lily. She took the diary from my hands and clasped it tightly to her chest.

"I knew it!" she announced, passionately. *"I knew it!"*

And then she got up and went directly to bed.

I was tipping cold tea down the sink when the pealing of the doorbell startled me.

It was quarter past five in the morning. Why was William ringing the bell when I'd left the latch unlocked in case he came home before we woke?

I wrenched the door open. "About sodding time!"

Theo Christensen stood there holding a bloodied towel over his right eye.

The cup in my hand fell to the floor and shattered. "Good God! What happened to you?"

Theo steadied himself, one hand flat against the wall. He sounded faint.

"I must talk to you, Frith."

"Is this to do with William? *Shit!* It is, isn't it?"

He stood immobile. Dry, black blood in his hair and beard. A caked stream plastering the right side of his throat. His shirt was splattered with dark Rorschach splotches.

Shakily, I stood aside. "You'd better come in."

CHAPTER THIRTY FOUR

FRITH

Theo followed me into the sitting room and sank into an armchair.

"Is he asleep, your brother-in-law?"

I took a deep breath. "He didn't come home last night. I've no idea where he is."

"I see." He grimaced.

"Make you a coffee?" I asked, inanely.

"Brandy, please, if you have any?"

There was an unopened bottle in William's drinks' cabinet. I poured half a tumbler and watched him gulp it in two mouthfuls. "Thanks, I needed that."

"What have you done?" I motioned at the gory towel against his forehead.

He lifted the cloth to show a wide gash above his right eyebrow. His temple and eye socket were purpling in an ugly bruise.

"Ouch. That looks painful. You need stitches."

"Yeah, I'm on my way to the hospital. I need to explain something first." I sat facing him, back rigid, hands in my lap. "I'm listening."

Call it sixth sense. When I saw Theo on the doorstep, my mind immediately flashed back to the bicycle at the gate, the night William had followed me.

Many times, I've imagined him creeping up the driveway to the side of Olivia's house where Theo has his studio, two narrow windows, shining in the dark. He'd have been bobbing and ducking in the shadows, peering into those windows, seeing me inside with Theo.

"Your brother-in-law visited my studio last night. It was about half-ten when I heard him knocking. I didn't recognise him at first, not until he stepped into the light. He didn't look well. I could see he was upset about something. I asked if he'd join me for a drink and offered wine but he made it clear he didn't plan on staying. "So, what's up?" I asked. He said he knew about me and you. "You've been sleeping with Frith," he said. I asked, "What's it got to do with you?" I was pissed off. Didn't like his tone – he sounded...*accusing*. He asked when I'd last seen you and I said, "Not for a while." He called me a liar – said we'd been together last week. I tried to keep my cool. Said we'd met only to talk and hadn't had sex. He asked if I was in love with you and I said 'no' and reminded him I'm married to Olympia. That's when he lost it."

Theo held out his glass and I poured another two fingers of brandy.

"He told me I was a 'cold, fucking bastard'! Said I'd 'forced you to prostitute yourself for my silence.' That made no sense. I laughed and told him you've always been a very willing accomplice. He started shouting. 'Go to the police! Tell them everything. But leave Frith alone! Stop blackmailing her. She has nothing to do with my past.' That's when things started spiralling out of control. His eyes were glittering. He looked...unhinged. I tried to keep a lid on it. 'Calm, down, man!' I said. 'This isn't making sense. There's been no *'blackmail'* – as you call it. I don't know what Frith's told you but it's not true.'" He picked up the statue Olympia gave me. Seemed to be testing its weight in his hand. I told him to get out before he did something he'd regret. He said he wouldn't and came at me with the statue in his fist. I saw stars and then nothing. I was out cold."

My mouth was parchment. "God," I said. "This is terrible. I don't know what to say."

"What have you been telling your brother-in-law?"

Where to begin? I licked my lips. "It's a long story, Theo." I sighed heavily.

It would've been like watching an oak being felled – Theo falling to the floor in that dark, pokey room. He'd have been unconscious, bleeding from the gash on his temple. William probably thought he'd killed him.

Theo's face had a waxy sheen.

"You need stitches." I got up. "I'd offer to drive you, but William has the car."

"No problem. Olympia's waiting."

"She's been out there all this time?"

"It didn't seem right to bring her in. She heard the commotion last night. Found William bending over me, slapping my face. He ran off in a panic when he saw her. She heard his car start up. Saw headlights in the darkness. Then he was gone."

"I don't know where he is," I said. "I've no idea where he would go."

My teeth began chattering. I had my arms wrapped around my chest, my hands buried in my armpits. "Thank you…" I managed. "Thanks for letting me know."

Theo touched my shoulder briefly. I looked at the criss-crossing of lines around his mouth. The wing of hair over his eye stained black with dry blood.

"I'm sorry," I told him. "I'm really sorry for…for all this trouble."

"You've had a shock. That's why you're cold. Pour yourself a brandy."

I shook my head. "It's this house. It's always cold."

As soon as he'd left, I bolted upstairs to William's room. *Please, please, let him have gone to the airport to catch the next flight to Heathrow. Make him call me from London. "It seemed the only thing to do, Frith…Venter's brother, now this…I had to get away."*

Wills keeps our passports in a clear, plastic pouch in the top drawer of his desk. They were all there. Three little burgundy books emblazoned with the gold coat of arms. William's was on the top. *Christ! Where was he?*

PLUM

I was scared of getting to the end of her diary and now I don't feel like Plum anymore and it's hard to say who I do feel like. I could be a chair or a sack of potatoes cause it's like all my human feelings have been sucked up by a hungry vacuum cleaner and if I was normal I'd have tears dripping down my face like my aunt after that last page but I'm...*nothing*.

I was right about Charlotte – she *is* our spirit, like I said – but I wish she hadn't shot herself with Edward's gun and died with her unborn baby inside. I think God must have sent her back to *North Wind* to atone for her sins – a*tone* is one of my new words – it means being sorry for doing something horrible like murdering your husband and your baby.

Now Dad will have to change his mind about energy leaving your dead body and being absorbed by plants and stop saying ghosts are made up by people who want to scare the shit out of you after I explain why Charlotte's still hanging around at North Wind years after she shot herself.

It was still dark outside when the sound of Dad's car woke me and I was going to run down and say 'hello' but I was cross with him for making us worry so I left my door open a little so he could tuck me up the way he always does. I heard them talking and knew Aunt Frith would be giving Dad the gears and I thought 'Serve him right!'

When I woke my room was dazzling bright which made my antenna vibrate because I'm not allowed to stay in bed after six on a school morning... unless...unless *something's wrong!*

She was in the kitchen talking to Birdie who was holding her hands together like she was in church praying and when she spotted me she chirped in a high warning voice, "Oh, look! Here comes Miss Sleepy-head!"

Aunt Frith stopped talking and from her racoon eyes she hadn't slept last night or brushed her hair which isn't like her so I asked, "What's wrong?"

She looked at Birdie who stared back and when they didn't speak I said, "Something's happened to Dad!"

"He's not home yet," Aunt Frith said. "I've left umpteen messages but he's not answering."

"But, I heard him," I told her. "I heard his car and then I heard you and him talking in the sitting room."

Aunt Frith said, "That was Theo Christensen."

That sounded really weird and Birdie sent her eyebrows flying and asked if I could manage a nice hot bowl of oatmeal.

"What's going on?" I yelled. "Why won't you tell me what's happened to Dad? *Where is he?*"

Aunt Frith pulled out a chair and patted the seat and said, "Sit, Plum," and I knew she was going to deliver bad news.

She said Dad and Theo Christensen had had an argument last night and Dad had hit Theo on the head with a statue and now nobody knows where Dad's gone.

I couldn't breathe. "Oh, Aunt Frith!"

"I know. I thought of ringing the police but…"

"Why don't you?"

"Because I think you've got to wait twenty-four hours before you can report someone missing. And besides, your Dad would have a fit if I asked the police to go looking for him."

Birdie put a plate of toast on the table and said she was off to tidy upstairs because all of the drama and upheaval was making her feel queer.

I asked Aunt Frith if I had to go to school and she said no, not today and she spread honey on my toast and I had a slice with tea and told her I was going to sit in the attic and talk to the spirit. Aunt closed her eyes like she hadn't slept for a year and asked in a tired voice, "What do you want to talk about?"

"Maybe she knows where Dad's got to."

FRITH

It's like a film that keeps looping in my head.

William balancing that cat in his hand and then, in churning fury, slamming the lump of pewter against Theo's cranium. The light fading in Theo's green, hooded eyes. Blood darkening his brow. William terrified at Theo collapsing and losing consciousness. Olympia at the door…a spark of recognition between them. William's shoes thudding on the path.

A scream of brakes as he sped away.

Then what?

He's been disappearing for hours upon end, driving mindlessly into the countryside.

Presumably, he followed this instinct and kept driving through the night. He could have taken one of the roads winding through the wine valleys: McGregor in the south, Gouda to the west, turning east for Montague, north for the Karoo.

But, why hadn't he called?

I heard footsteps. Birdie was flapping her hands like an agitated moth.

"Two gentlemen at the door."

"What?"

"Two gentlemen…detectives, they said…at the door, waiting." Birdie gave me an awkward hug. "Best see what they want."

As I got up, my knees buckled. She offered a crooked elbow, thin as a wire, for me to cling to.

Two sober-faced, plain-clothes detectives stood in the hallway. They were from the Berg River Road Station, they said. One asked if this was the residential address of Mr William Westwood. I said it was and he asked what my relationship with Mr Westwood was. I told him I was William's sister-in-law.

"Do you know the whereabouts of your brother-in-law?"

My knees started shaking. "No. He didn't come home last night."

"Do you know if he was driving a black BMW sedan, registration, CA 742 619?"

That's when my stomach plummeted. I nodded. "He has a black BMW."

The taller detective spoke softly, "I'm sorry to inform you but, at 9.45 this morning, Mr Westwood's car was involved in an accident. A head-on collision with a truck on the R60. The driver of the BMW was killed immediately."

I opened and closed my mouth. It took a few moments before I could speak. "Do you know for certain William was the driver?"

The men shared a glance. "We found his driving licence and identity document in his pocket," one answered quietly.

The hallway had a dizzying list. My mouth and ears were stuffed with cotton wool.

This is how life changes. It takes seconds. Nothing is ever the same again.

I don't remember anything else the two men said. I watched their open mouths moving but heard no words. One touched my arm in sympathy. The other kept his eyes lowered.

They left a few minutes later.

I ran. It's what I do when I can't face something – I run like the yellow coward I know myself to be.

I grabbed Birdie's keys from the peg, started up and jerked her wretched car down the driveway and into the road.

There was a harsh wind blowing that shook the car. Rain began sleeting down, drumming on the roof and painting the windscreen with a dense, frosty mist. The ancient wipers struggled to clear the glass. When I could no longer see ahead, I pulled onto a grassy verge and collapsed over the wheel, sobbing.

"Help me, Lil! I don't know what to do. Shit, Lil, this wasn't supposed to happen! You have to believe me. God, Lil, tell me what to do! I didn't mean this to happen!"

She didn't answer. She'll blame me for William's death. Probably never speak to me again.

I wept until my throat hurt and then lifted my head and saw through steamy windows, a procession of cars inching slowly past. *You can't sit here all day*, I told myself, grimly. *You've got to get it together…go home and tell her.*

My face in the mottled rear-view mirror looked like nobody I recognised.

One glance and Plum would know something was terribly wrong. I blew my nose and scrubbed my cheeks with my sleeve before cautiously easing into the traffic.

All the way home, I skirted fallen branches while slip-sliding on Birdie's worn, smooth tyres. I kept going over what I'd say.

'Plum, darling, I have bad news. Dad was in an accident. I'm so sorry, Plum. It was a bad accident. He died right away. The police were here. They said it all happened so fast, he wouldn't have felt any pain. He may have heard a loud bang, they said, but wouldn't have known anything else. They were sure about that, quite sure he didn't suffer.'

CHAPTER THIRTY FIVE

PLUM

I can't feel the spirit – *pouf* – she's gone like the silky threads of a dandelion when you blow on it. I spent a long time in the attic waiting for her but she didn't come. All the same I told her Dad had punched Theo Christensen in his stupid fat hairy face and got in his car and driven away and now nobody knows where he is. I also told her punching Mr Christensen will land Dad in more trouble which why he's gone AWOL – that means *'absent without leave'* – and it's what Dad does when he gets muddled or ashamed.

It's also what he used to do when he and Mom had a fight. They had lots of fights and once she called him a common criminal and he said my darling there's nothing common about me and she threw a jug that missed and hit the wall and started crying and he drove away and didn't come back for three whole days.

And I remember another time when Mom was sick and she said she wasn't going to last forever and if he was locked away for fraud I'd be left an orphan unless Aunt Frith stepped in but since she had the nurturing skills of a cuckoo that was hardly likely. That time Dad started crying and drove away but it wasn't long before he was home telling Mom he was sorry and making us laugh.

There are lots of orphans in books. Harry Potter after his parents were killed by creepy Voldemort and Anne Shirley when she went to live with Matthew and Marilla at *Green Gables* and Pip and Estella in *Great*

406

Expectations. You could say if I was an orphan I'd be in good company but I wouldn't be happy. Most girls at school have parents and grandparents and aunts and uncles and cousins and half-cousins and even godparents but in our family there's only me, Dad, Aunt Frith and my grandad who lives in Melville and doesn't count because I've seen him like five times in my entire life.

Aunt Frith is not as bad as a cuckoo but she's nothing like Mom and every day she asks, "You okay, Plum?" and I say 'yes' so she can tick the 'Plum Box' and there's less chance of her getting what she calls a *lobotomising* headache – that's a new word and something to do with brains and zombies, I think.

This thing with my aunt being nicer makes me wonder if she's trying to make up for Dad's weirdness. Here's an example – the other day I noticed the little ghost face I'd added to the window of her painting of North Wind wasn't there anymore so I shot her a quick look and she winked at me and I was like, '*Is this really you?*' because if I'd touched that painting a month ago she'd have gone through the roof.

Birdie was cleaning like mad and banging the Hoover into the curvy legs of Dad's new Stinkwood writing bureau and I knew he'd roar like a lion if she chipped the wood because he told me that desk cost as much as a kidney meaning an organ for transplanting not one from a poor dead animal.

Then Aunt Frith walked in and she looked all blotchy with pink mouse eyes so I said, "What's happened to Dad?" and my aunt made a funny croaky heaving noise like she wanted to talk but couldn't get the words out Birdie said, "Oh, pet, my poor, poor pet!" and pressed me to her apron that smelled of baking and I said, "Am I an orphan now?"

FRITH

That night we slept together in the same bed. I gave her an overdose of Rescue Remedy and she was out in minutes, thank God.

Worst night of my life, I think. Worse even than the night Lily died. Lily was desperate to go and I wanted her free from that excruciating pain – but *this!*

Too frightened to close my eyes, I kept them open as the hours ticked by. A wind came up. Trees thrashed and dry branches scraped the walls. The room changed in proportion, becoming large and shadowy. Familiar pieces of furniture – the bookshelf, the table – grew cumbersome and looming. Beams bowed from the ceiling. A spindly chair mutated into a stalking animal. My dressing-gown, hanging on the back of the door, looked like… like our mother, bloody Julia, taking quick, nervy drags of her ciggie. "Give me one of those," I said, and then laughed out loud because, thanks to my mother, I've never smoked.

How will you live with this? That flat, cold, leaden voice – my judgemental self. *You drove him to the edge. Let him think you'd been forced to have sex for his sake.*

The antique ormolu clock on the bedside table became a face, glaring spitefully. *This is your punishment, my girl. She's your responsibility until she turns twenty-one.*

When she woke, Plum asked to be taken to the place where William had died.

"I don't know where it happened, exactly. Somewhere between Ashton and Montague they said, but I can't be sure."

She looked shuttered. Pale as flour. "You have to find out."

They gave me details at the police station. We made a pilgrimage in Birdie's car, stopping for flowers on the way. We didn't speak. Plum positioned herself away from me, pressed against the passenger door, her nose almost touching the window, her face raw with shock and grief.

I found the spot on route 62 where weaving skid marks were still visible on the tarmac. A barrier at the side of the road had been jaggedly sawn in half.

I pulled to the side of the road and switched off the engine.

"We have to talk about this," I said. "About Dad's accident."

She shook her head. "It wasn't an accident," she said. "He did it on purpose."

Feebly, I touched her arm. "You don't know that."

Her eyes met mine, briefly. "I do," she said. "And so do you."

I sagged in the seat. Closed my eyes. It was like falling into an abyss of shame and sorrow.

Plum took the straggling bouquet from the back seat and knelt at the side of the road near the barrier. She dipped her face into the wilting flowers. I watched her lips move. Cars came and went. Eyes still tightly shut, I listened to the swish of traffic and shuddered.

Christ! I can't bear this! I should be there with her. Holding her. Saying a prayer or something.

I couldn't move. I sat hunched over the wheel, gazing in disbelief at Lily's daughter placing flowers for her dead father in a clump of swaying grass. Her hair blew around her face.

Lily's voice. *"What's wrong with you? Get your fucking act together and start behaving like the grown-up! Get out of the car and comfort her. She needs you, Frith. You're going to have to start thinking about someone other than yourself now. You hear me?"*

I don't suppose many people have a conscience that speaks in the sharp, clear tones of a twin sister. Whenever I hear her voice, I know truth is being told. Even so, I couldn't move.

PLUM

After you're born there's your mother and she's like the sun until your Dad starts to peep in like the moon and there's twice the love in your life until one dies and the love shrinks by half and then – if they both die – it's like there's no light in the world.

"How are you feeling?" she kept asking and what I really wanted to say was, "I've got all this love inside and nobody to give it to," but I didn't answer. You can't take words back once they're out and you shouldn't tell the truth if it's going to hurt and that's where white lies come in and I can't decide if it's a good or bad thing but I'm getting pretty good at telling them.

Here's an example. When I asked Dad what depression's like he said it's like looking down from a far-flung planet to a warm sunny place where everyone is normal and happy and laughing you're stuck miles away on an sunless mountain of rock with icy drafts swirling and you want to shout, *'Save me!'* but you can't because it takes too much effort and your tongue is too big for your mouth and you don't want to call attention to yourself and have all those normal jolly people staring as if you've gone bonkers.

Dad said, "Ever felt like that?" and I said, "School's like that sometimes," but that's a white lie because school is never that horrible.

I told him I'd love him forever and left the flowers in the place on the road where Dad died and on the way home we got stuck behind a donkey cart full of hay with loose stalks sliding from the back leaving a golden trail and I was thinking if we were living in a fairy story we'd follow the glittering hay to a magic place where Dad would be waiting and I was imagining Dad running with arms open to hug me and rubbing my cheek on the soft nubby wool of his jacket when Aunt Frith revved and Birdie's car gave a wheeze and clattered along beside the donkey cart before we zipped in front and I saw the white of the donkey's eye as we passed and knew he was as terrified as I was. My aunt's voice was so soft I had to strain my ears to hear. "This is nothing to do with you. You do know that, don't you, Plum?"

I don't know because I haven't had time to think so I said, "Was it a truck Dad crashed into?"

"Yes. Some kind of long distance tanker, I believe."

"Did it have a picture of a cow on the side?"

She gave me a quick look. "Why would you think that?"

I shook my head.

"He was depressed. He didn't mourn for Lily properly. Didn't give himself time or permission to weep, shout…grieve in private. He had to be strong for you while you were being strong for him. This is what comes of holding everything in so tightly and never letting go."

I asked her, "Is that why he hit Mr Christensen?"

She bit her lip. "That's my fault. I'll never forgive myself."

There was a green space at the side of the road. No fence, just long grass for miles.

"Can you stop for a bit?" I asked.

"Do you need to pee?"

"Yes," I said though I didn't but there was something I'd forgotten to tell Dad. I walked into the field and stalks of grass crackled and crunched as I trampled them down. "I know you did it to be with Mom," I told him. "But you're supposed to be looking after me so you'll have to make it up to her. Give her a hug and let her know you're sorry and she'll forgive you in the end like she always does."

My aunt started yelling my name so I went back to the car.

"We can go home now," I told her.

FRITH

The time after William's suicide passed in a blur. Birdie helped organise the memorial service. There were only seven – the three of us, one of William's carpenters, his banker, the woman from the real estate agency and, of all people, Louis Venter.

He leaned towards me, looking intent. "I'm truly sorry for your loss," he murmured, respectfully.

I had a sudden and inexplicable urge to fall upon him and weep onto the shoulder of his elegant, poplin navy blazer. He must have seen something desperate in my eyes – he took a few steps back. "Meet for a coffee sometime?" he said, pressing my hand briefly. "Give you a call."

Plum stood stiffly, hands clenched at her sides, enduring kisses planted awkwardly on her cheek. Birdie, leaking tears, kept blowing into a rainbow of coloured tissues balled into a bulging pocket. "There, there, pet," she whispered to Plum. "You hold on. This will all be over soon and, mark my words, the memorial is always the worst of it."

I took myself to bed after the service and slept like the dead through that afternoon and the next day. I had that awful recurring dream, the one where the earth gives way beneath your feet as you plummet into a dark, vertical tunnel, falling, falling, falling until, mid-flight your eyes spring open and you're jerked awake with your thudding heart echoing in your ears.

William died without leaving a will. I called Louis Venter who referred me to the Julie Christie lookalike, Katrina Burger.

"She's the one you want. Handles estates. You've met her before, which is an advantage."

"Except I don't like her. And the feeling's mutual."

"You don't have to like her. Just take her advice."

This time, she looked nothing like Julie Christie with black hair, sleek and straight to her chin. Maybe she wears wigs. There was no mistaking the haughty chill in her expression, but she knows her stuff. She rattled it off. The death reported to the Master of the High Court. An executor appointed to assess the value and administer the deceased estate. A new bank account opened by the executor in the name of 'Estate Late William Westwood' – all bank accounts transferred into this one.

I gasped in relief. "Thank God! So, I'll have access to William's money for living expenses and such?"

She beat a tattoo on her desk with jade green fingernails. "You'll be granted a cash advance to cover living expenses."

"What's that mean?"

"The advance will pay for funeral costs and four months' living expenses."

"The house is with an agent. What happens to the money if it's sold?"

"Mmmm – your niece will be the prime beneficiary. It's most likely proceeds from the sale will be kept in a trust until she turns twenty-one."

A wave of panic engulfed me. "How am I to look after her until then? There are school fees and…*Jesus!* This is another of William's royal fuck-ups!"

The bank manager provided statements showing how much William had in his current and savings accounts. The amounts were less than I'd expected. "No other accounts?" I asked.

"I'm afraid that's the sum of Mr Westwood's investment in *this* bank," the manager said meaningfully.

I left the bank with a credit facility in my name, from which I could draw living expenses until an executor was appointed by the court. That was something. At least we wouldn't starve.

At home, I trawled through William's things, searching for evidence of his overseas accounts. Lil had told me that, for tax purposes and to protect his anonymity, he'd always banked offshore. They shouldn't have been hard to find. William kept hard copies of all quotations, accounts, invoices and references of payments, stapled and bound into alphabetised lever-arch files. I found nothing. And there was no proof of offshore investments on his computer, though there were a few locked files asking for a password. It finally dawned. William had gone to his grave with these account numbers securely stored inside his brain. How ironic! I can't touch any of the money I'd once turned my nose up at – all those ill-gotten millions made at the expense of William's duped clients.

The funeral home called me to collect his ashes. They sold me a silver box to keep them in.

"These are your Dad's ashes," I told Plum.

She opened the box and took out a clear plastic bag containing what looked like silky white sand strewn with pearly chips and seeds of bone.

"Is it all that's left of Dad?"

I shuddered. It looked so meagre. Was the modest heap a token? Or was it really all that remained after William's body had been cremated, his skeleton, organs, skin and viscera reduced to three tablespoons of pale ash?

"I want to scatter some of him in the garden," Plum said.

She untied the metal loop securing the plastic and I followed as she walked slowly past the bank of pink and blue hydrangeas, past the tumbling wisteria, stopping at the Oom's rose bushes. Here she strewed William's ashes between the roses and at the root of a honeysuckle hedge. She walked around the patch, head high, back straight, gently shaking out cloudy puffs.

"Not all of it, Plum," I said. "We should keep some."

Plum held up the bag, empty but for a couple of teaspoons of sediment.

"Is this enough?"

A residue had blown over Plum's face. She looked like a ghost. Her hair and clothes were filmed in white. I heard myself wailing: "Oh, God, Plum! Oh, no, no!" My hands were everywhere, beating at her clothes, her hair.

Plum asked hopefully, "Did I breathe some of him in?"

We stayed in the garden until late, collapsed on deck chairs, watching the sunset.

"The house feels sad," she said.

"Yes."

"The garden too."

I nodded.

"I hope he's not too cold. I didn't think about that." She nodded at the silver box on my lap. "I bet it's warmer in there."

The light grew dimmer until the last of the sun vanished and she became a silhouette.

The garden fragmented into blackness. The shape of the house loomed.

"Is this what it's like when you die?"

"What?"

"Darkness and quiet and nothingness."

"Maybe."

"And then you see the light and that's when the angel comes."

I smiled though she couldn't see.

This *is* probably how it is. Dark. Silence falling. Everything shutting down. Life ebbing.

All light extinguished.

"What are we going to do?" she asked.

I've been dreading this. "I don't know."

"When will you know?"

"It will come to us." I tried to sound confident. "We'll have a long think, you and me. And then we'll talk about things and when we've said all that needs to be said, we'll know what to do."

"Okay," she said, doubtfully.

We sat in the dark for another five minutes or so, in complete silence.

She gave a sigh that ended in a sob.

"There's nothing wrong with having a good cry," I told her.

"I don't want to cry." Her voice sounded thin and empty.

"Fair enough. Let's go inside and make some supper."

When I switched on the lights indoors, her face was wet.

"Let it go," I said. "You can't hold in all that pain, Plum. Let it go."

She fell against me and sobbed into my chest.

Oh, Lil…are you watching? Her shoulders were heaving. Hot tears on my blouse.

I held her tight and for the first time, she didn't push me away.

CHAPTER THIRTY SIX

PLUM

I wish I hadn't scattered most of Dad in the garden. I should've thought first and kept him safe in the silver box – you can take that box anywhere and you'd never have to leave him on his own in the wind and rain and the cold.

Aunt Frith says we'll probably have to sell the house because it's too big and expensive and we might decide to live in another country like England or France.

"That's you," I told her.

"What do you mean?"

"*You* might decide to live in another country like England or France – not me."

She didn't answer which means there's a chance we're going to move to her flat in Paris.

I've been saying goodbye – like Charlotte did before she died.

Goodbye soupy fishpond with your crown of water-lilies curling muddy brown at their edges. Goodbye white stones on graves nobody knows about where dusty prickly pear bushes grow. Goodbye crumbly stone pots at the edge of a driveway that spits up biting pebbles when you whizz too fast around the curve.

Goodbye attic where spiders are still spinning…goodbye cradle…creaky rocking horse…the cupboard where I found the diary and the half-finished painting of *North Wind* that Aunt Frith kept for herself even though there's a 'finders keepers' rule that says that painting is mine. Goodbye…goodbye!

The spirit's gone and I should be sad but I'm not really because I've had the most awesome *revelation* – that's like a holy way of saying I've figured things out. It came when I woke up this morning and was lying in bed listening to bird claws on the roof and tree frogs playing castanets and thinking back to all those moments when the spirit came close enough to warm my skin and make my spine tingle and that's when I knew the spirit wasn't only showering me with love she was healing me because I haven't had a blank for ages not one – *nothing, nada, zip, zilch, zero.* Aunt Frith says I've probably grown out of them but it's *her*…the spirit…she's the one who's cured me, swear to God.

So here's what I think. She waited for us to find her diary and once we'd read to the last page she knew she was free to float up to heaven like a balloon when you let go of the string. There are two of us who know what truly happened to Charlotte Butler though my aunt doesn't believe in spirits which means I'm the only one who understands and one day cross my heart I'll tell her story to the world.

We were all sad. Birdie sifted her sadness into Bakewell tarts we couldn't eat so she gave them to the Oom who spooned up the filling because his gums couldn't mash pastry.

My aunt went to bed – migraines she said – but we heard her crying into her pillow and Birdie said leave things be until she gets over the hump. "Life's thrown a lot at her lately," she said. "She's going to need some time to herself, pet."

She stayed in her room for two days and I got a shock when I saw her sitting on the queen's staircase in the space where coffins were turned when people died at home in their beds – *'with their boots on'* – as Dad says – no – that should be *said.*

She was like a rag doll all boneless and floppy with her head on her knees and hands around her ankles making gulping noises though she stopped when she saw me and looked through puffy squinty eyes and mumbled, "Sorry I'm such a wet blanket."

She grabbed the banisters and heaved herself up and went slowly to her room and from the tottery way she was walking she looked terribly tired and like what Birdie calls a 'dying duck in a thunderstorm'.

417

The Oom said my Dad was a good man and too young to go and asked if I'd like to pick mushrooms in a secret place.

"What kind of mushrooms?" I asked because lots are poisonous.

"Penny Bun," he said and made a slapping noise with his lips to show how good they taste.

We took a basket and I thought we were heading out to a field but he led me to town and down a crooked side street with a gutter full of chip packets and beer cans and chocolate wrappers and burst balloons he said were condoms and I even spied a doctor's syringe with a needle which means drugs. There was an old house behind a thorny tangle of trees and I said we'd have to hack our way with a panga but the Oom opened a gate under a scraggy rosemary bush with a padlock so rusty it fell to pieces when he tugged it.

The house was splashed with pigeon poo and the garden a mess of dead stuff and broken chimney pots with old birds' nests inside and a mouldy sundial but at the back of the house mushrooms were growing in green boggy patches and there was even a big clump of strawberry plants with mean bitter berries not yet ripe. There was also a stink I didn't want to think too much about.

We picked mushrooms and the Oom ate some raw and nodded for me to do the same and they didn't taste too bad – kind of meaty and woodsy – but I had to keep spitting out bits of black soil and I wasn't sure about the smell so I had only one.

"I'll miss you," I told the Oom. "You taught me weeding and sweeping and gardening and I'm honoured you showed me the graves."

He put his funny old hat on my head. "Yours," he said and then I gave him the key charm from my silver bracelet and he showed his gums in a lovely pink smile.

FRITH

There were a few days when I didn't give a monkeys about getting out of bed, when it all seemed too much. Thank the Pope for Birdie who kept it together for Plum.

The Oom stepped in too. Showed Plum how to make nosegays. Took her for long walks. Made up chores to keep her busy in the garden. Get her mind off things. I've seen another side to the old man – he's a gentle soul, dignified and kind without a pinch of self-pity.

I've been thinking about what to do. There's my flat in France. I yearn to go back. I've totted up the cost of two one-way plane tickets, school fees, groceries, transport, month-end utilities and what-have-you. I'm hoping I can persuade the executor of William's estate to provide sufficient for us to live on until I find a job.

There's a gallery not far from my flat – *Passage de Retz*. You pass through a hotel courtyard before coming upon a maze of spacious, light-filled rooms displaying art. There's a chance, albeit a slim one, this gallery may hang my work on their walls. If my work sells, we can probably survive on my paintings for a while. Perhaps I can give lessons?

I can't think about the future without wanting to cry or scream or jump out of a window into traffic. She's twelve. School until she's eighteen. University after. Twenty-one is the earliest I'll be able to let go. That's *nine* years!

Jesus, Mary and Joseph!

It was Birdie who found a brown-paper wrapped parcel with a blank sealed envelope attached. She discovered the parcel at the back of William's cupboard where she'd been tidying, folding his clothes and boxing them up for some charity or other.

I thought it was a suicide note and couldn't open it for a couple of days. Then I mustered the courage and gulped a strong coffee before I sat down with the letter – even so, my hands shook as I tore open the envelope.

I recognised her scrawl at once.

"My Darling Frith,

I told William to give you this letter only after you had learned how to love Plum. The fact you're trying to decipher my awful handwriting means I was right all along in believing time and living with our daughter would change you in ways you couldn't begin to imagine.

Remember when I asked you to take care of Plum for me? You didn't answer for ages and then said, 'I'll do my best, Lil, but we know I'm not the mothering type.'

That wasn't what I expected to hear. I wanted to shout at you for being so fucking cold and distant but when I looked into your face I knew I was seeing the real you with all your superficial layers pared away, exposed and scared. We had that in common. You also saw right through my Mother Teresa act – dying gives me the heebie-jeebies – but leaving Plum is the worst and fills me with unspeakable sorrow.

So, my daughter is my true gift to you, Frith, the most precious gift I have to give to anyone in this lifetime. If you cherish her as I do, she'll love you as ferociously as she does me.

Now, this part is important…

You have an urge – through some misguided sense of what's right and proper – to tell Plum she's adopted. Please don't.

Truth is, Wills and I made up the story about the Russian ballerina who'd had an affair, got pregnant, delivered her baby and fled back to Moscow or wherever we said she was from. (I've forgotten some of the details we concocted – my brain is porridge from morphine.)

We told the lie about the Bolshoi dancer so if Plum were to ever discover she's adopted and search for her birth mother, she'd hit a blind alley from the start.

They found her in a cardboard box, a grape box, to be exact, one used for packaging export quality white, black or red grapes. Not a bad choice as boxes go – best quality cardboard, waxed inside to prevent water damage, sturdy and stable to protect fruit in transit.

There was a fluffy blanket doubled at the bottom of the box – white with a repeat motif of pink and yellow hopping rabbits. No note or bottle or toy.

The box was left outside a police station which, I suppose, is as good a place as any to leave a baby you can't keep or don't want. The policeman who found her said he took care of her for a few hours until a social worker arrived. In all that time, he said, she didn't cry once.

420

She came to us because we were next on the list. William took her while I wept, overcome with emotion, until he gently pressed our daughter into my arms. The day Plum became ours – that's when I discovered joy for the first time.

I get a jolt when I see a grape box with a flat colour picture of improbably round grapes stamped on the side. I've agonised over that box for years. Where did she find it, Plum's birth mother?

At a market? In a trash can? In a storage room, piled high with cardboard?

Another thing I'll never know, when this tormented mother set our baby down in front of the shabby municipal building, did she touch her face, kiss her cheeks, stroke her arms? Did she say a prayer or whisper goodbye? Did she walk away wracked with sobbing?

So now you know, Frith. This is why we've never told Plum the truth about how she came into this world. Hers is a story too tragic to repeat. I know I can trust you to keep silent.

Now for the parcel...

From its blocky shape and weight, you can tell it's the painting Ma gave me.

I promised you could have it but you slept with William and, for a while, I hated you enough to alter my will. I insisted William keep the artwork in a trust for Plum along with bits and bobs of my jewelry, my wedding rings and granny's pearls.

But then I changed my mind. I know you well enough to guess how much you've suffered from that one mistake. And you'll need the money you'll make from the sale. William has a small fortune squirrelled away in tax havens but there's blow-all in your bank account. Christie's, the Tate or Saatchi's will pay handsomely for that murky old master.

Don't for God's sake get maudlin and keep the painting because it was once mine. It belonged to her first. Reason enough to get rid of it.

One last thing you should know.

You're number two after Plum and Wills comes next. You probably shouldn't love a sister more than a husband – but he never needs to know. Besides, how could he compete when there's so much of me in you and you in me? We could be one and the same person.

After I've gone, you'll feel sliced through the middle with only half of you left. That's because we've never been an 'I' – we're a 'We' – and when you look in the mirror my face will stare back so, in a way, I'll never really die, but I won't be there either, if that makes sense.

I give you my word if there's an afterlife, I'll be watching over all of you and waiting for a time we can be together again. Your loving sister, Lily."

I felt hollow. By the time she had written the letter, Lily had forgiven me but, even so, I could sense her disappointment. '*Learned* to love Plum,' she'd written, as if I'm incapable of loving naturally. '*Fucking cold and distant*' – not the first time she'd used those words to describe me. And then that scathing, '*You have an urge – through some misguided sense of what's right and proper – to tell Plum she's adopted.*'

Her words set me off weeping again. *Twelve years* since Plum was adopted and all that time Lily didn't trust me with the truth. *Jesus,* that hurts. All her talk about us being '*We*' – you'd think she'd have known better. I'd never have breathed a word had I known Plum's birth mother was more likely a terrified teenager than a Russian ballerina with a face like a Bond girl.

I didn't open the brown paper parcel. It's a life-line, that painting. It will keep us afloat for a good many years. But I couldn't look at the picture of that murky estuary with water birds lifting in flight. It would bring back too many memories, not all good. Lil's letter drove me back to my room. I pulled up the coverlet and closed my eyes.

I must have dozed off. I woke with a start to the sound of a thud and the splash of water.

Groping for my shoes, I saw my water jar upended on the floor with strewn paintbrushes floating in blue-green water pooling on the tiles. The windows were shut. No draught coming under the door. The surface of my table was scattered with pencils, charcoal, tubes of paint, photographs. I must have placed the jar half resting on top of something until it overbalanced. I went down to fetch a bucket and mop.

"Thought you were getting a little shut-eye," Birdie said.

"I was. But my water jar seems to have taken a dive off the table."

"Clumsy," she smiled.

"Not me. I was asleep. It must've tipped over."

She gave a quick, wide-eyed glance. "You don't think…"

"No," I said firmly. "I do not!"

PLUM

I'm drawing a map of *North Wind* in case we have to sell the house and live in France where she has her flat and that's most likely what we'll do because she doesn't care about anyone except herself.

Birdie's been working on her and says the grass isn't always greener and it's safer in Paarl because there are terrorists in Paris who blow you to smithereens when you're in a café or walking on a street just minding your own business but my aunt says terrorists are everywhere and France is a lot safer than South Africa.

I've drawn my map like it's been photographed by a drone flying over the roof. You can see tops of chimneys and shingles slotting together like scales on fish and from where the drone flies you can make out stones in a crooked path to where the fountain spills into the green frogspawn pond.

I've copied the Oom's wonky old wheelbarrow full of leaves though from this angle it looks funny because you can't see the wheel in front so you don't really know what it is though my aunt will guess because she's a clever clogs.

They've been nice at school since Dad's accident and Bronte told me her mom said his fight with Mr Christensen is water under the bridge and there's lots who'd like to take swing at that oaf but Dad was the only one brave enough.

"People are saying your Dad was a swashbuckling hero," Bronte said. "A sort of Captain Jack Sparrow only not so skinny," and that made me proud.

We went to the hall for one last assembly before the holidays and as we were filing out our drama teacher shouted, "Plum Westwood! Over here, please."

Miss van Reenen crooked a finger at me and my hands got sweaty but I never smoke in the toilets or pass notes in class so I went up and made myself look right into her face.

"We're putting on *Aladdin* next term. Would you like to try out for the Genie of the Lamp?"

I didn't even have to think. "Yes, please Miss!"

"Here's the play. You'll want to read it." She gave me a bunch of stapled pages with *Aladdin and His Magic Lamp* on the front. "See you in three weeks."

The drama teacher smiled and for the first time I saw a she had this big gap between her two front teeth like a rabbit – you miss those things if you never look a person right in the face.

After dinner, Aunt Frith said, "How do you feel about leaving *North Wind*?"

"I've done what you said," I told her. "I had a long think and got a pain in my chest." I showed her where I think my heart is. "Right here," I said.

She frowned. "Go on."

"Dad used to talk about having a pain in his chest," I tried to explain. "He said it felt like a sack of flour under his breastbone. It's called 'heart-ache', he said."

She sort of smiled. "Mmmm. That sounds like your Dad."

"I don't know how we can leave when Dad's in all the rooms and we scattered some of him in the garden. And there's the diary and Charlotte and the spirit and I never want to forget what happened here long ago."

She didn't say anything.

"Then there's Birdie and she'll be on the bones of her bum without this job and the Oom needs us too and they're both like the only family we have. I'll miss school and my friend Bronte and Miss van Reenen – you know her – she's my drama teacher – she asked if I'll try out for the Genie in *Aladdin* and that's another reason I'd like to stay."

My aunt seemed far away with her eyes kind of cloudy not really looking at anything.

I sent a message – *please, please, please.*

"The real reason to stay here…" she said and I could hear in her voice she wanted to cry. She took a deep breath. "…the real reason to stay is because it's what your mother wanted for you."

CHAPTER THIRTY SEVEN

FRITH

It was inevitable, I suppose. I feel as if I've been propelled to this place by an unseen and unstoppable force. It's not where I want to be but there's bugger all I can do about it.

She hugged me with surprising intensity. "Thank you, Aunt Frith."

We stared at each other for a few seconds.

"I'll do my best," I said.

"Me too," she said and then added, "Can you sew?"

"Why?"

"I'll need a purple turban with a plumy feather and a flowing red cloak to play the Genie."

Birdie overheard. "I've an old Singer," she said. "I can whip up that cloak and a pair of silky harem pants in no time. And I'm a dab hand at decorating with beads."

They started talking about the school play.

"I come on when Aladdin rubs the lamp."

"Oh yes?"

"There are billows of pink smoke and I say, 'Oy! Ten thousand years will give you such a crick in the neck!'

"Sounds as daft as a brush, your Genie."

"No, Birdie, he's been trapped inside a lamp for ten thousand years."

"Oh well, that would give you a crick in the neck I suppose."

I'll have to sell my flat. Place an ad with pictures on line. *'Napoleon III Furnished Studio Apartment for sale, Upper Marais, near Hotel de Retz. Upstairs balcony, two bedrooms, courtyard with small garden – quiet sanctuary in the heart of Paris.'*

A lump in my throat. Tears crowding behind my eyes. Nothing will ever be as it was again.

Next morning, I asked Birdie if I could borrow her car. She was making pastry for a chicken pie with half an ear tuned to the radio news.

"As long as you don't mind the pong of dog vomit!"

Her Pomeranian had thrown up when she'd taken him to the vet for his Rabies shot and she'd only discovered the mess a day later. Even a blast of *Jo Malone* couldn't mask the sour odour, so I drove with the windows open.

I've become oddly attached to this car. She's like an old friend who keeps going despite falling to pieces, bit by bit. This morning, after being hooted at by drivers behind me, I discovered the exhaust had fallen off. It'll have to be replaced. Without an exhaust Birdie's Mini sounds like a 747.

I drove Birdie's car to an auto repair shop for a new exhaust to be fitted. They told me to come back in an hour so I bought some art supplies and went for a coffee.

On the way, I heard footsteps behind me. A touch on my shoulder.

"Thought it was you." Louis Venter smiled warily. "Buy you that coffee?"

He gave me his arm and I took it. His manners are impeccable. He pulled out a chair and adjusted the umbrella to shield the sun's brightness. But then he ruined everything by snapping his fingers at a waiter.

"I wish you wouldn't do that," I said, testily.

He grinned. "I find it the only way to command respect from the proletariat."

I sighed. "I'd forgotten how opinionated you are."

He turned to the waiter: "Usual for me, thanks. And the lady would like…" He glanced quizzically.

"Cappuccino, please."

The waiter set an ashtray before Louise who winked and tapped a packet.

"Mind if I smoke?"

"Do people still smoke?"

His face twitched with amusement. "These are mentholated. That makes them medicinal. I allow myself three a day on the pretext they're good for me."

He lit a cigarette and blew a cloud of smoke away from me.

"You've been on my mind. I find myself wondering how you are and what you're doing." He looked me up and down. "Have I crossed your mind at all, these past few weeks?"

"Sorry, no."

We regarded one another before he burst out laughing.

"Let's start over. How are you Frith?"

"*Comme Ci Comme Ca.*"

"It will take a while," he said, quietly.

The waiter arrived with coffee. Mine had a perfect cinnamon heart resting on waves of whipped cream.

I had to know. "I suppose everyone's talking about the drama between William and Theo...and...and the car accident?"

"You've a smudge of cream...just here." He touched his top lip, passing a serviette. "It's no secret our community relishes salacious gossip so yes – this incident has been discussed. Most think Theo's a troll and got what he deserved. Your brother-in-law's untimely death is a tragedy." Louis narrowed his eyes against a plume of blue smoke. "Was it suicide?"

"I think so. William was...infinitely sad after my sister died."

"Depression is a torment. After my wife died, I had a powerful desire to kill myself until I found the courage to live."

I blinked, surprised. "I'm sorry."

"We know so little about one another, Frith. Suicide kills more people than colon, breast and stomach cancer combined."

I took a sip of coffee. "We're staying in Paarl," I said. "I've come into some money. That painting I told you about. I had it all wrong. William wasn't trying to cheat me. Just waiting for the right time to give it to me. Anyway...I promised my sister Lily her daughter Plum would grow up here."

"You don't sound happy."

"*'Id est quod id est.'*"

He looked quizzical.

"It is what it is," I translated.

"I know what it means." Louis' eyes, on mine, were serious. "Ever considered spending time with a bachelor like the one sitting across from you?"

I glanced at the man at the next table.

"*This* bachelor!" he tapped his chest.

"Oh," I blushed hotly.

He looked injured. "You haven't guessed? My overtures have been anything but subtle."

Sparks flew as Louis stubbed out his cigarette. He leaned towards me. I caught a whiff of cologne. "What about dinner? You look like you could do with a square meal."

"Thanks," I said.

"C'mon Frith. What's say we get to know one another?"

I smiled. "I suppose we could give it a try."

His eyes roamed my face as if committing it to memory.

"I knew," he said, decisively. "First time we met. Felt a connection. I know you didn't and haven't yet, but – trust me – you will."

At home, I took a pair of secateurs outdoors and gathered an armful of roses.

"I'm staying, Lil," I whispered. "I'll take care of her, promise. Won't let you down."

I arranged the blooms in one of Lily's vases – Wedgewood, fine bone china, hand-painted with butterflies tipped in gold. She used to make a production of arranging flowers. She'd disinfect the vase and lay a bed of spongy oasis in the base. Flower stems were cut at a jaunty angle and she always sprinkled half a teaspoon of white powder in the water to make them last. I held Lil's vase under the cold tap, filled it with white roses and set it on a coffee table in the sitting room. To my eyes, the arrangement looked lovely.

'These are for you, Lil.'

After Plum had gone to bed, I sat alone, swirling dregs of cold tea in my mug. I flipped to the newspaper for the date. Friday 29th September. *Remember this date*, I thought– a life-changing day in the thirty-ninth week of the year when a new moon was promised that evening.

I yawned, stretched and got to my feet and as I did, my knee bumped against the coffee table, jostling the roses in their Wedgewood vase. I bent to slide the vase into the centre of the table but it skimmed across the glassy, polished surface and fell to the floor.

Instinctively, I screwed my eyes against the crash of china. There was no noise, only a ringing silence. Holding my breath, I opened my eyes and stood frozen as a damp fog nestled into the back of my neck. My hands shook.

The Wedgewood vase stood upright. The roses were just as I'd arranged them, not a petal out of place, not a drop of water spilled.

I took a breath and in that ragged inhalation, smelled the faintest trace of her perfume.

"Lily," I whispered. "Lil…is that you?"

26027462R00258

Printed in Great Britain
by Amazon